TAKEN FROM FATE...

Something slammed into the earth beside him. Shaken, Matt spared it a quick glance; it was a fallen gargoyle.

The stranger shouted another verse. Fire burst from the ground. Some sixth sense gave Matt just enough warning; he was already leaping back as the flame roared upward. Even so, he howled as it singed the side of his leg before he landed on the far side of the stony monster. But the gargoyle gave him an idea; he chanted,

> "Thing of stone, arise and walk you!
> Let no spell or magic balk you!
> Seize that man who struck you down!
> Stop his voice and see him bound!"

With a grinding of granite joints, the half-human, half-dragon sculpture rose to its hind feet and spread its wings . . .

By Christopher Stasheff
Published by Ballantine Books:

A Wizard in Rhyme:
HER MAJESTY'S WIZARD
THE OATHBOUND WIZARD
THE WITCH DOCTOR
THE SECULAR WIZARD
MY SON, THE WIZARD
THE HAUNTED WIZARD
THE CRUSADING WIZARD*
THE FELINE WIZARD*

Starship Troupers:
A COMPANY OF STARS
WE OPEN ON VENUS
A SLIGHT DETOUR

The Star Stone:
THE SHAMAN
THE SAGE

forthcoming

THE HAUNTED WIZARD

Book VI in *A Wizard in Rhyme*

Christopher Stasheff

A Del Rey® Book
THE BALLANTINE PUBLISHING GROUP
NEW YORK

A Del Rey® Book
Published by The Ballantine Publishing Group
Copyright © 2000 by Christopher Stasheff

www.randomhouse.com/delrey/

Library of Congress Catalog Card Number: 99-091068

ISBN 0-345-39248-5

Manufactured in the United States of America

First Edition: January 2000

10   9   8   7   6

CHAPTER 1

The moon rose high over the low hill at the edge of the plain, and over the cluster of rocks at its foot. Within that rough ring half a dozen men in white robes stood chanting, hoods covering their heads, gilded sickles at their belts, chanting a petition to a forgotten god.

"Why have you turned away from us, O Toutatis?" the leader called, and the others answered, "Because our fathers' fathers turned away from you."

"Remember us, Toutatis!" the leader cried, and the others chanted, "Toutatis, remember."

"Our ancestors built great stone rings in which to worship you, Toutatis, but we must hide in these circles you have given us by the mountains."

"We must hide in the mountains," the watchers chorused.

"For we who remember you are few, and weak thereby, Toutatis!"

"We are few and weak," the watchers agreed.

"We pray you, give us strength, Toutatis, that we may increase!"

"That we may increase!"

"That we may regain our dominion, and worship you openly in the great stone rings!" the leader cried.

"In the great stone rings," the watchers echoed.

"We shall serve you as well as we may, Toutatis!"

"As well as we may," the followers echoed.

"We shall give you our richest gift, Toutatis!"

"Our richest gift." Eyes glistened; one or two of the men moistened their lips and swallowed thickly.

"A virgin!" the leader cried. "A fine girl, not yet eighteen, preserved from man's touch for you!"

1

"And because her father's an ogre," one of the men muttered.

"Be still!" his neighbor hissed.

"Do you suppose this is really how the old druids did it?"

"Of course it is! Niobhyte has read all the old books of runes they left! Now be silent, before he hears you!"

"Bring forth the virgin!" Niobhyte the leader commanded.

"The virgin comes," cried a voice from beyond the rocks.

"The virgin comes," the other men chorused. All eyes turned toward the source of the voice.

A high-pitched drum began to beat, and three figures came into the rock circle, all in white cowled robes, but the one in the center wore a much finer cloth. The man to the left kept a firm hold on the arm of the central figure; the man to the right beat slowly on a small, flat drum. The central figure seemed to be wading through an invisible stream, stumbling now and again, but steadied by the hand on the arm. As the drum tapped out a solemn measure, the three came to the low, flat rock in front of Niobhyte and stopped a little to one side, facing both him and the small congregation.

"Unveil the sacrifice!" Niobhyte commanded.

The guard stepped behind the central figure and drew the hood back, revealing a heart-shaped face with huge eyes, retroussé nose, and full lips. A wealth of blond hair tumbled out.

The watchers caught their breath at her beauty. They had all seen her before, of course, seen and yearned, but by moonlight she seemed even more lovely than ever, with an almost supernatural quality. Now, though, her eyes were dim, unfocused, and she wore a bemused, faintly puzzled expression.

"See how Toutatis enhances the beauty of she who goes to him!" Niobhyte intoned. "Unveil her, unveil her!"

Slowly, the guard drew the robe down to reveal smooth shoulders, so pale in the moonlight, then further to expose a wealth of swelling curves and expanses of pale skin, on down to small, bare, dainty feet.

The men caught their breath; the youngest groaned. His mates silenced him with furious hisses. He wondered how Niobhyte had seduced her into slipping out of her father's house—with promises of a handsome prince awaiting her, or of wealth and power? No matter—once out, he had given her drugged wine, and his henchmen had borne her away to this ring.

"Lay her down on her nuptial bed," Niobhyte intoned.

The girl stumbled as they turned her about, then blinked, confused, as they laid her down. Several of the men moaned, looking at the moon-glowing body stretched out on the stone table. The girl looked about her, puzzled; then the drug-haze cleared for a second and alarm filled her face, but Niobhyte stepped forward to touch her forehead with a forefinger, reciting a phrase none of the men could understand, and her eyes dulled again, her body relaxed.

"Toutatis, we send you this gift!" Niobhyte swung the knife high.

The youngest watcher cried out and leaped to protect the woman. His companions, ready for it, caught and held him.

But they couldn't catch the peasants who leaped down from the tops of the rocks, howling in anger. More of them came pelting between boulders and into the circle, and a huge, brawny, grizzle-haired man caught Niobhyte's wrist and twisted. The knife fell and Niobhyte cried out in pain— but the cry changed to a staccato chant as his left hand came up, and light exploded from his palm.

The peasants shouted in pain, covering their eyes. The older man threw himself across his daughter, blinded and in panic. He heard the leader shout a command, but didn't dare rise to try to catch the scoundrel, blind as he was.

Then the green afterimage circle that filled his vision faded, and he could see the rock circle again—with peasants looking about in astonishment. Some began to mutter in fear.

But the father's fear was all for his daughter. Looking down, he saw with relief that she was alive and untouched, though still dull-eyed. He caught up the white robe to cover her and lifted her in his arms. "She is saved! I thank you all, neighbors, for helping me, for my daughter is unharmed, and only frightened!"

"By what magic did they all disappear?" one of the neighbors quavered.

"You know that mushroom that flares so brightly when you dry it and throw it into the fire? That's all he needed, in the dark like this, and he and his men ran away while we were

blinded. Come on, let's take this poor child home!" The father
headed out of the circle, cradling his daughter in his arms,
and the others followed, but with many fearful glances back
over their shoulders. Mushroom or not, they feared magic,
and considering what the white-robed murderer had been
trying to do, they feared it was magic of the worst kind.

In a grove of young firs higher up on the mountain, the
youngest acolyte stumbled in and collapsed on the floor,
panting. The others scarcely noticed; they were too busy
trembling and wiping away sweat. One older acolyte did pay
attention, though, and helped the lad up. "It's all right, now.
They won't think to look for us here, if we're quiet."

"We will not always have to be silent!"

The worshipers all looked up in surprise. Their chief sat,
hood pulled forward over his face, but a stray moonbeam
showed burning eyes and bristling beard.

"Our day will come," he told them. "Our cries and prayers
shall waken the old gods, and they shall come roaring into the
sky against this meek milksop who let mere mortals hang
him on a cross!"

The acolytes gasped at the blasphemy and huddled in on
themselves. Some of them glanced at the sky as though expecting lightning to strike them dead even for hearing such
words.

"Oh, a brave gaggle of Celts are you!" the leader said, with
curled lip. "How staunchly you worship Toutatis, when you
recoil in horror at the slightest word against the Lord of the
priests' book! Do you not wish Toutatis to rise again, and all
the old gods of the druids with him? To rise, and raise you to
power and wealth? The finest garments shall be yours, the
squires' houses, the most beautiful maidens!"

Avarice and lust overcame fear. Several of the acolytes
licked their lips, trying to pluck up courage, but two or three
took fire, crying, "Aye, we wish it!" with burning eyes.

"Then put aside your fears of these clodhopping peasants!" The "druid" overlooked the fact that all of his followers were plowmen themselves. "Put aside fear, and let
your spirits rise in hope! Our day will come! The old gods
will waken! We will win the protection of a prince! He is
swayed by my promises of power and glory, already half won

to our cause! He shall come to the throne, and we shall rise to dominion with him!"

The men stared; the "druid" had mentioned the princely patron before, but never so clearly. It had to be the heir to the throne, it had to be Prince Gaheris!

"We shall have the protection of a prince," the leader promised, his eyes glowing. "We shall have the protection of a king! Then shall we worship in the open with king's soldiers to guard us from these ignorant peasants, then shall we gather in the old stone rings to enact our sacrifices openly and for all to see—and without interruption!"

He stood, arms upraised, eyes searching the sky, and his followers rose with him, caught up in his excitement, in the visions of beautiful naked virgins that his words conjured. They held their arms up, eyes lifted to the cold, cloud-covered moon, and chanted with their leader, though softly, begging, "Toutatis, come!"

A month later Queen Alisande sat at table, not in the Great Hall, but in a smaller chamber, richly furnished, walls hung with bright new tapestries, carpets covering the stone floor, table and chairs of oak polished to glowing. Her husband and royal wizard, Lord Matthew Mantrell, had recommended such a chamber as an aid to negotiation at state dinners—and also a place for the family to gather by themselves. She sat with him and his parents—and with some very unwelcome guests from the neighboring kingdom to the north. The latter had virtually invited themselves, by the stratagem of inviting her when they knew she would be tied up with the bishops' council, convened because of the heresy that had cropped up in the south. Since Alisande was too busy to go to them, she'd had to invite them to come to her—for they were the King and Queen of Bretanglia, with their poisonous brood of three wrangling sons, and Rosamund, fiancée to Gaheris, the heir apparent.

Of course, in their quarreling and backbiting, the boys were only demonstrating that blood runs true, and it was shaping up to be one of the most unpleasant state dinners Alisande had ever experienced. In this universe there was no English Channel, but Matt was beginning to wish it existed, and

that their unwelcome guests were safely on the other side
of it.

Maybe they did, too. "It was a rough ride," Queen Petronille told Alisande. She was a tall, stately woman, still beautiful in middle age. Her auburn hair showed no trace of gray,
though that was probably due more to dye than to youth. She
wore a gown of maroon brocade with long, bell-shaped
sleeves, and a golden tiara set with diamonds. "The old im-
perial highway from Dunlimon was smooth enough, though
here and there a paving-stone is tilted. Still, our armies keep
it free of weeds and trees. But from Laiscal southward it is so
overgrown as to be scarcely a trackway."

Laiscal was the first major town on Alisande's side of the
border—but she let the sally pass with a gracious smile.
"How trying for you! Perhaps a palanquin would have been
more comfortable than riding."

Petronille eyed her narrowly, trying to decide whether that
had been a dig at her age. "Perhaps, my dear—though I have
found that the bearers jounce one about in a palanquin even
more than does a proud stallion."

Typical of the woman, Matt thought—emphasizing that
she was so fine a rider that she didn't need a palfrey or even
a spirited mare, but could handle a stallion of fettle and
mettle. There was also the little matter of calling a reigning
monarch "my dear" instead of "Your Majesty"—a very obvious breach of protocol.

Alisande took it in stride, though. Smiling sweetly, she
said, "Still, a saddle makes one ache so, when one is in it all
day. At least, mine does, whenever I must ride on campaign or
progress. Do you not find it so, Your Grace?"

Matt tried to hide a smile. His gentle wife had adminis-
tered a very mild rebuke for Petronille's breach of manners—
and had reminded her that she might be a queen in Bretanglia,
but was only Duchess of Pykta here in Merovence, and Alisande's vassal to boot. Further, Alisande, riding on military
campaigns whenever her country was threatened, was a sovereign, not merely the consort of one. Of course, she had also
reminded Petronille of her own abilities as a rider.

Petronille only smiled sweetly. "Of course, my dear. How
very boring for you." Then, unable to counter her role as a

king's consort, she turned to score on *Alisande's* consort. "Do you not find it tedious to accompany your wife on such processions, Lord Wizard?"

"Why, no," Matt said, smiling. "I enjoy travel. Of course, I do wish more of it could be peaceful, but I'll take what I can find."

"As did your royal wife, no doubt," Petronille said, with a poisonous smile. She turned to Matt's parents. "You were not born of the nobility, were you, lord and lady?"

"Not in Merovence, no," Papa said, which was strictly true, but left the impression that he had been a nobleman in his homeland.

Before Petronille could pin him down, Mama said, "Of course, one must abdicate all aristocratic titles when one decides to devote oneself to scholarship, Your Majesty."

Papa nodded, picking up on her lead. "When one commits one's life to being a professor, 'Doctor' should be title enough."

Matt smiled, once again elated to see how well they worked together.

"Indeed," Petronille said archly. "And what title would you have claimed in your homeland, if you had not chosen to leave the wider world for the cloisters of the university?"

Mama shrugged, careful of her phrasing. "I would not have chosen to be a countess, Majesty, but with that I should have been content."

Again, strictly true, but creating one hell of a false impression. Matt caught his breath in admiration of his mother's skill with words. No wonder she had turned out to be a top-ranked wizard once she arrived in a universe in which magic worked by poetry.

"Ah yes, you are of Ibile, are you not?" Petronille wouldn't give up. "What province would you have held there?"

Papa smiled. "My father was of Ibile, yes, and his city was Castile—but I grew up in my mother's land, far to the west."

King Drustan frowned. He was tall, well into middle age, but still broad-shouldered, and the bulk that had come on him in his fifties was only slightly flab. His hair was chestnut streaked with gray, and he wore it to his shoulders. His beard was grizzled, full and square-cut, his nose long and straight, his lips full and sensuous, his gray eyes bright and alert for any opening. "I have heard the rumors. Can there truly be a great land so far over the sea?"

"There is," Papa told him, "and my wife and I are both its natives."

"And what would have been your province, my lady, if you had not wed the doctor?" Petronille asked Mama sweetly.

Give it a rest, Matt thought, exasperated.

But Petronille wasn't about to change topics until she'd pinned Mama and Papa down to admitting they weren't of the nobility.

"Havana, if Castro had not stolen it from us," Mama said, allowing the old bitterness to show.

"A robber baron, then?" Petronille gave her a smile that oozed sympathy. "How fortunate for you that you met the good doctor!"

"Then you have come to Merovence to seek asylum?" Drustan asked.

Matt bit back the urge to say that an asylum was where Drustan and Petronille belonged.

"Why, no," Papa said. "We are here because of our son."

"Indeed!" Drustan said, with genuine surprise. "I had heard that you were of great assistance in purging Ibile of the Moors, but I thought you had returned to your homeland for that purpose."

"No, my lord, we did not know that the Moors were invading Ibile until after we had arrived," Papa said truthfully. "Even then, I only went along on campaign to be with my son."

"I am amazed to hear of a parent so dedicated," Gaheris said, with an acid glare at Drustan. He was lean and weasel-faced, with his father's long nose but a receding chin, and scarcely any lips at all. His eyes were small and constantly shifting.

The king glared back. "I, too, am amazed, for it is usually I who must insist that my sons accompany me when we march to war!"

Petronille rounded on him. "You should not force them, Drustan. Brion, yes, he has a fondness for battle, but Gaheris and John find it repugnant."

"Not John!" Drustan beamed at his youngest, sitting at Matt's right hand at the foot of the table. "He rejoices in the weight of his armor and the lance in his hand, do you not, boy?"

If Gaheris looked like a weasel, John looked like a pig. He wasn't terribly fat, only a little plump, but his nose was short and tilted sharply up, his eyes were small and close set, his forehead low under black hair worn, like his father's, at shoulder length. His only attractive feature was his beard, glossy black and silky, which had the double advantage of hiding his cheeks and chin. His doublet was already stained, though they were only on the second course.

He forced a smile in response to his father's question. "You have taught me well, Father."

Resentment flared in Gaheris' and Brion's eyes.

Before they could speak, the nobleman beside Gaheris exclaimed, "Ah, would I could have taken part in those battles!"

Matt looked up at him in surprise; he spoke with the accent of southern Merovence. He was lean but muscular, perhaps in his thirties, and handsome in an angular way, with dark hair cut short.

"You would, Orizhan," Gaheris said sourly. "You're almost as bad as Brion in that."

"Yes, *Sir* Orizhan is a true knight," Brion snapped. Like Orizhan, he wore his brown hair short, but was even more muscular—in fact, built like a carnival strong man. He wore a dark brown doublet with green facings, and his face was both handsome and regal, his nose as straight as his father's but not as long, his hazel eyes large and long lashed, his face clean shaven, showing high cheekbones and a strong, cleft chin.

Gaheris and John bristled at the implication that neither of them was truly worthy of knighthood.

Alisande stepped in to defuse the situation. "But one would expect Sir Orizhan to yearn for battle, when his homeland is so close to peril."

"Indeed, Majesty!" Sir Orizhan said fervently. "That our province of Toulenge was spared the Moors' rule, I thank God!"

"Then go to a church," Gaheris snapped, "and spare us your piety!"

Again Alisande stepped in. "I hope time does not hang too heavily on your hands, Sir Orizhan, for your ward must be quite safe in Their Majesties' keeping."

"I keep Rosamund close indeed," said Petronille, with a glare at her husband, a glare which he returned.

Rosamund kept her gaze fixed on her trencher. She seemed cowed and apprehensive, a mousy little thing whose blond hair had lost its luster and whose eyes had dulled, but Matt thought she might have proved quite a beauty if she'd had some spirit. She said not a word, and considering the company, Matt could sympathize. He just had to endure them for the evening, though—she had to live with them every day!

Sir Orizhan pulled attention away from her before she could be forced to talk. "King Drustan has been kind enough to find employment for me, Your Majesty, so that the time does not hang too heavily on my hands."

"You'd be better employed minding your own business," Gaheris snarled.

"Instead, he minds yours," Brion shot back.

King Drustan gave a shout of laughter. "Aye, Sir Orizhan minds all your businesses, my young bawcocks, and I daresay you embroil yourselves in far less trouble because of it."

"It isn't always pleasant to have an old man dogging our footsteps, Papa," John said, pouting.

Matt stared at Orizhan again. The man couldn't have been over thirty-five.

"Unpleasant and pointless," Gaheris snapped. "Nothing can prevent Brion from picking a fight."

"Nothing except the code of chivalry!" Brion returned. "A true knight never strikes the first blow, except in defense of the weak or innocent."

"The innocent?" Gaheris gave him a nasty smile. "What would you know about innocence?"

"Or weakness?" John asked, still pouting.

"Brion wears a mail shirt throughout the day," Petronille said quickly, "the more to strengthen his body."

"Indeed," Mama said, all enthusiasm. "I have heard him acclaimed as one of the finest knights in Europe—and he so young."

"Yes, it is a pleasure to see one's children excel." Petronille tilted her chin a little higher, preening. "You have only the one, have you not, Lady Mantrell?"

"God has granted me no more," Mama sighed, "but I thank Him that the one He did send me is so good a man."

Drustan frowned. "Oddly phrased, though I am sure the Lord Wizard is goodly. Are you not more concerned with the strength of his arm than with his saintliness?"

"No, Your Majesty," Mama snapped, eyes flashing. She caught herself and forced a smile. "Moral strength is the greatest, and that of the mind is second."

"You speak as a priest would," Gaheris said in disgust.

"I should hope so, for I am a devout Christian!" Mama turned on the prince. "Are you not, Your Highness?"

"Well, of course," Gaheris answered, nettled. "Isn't everybody?"

"But some more than others." Brion gave him a dark look.

"Yes, and some never relent in their holier-than-thou attitudes!" Gaheris snapped.

"Nobody ever asks if *I* go to church," John whined.

"With respect, Your Highness, I don't think they're talking about going to church," Matt told him.

Alisande tried desperately to move the conversation back toward a safer topic. "Surely the strength of the body means something, Lady Mantrell!"

"There speaks the warrior!" Drustan said heartily, and Petronille gave him a glare.

"Of course a strong body means much, Your Majesty," Mama said, smiling, "and Matthew has always been healthy— but he has gained so much since he came here! I think your climate is good for him."

Alisande smiled, with a trace of a blush—she understood that Mama spoke of the emotional climate as well as the weather.

"But you are a knight also, Lord Wizard." Brion frowned. "Surely you have learned the arts of warfare!"

Rosamund hadn't said a word so far, but now she shot at Brion, "Is there nothing for you but swords and maces?"

Brion reddened a little but said, "There is also the lute."

"Yes, the most perfect knights are poets as well as swords-men," Matt interposed smoothly. "I've learned the arts of war since I came to Merovence, Your Highness—but I do agree that chivalry means cultivating the sensibilities as well as the body. Still, I count myself an indifferent poet. I acknowledge you my superior in verse."

Brion reddened again, this time with pleasure. "Surely not, milord! You are so much more experienced than I!"

Matt laughed. "Experience counts for nothing without talent, Highness. I know many excellent poems, but in composing them, I may be clever, but I have no genius."

Brion leaned forward, suddenly intent. "I must hear these poems that you count great."

"Then you must find some time alone with the Lord Wizard," Drustan snapped. "There are some of us who can do with just so much rhyming."

"There are some of us who could do with a good deal more!" Petronille said, with another glare.

"*I* could do rhymes," John said, pouting, "but nobody ever asks *me.*"

"There are more important things in this world than verses, madame," Drustan said in a frosty tone, "as you would know, if you ever left off listening to your troubadours!"

"I govern the Pykta very well, thank you!"

"No," Drustan said, with a cynical smile, "you send Brion to do it for you."

"I do not order my children to run errands for me," Petronille snapped. "Brion goes where he will!"

"As a prince should." For once, Drustan seemed to agree with her.

"Yes, but Brion does not wed to gain what he lost in battle!"

Drustan reddened. Matt guessed the reference had been to the king's proposing to Petronille, and her lands, right after he had tried to conquer Erin—the Ireland of his own world—and failed. The king snapped, "No prince weds where he is not welcomed! Perhaps that is why Brion travels so widely!"

"He certainly does." Gaheris made it an accusation. "Myself, I would rather see to the management of my estates than go gadding about to every tournament or battle that crops up."

"Yes, because you fear the pain of a wound!" Brion snapped. "You fear even the sound of battle!"

"And you, brother, should beware the knife between your ribs." Gaheris made it a threat.

"They always go on like this," John confided to Matt. "It makes dinnertime so nasty."

"I can see that it would," Matt said politely. For himself, he was tired of it already.

"The knife between my ribs?" Brion gave his older brother a wolf's grin. "Who would dare wield it?"

"Anyone," Gaheris said flatly. "You may have already carved out a name as the perfect chivalrous knight, brother, and the people may love you because of the songs you give the troubadours to sing about you, but anyone who knows you in person finds little to love!"

"When you speak of yourself, brother, don't attach my name to it," Brion countered. "Even your fiancée can find nothing to love in you!"

Rosamund looked up in alarm.

Gaheris gave her a shark's grin and looked her up and down, letting his gaze linger over her contours, where her loose gown hinted at them. "She need not love me, brother. I shall do what loving is needed."

"None shall be needed!" Drustan barked. "Wait till you are wedded for such talk, boy!"

"Is it not his right?" Petronille challenged. "Or are you so prickly about every slightest comment made about every pretty young thing?"

"Should you not see to the protecting of this child you have reared as your daughter?" Drustan demanded.

"How can I, with you about?"

Rosamund turned on Brion. "See what you have done now! They're back to their old wrangling because of you!"

Brion bent his brows as he turned to her. "They will wrangle no matter what I say or do not say. Is it I who have sent you to be tossed about like some pawn in a chess match?"

Rosamund flinched as though she'd been slapped. "What parent would not wish his child to be a queen?"

"Your father might have taken the precaution of meeting the groom first."

"Speak no ill of the dead, boy!" Drustan snapped.

"It is not the dead of whom I speak ill." Brion regarded his elder brother narrowly. "Even at twelve years, no one could have thought Gaheris a true knight!"

"Oh, aye, chivalry is the only measure of worth for you, isn't it?" Gaheris sneered. "Never mind the dealing of justice, the prosperity of the people, or the good governance of your own province!"

"The people of Yorkshire are quite happy, thank you, and quite prosperous and safe!"

"They are, for you have had the luck to find an excellent seneschal!" Gaheris snapped.

"Whereas you have not bothered to choose one at all, Prince of Wales—and the Welsh toil in misery because of it!"

"Oh, stop it, stop it!" Rosamund clapped her hands over her ears, glaring at Brion. "Can't you give even a little respect to your future sovereign? Will you scold him so when he is your king?"

Brion reddened with anger and hurt, and Gaheris grinned, crooning, "Do not give a lady a cause for grief, O Chivalrous Knight! Nay, do her bidding and speak with respect to your elders!"

Brion gave him a whetted glare, but said only, "I will do as my future sovereign wishes."

"Silence is golden," John sighed. "My future sister-in-law has a knack for making it."

Only because Brion was willing to listen to her, Matt thought—and for this she snapped at him?

"You speak as a true knight should," Alisande told Brion, and turned to Petronille and Drustan. "You have cause to be proud of him."

Petronille fairly glowed at the compliment, turning a doting gaze on her middle son, but Drustan frowned, displeased.

"Yes," Gaheris said acidly. "It's just as well the troubadours don't know what a bully Brion really is."

"Why, for interrupting your pleasure when you were whipping that peasant?" But Brion glanced uneasily at Rosamund, and Matt had no doubt as to the peasant's gender. Rosamund didn't see it; she had gone back to staring at her trencher.

Gaheris gave him a black glare.

It made sense, Matt supposed—if the second child tends to be a rebel, then in this family, Brion would opt for being noble and upright.

"No one ever talks about me," John whined to Matt.

Matt bit back the temptation to say that he could see why, and started a polite rejoinder, but Gaheris snarled at Brion, "As I recall, you were wearing a mail shirt at the time and had your sword at your belt, while I was unarmed!"

"If you would strengthen your body, you too would be able to wear a mail shirt whenever you go out to—" Brion glanced uneasily at Rosamund, and changed whatever he had been about to say. "—whenever you go out among the people."

" 'Go out,' forsooth!" Drustan chuckled. "That's as much as to say a rooster 'goes out' in a hen house!" But he was watching Rosamund as he said it, and her cheeks burned with embarrassment, which seemed to gratify Drustan.

But if he was watching Rosamund, Petronille was watching him, and her face darkened at his attention to the princess. "So you think the lad should take pride in philandering, *husband*?"

Drustan turned to her with an easy grin. "Surely it is better that he do so before he marries than after, wife."

"Yes," Petronille hissed, and her gaze shot icicles, points first. "It is far better not to stray once one is wedded."

"More wine," Alisande said quickly, holding her standing cup toward the steward.

"The butt is out, Your Majesty," the steward said apologetically. "Shall I draw from a new?"

"No, I think it is time for brandywine." Alisande rose, and the others perforce rose with her. "Majesties, shall we leave the young folk to their sport and discuss the more sedate topics that accord with age?"

"Well, with rank, at least," Drustan said. Then, gallantly, "You could scarcely be numbered among those who carry the weight of years."

Petronille glared more icicles at him—she was considerably older than he.

"You are gracious, Majesty." Alisande turned to Rosamund. "Shall I bid the fiddlers play for dancing, lady?"

"Not on my account, I pray you, Your Majesty," Rosamund said quickly. "I find that my head has begun to ache, and think that I shall retire directly."

Lucky kid, Matt thought. This kind of table talk would have given anyone a headache. He, of course, couldn't beg off from the rest of the evening even if he'd had a migraine.

"I shall retire, too." John cast a covetous glance at Rosamund—and Gaheris stepped on his toe. John clamped his jaw shut in a way that spoke of long practice.

"Yes, do retire, brother," Gaheris said, with a nasty grin. "Leave the life of the night to those who are lively enough for it."

"Beware, Gaheris," Drustan said, chuckling. "I've been practicing swordplay with the lad. He might have more energy than you think."

"Then let him spend it by himself." Gaheris turned away to Brion. "Come, brother! Let us seek a chessboard and turn to gaming!"

Matt didn't doubt for a second that they would be playing games late into the night, but somehow he suspected that those games wouldn't involve a chessboard.

CHAPTER 2

The royal couples retired to Alisande's solar with Mama and Papa to act as buffers. A servant poured the first round of brandywine, then left the decanter and, at a sign from Alisande, departed.

"What a pleasant chamber, Your Majesty!" Petronille looked around at the wainscotted walls hung with tapestries, the Persian carpet that covered the hardwood floor, the huge clerestory window with its draperies closed now against the night. Opposite it was the fireplace and the tall bookcase that stood between it and the heavily carved table that served Alisande as a desk. Six hourglass-shaped chairs stood about in a rough circle.

"I thank you, Your Majesty." Alisande smiled, sitting in a chair a little taller than the others, with the crown and lilies carved in its back. The rest of the chairs were spaced equally around the room, so there could be no concern about rank in the seating—none would have denied Matt's right to sit next to his wife, and Papa and Mama were careful to take chairs across from them, to avoid having Merovencians on one side and Bretanglians on the other.

They sat, and Drustan sipped at his brandywine and smiled. "Excellently brewed! But now, Majesty, we must discuss the future."

"If we must, Majesty," Alisande sighed. "At times it seems all I can do to cope with the present."

"Indeed it does," Drustan said wryly, "but the future will become the present all too soon, and we must plan for it before it comes."

"Of which matters do you speak, Lord of Bretanglia?"

17

"Of the inheritance of Pykta and Deintenir, Sovereign of Merovence." Drustan lost his smile.

Matt braced himself, even though he'd known this was coming. By a quirk of history, Drustan and Petronille had inherited provinces in Merovence, and Alisande naturally did not want them to become part of Bretanglia. More to the point, she didn't want to lose any of her people to the rule of a monarch she didn't trust, or his heir, whom she trusted even less.

"Do you speak as Duke of Deintenir or King of Bretanglia?" she asked.

"As both," Drustan snapped. "Deintenir must go to my son when I die!"

Alisande's eyes flared at the word "must," but she kept her voice level. "I care not, so long as he acknowledges me, or my heir, as his suzerain in those provinces, even as you do, Duke and Duchess."

"I hold Deintenir from my childless uncle," Drustan said, "but my son's claim will be far stronger. He will inherit his provinces from both his parents, and therefore should hold them in his own name as part of his own kingdom."

"He will hold Deintenir as your son, and Pykta as Petronille's." Alisande sounded weary. "Therefore he will hold each province from only one parent. Am I to give all my northern coast to your line for no greater cause than half kinship?"

"Give the province to itself, Majesty!" Petronille urged. "I have inherited Pykta from my father, and am your vassal, but I have more sons than one. When I die, let Brion hold Pykta in his own right, and let it be a sovereign princedom in itself!"

Drustan rounded on her. "Would you split the domain only so that your favorite need not kneel to his elder brother?"

"Would you deny Brion everything?" Petronille returned. "You have granted all of Wales to his brother already, and refused him Scotland!"

"Scotland and Bretanglia became one kingdom when my Scottish father married my Anglian mother," Drustan retorted. "They must not be sundered again!"

"Then spare him Pykta as his own princedom!"

"Done!"

"But not by me," Alisande said, as he had known she would.

Her voice rang with iron. "Pykta is mine, but I shall be proud to name Brion my vassal, if he will take seizin from me."

Drustan surged to his feet, face red with rage, bellowing, "Do you dare deny my right? If I say my son shall have Pykta, he shall have it, by your leave or no! And when he weds Rosamund, he shall have Toulenge, too!"

"Deintenir, Pykta, and Toulenge?" Matt cried, scandalized. "That's a third of Merovence!"

"The law of inheritance is clear!" Drustan thundered. "If a third of your realm is my son's birthright and his wife's dowry, that is your bad fortune!"

Alisande sat unmoving, face stony, eyes gimlets. Matt rose with a feral grin, stepping a little toward Drustan, but before either of them could speak, Petronille declared, "Brion must be his own master!"

"Pykta is a small province, with rocky soil and no mines," Alisande pointed out. "It has little wealth and few soldiers. If it were a separate land, it would be quickly conquered by Merovence or Bretanglia or, worse, by a foreign power, most probably Ibile."

"Pykta shall triumph and remain free," Petronille returned, "if mighty Brion defends it."

"Is he a superhuman warrior, then, this perfect knight of yours?" Drustan demanded.

"Are you jealous of your own son?" Petronille retorted, and they were off again.

Alisande leaned back, unable to hide her weariness.

They all knew that neither side would yield, and that the issue could only be settled by battle. Drustan and Petronille were simply trying to provoke Alisande into giving them grounds to declare war, and she was determined to avoid it. Fortunately, the two of them couldn't agree long enough to force her hand.

Matt sighed; it was going to be a long evening.

The common room at the Inn of the Courier Snail boomed with laughter, ribald verse, and off-key song. Smoke from a wide fireplace curled along the low rafters, darkened with a century and more of poor ventilation. The hearth held a fragrant kettle of stew and a variety of fowls roasting on spits.

Minstrels sang in two different corners with no fear of anyone more than twenty feet away hearing them—and if the streets outside were not the safest nor the neighborhood quite the most refined, well, the kind of amusements the northern soldiers sought could scarcely have been found at a more luxurious hostelry.

Serving wenches threaded their way through the crowds in excellent form. The landlord filled one tankard after another from a huge barrel of table wine. He was rosy-cheeked and sweating with warmth, smiling with great good cheer—the Bretanglian soldiers of the royal bodyguard were good for business. Oh, there had been the predictable quarrels with the locals, about beef and ale being better than frogs' legs and wine, but they managed to avoid coming to blows, partly because the prostitutes had beguiled the more quarrelsome away upstairs to another kind of conflict, and the Bretanglians were now playing at draughts and at dice with good fellowship and amiable insults. After all, each side could claim not to understand the other because of its barbarous accent.

The scream tore across the common room, and Laetri, the most skillful of the inn's prostitutes, came tumbling down the stairs against the back wall. Everyone was instantly silent, all eyes turned to the scene of sudden violence, as the Bretanglian nobleman came striding down the stairs, his dagger raised. Oh, he wore the livery of a common soldier, but his bearing marked him as an aristocrat, as did his accent as he snarled, "Little thief! Give back my purse, or I'll cut out your heart!"

"I didn't take it!" Laetri stumbled to her feet, clutching the rags of her bodice to her, and men stared at the bruises on her face, the streaks of blood on her back and arms. "I didn't touch your purse," she cried, "and you gave me nothing from it! Pargas, help me!"

Her pimp stepped between her and the nobleman, pulling two small clubs from his belt, one in each hand. "You'll not get out of paying her wages simply by crying thief, milord."

"What lord?" the Bretanglian cried, enraged. "I'm only a common soldier, you fool!"

"Oh! Well, if you're only a trooper, then I might as well give you a drubbing till you pay!"

The Bretanglian soldiers came to their feet, hands going to their daggers. Their Merovencian fellow gamblers stood up, too, reaching for clubs and dirks, suddenly much less hospitable.

The landlord, seeing a riot coming, stepped up, crying, "Please, goodmen, not in here!"

A tall, older man in peasant dress stepped up to the nobleman. "Your Highness, this is not fitting! You shame yourself!"

"Get away from me with your mealy-mouthed preaching, Orizhan," the nobleman snarled, and shoved the disguised knight away. He stumbled back and fell.

"I do not preach, and my mouth has no meal!" a Bretanglian sergeant said, stepping up to glare at Pargas. "I am Sergeant Brock, and I shall grind your bones if you defy my lord!"

Sir Orizhan scrambled to his feet, his face red. "We are guests in this land!"

But the nobleman took courage from the sergeant's support and snarled at Pargas. "Insolent fellow! I'll teach you some manners, and your whore some honesty!" He leaped on the pimp, dagger flashing.

Pargas howled, stumbling back against the wall, blood spreading from a gash in his left shoulder—but his right arm swung its club.

The Bretanglian sergeant shouted and leaped in to block the club, his own dagger stabbing. Two Merovencian toughs bellowed in anger and jumped him.

Sir Orizhan ran to help Sergeant Brock, crying, "Put up your weapons, I beg you!"

A Merovencian tough whacked him with a club. He fell back into the arms of the nobleman, who tossed him aside in disgust, leaving him to rise again or not, as the fortunes of battle might have it. Then the Bretanglian nobleman took a firmer hold on his dagger and went after Pargas again as two Merovencians jumped on Sergeant Brock. Two of Brock's troopers ran to help, and four Merovencians fell on them.

As one, the foreigners turned on the locals, and in seconds

the whole room was one huge brawl. Stools swung as weapons. Men lifted other stools as shields. Knives streaked, clubs cracked, and men bellowed rage at one another.

Then a scream cut across the shouting, a scream of such horror and anguish that all the men froze and turned to stare.

Laetri was shoving herself into a corner, screaming and screaming, and Pargas, bleeding from half a dozen knife cuts, stood in front of her, panting but with his club still raised—and staring, appalled at the same sight that terrified Laetri.

The Bretanglian nobleman lay on his back in a pool of his own blood, a bruise on his forehead, his eyes wide and staring but seeing nothing, nor would those eyes ever see anything again.

The silence of shock gripped the whole room. Then Sergeant Brock shook off the brawler who had fallen on top of him, shoved himself to his feet and sprang to the fallen man. "Your Highness!"

Sir Orizhan moaned, sick with dread.

"Highness?" Dread washed over Pargas' features.

"Of course!" the sergeant shouted. "You knew he was no common soldier, no matter how he was dressed!" He glared at Laetri. "You have been honored with the touch of the heir to the throne of Bretanglia, woman—Gaheris, Prince of Wales!"

"Hon—Honored?" Laetri could only touch the bruise on her cheek, a sob catching in her throat.

Then the innkeeper pointed, howling. "Stop him!"

Whirling, everyone saw the man just as he sprang out the window and into the night. With the howl of the hunting pack, locals and visitors alike tore out the door to give chase.

The innkeeper turned to Pargas and Laetri, shooing them toward the kitchen. "Out of my house, scoundrels! Out the back door and into the alley, for I'll have no more of your troublemaking here!"

Half a dozen Bretanglian soldiers stepped into their path, and a hard hand caught the innkeeper's arm. He turned to see Sir Orizhan, flint-eyed and grim. "A nice try, landlord, and you might indeed have helped your friends escape—but I am the companion assigned to protect the prince, and I'll not take the blame for this alone! Corin! Ferol! Bind these three and take them to the castle—and do it quickly, before that rat pack comes back!"

Alisande's lady-in-waiting laid down the brush. "There! Your Majesty's hair glistens like the sun! Shall I braid it?"

"I shall do that myself tonight." Alisande stood up, clad in only her shift and long blond hair. "I thank you for your ministrations, ladies, but I shall tell you good-night now. It has been a long and wearying day."

"Good night, then, Your Majesty." The senior lady curtsied, and the others after her. They went out the door, already beginning to murmur in amazement at their young sovereign's strength in standing against the worst arguments and tempers of her royal guests.

The door closed behind them—and Alisande turned to throw open the other door, the one that connected to Matt's suite. He stood there waiting and came in, arms up to embrace. Alisande all but fell into them, buried her face in his shoulder and let herself go limp at last, let herself stop being strong, let herself take refuge for a few moments in her husband's love. "What a horrible family!" she said into Matt's chest.

"Not the worst I've seen, but certainly in the running for second place," he agreed. "With so much bickering, it's a wonder they can govern their kingdom at all!"

Alisande pushed herself a little away, though not far. "You cannot entirely blame Petronille if she is a virago, though—not with a husband like that."

"What—aside from the fact that she doesn't dare turn her back on him for a second? Look at it this way, Drustan's entirely dependable—she can depend on him to betray her anytime he takes it into his head to want something that might hurt her!"

"Well, be fair to him," Alisande said with a half smile. "He never stops to think whether or not his actions will hurt her, or anyone else."

"Right. He knows what he wants, and he sets about getting it, and if anybody gets in his way, too bad."

Alisande shuddered. "How could a woman marry a man like that?"

"Oh, I expect he looked a lot better twenty years ago," Matt said, "when he was new to kinging, and didn't realize how much power he had yet."

"Which he may have learned from her, if the tales of her former marriage are to be believed," Alisande said.

"She did kind of run her first husband, didn't she? But after all, she was the one who'd been born with a title."

"Yes, and he was only a knight errant, though a handsome one by all accounts." Alisande sighed. "One wonders why he died so young."

"Delayed action from an old wound, no doubt. Riding the tournament circuit can be dangerous."

"So can Petronille," Alisande said darkly. She went to sit down and stare into her mirror. "Could I ever be like that, husband?"

"Only if I didn't do my job right." Matt came up behind her, caught a stray blond lock and began to wind it about his finger. "No, I don't think you could ever be that selfish, love. You're too busy fighting off rebels and invaders, and trying to find some way to make life better for your people."

"Sometimes it is hard to know right from wrong," Alisande said, "and one step to the wrong can begin a long slide to perdition and tyranny. What of our children, husband? How can we prevent them from becoming like those boys?"

"By being as loving to one another and to them as we can," Matt said, remembering his own parents. "I don't think the Bretanglian princes learned insulting and pettiness on their own, after all. They tend to do what they see their parents do."

"There's truth in that," Alisande said somberly. "I've never seen a man who matched that Gaheris for pure malice. How could the Prince of Toulenge ever have betrothed his daughter to such a one?"

Matt shrugged. "She was only ten at the time, and I suspect Gaheris looked a lot better at fourteen. Only his parents and the servants knew the truth then."

"And perhaps he had not begun to be such a monster, when he had little power." Alisande sighed. "Poor Rosamund! How she must have suffered in that household!"

"You don't mean she was raised with that family!"

"It is the custom for the fiancée to dwell with her new kinfolk as soon as they are betrothed, husband." Alisande gave him a sad smile, to reassure him for not knowing all her people's customs yet. "She must learn the ways of her new land, you see."

"A ten-year-old girl, being torn away from home and raised among strangers?" Matt shuddered. "At least Petronille kept her close by her side."

"So you felt that, too?"

"Oh, yes. Besides, she had some ladies from Toulenge for company, didn't she?"

"Aye, but King Drustan sent them all packing. He could not send Sir Orizhan away, but the ladies he could, and did."

"I've been wondering where he came into the picture. You don't expect to find a man with a southern Merovencian accent living with the Bretanglian royal family. So he was part of the entourage that delivered little Rosamund to Bretanglia?"

"He was appointed as her bodyguard," Alisande told him. "However, King Drustan claimed that there was no need for such while the little lady lived under his protection."

"But he couldn't send a knight away when he was under orders from his own duke?"

"Not without grievous insult to his new kinsman, no. Instead, Drustan assigned Sir Orizhan to tutoring his own sons in chivalry, and to keeping them from harm."

"Broadened his assignment from one child to four, eh?" Matt frowned. "Could be that worked out for the best. If he kept an eye on the princes, he could make sure they didn't bother Rosamund too much."

"There is that saving grace," Alisande agreed. "However, since she is so very reserved, it would appear there were times when he could not protect her."

"Sure—whenever King Drustan or Queen Petronille were there. Maybe the queen dotes on her sons a bit more than she seems to."

"I would say she does not seem to dote at all," Alisande said tartly, "except for her favorite, and he has not turned out so badly."

"Brion? Yeah, he does seem to have some sense of right and wrong. I have to give the code of chivalry that much credit. Of course, his brothers know right from wrong, too. They just happen to choose Wrong."

"John makes my skin crawl," Alisande said with a shudder. "No doubt I wrong him—he seems harmless enough, in spite of his constant whining . . ."

"Not smart enough to be any danger? Hey, I've known some pretty dumb monsters, dear."

"Perhaps," Alisande allowed, "but it is not his fault that his face is a mass of pimples and his body inclined to plumpness."

"Still, it doesn't exactly speak of good hygiene or healthy habits," Matt pointed out. "How anyone who claims to practice swordplay out in the tilting yard so much can still have a pasty complexion with a poolroom pallor, I can't understand."

"He certainly seems to be a horrid little man." Alisande frowned. "What is a 'poolroom'?"

"A place for indoor recreation, dear, like the board games that keep our knights from chopping each other to bits during the winter."

"Only chess and the like?" Alisande smiled up at him. "I had hoped for another form of indoor recreation tonight. I need the consolation badly."

"Well, I hope I don't do badly with my consolation." Matt leaned down to kiss her—but before his lips touched hers, there was a knock at the door.

Alisande's lips went stiff. Matt froze for a second, then straightened with a sigh. "I could wish that the world would leave us alone for a day or two."

"I would be glad of an hour!" Alisande turned her chair to the door and sat, squaring her shoulders. "Enter!"

Lady Dulcet opened the door and stepped in, her face drawn and pale. "Your pardon, Majesty, but Sir Orizhan is come from town with urgent news . . ."

Alisande whirled to snatch up her robe and slip her arms through the sleeves. "Bid him enter!"

Lady Dulcet stepped aside with an air of relief. Sir Orizhan entered, stiffly erect, face taut with strain. He fell to one knee. "My liege!"

"I am, and great is the loyalty of one who remembers such when he has sojourned nearly ten years in a foreign court,"

Alisande assured him. "Whatever your news, speak it straight out, no matter how grim!"

Sir Orizhan braced himself even more. "It regards Prince Gaheris."

Alisande stiffened. "What of him?"

"There . . . there was a brawl in a tavern," Sir Orizhan told her. "The prince sought to defend the honor of a maiden, and . . . in the melee . . ."

Alisande started out of her chair. "How badly is he hurt?"

"The worst, Majesty. He . . . he is . . ."

"Not dead!"

"I fear so, Your Majesty." Sir Orizhan bowed his head as though waiting for the headsman's axe.

Alisande sank back in her chair with a moan. She started to bow her head into her hand, then caught herself, unwilling to show such a sign of weakness even to her closest lady-in-waiting.

Matt rested a hand on her shoulder. "I think we should take a few minutes in private, to consider the news."

"Indeed!" Alisande said. "I thank you, Sir Orizhan. Please leave us now."

The knight rose and started to back away, then hesitated. "I must tell Their Majesties of Bretanglia."

"You must not." Alisande sat straight again. "I shall tell them—yet I must have a few minutes to consider the way of it. Leave us."

"Thank you, Your Majesty." For a moment Sir Orizhan's emotional armor cracked enough to show great relief, and Matt was sure he would be even more loyal to Alisande in the future. The knight backed out, closing the door behind him.

Alisande folded in on herself, letting her head sink into her hands with a groan.

"Yes." Matt rested both hands on her shoulders, trying to ignore his sudden queasiness. "What a mess! I could almost feel sorry for Gaheris."

"I, too, had he not brewed such a coil for us by his passing." Alisande straightened, slamming one fist on the table-top. "Why could he not have stayed within the castle for his amusements!"

"Because his idea of fun was the kind of thing you'd start a war to prevent," Matt said grimly.

"Start a war indeed! We shall be most fortunate if his parents do not declare war on Merovence on the instant!" Alisande stood up slowly, shoulders bearing up bravely against the invisible mantle of authority with its huge weight of responsibility. "Let us face them now."

In only her robe and slippers, she went out into the hall and turned toward the chambers reserved for guests of state. Three steps down the hall and they could hear the muted voices shouting at one another, though they couldn't understand the words.

"Even at bedtime they quarrel?" Alisande stared.

"Of course," Matt said. "Why waste a perfectly good chance for a fight?"

But as they said it, a Bretanglian sergeant came panting around the corner with half a dozen troopers following. Ignoring his fellow soldiers who guarded their monarchs' portal, he pounded his fist on the door. The arguing inside cut off abruptly.

"Oh, no!" Alisande moaned.

"Maybe it's better if we aren't the ones to tell them the news, anyway," Matt consoled her.

The door opened and the sergeant hurried in.

"One." Matt counted seconds, holding up fingers. "Two . . . three . . . four . . ."

A scream tore through the door and wrenched at their heartstrings, but the roar that followed it should have shattered the panel. The sergeant stumbled out backward, pressing one hand to his cheek and the other to his forehead, then fell unconscious. Petronille stepped over his body and turned toward Alisande. She saw her hostess and screamed again, running toward her, hands hooked into claws. "You have slain him! Your vile people have slain him!"

"Traitors! Poltroons!" Drustan roared, only one step behind her. "Have you no guards, have you no Watch? How could you let your scum slay a true prince?"

"Your Majesties, I am most deeply sorry," Alisande said, face pale. "I share your grief."

"Be sure that you shall!" Drustan bellowed. "Be sure that you shall share it at spear's point!"

Every Merovencian soldier in the hallway slanted his pike or halberd to guard position. The Bretanglians saw and readied their own weapons.

"Nothing can console you for such a loss," Matt said quickly, "but I shall find the murderer and haul him before you for your vengeance!"

"We have the murderer," one of the Bretanglian soldiers snapped. "It's the pimp who—"

Petronille spun to face him, eyes wide and wild.

"—who fought him trying to ravish the maiden," the soldier ad-libbed quickly. "We have both him and one of his doxies in custody, Majesty!"

"I shall see him drawn and quartered!" Drustan thundered, glaring at Alisande.

"That is the punishment for treachery or the slaying of a prince," she agreed, wooden-faced.

"The surgeons must save him first," the Bretanglian soldier said in his heavy accent. "Your son gave the man quite a drubbing, Majesty, and slit his weasand for him."

Something about the way the man said it set Matt's built-in lie detector shrilling.

"Call out all your surgeons!" Petronille commanded. "We must preserve the louse for royal vengeance!"

"Indeed we must," Alisande returned. "Death in combat is far too gentle an ending for a prince-killer."

"Did he act alone?" Matt asked.

He said it softly, but the whole hallway fell silent. Then Petronille asked in a strangled tone, "What do you mean?"

"Only that," Matt told her. "Princes are trained in fighting; alley urchins only learn it by winning often enough to stay alive. I don't think a street fighter could have killed a skilled swordsman without help."

"The prince had no sword," the Bretanglian soldier said instantly, "only a dagger. He was disguised as a peasant."

Again Matt's alarm rang, but this time because he was guessing right. He ignored the question of why the prince had dressed down for his evening's recreation and said, "With or without a sword, he should have been more than the equal of a gutter rat. Who came at his back?"

The hall was silent, the Bretanglian soldiers staring at one another.

Finally Drustan smelled a running rodent, too. He turned on his guardsmen, demanding, "Well?"

"There was the man who went out the window," one of them said hesitantly.

"And you did not pursue him? Fool!" Drustan backhanded the man across the chops so hard that he fell back into his mates. "No one will find him now! The trail is cold!"

"Cold or hot, I'll find him," Matt assured the king. "If you don't have one murderer to chop up, you'll have the other."

"Then you shall accompany him!" Drustan jabbed a finger at Sir Orizhan. "You, disgraced knight who failed in your charge!" He kicked the fallen sergeant. "Wake this one and send him, too."

The assignment spoke of a lack of trust, but under the circumstances, Matt could understand it. He stepped around the king to the Bretanglian guardsmen. "Tell me about this man who went out the window."

They eyed him warily, and one said, "How could you catch him when the trail is more than an hour cold?"

"I'm the Lord Wizard, remember?"

"Tell him!" Drustan shouted.

They told.

CHAPTER 3

If anyone happened to be awake and noticing Matt through their windows that midnight, they must have shuddered and pulled the drapes shut, muttering a quick charm. Dressed in a dark brown leather jerkin and black hose, Matt looked pretty grim. Sir Orizhan wore similar clothing, and Sergeant Brock's indigo livery was just as gloomy. It didn't help their image that they were nosing around under the tavern's window.

"What do you think to find, milord?" Sergeant Brock asked, but there was no respect in his tone.

"I was hoping for soft ground and a footprint," Matt told him.

The sergeant gave a mirthless laugh. "In a back alley in the roughest section of your town?"

"He is correct, I fear," Sir Orizhan said. "You will find only hard-packed earth with a light coating of garbage."

"Gotta remember to tell the queen about a public health program . . ." Then Matt grinned. "Whattaya know! Cheese rinds and horse dung work just as well as the soft dirt in a garden bed." He pointed.

The other men stared down at the footprint in the garbage.

Sergeant Brock frowned, doing some pointing of his own, farther away from the wall, sweeping his finger in a broad arc. "There are more footprints there, many more. What makes you think this one was made by the foot of our runaway?"

"Because those are all going to left and right," Matt said. "This is the only one going away from the wall. Besides, it's cutting into the others and over them, which means it's much newer."

"Good enough," Sir Orizhan said, frowning, "but I see only

31

two prints going away; then they join the others. How shall you follow them?"

Matt took a vial of powdered chalk from his pocket, tapped a few grains into the footprint, then set the bottom of the vial on top of them chanting,

> "Marking powder carbonate,
> With this footprint resonate!
> On rocky road or bog path sodden,
> Show me where this foot has trodden!"

Sergeant Brock frowned. "You use wizard's words among common ones, but what good will they do?"

"There!" Matt pointed.

The others looked and saw a trail of tracks gleaming brighter than the rest, reflecting moonbeams as though they, too, had been dusted with chalk.

Matt put the vial back into his wallet. "Let's go!" He set off through the moonlit night, imagining sinister presences looking over his shoulder and watching him from the shadows— at least, he hoped he was imagining.

They came to a patch of shadow, and Sir Orizhan stared. "The footprints glow without light!"

"It's a useful spell." Matt glanced at Sergeant Brock. The man's face was set and grim—maybe his response to fear of the supernatural; Matt had seen people react to his spells in a host of different ways.

The footprints came out of the shadow and gleamed in the moonlight again, and the knight and sergeant relaxed a little. Matt blessed the silver crescent and wished it could stay up a little longer, but it was a young moon early in the month, and had to be in bed at a decent time. If it stayed with him another hour, he'd be lucky. Of course, Sergeant Brock was holding a torch to guide them after that.

Matt's spine prickled as he remembered that the man he was tracking wasn't the only footpad in this part of town. "Y'know, men, we may be dressed for rough work, but our clothes are much better quality than most of the garments people wear around here."

"What of it?" Sir Orizhan asked, frowning.

"He means that our garments show us to have money," the sergeant explained. "Do you track a murderer, yet fear simple footpads, Lord Wizard?"

"Good clothing might be enough to put a small gang with clubs and daggers on our trail," Matt told him.

"You are a knight as well as a wizard," Sir Orizhan said softly. "You should have no need to concern yourself over peasants."

"Don't underestimate the poor, Sir Knight," Matt answered. "They can be tougher than you think, especially if they travel in packs—and they could slow us down a lot."

Sergeant Brock looked pleasantly surprised—he was a peasant himself, and not used to having knights view his kind with anything but contempt.

Matt rested a hand on his sword just in case.

Sir Orizhan couldn't believe his ears. "Surely you do not fear them!"

"Of course not," Matt said, nettled. He'd been knighted, after all, and courage was one of the side effects of the knighting ceremony, at least in this universe. "I think of peasants the same way I think of electr—uh, lightning, Sir Orizhan. I don't fear them, but I do treat them with a very healthy respect."

Sir Orizhan looked scandalized, but Sergeant Brock almost smiled.

The footprints led out of the alley and into the street, which wasn't much better—but the center was clear of refuse, and the footsteps disappeared as they hit hard-packed dirt. Matt sighed, wishing there had been a little rain early in the evening. Since there hadn't, he took out his vial of chalk and sprinkled it lightly before him, chanting,

> "Powder of the old antacid,
> Show me where the foot has pass-ed!"

A few grains glowed dimly in the night.

Sergeant Brock gawked. "What are those spots that glow so?"

"Grains of the powder I sprinkled, that landed where the fugitive stepped," Matt told him.

"How can they tell his steps from all the others?" Sir Orizhan was striving for composure.

"The Law of Contagion," Matt explained. "I made the powder identify his footsteps back beneath the window, so it still does, even though we can't see them."

Sir Orizhan frowned, not understanding. Matt wasn't sure he did himself, so he let it pass. He set off following the trail, sprinkling a little powder and chanting a couplet every ten feet or so. Sure enough, the faint glow confirmed that he was still going in the right direction. "Just hope our man went to ground nearby."

"Why?" Sergeant Brock asked.

"Because he has a two-hour lead," Matt explained. "If he just kept going, I can't possibly catch up with him before I run out of chalk."

"Is that all that substance is?" Sir Orizhan asked, wide-eyed.

"Just powdered chalk," Matt assured him. "The magic is in the verse I made up, not in the powder itself."

The footprints led him out of the maze of crooked alleys and into a nicer part of town, or one that was at least a little less run-down.

"Luck is with us." Sergeant Brock pointed at the faint glow of the powder. "Either that, or your spell has weakened."

The footprints stopped at the door of the first decent-looking inn.

"Or," said Sir Orizhan, "our quarry is overconfident."

"I don't think it's my spell." Matt started to knock on the door, then hesitated; Sir Orizhan's words raised a doubt.

"Yes, you see my point," Sir Orizhan said. "The man we are hunting must be supremely overconfident to have done no more to escape than to take a room in an inn for the night."

"You might be right," Matt admitted. "I would have expected him to try to climb the city wall, at least."

"The lout didn't even choose a bolt hole that would be hard to find," Sergeant Brock grunted.

Matt nodded. "We could have done nothing more than send a dozen soldiers knocking on the door of every inn in town, asking if a man had checked in within the last two hours. What would he have done then?"

"Gone out the window and into the night again," Sergeant Brock answered.

Sir Orizhan agreed. "Soldiers asking questions would have been all the warning he needed."

Matt couldn't very well disagree, considering that their quarry had already gone out the window once that night. "I still can't help feeling that we might be stepping into a trap."

Sir Orizhan looked up, startled. "Why, so we might!"

"Aye, now that you mention it," Sergeant Brock growled. "That might be reason enough for hiding so plainly, might it not?"

"I think we'd better take precautions," Matt told them. "Sir Orizhan, you pound on the door and wake the landlord. When he lets you in, find the inside door to the yard."

"A distraction?" The nobleman frowned.

"That," Matt told him, "and enough noise to flush our quarry like a pheasant from a brake."

"And you and I shall watch the windows?" Sergeant Brock asked, teeth gleaming in a grin.

"No," Matt said. "If someone's pounding on the door, he'll expect soldiers outside. He'll jump down into the innyard and hide in the stable or try to go out the wagon door."

"Where we shall be waiting!"

"Right." Matt stepped back, addressing them both. "Let me confront him. You two stay in the shadows and be ready to help out if he tries to fight."

Sir Orizhan nodded. "Surprise is always the best weapon."

"Right. Let's hope he thinks he's safe. Give me a few minutes—count to two hundred slowly, then start pounding and yelling." Matt turned away from the door. "Come on, Sergeant."

They went around the side of the building to the great wagon door—like most medieval inns, this one was built around three sides of a courtyard, with the fourth side closed off by stables, and doors wide enough to admit carts and wagons. They were shut, of course, but it didn't take Matt more than a few minutes to swing over the top and land lightly inside. He heard the soft thud as Sergeant Brock landed behind him, but didn't look.

Stables blocked his view to either side; he went past them

and looked about the innyard. The moon was still helping out, though it was very low, and he could make out the shape of the well with its watering trough, the railed balconies outside the guests' rooms, and the dark shape of several wagons. But the moonlight struck only the center of the yard, making the shadows all about seem even darker. Matt noticed movement in those shadows, off to his left, and felt reassured that Sergeant Brock was sliding into place.

Then he remembered that the sergeant was one of King Drustan's men, and the feeling of reassurance evaporated. He found himself wishing that he'd picked the Merovencian knight to steal into the courtyard with him. Then a form in black tunic and hose separated itself from one of the dark looming shapes and stepped out of the shadows. Moonlight flashed off a gloating grin, and Matt felt his stomach sink.

"You're late, Lord Wizard." The fugitive spoke with a strong Bretanglian accent. "I expected you when the moon was still high."

"Well, you didn't make an appointment," Matt said, somewhat nettled. "Besides, the guardsman who reported the murder had to nerve himself up to telling us, and that took a while. It took a longer while to calm down Drustan and Petronille enough for them to start making sense."

"Ah, were they distressed, then? Good, good!" The man grinned wide, fists on his hips, cocky as a bantam rooster.

Matt frowned and came closer, peering through the darkness, wary of traps and ambushes, but very curious about the man. At the very least, he wanted a good look at his face. "I take it you don't like your king."

"Who could?" the man returned. "His soldiers are everywhere!"

"Yes, I expect it's gotten so a man can't pull off a decent rape or burglary without some oaf in a uniform interfering," Matt said dryly. He stepped to the side, but the fellow was standing in shadow, indistinct and menacing, his face invisible.

"The day will come when those soldiers will answer to me!" the man snapped. "Milksop kings have reigned too long over Bretanglia! It is time for a monarch with hot blood in his veins!"

If Drustan was a milksop, Matt surely didn't want to see a tyrant. "What makes for being wishy-washy? Putting down bandits and punishing murderers and thieves?"

"Oppressing strong and lusty men, and letting courts and juries say who shall be punished and who not!" the man declared.

"Oh?" Matt realized he might be able to work him up to such an emotional pitch that the man wouldn't think about what he, the pursuer, was doing. "How would *you* decide who's right and who's wrong?"

"The old ways—trial by combat, and trial by ordeal!"

"So that the man who's stronger and has a higher pain threshold will always go free to beat up his neighbors, eh?"

"Have not the stronger the right to thrive?" the man demanded, his voice rising. "Have not the . . ."

Matt let him rave while he muttered,

> "Let a sudden fire grow
> Right beside this fellow's toe,
> So that its flame and ruddy glow
> Shall light his face up from below!"

Light burst between the man's feet, and Matt had half a second to study the face—square and blocky, mature, a little gone to fat, with a tawny jawline beard and close-cropped moustache. Bushy brows cast shadows over deep-set eyes.

Then he shouted, leaping back into the shadows—shouted a singsong verse in a language Matt didn't know, and the fire died. The courtyard seemed much darker, for Matt's eyes had started to adjust to the sudden glare. He could scarcely see his opponent at all. Alarm shot through him—his fugitive was a sorcerer!

"Aren't we clever now, managing a bit of light to see my face?" the man snarled. "You'll wish you hadn't, my bawcock!" And he rapped out another verse.

Matt hated not knowing what spell he had to counter until it happened. On general principles, he chanted,

> "Avaunt, avoid! What e'er befalls,
> Turn aside from my frail frame!

Strike me not! Confound the calls
Of him who seeks myself to maim!"

Something slammed into the earth beside him. Shaken,
Matt spared it a quick glance; it was a fallen gargoyle.

The stranger shouted another verse. Fire burst from the
ground. Some sixth sense gave Matt just enough warning; he
was already leaping back as the flame roared upward. Even
so, he howled as it singed the side of his leg before he landed
on the far side of the stony monster. But the gargoyle gave
him an idea; he chanted,

"Thing of stone, arise and walk you!
Let no spell or magic balk you!
Seize that man who struck you down!
Stop his voice and see him bound!"

With a grinding of granite joints, the half-human, half-
draconian sculpture rose to its hind feet and spread its wings.

The stranger leaped back, arm snapping down to point at
the gargoyle as he shouted a verse.

Matt was ready for him this time, though—the man couldn't
aim a verse at him when he had to stop the gargoyle. Matt had
the precious moments he needed to seize the offensive. He
pointed at his enemy and shouted another verse.

"Wee, sleekit, tim'rous, cowerin' beastie!
Ah, what a terror's in thy breastie!
Thou must become four-foot and furry,
And in the dust must surely scurry!"

The gargoyle froze, its eyes glazing as it turned to stone
again—but the sorcerer screamed as he shrank, his body
transforming. Those screams turned into a chant, though,
in that strange musical foreign language, and he stopped
shrinking, two feet tall and with paws instead of hands
thrashing their way out of sleeves three times too long for his
arms—or front legs. His face bulged into a muzzle with a
sharp nose, but his tongue was still human enough to intone
another verse in a high, squeaky voice as he pointed upward.

The picture he presented was so ludicrous that Matt couldn't help but laugh. He was still laughing as the end of the hayloft broke off from the stables and buried him under several hundred pounds of wooden beams.

The invisible envelope of his first spell kept the boards from hitting Matt, but they knocked him to the ground anyway—hard, since the beaten earth of the innyard hadn't been trying to do him any harm. He landed on his back, pain shooting through his abdomen, and he fought to breathe, but his diaphragm wasn't cooperating. He heard a howling battle cry with a Bretanglian accent, but it was cut short. Then Sir Orizhan shouted in anger, but the sorcerer shouted back in his own language, and Sir Orizhan's voice cried out in pain before it fell silent.

Matt struggled for breath, but couldn't pull in enough to speak.

Footsteps came near, and the enemy sorcerer's voice said, "I know you are alive and whole in there, for you spoke a spell that told anything falling not to strike your body. Listen well, Lord Wizard. I know who you are, but you do not know me. You will, though, be sure of that—for King Drustan will declare war on Merovence now, in revenge for the death of his son. He has wanted to battle Alisande for some time, for he seeks to rule both Bretanglia and Merovence. Now he has an excuse, and will defy you to find a way to keep him from it." There was a sound of gloating in his tone as he went on. "Try to stop this war, and you will find yourself fighting me at every turn. Let the war run, and you shall meet me on the battlefield. In either case, we shall meet again, and fight. I cannot kill you now because you have cobbled up some sort of spell to defend yourself, but I shall be ready to counter it when we meet again."

Matt caught his breath and shouted,

> "With downcast looks the joyless victor sate,
> Revolving in his alter'd soul
> The various turns of chance below . . ."

"Aroint thee!" the enemy sorcerer cried, and chanted a couplet in his flowing language. A soft explosion sounded, and Matt ended his verse with a curse, knowing his enemy had escaped and thereby won the fight.

Matt resolved the man wouldn't win the war. He tried crawling forward, and beams bounced off the unseen bubble that protected him. At the edge of the pile Matt shoved himself to his feet, and boards fell around him. He stepped out into the moonlight, gratefully drawing a breath of clean air and looking about him.

He saw Sergeant Brock lying facedown in the dirt, and ten feet across from him, Sir Orizhan, on his back and unconscious with his sword by his hand.

Matt stared in alarm, then ran to the sergeant first, to flip him over and make sure he had clear breathing. He did, so Matt checked for a pulse, found it, then went over to Sir Orizhan, still concerned—but as he came close, the knight sat up suddenly, shaking his head. "What . . . where . . ." He looked about, then shoved himself up, catching his sword as he looked about wild-eyed. "Where did he go?"

"Disappeared," Matt said. "He's a wizard."

"I saw," Sir Orizhan told him. "He struck me down with a chant and a wave of his hand. Why did you not call us to attack him sooner, Lord Wizard?"

"I thought I could handle him by myself," Matt answered, and the words were gall on his tongue. "He turned out to be a better sorcerer than I thought."

"A sorcerer?" Sir Orizhan frowned. "How can you be sure that he uses his powers for evil?"

"Just a feeling," Matt said, "but when you've held magic duels with enough sorcerers, you begin to recognize that feeling. Besides, he helped murder a man, maybe even did it himself, and is trying to start a war." He started toward Sergeant Brock. "Come on, let's see if we can get this soldier on his feet again. We have to go back to the castle and tell the king—" He broke off, gritted his teeth, then forced himself to say, "—tell the king I lost, and the murderer got away."

"He will not like that." Sir Orizhan joined him, scooping an arm under Brock's shoulders and pulling him up.

"No, he won't." Matt shuddered at the thought of facing the king. "He's going to like it even less when I tell him the man was Bretanglian."

"He will not believe you," Sir Orizhan said flatly.

"No, he won't," Matt agreed, "but you heard his accent—didn't you?"

"I heard most of what passed between you, yes."

Matt started patting Sergeant Brock's cheeks. "Where would you say the man came from?"

"Bretanglia—but I have seldom heard so strong an accent."

Matt paused. "You mean he might have been laying it on too thick because he wanted me to think he was Bretanglian when he wasn't?"

"That, or making sure you could not mistake him."

"Makes sense, if he's trying to start a war," Matt said grimly, "which is what's going to happen, when I have to tell the king I failed."

"Are you sure the man you fought was indeed the murderer, though?"

Matt froze, the light dawning. Then he turned to Sir Orizhan with a smile. "No, I'm not. We really should try to make sure before I report in, shouldn't we? Come on, let's wake up this man and visit the crime scene."

Matt cured Sergeant Brock's headache by massaging his temples and reciting a verse. Then the two men led him deep into the twisting alleys of the oldest part of the town, to the Inn of the Courier Snail. They came in to find the common room silent, with sixteen very glum patrons, an extremely worried landlord with trembling serving wenches, and a dozen grim-faced soldiers stationed around the room, their halberds on guard, Merovencians on one side, Bretanglians on the other.

"I guess it really is a good thing we came," Matt said.

"Aye, milord, unless you wish the war to start here," Sir Orizhan said.

The soldiers all looked up. The Merovencians smiled with relief, the Bretanglians glared. The civilians quaked.

Matt decided it was time to be authoritative. "I am Matthew Mantrell, Lord Wizard of Merovence, come to investigate this night's doings."

The Bretanglians turned surly. Matt was a lord and a

knight, so they had to do what he said, unless they'd had orders not to—and they hadn't.

Matt strode up to the landlord. "Okay, mine host. Tell me what you saw."

"Very little, my lord," the man said quickly. "We were very busy, no time to be nosing into anything but business, when this horrible scream tore the room and we all turned to see the prince—well, we didn't know that's what he was then, did we? But we saw Laetri come flying down the stairs and slamming into the wall, with the prince stalking after her calling her a thief."

Matt frowned. "Who's Laetri?"

"One of the regular prostitutes who visits here, my lord," the innkeeper said.

Well, Matt hadn't really believed Gaheris was killed defending a maiden's honor. He fixed the innkeeper with a steely gaze. "And you didn't chase her out?"

The innkeeper squirmed. "This is a public house, my lord. I serve all who come."

"Of course, and I'm sure you don't charge extra for letting them use the rooms upstairs—which they must have done, or the prince wouldn't have thrown Laetri down the steps." Matt said evenly, "You know that pimping is against the law, don't you?"

"I know," the innkeeper said with dread.

"And visiting a prostitute, too?"

"Yes," the innkeeper said in a faint voice. Then he rallied. "Why does the queen not make it a crime to be a prostitute?"

"Because prostitutes are usually victims, not perpetrators," Matt told him. "Very few of them choose their line of work. Most of them are forced into it by their pimps. For the rest, it's whore or starve."

The innkeeper didn't look convinced, but few men wanted to believe the facts when it came to sexploitation. Matt said, "What happened when the prince caught up with Laetri?"

"He raised his hand to strike her again," the innkeeper said, "but Pargas, her pimp, stepped in to stop him and ask the reason for his anger, and the prince told him that Laetri had stolen his purse. She denied it, of course, and Pargas sided with her, again of course, and the prince struck at Pargas.

Well, Pargas didn't know the man was royal, so he struck back, and this sergeant here"—he nodded at Brock—"stepped in to protect his prince, and in a few seconds the whole common room was one big brawl. I tried to stop it, but it was like spitting into the wind. Then Laetri screamed again . . ." He shuddered. "It was the worst scream I've ever heard, sir, and when we turned around, we all saw why—the prince lay there in a pool of his own blood, and Pargas stood over him, bloody but with his club in his hand. Then I saw a man trying to climb out the window, so I raised the hue and cry, and everyone ran out into the night to catch him—except Pargas and Laetri, of course, and I tried to kick them out to end the trouble, but this nobleman stopped me." He pointed to Sir Orizhan.

"Even so." Sir Orizhan nodded. "The man Pargas had clearly killed the prince, and I wasn't about to let this fellow help him escape."

"And that was the end of it?"

"As far as I know," Sir Orizhan said.

Matt turned back to the innkeeper. "How did you get all your customers back?"

"The soldiers brought them, sir, when they couldn't catch the one who went out the window."

"All?" Matt turned to Sergeant Brock.

"We lost him quick enough," the sergeant said, "and herded the rest of the civilians back in here, though you may be sure they didn't like it. We might have lost one or two, but no more, I'll wager."

"Yeah, but that one or two might include the murderer." Matt turned away with a sigh.

"The murderer?" Sergeant Brock stared. "Are you ma— I mean, it's clear Pargas killed him, sir! . . . Isn't it?"

"Then why did you all chase the man who went out the window?"

Sergeant Brock stared at him, at a loss. Everyone else stared, too, and Matt could see they were all asking themselves the same question.

"It's an instinct," Matt explained. "If somebody runs, it's natural to chase them, because why would they be running if they hadn't done anything? But in this case the man was trying to decoy you all out of the inn so the real murderer could escape."

Sir Orizhan frowned. "How can you be sure it was not Pargas who struck the fatal blow?"

"Because you said the prince was lying in a pool of blood," Matt told him, "and Pargas only had a club."

CHAPTER 4

Sir Orizhan stared, then whirled to exchange glances with Sergeant Brock, who only stared back at him.

"Where did the prince fall?" Matt asked.

"Over here." Sir Orizhan led the way to the foot of the stairs, where a dark stain covered the floorboards, three feet across.

Matt looked down, nodding. "Pool of blood, all right. What time did it happen?"

"Time?" Sir Orizhan frowned; the medieval mind scarcely thought in terms of hours, let alone minutes. "In the middle of the night, my lord. What more can we say?"

Matt raised his voice. "Is there a man of the Watch here?"

"Here, my lord." One of the Merovencians stepped forward. He didn't wear livery, like the soldiers, but only a brassard to show his office.

"How far into your Watch did this happen?"

"We were almost done, my lord, when a pot-boy came running to summon us. We were in time to see the folk come streaming out of the inn."

"An hour before midnight, then." Matt had set up the duty rosters himself. The first Watch began their shift at dusk, which would have been about seven o'clock in this season. "Where is the body now?"

"We brought it back to the castle, milord," Sir Orizhan said. "We thought his parents would wish it."

"I'm sure they do. And Pargas and Laetri?"

"At the castle also, milord," Sergeant Brock said, "but in the dungeons."

"Of course," Matt said sourly, gazing down at the stain. "But you saw the prince's body. Where was the wound?"

"In his back, my lord." Sir Orizhan's face writhed with disgust, and he spoke with contempt. "It was truly the stroke of a base coward."

"But Pargas fought the prince face-to-face, with only a club."

"Two clubs, milord," Sergeant Brock told him. "Small ones. I fought him myself, till some fool of a Merovencian pulled me away and stabbed at me."

The Merovencian soldiers' faces darkened, and Matt hurried on. "Two small clubs? Why did he only have one when he was standing over the body?"

"Because someone had stabbed his left shoulder, milord."

"You?"

"No, milord," the sergeant said. "He had both clubs when I was torn away from him. Then another brawler came at the prince's back, felling the soldier who warded him there, and I had to leap to guard him from behind until I was laid low in my turn by some other Merovencian bully boy."

"Probably the prince who stabbed Pargas, then." Matt turned away before the sergeant could object, and measured the distance from the stain to the bottom step with his eyes. "Ten feet clear of the stairs, at least. The prince fought a good way into the room."

"He was a decent fighter with a knife, milord." The sergeant's tone was neutral.

"And not very many noblemen are good knife-fighters, hm? Not his first tavern brawl, no doubt. Unfortunately, he made it far enough away from the walls so that virtually anyone could have come at his back."

The room was very quiet.

Into the silence, Sir Orizhan said, "Then anyone here might have struck that blow?"

"Anyone," Matt agreed. "Start asking questions, Sir Knight. You, too, Sergeant. I want to know where everyone was when the prince fell."

They started asking. Half an hour later Matt had a complete picture of where everyone had been. Each one of them remembered whom he had been fighting, and their stories all checked—except for two men whose opponents had disappeared chasing the fugitive, but Matt was inclined to believe them, so the escapees couldn't have been the murderers. One of the Bretanglian troopers even remembered that he'd been fighting Pargas when Laetri screamed, and that he'd seen her over the pimp's shoulder the whole time. The serving wenches had all been hiding behind the bar, and all remembered each other's presence.

"It would seem that the murderer was the man who went out the window after all, milord," Sir Orizhan said.

"That," Matt agreed, "or somebody's lying. Let's go back to the castle, Sir Orizhan. I want a look at the body before I talk to its father."

"A look at the body? But why?"

"Tell you outside," Matt muttered, then snapped, "Come on, Sergeant. Let's go!"

They strode out into the night—and Matt halted, turning to face the two men. "I didn't want to say this where the bystanders could hear—but if the man who went out the window didn't stab the prince with his own hand, and everyone else remembers who they were fighting, there's a very good chance the prince was killed by magic."

The knight stared, face sickening, eyes filling with dread—but Brock's expression turned stone cold.

Prince Gaheris' body lay in state in the Great Hall, surrounded by candles and Bretanglian guards. His face and hands had been washed, but the servants couldn't undress him to bathe because of rigor mortis. Sir Orizhan had to do some fancy talking to keep the guards from objecting to Matt's inspection, and Sergeant Brock had to order them away from the casket—all the way to the edges of the room, so they couldn't hear the muttered conversation.

Matt turned the body over and stared at the wound in the back. Doublet and cut alike were stiff with dried blood. He swallowed heavily against nausea and whispered to Sir Orizhan, "You really think a knife did that?"

"Assuredly not!" The knight's face turned gray. Even Sergeant Brock turned pale.

It was a huge, gaping, horizontal cut, at least six inches long. The edges were ragged, as though someone had cut in with a saw instead of stabbing.

"What weapon made that?" Sir Orizhan whispered.

"A sword," Sergeant Brock told him, "or a spearhead. Even then, the murderer must have twisted it and hacked a bit, to make the edge so ragged."

Matt turned the prince faceup again. "A lump on the left-hand side of his forehead—Pargas scored once, at least. A few more bruises, but I don't see any blood on this side."

"No," Sir Orizhan agreed. "I have seen sticks hit men hard enough to make them bleed, but nowhere nearly as much as the prince did. The pimp could not have slain him, then, could he?"

"A club doesn't cut into a body too well, no," Matt acknowledged, "and it's hard to hit both the front and the back of a man at the same time." He scanned the body, frowning. "Notice what's missing?"

Both men stared down, thinking. Then Sir Orizhan said, "His purse!"

"Right." Matt nodded. "Sergeant, send somebody back to the inn to search. Might be the prince really did think he'd been robbed."

"Why else would he have accused her?" Sir Orizhan asked. His face sickened as he realized the answer.

"Right again." Matt nodded. "Gaheris wanted an excuse to beat up on her."

"I assure you, this prince never troubled with such an excuse."

"A real sweetheart," Matt said grimly. "Still, it might be interesting finding out where that purse is. Send someone, would you, Sergeant?"

"There's no need," Brock said, voice very low. "I watched you fight the sorcerer from the shadows. I wondered why he needed two purses. I thought perhaps one held magical powders."

"Not a bad guess, but wrong this time." Matt nodded with satisfaction. "You've got sharp eyes, Sergeant. So whether or not the sorcerer struck the death blow, he did provide the excuse for the brawl." He stepped away from the corpse. "Okay. I can't put it off any longer. Time to tell his parents."

They went out of the Great Hall, but Sir Orizhan said, "I can see you do not believe all you have seen, Lord Wizard."

"Oh, it's believable," Matt told him. "I've seen knives big enough to make a wound like that."

"Short swords, more likely," Sergeant Brock grunted, then stared in surprise at his own words.

Matt nodded. "Could have been a short sword, like a Reman gladius, yes."

"But you do not believe it," Sir Orizhan pressed.

"No, I don't," Matt told him. "It's much more like the hole a scissor blade would make, or maybe a paring knife, if you stuck it into the back of a straw doll and jabbed it around a little for good measure. It wouldn't even be an inch long, of course, but on the real body . . ."

"Witchcraft!" Even the toughened sergeant shuddered.

"Or sorcery." Matt nodded. "No way to defend yourself against it, is there? And all three of us know the man who went out the window was a sorcerer."

"Then you must tell the king that his son was slain by one of his own countrymen!" Sir Orizhan exclaimed.

"Yes," Matt said heavily, "and I don't think he's going to like that. In fact, I don't think he's going to believe me at all."

"You lie!" King Drustan cried, and Queen Petronille declared, "You seek to shield a man of your own!"

Their rage was frightening, but Matt felt a surge of anger at being called a liar. "If I had the man here, you couldn't deny it."

"If you had him here, aye!" Drustan roared. "Lord Wizard, do you call yourself? When a peasant sorcerer can outdo you in magic? Or did you let him escape in order to shield your country from war?"

"Ask your own man." Matt nodded at Sergeant Brock. "Ask him how I fought."

"He wrought wonders," the sergeant told the king. "It was pure bad luck that he lost, and good luck he lived."

Matt flashed the man a look of surprised gratitude, but Drustan roared, "*Bad* luck for him, for he'll die in battle on a Bretanglian lance!" He struck Brock backhanded.

"How dare you insult us by saying our son was slain by our own countryman!" Queen Petronille cried, white-faced and trembling.

"There can be no question of peace between our countries now!" Drustan shouted, and turned to Alisande. "We go back to Bretanglia at first light—to gather our armies, and march in vengeance!" He spun to Sir Orizhan and Sergeant Brock. "You have failed in your duty, knight and soldier! You were set to guard the prince, and he is dead! Do not think to come back to Bretanglia until you have found his murderer, or avenged his death!" He whirled back to Alisande. "Prepare your people for war, *Your Majesty*!" He made the words an insult. "Prepare for war—and defeat!"

Matt stood beside Alisande on the battlements, watching the Bretanglian royal family ride away from Bordestang surrounded by their entourage—knights, soldiers, servants, and ladies-in-waiting. "So the sorcerer gained what he wanted— war."

"Not the sorcerer alone." Alisande gazed after the departing party, saddened and troubled. "They came to seek an excuse for war, Drustan and Petronille both."

Matt stared at her. "You don't think they *planned* on their son being assassinated!"

"Of course not!" Alisande looked up, shocked that he could even think of such a thing. "They meant to rely on their own tempers and insults to provoke me into declaring war." She turned to look after her erstwhile guests. "Nonetheless, my heart is heavy with their sorrow. I have a son now, and know how Petronille must grieve."

"That heart is too good," Matt said softly.

She looked up and found his eyes doting, and smiled, taking his hand. "You are a greater comfort than you know, husband, and I have need of such reassurance now." She turned to look after the Bretanglians again. "Unpleasant though he may have been, Gaheris was my cousin, for so is his mother, though rather distant kin. I am overcome with guilt that he should have been slain in my capital."

"You couldn't prevent it," Matt assured her, "if someone in their own party was planning it all along, and just waiting for this trip to set that plan into motion."

Alisande turned to him with a frown. "Do you truly think so?"

"I do, but how's for me telling you about it inside? This spring wind is brisk, and a warm fire would be a great comfort, too, just now."

Alisande smiled again and laid her arm on top of his. "Let us go down to the solar, by all means."

The huge clerestory windows justified the solar's name, letting the sun bathe the room in early morning light. With a roaring fire to warm them outside and spiced cider to warm them inside, they could relax with Matt's parents and mull over the night's events.

Alisande sat back with a sigh. "I confess it is a relief to have them gone, though that relief will be short-lived."

"Yes, you must prepare for war," Mama agreed, "though we hope you will not have to wage it."

"An honest, open battle would be better than this skulking in shadows and stabbing men in their backs," Papa huffed.

"Now, husband!" Mama reproved. "There has been only one man stabbed."

"Yes, but how many were waiting their turn?"

"Everyone in that inn has an alibi," Matt said, "even the two who managed to slip away. Sir Orizhan and Sergeant Brock questioned them with me, and each one remembers who he was fighting when the prince was killed. Their stories check out—both opponents remember each other, and the only two whose foe wasn't there, remember fighting one of the two men who escaped."

"Rather convenient," Papa sniffed. "Who remembers fighting this man who went out the window?"

"No one. Boosts his chances of being the murderer."

"At whose command?" Alisande said quietly.

Mama and Papa turned to her in surprise, then looked apprehensive. Mama said, "Surely you do not mean someone in his own family hired the killer!"

"It's been known to happen," Matt said with a smile of irony, "and I don't see any great love lost between those siblings."

"Petronille does not seem all that fond of either her eldest or her youngest," Mama admitted. "Odd. The second child is usually the rebel, and rarely the favorite."

"Considering what Brion is rebelling against, any mother would favor him," Matt told her.

"Do Drustan and Petronille remember this sorcerer being with their party?" Alisande asked.

"I didn't think I should mention the issue," Matt said apologetically. "They were too upset."

"Upset? They raged as soon as you told them the man had escaped," Papa exclaimed, "and they kept raging! You had no chance to ask!"

"Well, I could have asked before I told them the bad news."

"Without the culprit there? Do you think they would have said anything but ranting?"

"Thanks, Papa," Matt said with a warm smile. He shrugged. "Anyway, why would a king or queen remember one soldier out of all the rest? I don't expect he went along wearing sorcerer's robes."

"Surely this sergeant you speak of would remember," Alisande said.

"He should," Matt admitted, "but he saw the man's face in the moonlight, too, and tells me he wasn't one of their soldiers. Says he doesn't remember him being with the entourage at all, in fact."

Papa stared. "You don't mean he was already in Bordestang, waiting for them to arrive!"

Matt sat still for a minute. Then he nodded slowly. "Now that you mention it, that's a distinct possibility."

"Perhaps not," Mama offered. "If he is a sorcerer, as you say, he could have come at any time, or even been with them, but invisible."

Matt threw up his hands. "Almost anything is possible, when you're dealing with magic! Whenever he came over, though, I think he waited his chance, and when the princes went tavern-hopping, he stole Gaheris' purse while he was, uh, distracted, and waited for the brawl to start. Then he pulled out a doll that already had a lock of Gaheris' hair on it and stabbed it with a paring knife. Stabbed two or three times, just to make sure."

Papa shook his head. "It seems so improbable! Why be there at all? And if he was, why not simply stab with a real blade?"

"I was not aware that stabbing a doll made the wound show," Mama said slowly.

Matt sat still again. Then he said, "You're right—it doesn't. That would have taken an extra spell."

"Which your sorcerer might have cast, if he wished to place the blame on a man of Merovence," Papa pointed out.

"I suppose so," Matt said, "so it cancels out."

Alisande nodded. "The point was not the simple murdering of the prince—it was the provoking of war."

"Oh, I don't know," Matt said slowly. "Why not accomplish two objectives with one murder? As you pointed out yourself, dear, nothing says the sorcerer was working for himself."

Papa frowned. "Do you mean that someone else would have wished to kill Gaheris, and waited until his death could be useful?"

"Yes, and with impending war to distract people from looking for the murderer, there'd be less chance of either boss or hit man being found out!" Matt said. "Let's think, now—who wanted Gaheris dead?"

The room was silent a moment. Then Mama said, "Who did not?"

"That was unkind!" Alisande cried.

"Quite unkind," Mama agreed, "but probably true. Be honest, my dear—he was a very disagreeable young man. If you wish, you may count his friends instead of his enemies."

Alisande was silent for a moment, then admitted, "I cannot think of any—but I do not know them well." She looked up. "Sir Orizhan! There is one!"

"Sir Orizhan was assigned to be the princes' companion and watchdog," Matt said. "That doesn't say he liked them."

"But if he has known them for ten years . . ."

"He could learn to really despise them," Matt finished for her. "But he's a very chivalrous knight. I don't think he'd let his feelings show."

"Can you not read him at all?" Alisande challenged.

"Well, I do get the impression that he didn't approve of Gaheris' taste in entertainments." Matt frowned, mulling it over. "In fact, I don't think he approved of Gaheris at all—but especially not as a fit husband for the princess Sir Orizhan had sworn to protect."

"Ye—ssss!" Alisande lifted her head. "A true knight would make the welfare of his ward his first duty, would he not?"

"Especially," Matt said, "if he liked her."

"Why would he?" Papa asked. "She seemed little more pleasant than her future family."

"How can you say that?" Mama challenged. "The poor thing spoke scarcely at all while we dined!"

"When she did, though, she spoke rather sharply," Papa pointed out.

"Only to Brion, and she is obviously in love with him," Mama said.

"She is?" Matt looked up in surprise.

"Aye, my husband." Alisande smiled. "She may not know it herself, but it is there in her eye, in the tilt of her head, but most especially in the sharpness of her tongue as she addresses a man she desires but knows she cannot have."

"She can now," Matt said softly.

The room was quiet as Mama and Alisande digested his comment, eyes widening in horror. Then both spoke at once.

"You cannot think she ordered him slain!"

"That sweet little thing couldn't have—have—"

"Oh, yes she could," Matt said in answer to both. "Stop and think, ladies—would you want to marry Gaheris?"

"Well, of course not!" Alisande said indignantly.

"But that does not mean I would slay him," Mama maintained.

"You're not a medieval princess being set up as an international sacrifice." Matt knew the Prince of Toulenge had died, and that Rosamund was officially the province's ruling princess, though her mother ruled as her regent. Apparently, though, the dead father's bargain with Drustan couldn't be broken—as long as Gaheris was alive. "I'd say it's quite possible that Rosamund hired the footpad to kill Gaheris so she wouldn't have to marry him. In fact, considering Gaheris' idea of fun, you might even call it self-defense ahead of time."

There was another short silence. Then Alisande admitted, "I could not truly blame her."

Matt had another thought. "Is Brion in love with her?"

"That is harder to say," Mama said. "He is so easily baited, at least by her—" She broke off, looking thoughtful.

"You spoke truly, my love," Papa said quietly. "To his brothers, he gave jibe for jibe, but to her, he could only protest, and that with some sign of hurt."

"His defenses aren't up to their usual standard with Rosamund," Matt agreed.

"Yes, I would say there is some sign that he is in love with her, then," Mama said, "though like her, he denies it."

"But he might be able to find an excuse to defend her," Matt said, "by killing his brother."

"The murder does make him heir apparent," Alisande agreed.

There was another silence as the next thought occurred to them all. Matt finally voiced it. "Does Rosamund go with the crown?"

"In law, the betrothal was only with Gaheris," Alisande said, "but it was made because he was the heir apparent."

"So it would have to be renegotiated with Brion, but probably will be?"

"It would," Alisande said, "but with a war, such negotiation will be impossible."

"Which means Brion gets to keep her."

"Or," said Mama, "that Drustan does—for if she is betrothed to no one, he can keep her near with none to bar him."

Papa turned to her. "Then you think Petronille's jealousy has some basis?"

"Oh, yes," Mama said quietly. "Did you not see the gleam in Drustan's eye when he looked at Rosamund?"

"Yes, I did," Alisande said darkly. "If this war serves no other purpose, perhaps it will allow us to rescue my cousin."

"Maybe Sir Orizhan thought the same way," Matt said.

Papa smiled. "We have come full circle, my son. The only two we have not suspected are Queen Petronille and young John."

Matt shrugged. "I don't see what John would gain by killing Gaheris."

"Might he be striking back at a bully?" Mama suggested.

"Might," Matt agreed, "and there's always sibling rivalry.

But since John seems to have established himself as Papa's pet, he has all the protection against Gaheris that he needs, and probably revenge, too."

"I cannot see that Petronille has anything to gain," Alisande said, "other than the beginning of war, which may gain her birthright, her quarter of Merovence, for her favorite Brion . . ." Then her eyes widened.

So did Matt's. He finished the sentence for her. ". . . or even the whole kingdom!"

"Yes," Alisande whispered. "If Brion is her favorite, she would wish to see him as King of Bretanglia—but surely she would not kill her firstborn to gain the crown for her second!"

"Brion becoming heir might not be motive enough in itself," Matt said slowly, "but if Drustan really does desire Rosamund as much as the queen seems to think he does, jealousy is all the reason Petronille needs."

"To slay Rosamund, perhaps." Alisande turned to him with a troubled frown. "Why would she thereby have Gaheris slain?"

"Who did Rosamund live with as long as she was engaged to Gaheris?" Matt asked.

"Why, with the king and his family."

"But what if the king and queen separated? Who would Gaheris live with then?"

"With his father." Alisande frowned. "He resents his mother, as you may have seen."

"Oedipus complex, no doubt," Papa mused.

"Who would she live with now that Gaheris is dead?" Matt asked. "If they separated, that is."

"Brion is his mother's darling, and would no doubt live with her," Alisande said slowly, "and if Petronille can bring about his betrothal to Rosamund . . ." She shook her head violently. "No! It is not possible that Petronille would have ordered her own son slain only so that she might take Rosamund away from Drustan!"

"If she disliked Gaheris as much as everyone else does, and feels at all protective toward Rosamund, I would say it is quite possible," Papa said softly.

"I think that is too much for any mother to consider," Mama said firmly, "even one so vindictive as Petronille."

"Let us trust so," Alisande said with a shudder. She rose. "So! Any of them might have hired an assassin, or none of them—but in any event, I must prepare for war." She looked up at Matt. "I thank you for counseling me to build a navy, husband. We may have only ten ships thus far, but they will do to harry the coasts of Bretanglia—and may distract Drustan enough to prevent his invading Merovence."

"Be nice if we had the English Channel in this universe," Matt said.

"You have told me of that." Alisande frowned. "A twenty-mile-wide stretch of water between the Bretanglia and Merovence of your own world, is it not?"

"In our version of this universe, yes—only we call them 'England' and 'France' there, and they speak two different languages."

Alisande nodded. "I can see how the speech would have drifted apart, if Bretanglia were an island. There would have been far less coming and going between the two lands."

"Yes, Bretanglia was part of Hardishane's empire here, wasn't it? After all, he could just march in and conquer."

"As he did in Ibile, Latruria, and Allustria," Alisande said, "overcoming evil kings who were devoted to sin and Satan. He even conquered far beyond, well into the lands of the Rus. It is small wonder we all speak the same language."

"No wonder at all." Matt frowned. "But there was never another invasion of Bretanglia, was there? After Hardishane's empire broke up, I mean."

"Well, the Danes and Vikings harassed their coasts," Alisande said, "and even carved out their own kingdom in the eastern counties, to both sides of the wall built by great Reme's soldiers."

"Truly?" Mama asked. "The Vikings held land in both England and Scotland?"

"There are Scots in the northern part of Bretanglia," Alisande acknowledged, "and it was a separate land until the Vikings came. They married into all the noble families, and Drustan's father welded them together into one kingdom. This Drustan, his son, is the sixth of his name, and still rules all one land."

"Does he have a Viking fleet?" Matt asked.

Alisande smiled. "The Vikings ceased sailing two hundred years ago, husband. I think Drustan may have a few warships, but nothing more. What need of them has he, when he can ride into Merovence at will?" She turned somber. "Now, though, I fear that he will come riding in earnest, with all his armies, and with fire and sword."

"I think I might be able to find some way to keep him from invading," Matt said slowly.

Alisande looked at him with misgiving. "I would welcome that, but not at the price of danger to you."

"We're in danger already, love. Besides, there shouldn't be all that much peril in this method of distracting him."

"Which is?" Alisande asked, misgiving yielding to dread.

"Gaheris' murder was definitely no simple tavern brawl," Matt told her. "Okay, maybe the Man Who Went Out the Window stuck the knife in Gaheris himself, but I suspect someone hired him to do it. In fact, there just might be a whole conspiracy underlying it."

Alisande's eyes lighted. "If you can learn who has wrought this conspiracy and what its goal is, you may set Drustan and Petronille to rooting it out so earnestly that they forget to attack Merovence!"

"Right." Matt nodded.

"But if there was no conspiracy?" Mama frowned. "If the murder was only the work of this Man Who Went Out the Window, for whatever reason he may have had?"

"That's even better," Matt said. "If the murder wasn't the product of intrigue, handing the assassin over to Their Majesties should bring the armies to a grinding halt, especially if he's Bretanglian."

"I see." Papa smiled. "No Merovencian to blame for the murder means no war."

"Right." Matt nodded. "Of course, after they've hanged the traitors, they'll remember that they wanted to conquer Merovence."

"But if the assassin proves to be a man of Bretanglia, Drustan and Petronille will have no cause to attack." Alisande smiled. "They shall have to discover a new one."

"Excellent!" Papa cried.

But Mama frowned. "How shall you go about discovering this conspiracy, my son?"

"Well, that is the knotty part," Matt admitted. "They've gone back to Bretanglia now. I'll have to follow them if I'm going to be able to track down who's doing what."

"No!" Alisande cried.

CHAPTER 5

"Now I say nay!" Alisande threw her hands up, turning her back. "I have waited before while you have gone into peril, and have lived with the threat of doom hanging over me every day you were gone! You cannot ask me to do that again!"

"I wouldn't if I didn't have to." Matt stepped around in front of her, eyes sad, hands reaching out for hers though not touching. "But it's the only way I see to protect you from war, darling—you, and our children, and all the country."

"That is unfair," Alisande whispered, "to extort my consent by reminding me of the threat to my children and my people!"

"Very unfair," Matt agreed, "but also very true, and unavoidable. There's no way around it, dear. I have to go."

For a moment the wife warred with the mother and the monarch inside Alisande. Then she gave in and let herself fall into Matt's arms. Face against his chest she said, "Go, then! But oh my darling, take care, take care!"

"I will," Matt murmured into her hair. "I have a lot to come home to."

Mama and Papa exchanged a fond glance and quietly slipped out of the room.

"You must not go alone!" Alisande commanded, still in Matt's arms. "I shall send that knight of Toulenge with you—he knows the land somewhat, at least! And that Bretanglian sergeant! Both have their honors to save, and will no doubt strive mightily to aid you!"

"Yes. Very good idea." But the thought chilled Matt—he wasn't entirely sure he could trust either man behind his back. It was better to have them where he could keep an eye on them, though, rather than here in Bordestang, where they might try another assassination—say, of Alisande.

"If you must go, then, go." But Alisande still made no move to leave his arms. Instead she tilted her face up, eyes suddenly burning. "But first, come to my bed, for it may be a month or more till I see you again!"

All things considered, Matt was very glad his parents had left.

The sun wasn't up yet when Matt gathered Sir Orizhan and Sergeant Brock and set them to packing for the journey. It didn't take long—both men were used to traveling light on campaigns, and both, as Alisande had guessed, were very determined to clear their own names, to atone for what they saw as a failure in their duty—to protect Prince Gaheris.

But Matt knew that earnestness could have hidden another kind of determination—to keep from being found out. Either man could have been the murderer himself—and if so, what better place to be than with the man who was trying to prove their guilt? If he came too close, the murderer would be right there to kill him, too. Matt didn't really think it was terribly likely, since both had been fighting to protect the prince when someone else stuck a sword in his back, but he resolved not to sleep too soundly. Just to be on the safe side, though, he sent out a carrier pigeon to call in a friend.

Inside the castle, Mama and Papa braced Alisande with determination. "My dear, my husband and I have decided to go with our son."

Alisande stared. "Mother Mantrell, it is bad enough that I must hazard my husband! Must I risk you, too?"

"Why, I thought you would prefer that he have protection," Mama said in surprise.

"He has Sir Orizhan and the sergeant! But if it is protection, surely Father Mantrell would be enough!"

"To protect Matthew against a sorcerer, yes," Mama said, "but to help him discover this conspiracy he suspects? A woman may learn things a man may miss, my dear, especially where a princess is concerned."

"You speak of Rosamund? Surely she is of little concern in this matter! But I, I am greatly concerned, for if Drustan marches before Matthew can prove who murdered Prince Gaheris and why, I must take my armies to meet his, and who will protect my castle and children while I am gone? Much worse, who will protect them should I not return?"

"Why . . . there is Saul, the Witch Doctor," Mama began.

"I should not tear him away from his researches and his family again! I pray you, Mother Mantrell, stay and help me ward my kingdom. Stay to guard your grandchildren!"

Mama glanced at Papa. He nodded—they both recognized an appeal for moral support when they heard one. Mama turned back to Alisande, reaching up to embrace her. "Of course, my dear, we will stay. We had thought to relieve your worries about your husband, but if you will fret less because we are here when he is not, we must certainly be by your side."

"Oh, thank you!" Alisande hugged her, doubly glad because they had not pushed the issue to the point at which she had to command them as their sovereign. "It means much to me that you will stay only because I ask it!"

"I am sure that it does." Mama touched her cheek lightly. "Just as it means much to us that you invited us to stay when we had lost our home. Now that we have a home again, and the daughter for whom I always longed, how could we leave unless you wished it? No, of course we will stay."

"Then we must tell Matthew good-bye," Papa said. "Let us hurry; he may be mounting even as we speak."

"I have said my farewells already," Alisande said, tears in her eyes. "I would rather not say them again—but go, by all means go, to give him a mother's and a father's blessing."

"We shall be back in a few minutes, then." Mama gave her a brief smile as they left the room.

Matt was checking the straps on his pack when they came out. Mama halted, staring. "Peasants' clothing? All three of you?" Then she lifted her head, understanding. "Of course! You go to track a murderer who may well be a peasant! But what if he is a knight or lord?"

"We're bringing a change of clothes." Matt tapped his pack. "I don't really expect to need them, though. Even peasants can ask shelter in a castle, and we can learn more from the servants than from their employers."

Mama glanced at Sir Orizhan, whose face was as impassive as a slab of rock, and at Sergeant Brock, who looked somewhat grim. She turned back to her son and stretched up to give him a quick peck on the cheek. "Go with God, Matthew, and may He bring you back to us in safety."

"Amen to that." Papa stepped forward to clap a hand on Matthew's shoulder. "May the Lord shield you with His wings, and may you walk through danger unscathed."

"Thanks, folks." Matt gave them each a quick embrace, then stepped back. "Do two things for me, will you?"

"Of course," Papa said.

"I didn't get a chance to question Pargas and Laetri— they're the prostitute and her pimp who were, ah, present, at the crime."

His parents understood on the instant; both their faces darkened. Mama said, "I wondered at Prince Gaheris dying while committing so chivalrous an act as defending a maiden. Have no fear, my son, I shall discuss the event with the woman."

"And I with the man." Papa had a very stern look about him. "We shall attend to it, be sure."

"Thanks," Matt said. He smiled, then turned to look up at the solar window, where a lone figure was silhouetted against the candlelight. He blew a kiss to her, then turned away toward the gate. "Come on, guys." He waved over his shoulder at his parents.

"What is a 'guy'?" Sergeant Brock asked Sir Orizhan.

"I have heard it used as a man's name, but not as a word by itself." Sir Orizhan shook his head and sighed. "I fear that is only the first of many strangenesses we shall encounter as we travel with the Lord Wizard, Sergeant. Let us go."

They came to the second strangeness half a mile beyond the town wall, as the sky was lightening—or rather, it came to them. They were passing a woodlot when a huge shape loomed out of it and into the roadway. Sir Orizhan leaped back with a shout, reaching for the hidden sword under his cloak, and Sergeant Brock whipped his staff up to guard. Matt only grinned, though, and raised a hand in greeting. "You got my carrier pigeon, then."

"Yes. It was delicious," the huge shape rumbled. "I could not resist so tasty an invitation."

"Even so, that was fast flying, Stegoman. Thanks for coming."

"Did you think you could go gadding about and leave me behind again?"

"Not really, no. Stegoman, these are my traveling companions, Sir Orizhan and Sergeant Brock."

"I greet you." The dragon bobbed his head. "I see from the plainness of your garb that you are setting forth on a mission of some danger."

Sergeant Brock only stared, but Sir Orizhan managed to find his voice. "So the Lord Wizard informs us, Master Stegoman. I am pleased to meet you."

"You are very courteous," the dragon said, "but a very poor liar. Please be assured that I do not regard knights as my natural enemies, no matter what manner of silliness you have heard in that regard."

Sir Orizhan couldn't help smiling. "Only the usual minstrels' exaggerations."

"Storytellers are to be blamed for many misunderstandings, I fear," the dragon sighed, a sound like a blast furnace. "May I inquire as to the nature of your quest?"

"Surely you outdo most knights in your courtesy!" But Sir Orizhan's face clouded. "Know, then, O Gracious Beast, that this sergeant and I were both set to guard a prince, and in spite of our caution, he was slain while we sought to ward him in the midst of a brawl."

"The prince was the heir apparent to the throne of Bretanglia," Matt explained, "and his parents have declared war on Merovence because he was assassinated on our soil, presumably by one of our people."

"So that is why the Witch Doctor has asked Narlh to fly over that land and discover what he can!"

Sir Orizhan frowned. "Who is Narlh?"

"A dracogriff," Matt explained, "a magically encouraged hybrid between a dragon and a griffin. He flies, but he doesn't like it. His best friend is Saul, the Witch Doctor." He turned back to Stegoman. "So Alisande called him in? I thought she was going to try not to."

"From what Narlh said before he left our rookery, I gather that Master Saul discovered the matter by himself," the dragon said. "So it is to be a war of retaliation, and you go to seek the murderer in hopes of stopping the war?"

"Yes, and before it starts, if we can."

"And you," Stegoman said to the knight and his sergeant, "go to redeem yourselves, and to recover lost honor."

"We do," Sir Orizhan admitted.

"Then I will be pleased to travel in your company, since you go in the name of chivalry," Stegoman said. "Will you ride?"

Both men fell back a pace, staring in alarm.

"That's the other reason we didn't take horses," Matt explained. "It's really quite comfortable, once you get used to it—his vertebrae make natural saddles, and it's a *lot* faster than walking."

With obvious effort, knight and sergeant screwed up their courage and stepped forward.

They climbed down much more stiffly, when the sun had fallen near the horizon and Stegoman landed by a small grove of trees. Sergeant Brock virtually fell off, and kissed the ground while he was down. Then he shoved himself to his feet, groaning. "How long will it take to become used to this manner of riding, Lord Wizard?"

"You'll feel fine once you get over this first set of aches." Matt took off his pack and pulled out a bottle. "Better rub your legs with this, or we'll have to lift you out of your blanket roll tomorrow."

"I thank you," Brock said, taking the bottle, then turned to bow to Stegoman. "I thank you, too, great beast, for carrying me this day."

"My thanks also," Sir Orizhan said, also bowing.

"I was pleased to have your company," Stegoman said gravely, "and honored by the presence of men of such courage."

"Yes, you were really very good about not looking down," Matt said, "and you got used to it very quickly, both of you. It'll be better tomorrow, Sergeant—I'll bet you won't turn green at all. You might even be able to eat lunch."

"And what is the matter with being green?" Stegoman intoned.

"It's not easy," Matt explained. "About eating, though. I'd better light a fire and get a kettle going."

"And I will seek a stray cow," Stegoman said. "You will pay the farmer in the morning?"

"Of course," Matt said. "Airline food always was overpriced. See you when you're finished with the entrée."

"I shall return when I have fed," Stegoman assured. His wings boomed wide; he ran across the field and launched into the air. Matt watched him go, feeling reassured—with a dragon apt to stop back any time, neither of his two companions was apt to try anything against him. Not that he suspected they would, of course—they had the same goal he had, after all—but it never hurt to be careful.

Sir Orizhan watched Stegoman climb into the evening sky. "I cannot believe I actually rode upon his back!"

"I can," Sergeant Brock groaned. He had already stripped off his leggins and was busy rubbing the ointment into very sore muscles.

"Not feeling stiff?" Matt asked Sir Orizhan.

"It is not much different from riding a horse," the knight told him. "I only needed to accustom myself to the fear of heights, and the—" He glanced at Sergeant Brock and lowered his voice. "—and to the sudden and unexpected ups and downs of it."

"That does take getting used to," Matt admitted. "In fact, I have a breakfast menu that should help a bit."

"That root you gave us to chew?"

"Hey, it helped, didn't it? But we'd better see about getting that fire going, or we won't get dinner, let alone breakfast."

Stegoman had dropped them in a pasture at the edge of a small patch of woods. They turned to explore the grove with no one suggesting it—they all felt the need to investigate. After all, there might be an enemy hiding in it, a bandit or other outlaw. They stepped into the shadow under the canopy of leaves, and all cried out in surprise.

"A cabin!" Matt cried.

"A cottage, at least." Sir Orizhan frowned at Matt. "What is a 'cabin'?"

"A cottage by any other name. Hasn't been used in a while, has it?"

That was obvious at a glance. The thatch was moldy and patchy, missing in several places, and the windows and doorway gaped empty. The shutters hung at an angle, leather hinges broken, or lay beneath the window. The door was gone completely, probably chopped up for firewood. The area around the little house was clear, but only because the shadow of the trees was too deep for anything to grow.

"It will give us shelter for the night, though," the knight said. "Come, let us rid the place of any unwelcome dwellers."

He advanced, sword out, ready for anything from badgers to bears. Matt and Brock drew and followed.

They didn't need their blades, though. The cabin was a single large room, empty except for the refuse of years. Bears obviously had lived there in the past, or some sort of carnivore, and lesser woodland creatures had been there before or since. A pallet of musty straw lay against one wall, but there were, of course, no blankets. There was no other furniture. Like the door, it had been chopped and burned by other travelers who had used the abandoned cottage for a night's shelter. The ashes in the fireplace were old, though, and crumbled to a bed of soot.

"Empty, but filthy." Sergeant Brock sheathed his sword. "I'll find a dry branch and some green leaves for a broom."

"I shall gather firewood," Sir Orizhan said.

"You've got all the tinder you need right here." Matt nodded at the moldy pallet. "I'll gather up the bones and toss them out."

They went, each to his own task. Matt hauled a double armful of cow and deer bones out to the edge of the trees. When he came back, he found all the old straw stuffed into the fireplace, and three pallets of fresh straw in its place. He was pleasantly surprised, and wondered which of his companions had managed the trick while he was out. Then he pulled his leather camp bucket out of his pack and set off to find a stream.

There was enough dry wood under the trees so that they had a fire burning brightly before it was dark. Dinner was

stewed jerky and toasted journeybread. As it cooked, Matt
said, "It was really nice of you to bring in fresh straw."

Neither man answered, but each glanced at the other, obviously waiting.

Matt frowned. "Okay. Who brought it?"

"I thought it was one of *you*," Sergeant Brock said.

"And I thought one of you two had done it," Sir Orizhan
said, very confused.

Matt felt his personal alarm bell ringing all the way up
his spine. In this universe, unexplained phenomena usually
wound up being explained by magic. What magus was trail-
ing them—and why did whoever it was want him to know
about it?

But he couldn't let his companions know, of course. He
didn't need to have them staying awake all night waiting for
the spell to fall. "Guess I must have wished too hard." He
stabbed a piece of jerky with his dagger and offered it to Sir
Orizhan. "Think that's tender enough?"

It was, and the aroma from the stewpot had revived
Sergeant Brock's appetite, sort of. As they ate, Sir Orizhan
asked, "How shall we find the trail of this murderer, Lord
Wizard?"

"I'll be using what spells I can," Matt said, "but I think he
magicked himself back to Bretanglia, and so far, all my own
charms can do is verify that." His enchanted compass needle
had pointed north. "At the moment, I'm trying to find him
from another direction—by figuring out who else was in on
the conspiracy to kill the prince, and hoping they'll lead us to
our assassin."

Sir Orizhan frowned. "But I thought you knew of only the
one murderer—the footpad who went out the window, and
whom you chased and fought."

"He denied it," Matt said, "though he would, of course.
That means I have to prove it."

"If he slew the prince by casting a spell, proving will be
difficult," Sergeant Brock pointed out.

"Right. As it is now, I can't even make a convincing case
that he had a reason to do it."

"To draw Merovence into war!" Sir Orizhan exclaimed.

"Well, he did challenge me to try to keep us out of it," Matt admitted, "but that might be only one part of an overall strategy. Could be he was just a hired hand—and if he's something more, what is he?"

Sir Orizhan stared at Sergeant Brock and Sergeant Brock stared at him. Then both stared back at Matt.

"Yes," Sergeant Brock said, "what, and who?"

"Do you mean to say this Man Who Went Out the Window is not the only one to have a reason for slaying Prince Gaheris?" Sir Orizhan asked, scandalized.

"It is mean to say it, I know," Matt said sympathetically, "but it's probably true. In fact, he might have been hired by another one of the people who had a reason. Let's start with Brion and John."

"You cannot mean his own brothers would slay him to gain the throne!" Sir Orizhan demanded.

"Yes I can," Matt said, "and so can you; we've heard of it happening in other countries."

"If I did not know Brion to be so honorable, I would say that he might; he would thereby become heir." Sir Orizhan gazed off into space. "John would not gain by it, though."

"He would now," Matt pointed out. "Whether Brion had Gaheris assassinated or not, they're probably both thinking up ways to kill each other this minute."

"Yes, John to gain Brion's place as heir, and Brion to save his own life," Sir Orizhan said. He shuddered at the thought, but pursued it relentlessly. "Even then, Brion is too chivalrous to strike before he is attacked, or to attack by treachery. John though, would gain not only the throne, but Rosamund, too."

"And Rosamund wouldn't like that," Matt said, "unless she has *very* odd tastes."

Sir Orizhan stiffened, eyes glinting dangerously. "Do you accuse my princess of murder?"

"Of course not." Matt backpedaled quickly. "Of course, if she did, she'd be planning the same little surprise for John— but since she didn't, she isn't."

"If she did, I could sympathize with her," Sergeant Brock said darkly.

"Indeed, so could I." Sir Orizhan shivered, the bodyguard gaining ascendancy over the honor guard for a moment.

"The only one of those three princes who was never repulsive in either looks or personality was Brion," Matt said, "and he's so arrogant that I can't say I was surprised when Lady Rosamund showed flashes of irritation with him."

"He is justly proud of his prowess as a warrior and troubadour," Sir Orizhan said slowly.

"But such arrogance might disguise weak self-esteem in other areas," Matt pointed out. "Sometimes the second child feels he can't possibly measure up to the first. Of course, when his mother favors him as obviously as Petronille favors Brion, that shouldn't be much of a problem."

"What if his father does not?" Sergeant Brock asked.

"Yes, let's think about Drustan for a minute." Matt turned to Sir Orizhan. "Rosamund didn't seem too happy about his attentions at dinner last night, nor did her fiancé, Gaheris."

Sir Orizhan stiffened again, and Sergeant Brock protested, "You cannot mean the king could desire Rosamund for himself!"

"In a country in which noblemen still practice the *droit de seigneur*, bedding each virgin on her wedding night?" Matt countered. "I'd say it's quite possible."

"But his own son's bride, milord!"

"I do not like to speak of such things," Sir Orizhan grated, "but I have indeed heard of men who have such feelings, and in an unscrupulous king who is accustomed to having whatever he wishes, such lust might be reason enough for him to have his own son assassinated."

"So." Matt looked directly into his eyes. "You've had to protect Lady Rosamund from her betrothed already, haven't you?"

"Young men are apt to be overeager," Sir Orizhan said stiffly.

"Meaning you never left her alone with Gaheris if you could help it. Bet you even used the pretext that a princess has to learn swordplay, too."

"Every woman who will grow to be a chatelaine must," Sir Orizhan countered, "for she must defend her husband's castle in his absence."

"But you couldn't defend her from her new king," Matt said quietly.

"There was no such need," Sir Orizhan grated.

"Only because you made sure there was no opportunity."

"My king is not such a villain!" Sergeant Brock rested his hand on the dagger under his tunic.

Matt turned to him and locked gazes for a minute. Then he bowed his head a little. "Of course not. I'm sorry, Sergeant—I was carried away by my zeal for finding Gaheris' murderer."

Sergeant Brock stared, completely at a loss; he had never heard a nobleman apologize to a commoner before.

Even Sir Orizhan seemed to be unsettled, and took refuge in duty. "Besides, with Gaheris dead, Rosamund will soon be betrothed to Brion."

"Which, as we pointed out, is a reason for Brion to have Gaheris killed," Matt said.

Sir Orizhan threw up his hands. "Why do you not indict Queen Petronille while you are about it?"

"Not a bad idea." But one glance at Sergeant Brock's expression was enough to persuade Matt to drop the issue. "Of course, it's possible that the Man Who Went Out the Window did kill Gaheris on his own, and for his own reasons only—but one way or another, we have to be sure."

"Yes, quite so." Sir Orizhan frowned. "At the moment, we do not know if this sorcerer-footpad even committed the murder."

"No, we don't," Matt agreed. "At the moment, though, he's the most likely candidate. Of course, any of the soldiers in that inn could have slipped behind the prince for a few seconds. It had occurred to me that the wound could have been made by a spear point."

"It is the right length," Sir Orizhan said, gazing off into space.

But Sergeant Brock shook his head. "I'll warrant that no soldier, Merovencian or Bretanglian, bore a spear or halberd into that inn. We leave them behind when we have liberty."

"Yes, it would be rather cumbersome hauling an eight-foot shaft through the streets," Matt agreed. "I don't suppose a man might have cut a spear point off with a foot of shaft for holding it?"

Knight and soldier exchanged surprised glances. Then Sergeant Brock said slowly, "It would have been possible, and such a sawn-off spear could easily have been hidden under a soldier's livery—but it would be quite unlikely."

"So is the killing of a prince, though," Sir Orizhan said. "You amaze me by your ingenuity, Lord Wizard."

"Thank you," Matt said with a wry smile, "but as the sergeant points out, it's more ingenious than probable. Our hypothetical soldier would have had to carry that weapon around every time he went to a tavern on the off chance that the prince might stop by for a brawl."

"No, for some wenching, no more," Sir Orizhan pointed out. "You yourself have shown that the theft of the purse was done deliberately to start the brawl."

"Why, so I did, didn't I?" Matt said in surprise. "And that the murderer waited until the royal family was on Bretanglian soil. Once they checked in at Alisande's castle, it wouldn't take much imagination to realize the princes would probably check out the high life in the continental capital."

This time knight and soldier exchanged glances of puzzlement. "Your terms are difficult to understand, Lord Wizard," Sir Orizhan complained.

"You get the gist, though, don't you? Once our murderer knew the royal family was going to visit Merovence, he saw his chance. Sawing off his hypothetical spearhead and taking it along on a night's carousing would have been easy then."

"So was the blow struck by magic," Sergeant Brock asked, "or by a stealthy hand."

"Yes," Matt said, "one or the other. We can't tell which until we catch up with the Man Who Went Out the Window, catch him at a disadvantage, and cadge a few more facts out of him."

"You truly think you can defeat him?" Sir Orizhan asked in disbelief.

"Sure, now that I know I'm up against another magic-worker." Matt spoke with far more confidence than he felt. "I'll go in with a round of spells prepared this time—and directions for you guys to knock him over the head while I've got him distracted."

"So we are not here merely because Queen Alisande wished you to be guarded," Sir Orizhan said, staring into Matt's eyes with sudden intensity.

Matt grinned back. "She had her reasons for insisting, and I had mine for accepting. What better company could I have than two men who have their own very strong and very personal reasons for wanting to catch the same man I'm after?"

The dungeon door grated open and Papa stepped into the cell. Pargas jerked upright from the moldy pile of hay on which he'd been lying. The guard who'd come with Papa took a very obvious and very menacing station by the door, spear very much in evidence. There wasn't much light coming through the little barred window high on the wall, but the guard managed to make his spear point catch it.

Papa unfolded his camp stool and sat down five feet from the pimp. "Good morning, Pargas. Did you sleep well?"

"If you don't count the bedbug bites and the rats scurrying by," Pargas grunted.

"Like will to like," Papa said grimly. "I am Dr. Mantrell, a wizard in the service of Her Majesty. I would advise you to tell me the truth, Pargas, so that I will have no reason to try to ferret it out of you."

Pargas locked glares with Papa, then shuddered and looked away. Papa didn't like pimps. Then, too, Pargas had no doubt been thinking what manner of ferreting a wizard could do.

"I see we understand one another," Papa said. "Now, tell me—who cut your shoulder so badly as to make you drop one club?"

"That corrupted prince who had disguised himself as a commoner!" Pargas spat. "If he'd been honest as to what he was, I'd never dared fight him."

"Perhaps he likes your trade no more than I do, and welcomed the excuse to punish you," Papa said.

"Welcomed the excuse to punish anyone! Laetri told me what he did to her. He enjoyed his cruelty, that one. I'm glad I had the chance to give him a knock or two before he died." Pargas glared at Papa in defiance.

"So you took pleasure in giving the prince what you thought he deserved?" Papa asked.

"That I did! But I didn't kill him, if that's what you're thinking."

"You must have seen who moved behind his back, though."

"If you think I noticed much but the man who came against me, you've never been in a fight," Pargas said with contempt.

"I have been in combat," Papa said, his voice neutral, "but I was trained to perceive all that went on about me, in case some second enemy should attack from the side. If you have not, you have shown more luck than skill in your fights."

Pargas darkened with anger and embarrassment. "I'll fight you any day of the week, old man, and with no more weapons than these!" He held up his fists.

"Don't tempt me," Papa grated. "So you saw no sign of anyone who came behind the prince?"

"There was a Merovencian soldier fighting a Bretanglian," Pargas said, "but they were busy enough with each other. The Bretanglian must have won, for he turned his back to the prince and fought there awhile, guarding the rear, until someone knocked him away."

Papa tensed. "What kind of man did the knocking?"

"A Merovencian soldier, but he went right on by with two more behind him. If he stuck a knife into the prince's back, he must have done it awfully fast. Besides, it was a good minute or two later that the prince screamed and snapped bolt upright, then leaned back to fall."

"So." Papa frowned. "A Bretanglian guarded the prince's back until a Merovencian knocked him aside—but you saw no one behind him when he cried out."

"None, and none after he fell," Pargas assured him. "Me, I was fighting him one-handed the whole time, and hard put to keep him from sticking me with that rat-tail dagger of his. Whoever came at his back must have come in low and run away fast."

"Or not been there at all?" Papa gave him a hard smile and stood up. "Well, we'll see if anyone else saw what you claim, Pargas."

"And won't find any, I'll warrant," Pargas snarled. "I know how these things go."

"Do you indeed," Papa purred.

"You learn the ways of the world fast, in the gutter," Pargas said, "and I know none of your lordly kind will take the blame for a prince-killing. You have to have a goat, someone to take the blame for it, no matter who really shoved the shiv between his ribs. You'll pin this murder on me somehow."

"We will not," Papa contradicted. "Much as I hate to say it, Pargas, I'm convinced you're guilty of no more than striking a prince with a stick."

Pargas stared, and hope flared in his eyes.

"There's a heavy enough punishment for that, of course," Papa said, "but Prince Gaheris *was* disguised. The judge might take that into account."

"You don't mean I'll go free!"

"I don't mean that at all," Papa said. "There still is the charge of pandering against you."

"Oh, I'm not worried about that." Pargas relaxed with a grin. "No man will punish a pimp too hard, or leave him in gaol too long. Judge or nobleman, respectable or chivalrous, he'll know he might want my services someday."

"Thank you for the tip," Papa said as the guard opened the cell door. "I'll see that you're judged by the queen herself. Rest well while you can, Pargas, for I'm sure you'll begin hard work soon enough—very hard, and for a very long time."

Pargas' face fell. Papa smiled and went out, listening with satisfaction as the guard closed the door behind him.

CHAPTER 6

The cell door opened, and Laetri jumped up off her bunk to push herself against the wall, trembling, face pale.

Mama stepped in, frowning. "Do not worry, child, I shall not—" Then she saw the bruises on the girl's face and cried out. "Who has hurt you so?" She stepped close, reaching up to turn Laetri's face so that the light from the single window showed the purpled aura around the eye, the dark blotch on the forehead, and the lavender spot on her cheek. "Surely the prince could not have done all this to you! Tell me who did! At once!"

"I dare not." Laetri's voice caught on a sob.

"I can guess." Mama whirled to the door and called, "Gaoler!"

Slow steps approached, and the gaoler pushed the door open. "Yes, milady?"

"Who did this?" Mama demanded.

The man looked at Laetri's battered face, and the shiftiness in his eyes told Mama all she needed to know. "Do not think to lie, young man! I can see well enough what you and your fellows have been doing. Tell me why!"

"She wouldn't give." The man refused to meet her eyes. "It's her stock in trade, after all, and if she's in our gaol—"

"If she's in a cell in your dungeon, you are to guard her, not despoil her! Must I set soldiers to guard her from her gaolers? Be sure that if I do, they shall be no more gentle to you than you have been to her!" Mama raged. "Do you understand, sirrah? If there is one more bruise on this woman's face or body, *anywhere* on her body, you and all your fellows will be fortunate to have your hides whole! What manner of rotten gibbering apes are you, to exploit a woman who is given into your care? What sort of mother did you have—a baboon who sold herself to any hyena who asked? I won't even ask about your father, for any man who would treat a woman this way can't have known *what* his father was, let alone who! No matter what she has done or has been, in the queen's castle she shall be safe, or you shall find yourself before a judge and become a prisoner in your own dungeon! Unless that judge is merciful, of course, in which case you might find yourself fortunate enough to spend your years mucking out stables till you can be sent to the front rank in the next war! Do you understand me, you moral cripple?"

The man's face burned with anger and shame, but he knew better than to talk back to the queen's mother-in-law, especially since she was a powerful wizard in her own right. "Yes, milady," he mumbled.

"And she shall be safe in your dungeon?"

"As safe as a princess, milady."

"None shall even *think* of touching her?"

"No, milady."

"Then go and tell all the other gaolers! At once! Or shall I come out and tell them myself?"

The gaoler winced at the thought of all his prisoners hearing this termagant railing at every single gaoler, one by one. "I shall tell them, milady."

"Go do it, then!" Mama pointed out the door, imperious in her anger. The gaoler shuffled out, muttering under his breath. Mama glared at the door as it grated shut, then turned to find Laetri staring at her in complete amazement.

"You may feel safe now, child," Mama assured her.

"I—I thank you, milady!" Laetri said. "But . . . but why would you . . . would you trouble yourself for . . . for a street whore?"

"Because every woman should be treated with respect, and no woman should be subjected to such abuse as you have been!" Mama told her. "Then, too, I suspect you have been far more a victim than a sinner." She watched Laetri closely for the quick, calculating look in the eyes that would show a jaded, cynical mind quickly estimating how much of a sucker this sympathetic rich woman was, how far she could be milked for money or freedom—so Mama was completely unprepared when Laetri virtually threw herself into her arms, sobbing her heart out.

"There there, child." What could she do but hold her and pat her back and make soothing noises? "There are some of us who know it wasn't your fault, not yours at all, that the worst thing you did was fall in love with the wrong man and do whatever he asked of you, as love bids us all do. Not your fault, not yours at all, but his, all his, for courting you and pretending love, only to make you into a commodity he could sell!"

The worst of the storm passed, and Laetri managed to push herself away and wipe her eyes with the hem of her dress. "How—How do you know all this about me?"

"Do you think you are the only pretty child who has ever found her love so abused, who has been decoyed by a handsome face and sugared words into becoming a virtual slave? Poor thing, you aren't the first, and won't be the last! It's an old tale, very old, but vulnerable creatures of the heart that we women are, it will always be told. Come, dry your eyes now and tell me the truth of these charges against you."

She sat on the camp stool she had brought, pointing to the heap of moldy straw that served Laetri for a bed—there was no chair, not even a stool. The prostitute sat down beside her with a certain awkwardness about her movements that made Mama wonder how old she could be—sixteen? Seventeen? Mama hoped she was at least nineteen, but doubted it strongly. "Tell me—which of those bruises did the prince make?"

"This one." Laetri touched her forehead. "And these." She pulled down the neckline of her dress to show five purple marks where a rough hand had squeezed far too tightly. "There are others." She lowered her gaze, blushing with shame. "I am sure you would not care to see where they are, though."

"I can imagine," Mama said, her voice hard. "He did not wait to see his purse was gone before he struck you, then."

"Oh, he did." Laetri touched her breast. "He did not make these by striking me. No, it was only when we began to dress again that he saw his purse was missing. Then he shouted 'Thief!' and struck me with his fist." She shuddered at the memory. "I screamed and ran, but he caught me at the head of the staircase and threw me down the steps, calling for his money, calling me a robber. Then Pargas stepped between us, and I was safe."

"Until Pargas decided to rent you to another sadist," Mama said grimly. "What did you see of the battle between them?"

"The prince accused me of stealing. I said I hadn't, and Pargas told the prince that if I said it, it was true. The prince struck at Pargas. If he'd been honest about who he was, Pargas would never have dreamed of striking back, but since he didn't know, he pulled out his little clubs and swung. He struck the prince on the arm. The prince yelled with rage and stabbed Pargas in the left arm. Pargas dropped his left stick, but gave the prince a knock on the head with the right before he could pull the knife out. The prince backed away, howling, and slashed at Pargas, but he blocked with his club. They traded three or four blows then, but neither hit the other until the prince screamed, arched his back, and fell. My man pushed back against me then, panting, ready to defend. That's when the sergeant and the nobleman stepped in and started asking questions. Then the landlord shouted and pointed to the man who was going out the window, and my man and I started for the kitchen and the alley door, but the nobleman stopped us and accused us."

"Pargas is not 'your man,' except as a dog might think of its owner as 'his owner,' " Mama said severely. "Have no doubts about that, child. Pargas is not in love with you. He only thinks of you as his property."

Laetri's eyes filled with tears. "Surely he has some feeling for me!"

Mama shook her head sadly. "Only lust for your body and greed for the money it can bring him. How many other women does he run?"

"Only two." Laetri had to force the words out, eyes lowered, face red.

"You may be his most profitable," Mama said, "because you are his youngest—but that is all. You must not go back to him, child, nor to any other pimp, or your life will be wasted."

"But what else can I do now?" Tears began to run down Laetri's face. "No man will take me for a wife, and my family would not take me back in their cottage! I must whore, or starve!"

"I shall speak to the queen," Mama said. "I think she may find you a place in her kitchens. You may have to scour pots, child, and endure the sneers of the other women till they begin to trust you. Can you steel yourself to that?"

"Oh, yes! But—But the men of the staff. Will they not expect . . . expect me to . . ."

"If the queen is willing to take you into her service," Mama said firmly, "she will see that all her menservants know not to presume upon you. If I can arrange it, child, will you accept it?"

"Oh, yes!" Laetri cried, seizing Mama's hand in both her own. "I shall labor long and hard for the queen, milady, you shall see! I was born a serf's daughter, and learned to work hard at washing and baking and scrubbing as I grew! I wish I had never left that life, that I could go back to it!"

"Why *did* you leave it?" Mama said, frowning.

"Because all the boys were brutish and foolish, and I longed for something more—but in the city, I have found less! Be sure that I shall scour and labor from dawn till dusk for Her Majesty, milady! I ask only enough food to stave off hunger, and a warm place to sleep—and that never, ever again shall I have to suffer the touch of a man!"

Dinner done and talk run out, the three men prepared to sleep. Matt offered to take first watch, and neither of his companions argued; in fact, they both looked relieved. But as Sergeant Brock opened his pack to draw out a whetstone, Matt noticed something gleaming. Looking more closely, he saw silver. "A sickle?" he asked. "Silver, too! That's a curious thing for a soldier to be carrying!"

Brock tensed, but forced a smile as he closed his pack. "Curious indeed, milord. It is a battle trophy from a band of perverts we broke up. Caught none of them alive, sad to say, but we slew a few and chased all the rest. I took that sickle off one of the dead ones."

"Perverts?" Matt frowned, ready to do battle for a misunderstood and oppressed minority. "What kind?"

"The kind that get their thrills from killing the innocent,"

Sergeant Brock said grimly. "They dressed up in robes and ivy crowns to do it, and set her out as a naked sacrifice to some pagan god under the full moon as an excuse, but they were going to kill her, right enough. Four of them were holding her down, one to each limb, and a fifth, their priest or whatever, was lifting his blade to do her, when we came upon the scene and routed them."

Matt struck the "oppressed minority" off his list. Even freedom of religion had its limits, and two of them were human life and pain. "That sickle's kind of odd as a sacrificial knife. The blade's too narrow for a murder weapon." But he thought it would make just the right kind of wound in a straw doll—right to match the cut in Prince Gaheris' back.

"That sickle is not what the priest wielded—he lifted high a knife with a stone blade. We found it afterward." Sergeant Brock sat down and began to sharpen his short sword. "You must do this every day, if you have no squire to do it for you—catch each speck of rust before it can grow."

"Yes, I know," Matt said. "Gives me something to do while I'm on watch. You take care of your weapon . . ."

"And your weapon will take care of you. Yes." But Sergeant Brock stopped stroking the blade with the stone, frowning off into the distance. "I suppose it would have been a different matter if the woman had been one of them, and going to the slaughter of her own will . . ."

"Not really," Matt said. "Hardly different at all. But she wasn't?"

"No; that's why the reeve called us in—because she'd disappeared, and his men alone couldn't find her, and there are some nasty bogs on the King's Own Lands." Brock started whetting again. "But we knew they'd kidnapped her, for we'd heard about other cases like this, and chased down three of them already, so we knew what we'd find before we went looking."

"Four cases?" Matt stared.

Sergeant Brock nodded. "They've sprung up all around the land this last year. Claim to be the Old Religion, and their leaders Druids who've kept the old knowledge passed down from father to son, but the bishop set his monks to looking in old books, and they found a dozen ways these kidnappers differ from the Druids of old. No, I think they're just a very nasty bunch who like to dress up in outlandish robes so they can forget who they really are and have some excuse for their twisted pleasures."

Matt shuddered. "Nice country we're going into."

"It is that." Sergeant Brock stopped whetting and lifted his head to look Matt straight in the eye. "It's a beautiful land of rolling downs and vasty old woods, of azure lakes and stone-walled fields, and the people are the salt of the earth, steady, hardworking, and always ready to help a stranger. Don't judge us by these bands of cultsmen, Lord Wizard. They're a sprinkling only, and the most of us are good folk indeed."

He might have said more, but the moonlight suddenly dimmed, and Sergeant Brock looked up in alarm. Sir Orizhan shouted an oath, then froze, staring up at the huge dark mass outside the doorway, sword in hand.

"The stray cow was near," the huge voice rumbled out of the darkness. "You owe the farmer who dwells in the cottage with two tall pines beside it, Matthew."

"I'll pay it." Matt grinned. "I've claimed first watch, Stegoman."

"Wherefore?" the dragon asked. "I have no lids to my eyes; even in sleep, I shall see what occurs."

"Dragons don't really sleep," Matt explained to his companions. "They just sort of slow down their systems and go into a trance."

"How reassuring," Sir Orizhan said in a hollow tone, and the two men slowly went back to what they were doing. Matt went to get out his own whetstone, feeling much safer knowing that Stegoman would be watching when he went to sleep. It wasn't that he didn't trust the two men, really—it was just that he couldn't trust anyone who hadn't proved his loyalty by saving his life a few times, the way the dragon had.

Both knight and sergeant rolled out their pallets and lay down to sleep. Matt rolled his out on the other side of the firepit, but sat up on his blanket, on watch. He let his mind wander, sorting through the various possibilities of who gained by Gaheris' death, and wondering where the Man Who Went Out the Window fit in. It all came down to him, of course. For a moment he had the crazy irrational notion that if the man hadn't gone out the window, none of this would have happened.

Then that thought vanished from his mind, because he saw the eyes watching him from the shadows.

They were perfectly nice eyes, seemed almost like those of a deer, large and brown, but what were they doing there? Sir Orizhan lay parallel to the hearth, Sergeant Brock lay at right angles with Matt's pallet opposite him, but the corners of the room lay in shadow, deepest opposite the fire and farther away from it, on the wall with the doorway. Matt was close to the hearth, and the eyes were watching him from the corner farthest away, where the darkness was most complete.

No, not perfectly nice after all, Matt decided—there was definitely a malicious cast to those eyes, or at least a mischievous one, and they didn't blink, they just stared, wide-open and calculating, staring right at him!

Matt didn't use his captured magic wand very often, so he never carried it, but he had found that any long, straight object would do reasonably well for focusing and directing a magic spell, so he rested his hand on the hilt of his dagger and waited, watching. After all, the eyes might be those of a sheep who had wandered in out of the cold while he wasn't looking. Not likely, he had to admit, but he hoped the only problem here was his own lack of vigilance.

Then the eyes turned away with studied nonchalance and moved toward the fire. They brought the whole creature along with the grace and silence of a prowling cat, and Matt stopped breathing for a moment.

It was humanoid, he could say that at least, though its legs were shorter than a man's and bowed; Matt couldn't see what shape they were, because the creature wore a ragged pair of trousers that came down to mid-calf—trousers, in a land where peasants wore leggins! Its arms were longer than a man's, almost to the proportion of a gorilla's—and it was just as hairy as a gorilla. But it walked with the upright posture of a human being, and its face was almost completely human. The ears were larger, and the head was very round, almost a perfect globe, covered with hair except for the face—but it grinned with a very human delight in its own mischief as it settled down near the fire, holding its hands out to the flames.

Matt was appalled, more than he would have been if it were so severely deformed as to be an outright monster. He could have accepted a different species more easily than a creature that was as much animal as human.

The creature sat on its heels, its legs folding like jack-knives, and rubbed its hands in the warmth of the fire, but its eyes stayed on Matt, and its grin widened.

Matt stared back, feeling the atmosphere grow tense and more tense, waiting, waiting. He was bound and determined that he wouldn't speak first, or take any hostile action—but a defense spell ran through his head again and again, ready to be shouted at the slightest false move on the creature's part.

Apparently the creature realized his resolve, because it finally said, "Ye might as well speak up, man. I know you're watching."

Matt only nodded.

"Fear not for them." The creature dismissed Sir Orizhan and Sergeant Brock with a glance. "They'll not wake till dawn. I've seen to that."

So it had magical powers, too. Matt nodded again, still holding the creature's eyes with his own.

Its lip curled in derision. "What's the matter, then? Have ye never seen a bauchan before?" It pronounced the word "buckawn."

Name magic thawed Matt; it was irrational, but having a word for the species reassured him. "No, I haven't. Are you a male?"

"That I am, and it's long since I've seen a female of my kind, I tell you. Centuries. Don't fear, though—I've no yen for human women. No yen for any kind of coupling, if no female bauchan is by me and in heat." It paused, but Matt didn't comment, so it said, "We do get lonely, though."

Suddenly, Matt felt sorry for the creature. To be the only one of his kind—as he must have been, if it had been hundreds of years since he'd seen a female—must have been very lonely indeed. "I can see that you would. But aren't there any other bauchans around?"

"There is one some four miles distant." The bauchan pointed north. "And one some ten miles east." He pointed another finger, looking like a semaphore. "But we have little liking for each other." He dropped his hands.

"Oh, great!" Matt said. "Two more near enough to do some good, and they're both grouches."

"Oh, nay." The bauchan grinned. "They're no worse than I am—but no better, either. Bauchans do not like other bauchans, you see."

Matt had read his share of folklore in his studies of comparative literature. "You mean you're solitary fairies?"

"Fairies!" The bauchan sniffed. "Why do ye mortal folk always lump all us magical folk together as fairies? We're spirits or spirks or pooks, nothing else! But solitary, aye, at least as regards our own kind. We'd much rather have mortal folk for company."

"Oh?" Matt felt the first tendrils of dread reaching out for him. "Tell me, why is that?"

"Because we've no wish to suffer one another's tricks and whims."

"Yes, I can see that would be a problem." Mentally, Matt tried to fight off the dread; he was a wizard, he could handle one country spirit! "But if you're so sociable, why are you hanging around this abandoned hut?"

"Because it belonged to my last family." The bauchan wiped away a tear. "They were good folk, grandfather and father and daughter, but none came to marry her, and she dwelled alone in this cottage until she died, a good old woman of three score years and ten."

That was the Bible's allotted life span. Matt wondered if she'd forced herself to hang on until she turned seventy. "Rough life."

"Aye. She had few friends, fewer who came to visit her."

The vagrant thought drifted through Matt's mind that the bauchan might have had something to do with that.

"She did try to slay herself once or twice," the bauchan said, his eyes glittering, "but of course I could not allow that."

"Sure, you wouldn't want to be lonely." Matt shivered. "What happened to the rest of her family?"

"Oh, they died, too. They were a very nervous lot."

"I'm beginning to see why. No one else has ever tried to stay the night here, huh?"

"Nay, they have not. The place has a bad name among the villagers."

"Gee, imagine that." But Matt and his friends had flown over the village, not ridden through it and heard the warning. "How long ago did she die?"

"Thirty years."

"Yes, that's a considerable length of time. Why have you stayed?"

"Why, because I'd adopted her family, do you see. There was no point in leaving without another family to go to."

"Very loyal of you, I'm sure." But Matt's doubt sounded in his voice. "How does a bauchan find a new family?"

"He waits until someone stays the night in his old family's house, then adopts that person and stays with him and *his* family."

The tendrils of dread whipped tight around Matt. Ever the optimist, he said, "And you've chosen the sergeant here."

Grinning, the bauchan turned its head from side to side.

"The knight, then."

Again the bauchan slowly shook its head.

"You can't be thinking of—" Matt swallowed. "*—me.*"

The bauchan lifted its head up and down, eyes glowing.

Matt stared, frozen, while a chill passed over him. He gave himself a shake, cleared his throat and said, "I'm afraid that's not possible."

"Oh, but it is," the bauchan assured him. "I've adopted you, you see."

"I'm not up for adoption," Matt said firmly.

"Ah, but you've no choice there." The bauchan's teeth glinted in the firelight. "I've adopted you, and there's no more to say."

"How about 'no'?"

"You could not; you'd regret it."

"I think I'd regret 'yes' even more."

The creature's eyes flashed. "Do you refuse the gift of my company, then? You'll rue it if you do, mortal!"

Those eyes really were like those of a stag. Matt cleared his throat, resolved to straighten out this presumptuous creature. "Now look here, Buckeye—"

"Buckeye I am!" the creature crowed with delight. "You'll

never be rid of me now, mortal! Buckeye you've named me, and Buckeye I shall be, as long as I stay with you and your family! That's the way the spell works, you see!"

The dread sank in around Matt and pooled in his belly. "Then I'll make it work backward."

"You cannot, for you've chosen to name me of your own free will! Try to break that bond, and you'll regret it sorely!"

"If I do," Matt said, "you'll regret it even more."

"Do ye not ken who brought yon pallets for your sleep?" The bauchan pointed at the piles of straw under the companions' blankets. "Do you not think I can make you rue the night you slept on them?"

"Maybe, but I can make you rue your threat." Matt pointed a finger at the creature and chanted,

"Away! The moor is dark beneath the moon,
Rapid clouds have drank the last pale beam of even:
Away! For night's swift steeds will ride the darkness soon,
And bear you off beneath the lights of heaven!"

Far away there was a sound like distant hooves that went on and on, coming nearer.

The bauchan frowned. "What is that?"

"Your exit approaching," Matt told him.

The sound grew louder.

The bauchan grinned, but a bit uncertainly. "Oh, is it now! And what do you think you are—a sorcerer?"

"No," Matt said, "a wizard."

With the thunder of a cavalry regiment, something unseen and unseeable swept through the cottage, darkening the firelight for a minute. The sound was so loud that Matt could scarcely hear the bauchan's angry squall of surprise. Then the cottage lightened, and the creature was gone.

Matt felt a twinge of conscience, but it only lasted a second—he hadn't specified that any harm come to the bauchan, only that it be relocated far away from him. He let himself smile—he had turned the tables neatly, using magic to banish a magical spirit. He just hoped Shelley wouldn't mind his making a few modifications.

Matt let himself relax, surveying the room, once again on

watch, noting Stegoman's sleeping bulk outside the doorway
and the slow rise and fall of the mounds that were Sir Orizhan
and Sergeant Brock. The bauchan hadn't been joking about
its own magical powers—whatever sleep spell it had cast on
Matt's companions had certainly worked well.

Then Matt felt a sting in his left buttock. He spun off the
pallet and onto his knees, brushing at every part of his anatomy
that had been in contact with the blanket. Looking down, he
saw that the straw had come alive with bedbugs, and very large
representatives of their species at that. He swore softly. Sleep
wasn't the only spell the bauchan could cast. He hadn't been
joking about his power over the pallets.

On the other hand, Matt had some influence over them
himself—and he needed to speak quickly before his companions were welted.

> "Hey! Where y'goin', y'crawlin' ferlie!
> Your impudence protects you sairly:
> I canna say but ye strut rarely
> O'er straw and hay.
> Though faith! I fear ye dine but sparely
> In such a place.
>
> Why not go where pelt is furry?
> Get you hence in hungry hurry
> To him who sent you.
> You'll find him savory as a curry.
> Quick, go to his venue!"

The bedbugs all froze in position, and Matt could imagine
their diminutive antennae sticking up straight in surprise.
Then, suddenly, they were gone.

Matt nodded with satisfaction, then cocked his head,
listening. After all, there had been more to the spell than
banishment . . .

Outside, he heard a howl of shock and anger which
broadened into a squalling that rose, then fell and dimin-
ished, fading away into the night. Matt grinned and settled
himself cross-legged on his nice, fresh, clean pallet again.
The bauchan wouldn't try its pranks on him again in a hurry.

Or would it? Uneasily, Matt wondered if, once having said it adopted him, the bauchan was bound to him whether it wanted to be or not. He resolved to be very vigilant for a while.

Mama woke at the knock on her door and clucked her tongue in annoyance with herself for sleeping so late. "Come in!" she called, pushing herself up in bed.

The door opened and a serving maid came in, caroling, "Good morning, milady!" with just the right degree of optimism.

"Good morning to you, Meg," Mama said, smiling.

Meg balanced the bed-tray dexterously while she closed the door with one foot, then came over to set the tray over Mama's lap and plump up the pillows for her to sit up. Mama leaned back with a happy sigh. Before coming to Merovence, she had only had breakfast in bed on Mother's Day and her birthday. It was a very pleasant way to start each morning.

In this case, it was also useful. As Meg bustled over to open the curtains, Mama asked, "Has the week been as difficult for you belowstairs as it has been for us?"

"Oh, a proper fright, milady!" Meg turned back to her, eyes wide. "No lass dared turn her back on those princes, not that it—" She blushed and clamped her mouth shut.

"Come, come, I too know the ways of men, both good and bad," Mama cajoled. "So even facing them did not protect you from their gropings? Well, there have always been noblemen who thought all women of the common folk were theirs to do with as they would. Was it only the princes, or their father, too?"

CHAPTER 7

"My lady!" Meg gasped, blanching.

"There are only the two of us here, and I will never say where I learned this news," Mama assured her. "Do I shock you by the mere thought, or only by the fact that I dare speak of it?"

"Well . . ." Meg turned away. "How did you know?"

"The tone of his voice, and the look in his wife's eyes when he spoke to a younger woman." Mama didn't mention that the younger woman had been Gaheris' fiancée. "So he did treat all the serving women as though they were there for his pleasure?"

"Yes, milady, though I will say he did not press us to come to his bed, as his sons did."

"No doubt because his wife was here," Mama said. "How did you deal with the princes?"

"We spoke to Sir Martin the seneschal, milady, and he spoke to the king. None knows what passed, but the servants in the hall spoke of hearing the king's shouting through a three-inch-thick door of oak, and of Sir Martin coming out looking more stern than usual, and the king being in a right royal rage when he sent for his sons. They ceased to press us to their beds after that, though they stole as many kisses and caresses as they could, and poured lascivious remarks into our ears."

Mama made a mental note to get to know Sir Martin better; apparently, his devotion to chivalry gave him such standing as a knight that even a king dared not seek to punish him. "Even Prince Brion?"

"Oh, he never troubled us, Majesty, though he did cast admiring glances our way." She blushed. "Perhaps more than admiring, but less than lustful. Then, too, we saw him often in conversation with Sir Martin and Sir Orizhan, quite earnest conversation, about chivalry and the meaning of a knight's vows."

"But not a knight's love for his lady?"

"Not *his* lady, no," Meg said slowly. "The talk was of loving from afar, of how a knight must acquit himself when he loves a lady he may not court—even, I think, of when that knight may wear her favor, and when he may not."

In tournaments, a knight could tie a lady's scarf about his arm to show she was hoping for him to win, even if they were not in love—but Mama strongly suspected that Brion was in love with his brother's fiancée, and this overheard remark confirmed that he would not have committed murder to gain her—it would have been unchivalrous.

Mama sighed, looking up at the ceiling with its pattern of stars, suns, and moons. "I cannot understand how a family could stay together when there is so much sniping and snapping at one another."

"They are royal," Meg said simply. "They need not stay together."

"True," Mama said thoughtfully. "They can live in separate castles." She smiled at Meg. "And who could blame them?"

"They were quite—" Meg bit her tongue again, reddening.

"Quite unpleasant? Say it, my dear—I have told you I shall not repeat it. Whether it is spoken or not, most of the people in this castle will think it, from the queen to the scullery maid."

"The scullery maid! She is not even pretty, but still the princes—" Meg cut herself off again.

"If you do not stop biting your tongue," Mama said, "you will wear a hole in it. So they pursued every woman, whether she had beauty or not?"

"Prince John did," Meg explained.

"Well, like will to like. No doubt the king blames us all for guarding our virtue, for if Prince Gaheris had found his sport within the castle, he might have felt no need to go out of it."

"He may feel that," Meg said grimly, "but it will not be

true. Gaheris was the sort to think that every woman is a conquest waiting. He could never be satisfied."

"Not as long as there was a virtuous woman undespoiled," Mama agreed.

"I do not think he insisted on virtue," Meg said, "though virginity might have added spice to his conquests." She shuddered. "Vile or not, though, his death has made a horrible ending to this week."

"Yes, but he and his family saw to it that it would be a horrible week. I will except Prince Brion from that, though, and Lady Rosamund." She shook her head in pity. "Poor child! I wonder where she was while her fiancé was out wenching."

"Oh, I can tell you that!" Meg said.

That was exactly what Mama had intended. "Really? Where?"

"When the princes went out to roister, she went to her room, pleading a headache."

"I can understand that." Mama shuddered at the memory of the dinner. "I hope it passed."

"She went right to sleep, it seems, for she locked her door, and when her chambermaid came with a draft of wine to help her slumber, Princess Rosamund told her through the door, voice thick with sleep, to go away, she needed no wine."

"Then she slept, which was well, for she had a very rude awakening." Mama shook her head. "And we thought it was a blessing when those three princes left the castle in peace for a few hours!"

"Oh, not all the princes, milady."

"Oh?" Mama looked up. "Brion stayed behind, then?"

"Brion? No, he went carousing with his brother, and Sir Orizhan to ward them, with a troop of guards." Meg shook her head. "It was Prince John who stayed behind."

"Prince John?" Mama demanded, suddenly intent. "Are you certain?"

"Quite certain, milady." Meg seemed taken aback by Mama's sudden intensity. "He was most surely in the castle until he took to his bed—he went nosing about in the kitchens, asking me to his chamber, and when I told him no, he went into the hallway and pressed his demands on poor Alia. She told him nay, too, of course, so he went to his chamber in a sulk. Then

Coquille fetched him mulled wine to help him sleep, and did not come out."

Mama stiffened. "You do not mean he held her prisoner!"

"Oh, nay," Meg said, with a little laugh. "Coquille is very hard and calculating. She threw herself away long ago, for the man who stole her maidenhead with a promise of marriage then jilted her, and she resolved to have gold from men, for she claimed she could depend on them for nothing else. She fairly boasted to us the next morning that she had sported in bed with Prince John until midnight, and that she took coins from him both before and after."

The assassin had killed Gaheris about eleven, so John had a very thorough alibi. Mama frowned; she had been expecting him to be patently guilty, and was rather sorry to hear he was not.

"He still might have hired the assassin," she told Papa when they went walking in the garden after breakfast.

"So might Drustan and Petronille," Papa reminded her. "I never thought they might have wielded the knife themselves, but it is reassuring to know that they were both with Alisande and ourselves until ten."

"After that, though? The murder happened only an hour later, after all."

"I shall check to see if either of them went out." Papa smiled. "It pays to cultivate the acquaintance of soldiers, particularly those who guard the chambers of royalty."

The dragon banked low, struck the earth, and ran a short distance as it slowed, folding its wings.

"Thanks, Stegoman!" Matt climbed down. "You may have cleared up another problem for me."

"Which, if I may ask?" the dragon rumbled.

"Well, I think you could say that if anyone wants to follow our trail, they'll find it very difficult when we've just flown fifty miles."

Sir Orizhan looked up, one hand steadying himself against the dragon's side. "Who will follow us?"

"You never can tell," Matt said. "How was your trip, Sergeant?"

"Better than yesterday's." Brock climbed to his feet; he had as much fallen off the dragon's back as climbed. "I should be quite used to it by tomorrow."

"Oh, don't worry—we walk from here on."

"Walk?" Stegoman fumed. "Wherefore, when you might ride?"

"Well, we're trying to gather information," Matt explained, "so we have to try to be inconspicuous. We'll be across the border and into Bretanglia soon, so we have to go on foot. But thanks for the ride."

"Can I do no more to aid you?" the dragon protested.

"Well, actually, you can," Matt said. "Saul sent Narlh to check out conditions in Scotland and to watch for any signs of invasion, but the local dragons probably won't accept him. Could you go along and see how bad things are there, and back him up if he needs it?"

"The valiant dracogriff? Of course!" Stegoman huffed. "Woe to any drake who seeks to singe him! Nay, I'll fly north immediately!"

"Oh, I don't think it's *that* crucial," Matt said quickly. "You could spend one more night with us—you know, have a cow and settle down for some chat."

"The journey has been long and tiring," Stegoman agreed. "Very well, I'll seek a steer and join your company for one more night."

Matt sighed with relief. If the bauchan did manage to find them, it would probably think twice about causing trouble with Stegoman near.

Unless, of course, it managed to put him to sleep again.

Hastings Castle was small, as royal fortresses went, but the castellan and his family lived in a lodge in the courtyard, leaving twelve rooms for the use of the royal family. The structure was quite well situated to be the first dwelling to welcome its king and queen on their return to Bretanglia.

King Drustan strode into the Great Hall, yanking off his gauntlets, hurling them at a squire, and snarling at everyone about him. "I could have ridden in here with an army, and none to stop me! Castellan, have you no more sentries for the walls? Confound you, steward, send your bottler for wine! You knew I was entering the castle, the goblet should have been ready for my hand! Or are the sentries so lax that you did *not* know I was coming? Be done with that curtsying, wench, and fetch me bread and meat! Ninny, do you think I care for your homage? Varlet, you barely nodded your head! Do you not bow to your king?"

Queen Petronille was right behind him, snapping, "How long is it since these walls have been scrubbed? Sloven, are those tapestries never beaten? I see rust on the trophies and dust on the royal coat of arms! You there, do you call yourself a gardener? I shall stroll through your handiwork after dinner, and if I see so much as one weed, you'll spend the rest of your life mucking out stables!"

Up the stairs they went, snapping and snarling at all about them, then into the solar, slamming the door behind them. There, Petronille sank into an hourglass chair, covered her face and loosed a torrent of sobs.

"Oh, be still!" Drustan snapped. "If you hadn't insisted on taking the boys along, this never would have happened!"

"I!" Petronille snapped bolt upright, glaring at him through her tears. "If you hadn't taken it into your head to go gallivanting off to Merovence, our son would be alive this day!"

"You were quick enough for the jaunt when I mentioned it!"

"Aye, to make sure you would not be trying to bed every wench you found!"

"At least they would not have made my bed a battleground!"

"Better your bed than our children!" Petronille blazed.

"Then why did you shower Brion with praise and John with criticisms? Not to mention poor Gaheris, which you did not, and look what has come of it!"

"Oh, indeed!" Petronille sprang to her feet. "And who was ever telling him that he must be cruel to be a man, and must prove his manhood by bedding every wench he saw?"

"Who told him he must never touch a woman at all?" Drustan returned.

"Save his wife!"

"Ah, but you did not tell him that!"

"You never heard! You were always far too busy planning your next slaughter and your next seduction—if you can so dignify commanding a helpless woman to submit to your embraces!"

"Submit?" Drustan roared. "They were glad enough to come to me, and you were too, till you saw I would not bow and scrape for it!"

"So because I would not shower you with honeyed words every hour of the day, you turned to Rosamund and sought to seduce a child under our protection!"

"There will certainly be no need for seduction now!" Drustan retorted. "Not when she must face the prospect of marrying your lapdog Brion!"

"See to it you dare not dog her lap, sirrah! Any woman would faint with delight at the thought of wedding Brion! It is the prospect of marrying your depraved little John that makes her faint with nausea!"

"A woman wants a man who is his own master, not forever the slave of his mother!"

"His own master, but not hers! Brion is a true knight and troubadour, chivalrous to the last, and will treat her with the respect due the lady she is!"

"Set her on a pedestal and never touch her, you mean! Let her pine and waste away! I'll save her from such a fate by marrying her to John!"

"To John?" Petronille screeched. "To yourself, you mean, for if she is betrothed to John, she will live with you, and you'll be quick to take advantage of her!"

"So that's why you want her for Brion!" Drustan's eyes glittered with malice. "You wish to keep her by you out of sheer jealousy!"

"Out of duty, you great ninny! My duty to protect the child from such libertines as you! That I shall do in any case—but I wish her for Brion solely because he is now heir, and she was betrothed to the heir of Bretanglia!"

"John, too, is the heir!"

"Aye, after Brion! Will you slay your second son, too, only to steal Rosamund for yourself?"

"I, slay my own son?" Drustan turned purple. "I would never so much as dream of such a thing! How corrupted and base your mind must be, that you think of it!"

"Corrupted by learning what a king may be!"

"Corrupted by years of marriage to a southern prince who taught you all manner of nasty games!"

"Louis? There was nothing he could teach me but the Bible! If he'd known any manner of games, I'd surely never have divorced him for you!"

"But you did, and liked my games well enough," Drustan said, with a vindictive grin.

"Aye, so long as you played them only with me! But it is a dance for partners, sir, not a crowd of maidens 'round a maypole, and little Rosamund shall not dance attendance upon you!"

"And how shall you prevent it?" Drustan challenged. "By betrothing her to Brion? Little fool, whether to Brion or John, she will still live in the same castle with me!"

Petronille narrowed her eyes. "Not if I do not."

"What choice have you?" Drustan countered. "If I say John shall be king, he shall, youngest or not! You may remove yourself from me, but Rosamund shall stay!"

"You would dare!" Petronille hissed.

"Of course I would." Drustan grinned. "I shall do it now!" He strode to the door, threw it open, and stepped out to the rail that overlooked the Great Hall. "Hearken one and all! Hear the word of your sovereign! Prince John shall succeed me! Prince John is heir apparent! Prince John shall be your new king!"

"Brion shall be king, by right of law!" Petronille shouted. She whirled out of the room to face Drustan, glaring up at him. "Will you or nil you, Brion shall rule! It is his right!"

Doors opened; John and Rosamund stepped out, eyes sleep-blurred, staring in fear. But Brion's door opened, too, and though his face was flushed with sleep, his eyes were bright and clear, ready for anything that might come, and there was no fear in his face.

"Away!" Somehow, Petronille had found a cloak, and swung it about her shoulders as she pivoted to Brion. "He seeks to disinherit you! You must fight for your right, and the welfare of your people!" She caught Rosamund's hand and pulled her away toward the stairs.

Drustan roared and came after her, but brought himself up short to avoid the point of Brion's sword. "Well, now we know with what mistress *you* sleep!"

"As always, my father, you are correct," Brion said. "Not right, but accurate."

"So you would stab your own father, would you?"

"Never," Brion assured him, "but if he chose to throw himself upon my sword, how could I interfere with his will?"

"Then obey my will indeed, and put up your sword! It is your sovereign who commands!"

"Your sovereign seeks to break the law of the land by displacing the legitimate heir!" Petronille cried from the stairwell. "In Bretanglia, no king is above the law! He has defied it, he is rightful king no longer! Hail Brion, true King of Bretanglia!"

There was a startling lack of response from the crowd of servants and soldiers.

"Stop them!" Drustan shouted at the guards.

Two dozen men moved forward on the instant.

"To me, men of mine!" Petronille cried. "Protect me, all men of Pykta! Guard your princess, all men of Toulenge!"

Thirty men leaped to surround the two women.

"Beware, woman!" Drustan bellowed. "Walk out down that stair and across that drawbridge, and this means war!"

"Then let it be war!" Petronille cried. "Let it be war for virtue and right, and the true king come to replace the false! Down with the disgraced king! Let the right prevail!"

"And you?" Drustan fixed his middle son with a vengeful glare. "Do you cleave to your true king, or to this rebel woman?"

"I am a knight," Brion said simply. "I must defend women in distress."

"A pox upon your chivalry!" Drustan roared. "I knew I should never have let your mother fill your head with that troubadour nonsense!"

"It is no nonsense, but the only possible salvation of the world." Brion backed away, down the stairs, sword still level. "It allies the might of the knight with the mercy of Christ, alloying the strength of arms with Christian charity."

"Yet the dauntless knight dares not turn his back on his unarmed father," Drustan sneered.

"I would never turn my back upon my sovereign," Brion rejoined.

"Guard him!" Petronille commanded, and half a dozen men broke away to meet Brion at the foot of the stairs. Armed and wary, they retreated to join her men at the door.

"Take one more step at your peril!" Drustan warned them all. "Leave this hall, and you are traitors one and all, rebels to king and country, who deserve only the noose or the headsman's block!"

"So speaks the man who seeks to break the common law and custom of Bretanglia!" Petronille cried. The words sounded strange in the accent of Merovence. "So speaks the traitor to his land, the tyrant who breaks his covenant with his people and his God! We shall remember your words, O Traitor, when you kneel before us on the day of your defeat and our triumph."

"I shall never kneel to you!" Drustan roared.

"You did once," Petronille reminded him, then stepped backward out of the Great Hall, pulling Rosamund with her. Her son and her men followed.

Out they went into the courtyard, where horses waited for them all, held by a score of Pyktish soldiers, the rest of Queen Petronille's private guard, save for the few who had already secured the gatehouse. They rode through it, under the portcullis and out across the drawbridge, the rearguard leaving the barbican and riding flat out to join them.

Inside, Drustan roared, and all his knights and men ran to saddle their horses, mount, and ride out into the night to catch the queen and her party.

They rode and searched till dawn, but the queen and her entourage had disappeared. Superstitious rumors began in the army and ran through the country in a week—that the queen had spoken truly, that Drustan had indeed violated the old law of Bretanglia, the bond between people and soil, and that the land itself had hidden the rightful king and his mother from the false king.

By that time a dozen discontented barons had rallied to Petronille's banner and Brion's command, while Drustan had called down his nobles all, and the armies had begun to march.

* * *

It wasn't a hard rain, only a gentle drizzle, but it was constant, and the boots and cloaks of the companions were almost soaked through, so they threw back their hoods with a sigh of relief as they stepped into the wayside inn.

"This will be far more agreeable than sleeping in an open field," Sir Orizhan observed, "or even that ruined cottage where we slept last week."

"It sure will." But Matt couldn't help glancing over his shoulder. He wasn't at all sure that Buckeye was going to stay gone. The "adoption" had sounded like pretty strong magic, after all, especially since he had been so careless as to give the creature a nickname. True, he hadn't seen the bauchan in days, but constantly had the feeling they were being watched. Also, he kept finding things—the stack of wood that appeared while they were setting up camp, the dazed rabbits that hopped into the campsite fairly asking to become dinner, the fourth shadow that joined theirs under the morning sun though there was no one to cast it. All in all, Matt was glad to have a lot of people around.

The big common room was noisy enough. Maybe it was the rain that made business so good, but Matt hoped it was the ale. The only seats he and his companions could find were at a round table where four peasants were already eating. They ordered a pitcher and the special of the day, which was what most of the people were eating, not having money enough for chops. The special turned out to be hash. Matt hoped for the best and started eating.

"Sad news from Bretanglia," one carter was telling another across the table.

Matt didn't bother pricking up his ears—Sir Orizhan and Sergeant Brock were tense as pointers in pheasant season.

"Aye, Ian," the other carter agreed. "War is always bad for business. I'll have trouble enough finding the merchant who ordered my cargo, let alone another load to carry home."

"If the soldiers let you into Bretanglia at all," Ian said darkly, "and you're lucky enough not to run into an army."

"The war has started," Sir Orizhan whispered.

"Not too much worry of that," the second carter said. "The news is all from the midlands now. The queen's army took the high ground at Lochlar and fought a pitched battle against the king's forces under Duke Golarrig. The duke retired in defeat, and the queen invested the town. She has her another stronghold now, and thousands of men to press into her army."

"War, yes." Sir Orizhan stared in shock. "But not between Bretanglia and Merovence!"

Matt stared, too. "*Civil* war?"

Sergeant Brock managed to keep the groan so quiet that only his companions heard it. "Alas, my poor country! For how long now shall Pyktans spill Anglian blood again?"

Matt's mind took refuge in the thought that he had guessed correctly about the origin of the country's name. Apparently the invading Angles hadn't won anywhere near the clear-cut victory in this universe that they had in his. They'd been forced to make friends with the country's current inhabitants.

"And what of Princess Rosamund, Much? What of the cause of this war?"

"There are some as say she's not the cause at all," Much said darkly. "Some say the cause is Prince Gaheris himself."

"But he is dead," Ian protested.

"Aye, but Rumor says he did not die quite as the proclamations say."

Ian shrugged. "There's no surprise in that. All knew of the prince's roistering. Not a man in all of Bretanglia believes he died defending a maiden's honor."

"The queen did, says Rumor, and fights because the king insists on the truth—that a pimp stabbed him in the back while he was beating one of the man's whores."

Matt was amazed that the rumor was even that accurate.

"If that were said of Prince Brion, the queen might fight to defend his good name," said Ian, "but Gaheris? He was never her favorite."

"Aye." Much grinned. "I think you had the right of it at first. With Gaheris dead, they fell to fighting over Princess Rosamund—whether she would marry Brion, and live with the queen, or wed John, and live with the king."

"He would wish that, surely," Ian agreed. "But where is she hidden, while they fight?"

"Rumor has it that the queen sent her to Castle Eastwind with a hundred men for guard, but while they were on the way, Earl Marshal attacked and stole the princess away for the king."

Prurient interest gleamed in Ian's eye. He hunched closer. "And what has the king done with her?"

"Nothing yet," Much answered. "He was already in the field, so the marshal took her to a moated grange at Woodstock, and set a strong guard around her—for her safety, says Rumor. Then he rode away to raise the west country."

"Woodstock?" Ian frowned. "There's a royal castle there."

"There is, and the moated grange is hard by its walls."

"How convenient for the king," Ian said with sarcasm.

"Aye, if he comes back to it alive."

"Surely the queen cannot win! The king must have five times the men and horses that she can call up!"

"You never know, in war," Much said philosophically. "At least their marching to and fro should keep them far from the borders."

"The news is old," Ian cautioned. "The fighting may have moved southward. Surely the queen must capture Dunlimon if she has any hope of winning."

"Small enough hope, I would say," the second carter replied, "though Queen Petronille is not the kind to ever consider defeat. Aye, she must capture Dunlimon—or the king."

Ian shook his head sadly. "She cannot do either, unless all the folk of Dunlimon are secretly for her, not with the king's armies so outnumbering hers."

"She can make a lot of Bretanglians suffer, though." His friend rose from the table, taking his mug. "I hear a minstrel tuning his lute. Let's approach and listen—I could do with a song."

"I, too." Ian rose and went with him.

"So my queen shall drive half the midlands before her against the king's men," Sergeant Brock moaned, "and the land shall drink their blood!"

"Maybe the king's a better general than you think," Matt consoled. "Maybe he'll knock her out in one quick battle."

Sir Orizhan smiled mirthlessly. "Or perhaps she will find a wizard who can capture the king without a battle. Come, my friend, let us talk in realities."

"Actually, your idea isn't all that far-fetched." Matt's eyes lost focus as he considered how to craft a spell that would transport King Drustan to him.

Another peasant sat down where Ian had been, a mug in his hand.

"Does the king have a wizard on his side?" Matt asked.

"Aye," said the newcomer, "but the elves and the pixies will fight for the queen."

Matt looked up in surprise, and felt a shock run all through him. The hood and tunic were those of a very ordinary peasant, but the hand that held the mug was covered with silky, tawny hair, and the face was Buckeye's.

The bauchan grinned. "You did not think I would stay banished, did you?"

Through stiff lips Matt demanded, "Where's the peasant who used to wear that outfit?"

"What outfit?" Sergeant Brock looked up, frowning.

"Don't fear for him," Buckeye said. "He sleeps in the stable, quite well, and will find his clothes by him when he wakes."

Matt turned to Sergeant Brock. "You see that peasant sitting across from us?"

"Peasant!" the bauchan said indignantly.

"The one whose hood hides his face?" the soldier asked. "He is nothing to worry you. You may speak freely, milord."

"Not too freely, 'milord,'" the bauchan mocked. "You would not want them to think you daft, now, would you? Or, by the rook! Haunted! Forfend!"

That made Matt mad. Blackmail attempts always had that effect. His eyes narrowed, his lips thinned, and he said to his companions, "By the way, have I told you I've picked up a mascot-spirit?"

"Spirit!" Sergeant Brock leaned away, eyes wide.

"Mascot?" Sir Orizhan frowned. "What is that?"

"A sort of a pet." Matt ignored the hoot from across the table. "It goes wherever I go. It's a bauchan."

"A bauchan!" Sergeant Brock turned pale.

"What is that?" Sir Orizhan asked, interested.

"It's a Bretanglian spirit," Sergeant Brock explained. "I knew they came down into the north of Merovence, but I never thought to have met one." His eyes widened. "That empty cottage! I should have known it would be haunted! 'Twas there you met him, was it not?"

"It was, yes," Matt admitted.

"The man is canny," Buckeye said with approval, letting the sergeant and the knight hear him.

"I am flattered." But the whites showed around Sergeant Brock's eyes as he glanced at their new neighbor.

"What, that fellow a spirit?" Sir Orizhan frowned. "I see naught but a peasant!"

"Look at his hands," Sergeant Brock said.

"He wears gloves with the hair on the outside. What of it?"

"Gloves with nails?" the sergeant asked.

Sir Orizhan studied the bauchan's hands. Buckeye grinned and, very slowly, raised the tankard to his lips and tilted his head back to drink, letting the light from the tallow lamps show them his face. Sergeant Brock shuddered.

"He is quite ugly," Sir Orizhan said, "but surely no spirit."

Matt's heart warmed to the man.

"Ugly!" Buckeye slammed his mug down on the table. "Forsooth! I suppose you think you are comely, fellow?"

"I am a knight." Sir Orizhan frowned and rested his hand on his sword. "I'll not have a varlet call me 'fellow.' "

"I don't think you want to draw on him," Matt said nervously. "Unfortunately, that face is the most human thing about him."

"If a sharp edge will not harm him, cold steel will," Sir Orizhan countered.

Buckeye frowned. "I like ye not, soft man of warm climates."

"It won't do any lasting good," Matt warned. "I tried to banish him right off the bat, but the spell seems to have worn off."

"He did not try a bat," Buckeye corrected. "That might have lasted a wee bit longer."

"A bat for a bit?" Matt turned to him, interested. "I'll remember that."

Buckeye's glance flashed with malice; then he was all mischievous grin again. "It will do ye no good."

"It will not that," Sergeant Brock agreed. "When a bauchan attaches himself to a man, he'll never forsake him—nay, neither him nor his family." He shook his head sadly. "I pity you, Lord Wizard. Not all your power will make this spirit flit."

"Oh, I'll find a way." Matt wished he felt as confident as he sounded. "But I can't ask you guys to suffer along with me while I'm trying. If you want to go off on your own, go ahead."

"Go off!" Sir Orizhan exclaimed, affronted. "When my queen has commanded me to accompany you? I am a better knight than that, Lord Wizard!"

"And I have my good name to restore." Sergeant Brock had recovered from his first fright. "I'll stand by you night and day, Lord Wizard, until we've hung the murderer by the heels and proved I fought my best to save my prince." His eyes narrowed and held steady on the bauchan's ugly face.

"A murderer and a dead prince?" Buckeye asked, interested. "I may have come upon more fun than I expected! Whatsoever it may be like to follow you, wizard, I doubt it will be dull!"

"You don't know how I've wished for some boredom," Matt sighed.

"Still, I cannot let you suffer that, can I?" Buckeye reached out with a long arm that stretched even longer and caressed a waitress' bottom as she was passing Matt.

The girl shrieked even as she turned and whacked Matt soundly across the face.

CHAPTER 8

"And you with a wedding ring!" the serving wench scolded. "My master has thrown men out for mauling girls who don't wish it!"

Matt glared at Buckeye, but the bauchan only grinned back. His lips moved, but the sound seemed to come from Matt in Matt's own voice. "Lasses who don't wish it, aye—but will he throw me out for stroking those who like it? Might you be one such?"

"I am none such!" the girl declared, and pivoted away crying. "Master! Here's an unabashed womanizer for certain!"

The innkeeper bulled his way to the table just as Matt's voice was saying, "None such is nonesuch, and a nonesuch is a thing of great rarity, and a virtuous woman is a rare thing indeed. Next she will be telling me she is a virgin!"

"I *am* a virgin!" the serving maid cried.

"I will not permit harassment, countryman," the innkeeper warned.

"Meant?" Matt's voice asked. "Well, if her—"

"I didn't say that," Matt interrupted.

"Indeed! Then how was it your voice I heard? I tell you, fellow, I'll not have my serving maids touched!"

"Saving them all for yourself, are you?" Matt's voice asked.

The innkeeper reddened. "Enough!" He grabbed Matt by the tunic and yanked him to his feet. "I'll serve you no longer! Out of my inn, fellow, and a cold wet night to you!"

"You may not speak so to a lord!" Sir Orizhan snapped, rising and grasping his sword.

"A lord, is it?" The innkeeper turned on Sir Orizhan. "A

lord, dressed in a peasant's smock? And I suppose you are his knight, and the other your squire?"

"Don't blow our cover!" Matt hissed.

Sir Orizhan ignored him. "You have guessed the truth of it, landlord. Now unhand His Lordship or—"

"Take him, then!" The innkeeper threw Matt at Sir Orizhan.

Sergeant Brock shouted in anger and swung his staff at the innkeeper, who leaped back, letting the staff swing by—to crack across the shoulders of another patron. The man leaped to his feet with a howl and waded in swinging.

The serving maid screamed and backed away, her tray up as a shield.

Matt spun away from Sir Orizhan and blocked the man's haymaker. "Now, wait a minute. We didn't mean to—"

"A coward!" the man cried, and slammed a punch at Matt's midriff.

The innkeeper yanked a short cudgel from his belt and swung at Sergeant Brock.

Matt blocked again and counterpunched. The man's mates howled and leaped into the fight.

Sergeant Brock blocked with one end of his staff and swung with the other. He caught the landlord on the hip. The steady customers shouted in anger and jumped on Brock.

The innkeeper stamped on Matt's toe and swung his cudgel. Matt shouted with pain even as he ducked. He heard the stick strike somebody, hoped it was the bauchan, and caught the innkeeper's wrist. He was about to twist when another fist caught him on the cheek. He staggered away, feeling somebody catch him. The spell he'd readied to use on Buckeye hovered on his lips, but he remembered that these were good, ordinary men fighting to defend their own, and choked it down. Whoever had caught him threw him back at the innkeeper just in time to meet the stick swinging down— but Matt doubled over and kept on going, butting the innkeeper in the stomach. The man's breath went out in a whoosh as he slammed back against the wall. The move lacked elegance and finesse, but it did give Matt a softer landing. He scrambled back up, cocked a fist—and felt a dozen hands grab him.

Five minutes later he landed in a puddle outside the door with a score of bruises. He started to struggle to his feet, but his pack came sailing to strike him square in the kidneys, knocking him full-length in the puddle. Four more splashes told him Sir Orizhan, Sergeant Brock, and their packs had landed, too.

"And stay out!" the innkeeper bellowed, then slammed the door behind him.

A hairy hand reached down for Matt. "Let me help you up."

Matt looked into the ugly grinning face of the bauchan, and snatched his arm away. "No, thanks. I can do without your kind of help."

"That's unjust." The creature actually sounded wounded. "I can be a great help, when I've a mind."

"Yeah, but I don't trust your mind." Matt struggled to his feet and looked down at his sodden, muddy clothes. "This isn't what I'd call assistance."

"Ah, but that was when I meant you ill," the bauchan said, grinning, "to show you what can happen if you seek to be rid of me. If I mean you well, it will be just as striking."

The look Matt gave him verged on mayhem. "Don't talk to me about striking."

"Nor to me," Sergeant Brock groaned, struggling to his feet. "Why did you not use your magic against them, Lord Wizard?"

"I thought of it," Matt admitted, "but I remembered that they're good plain folk, fighting to defend a friend and his inn. They didn't deserve to be blasted."

Brock looked up at him in surprise. "You're an odd lord, to be so caring about the common folk."

That's because I'm really a commoner, too. But Matt couldn't say that out loud. Instead he said, "I'm married to a queen who cares for every single one of her people, Sergeant, and that's one of the qualities that made me fall in love with her."

Sergeant Brock turned away, looking very thoughtful, and helped Sir Orizhan to his feet. The bauchan asked, "What sort of spell would you have used on them, wizard?"

"Oh, one like this," Matt answered.

"Pleasures are like poppies spread—
You seize the flower, its bloom is shed;
Or like the snow falls in the river—
A moment white—then melts forever.
Thus let be a bauchan's presence,
Here some minutes, then gone for pleasance."

Buckeye squalled in shock and surprise as an invisible hand caught him up and whirled him into a tiny dot that winked out. They listened to the sudden peaceful susurrus of rainfall. Then Sergeant Brock quavered, "He seemed to stay where he was, yet was also whisked far away."

"Very perceptive, Sergeant. That's exactly what happened."

"How can that be, Lord Wizard?"

"Oh, it's not hard. It's just a question of where he was being whisked, and in what direction."

"Where?" Sir Orizhan asked, staring in awe.

"Into another dimension," Matt said, "and as to direction, it was at right angles to the three we know."

"How can that be?" Sir Orizhan asked with foreboding.

"I . . . don't know," Matt admitted. "Hey, look—I just cast the spells. That doesn't mean I understand 'em."

"How can you not?" Sergeant Brock asked.

Matt shrugged. "It's like driving an automobile. I know how to make it go where I want, but I don't know how it works inside—not in detail, anyway."

"Oh." Sergeant Brock seemed to be thinking that over.

"I suppose that makes sense," Sir Orizhan allowed. "But, Lord Wizard . . ."

"Yes?"

"What is an 'automobile'?"

They found a barn, peeled off their wet clothing and set it to dry, rubbed themselves with hay, then put on their spare clothes and rolled up in more hay to sleep. Sir Orizhan took first watch, and Matt had absolutely no trouble dropping off to sleep. Unfortunately, he dreamed. At least, he hoped it was a dream.

In the darkness of slumber a voice ranted, "Pay attention, blast you! I haven't been shouting at you all these days for my pleasure!"

"Well, then, why have you been shouting?" Matt demanded.

There was a brief silence, but somehow Matt could feel the astonishment in it. Then the voice erupted with delight. "I've broken through! He has heard me! Do you know who I am, Lord Wizard?"

"I haven't the faintest." Matt was beginning to have a bad feeling about this.

"I am Gaheris! I am Prince Gaheris of Bretanglia! And I may be dead, but I'm not deaf! I heard you say you would find my murderer! Who is he?"

The bad feeling was proving true. Matt reassured himself that he must be dreaming and said, "Don't you know?"

"Know? How could I know? The villain came at me from behind! I felt the sword go in, felt a pain that seemed to rip the world apart—then all went dark. At last a dot of light broke that darkness and swelled to a hollow. I could see a long way into it, saw it was a tunnel with a sublime light at its end. I thought I heard voices that I knew calling from it, and my heart went cold within me. I turned my back on it with a shudder and fought to sit up, but my body would not answer. I thought I must have fallen asleep, and fought to waken, fought and fought—and bit by bit I regained my senses, but found myself looking down at my own body and hearing folk talking of who had slain me! I snapped at them that I wasn't dead, shouted at them that I wasn't dead, roared and bellowed at them that I wasn't dead—but they did not answer, and my stomach sank as I realized they had not heard me. Then I saw the wound in my own back, and knew that I was dead indeed."

Matt felt rather than saw the shudder. In fact, so far he wasn't seeing anything. "Why did you come to me?"

"I came to everyone! Mother, Father, Brion, John, Sir Orizhan—waking and sleeping, I came to them, ranted to them, howled at them, but none seemed to hear me! Well, I was scarcely surprised when it came to Mother and Father—if they hadn't heard me alive, why should they hear me dead? But I had always been able to rouse Brion's anger, or John's fear—yet now even they seemed not to hear!"

"Why me?" Matt said again.

"Because you're a wizard, blast you! And it worked!"

"Sure—all you had to do was catch me when I was asleep. How many nights have you been trying?"

"All day. This is the first night."

"Must be because ghosts are a sort of magic, or related to it," Matt mused.

"Never mind the why! Only tell me who slew me!"

"I'd love to," Matt told him sincerely. "Even more, I'd love to tell your parents, and rob them of their excuse to attack Merovence. Unfortunately, everybody seems to have had a reason to want you dead—"

"Aye. They all hate me, the jealous sods!"

"—and everybody has an alibi." From what Matt knew of Gaheris alive, jealousy hadn't entered into it. When you try to hurt people, they tend to resent you. "Can you think of any way I can tell who was there that I don't know about?"

"Whom do you suspect?"

"Everyone who was in the inn that night."

"How the devil should I know who was in the inn that night?"

"That's right," Matt sighed, "you were only there. Well, if you don't have a notion who killed you, how can you expect me to know?"

"Because you're a wizard, damn your eyes!"

"I'd be kind of careful with that word 'damn' if I were you," Matt advised. "Has the tunnel appeared to you again?"

"Aye, twice more." Gaheris' voice was hollow with fear. "But I ranted and railed at it, cursed my murderer aloud, and it went away."

"Unfinished business," Matt muttered.

"What did you say?" the ghost-prince demanded.

"Nothing important." Matt had a notion that if he found and punished Gaheris' murderer, the light-tunnel wouldn't go away the next time it appeared. All that was holding the prince's ghost to this universe was his anger at his murderer, and his thirst for revenge. On the other hand, Matt didn't particularly want the ghost to know that. He didn't like being haunted, dreaming or waking, and wasn't about to let Gaheris know he had a way of avoiding the afterworld. "Look, nobody can see you, right?"

"True." The ghost sounded wary.

"Well, then, you can flit around and watch them when they think they're safe and alone."

"Who would you have me watch?"

"Everyone in your family, for starters. More importantly, there was a sorcerer in the inn that night—"

"A sorcerer?" the ghost cried. "Of course it was he who slew me!"

"Why? Because he had magic? Believe me, I haven't found the slightest sign that he shoved the knife into your ribs, or made a knife stab you by itself. Besides, he denies it."

"Of course he would, you dolt!"

"Hey!" Matt snapped. "Do you want me to try to find your murderer, or not?"

"Of course I do! How dare you even ask?"

"Because I'm the one who can do it—maybe. You talk to me with respect, or I'm walking off the job."

"You cannot speak so to a prince!"

"I can when I'm married to a queen," Matt reminded him. "In fact, if you want to get technical about it, that makes me a prince, too—and one who's got a bit more power in this situation than you do. Just give me a good reason to drop this investigation and I will."

"If you do, I shall haunt you all your days!"

"You're a little late," Matt told him. "Somebody already got there—a bauchan. You want to cross horns with him over haunting territory?"

Gaheris spluttered incoherently, but there was a definite tinge of fear to it. Matt reflected that the superstition of the Middle Ages could be very useful. Here the prince was, a haunt himself, and he was still afraid of the bauchan!

"Go away," Matt grumbled. "I need my sleep. How can I catch your killer if I'm groggy?"

"You will rue this one day, wizard!" Gaheris blustered.

"I doubt it," Matt snapped, and mentally rolled over and pulled the metaphorical blanket over his head. "Go away."

Amazingly, Gaheris did—possibly because Sir Orizhan woke Matt for his watch. Half an hour later he decided that after that dream, being awake was very restful.

* * *

The army of Earl Salin, the Marshal of Bretanglia, came striding behind its knights along the high road—really high, for the ground fell away to both sides. Ahead, though, it passed through a cleft in the hills.

Atop one of those hills, Sir Gandagin, a knight in his forties, sat on his horse, shielded by a great boulder to either side, and counseled Prince Brion, "We may hold the high ground, Your Highness, but they still outnumber us by half, and Earl Marshal is the most excellent knight in Bretanglia. Saving your presence," he added hastily.

"Spare me flattery, Sir Gandagin," the prince said. "Though I might hope to equal a knight of Earl Marshal's excellence in chivalry, I know I cannot compare in prowess with a man thirty years my senior. I own you have sense on your side— but the marshal is all sense and no nonsense, with great faith in the order in which he has drilled his men. If we come upon him like wild Celts, we may do to him as Queen Boadicea did to the armies of Reme when she found they had cheated her of a whole county, by trading it for gems she discovered to be glass. She chewed them to bits, for they knew not how to counter her disorder."

"Soundly planned," Sir Gandagin admitted. "Still, my prince, do remember that Reme eventually brought Boadicea to heel."

"Eventually," Brion reminded him. "I need not win the war—only this battle."

Below, the vanguard of the marshal's army entered the notch.

"Out upon them!" Brion commanded, and swung his sword high with the same eerie, ululating battle-cry that had struck fear into the hearts of legionnaires a thousand years before, a battle-cry taken up by five hundred mouths, echoing from both sides of the road as men in half-armor came charging down, spears leveled.

"Close ranks!" the marshal bellowed, and the double file of soldiers pivoted to face outward, shields coming up to present a solid wall that bristled with spears.

But the attackers had spears, too, and were striking downward. They hurled their javelins, and a score of soldiers fell dead. Then they struck into the shield-wall, long spears stabbing down over the tops of the shields. Most of the soldiers snapped their shields up, deflecting the spears and striking back with their own, but a few were slow and fell, blood streaming down over their breastplates. The attackers caught the spears of the shield-wall on their own shields, though another score fell in trying. Then the two forces grappled one another in a desperate melee that filled the road. One by one, men fell and rolled down the sides, defenders and attackers alike.

Through the press rode the knights, hewing and hacking about them as they sought to come to grips with one another. They roared with anger, and footmen stumbled out of their way as quickly as they could, but stumbled and went down as often as they stumbled to safety.

Prince Brion chopped his way to Earl Marshal, blood singing high within him, head filled with visions of the honor of crossing swords with one of the finest knights in Europe. He chopped, he roared, and the marshal turned his steed at the last minute, shield rising to meet Brion's broadsword. Then they hewed and hacked at one another while their warhorses circled about and about until finally the old knight struck a third blow in exactly the same line on Brion's shield, and the metal and wood fell apart. Brion snatched at his dagger, better than no defense at all, but the marshal spurred his horse and struck the prince squarely with his own shield. Brion fell, and the marshal bellowed, "Surrender! Your prince is down!"

His knights echoed the cry, and the foot soldiers froze. Then, one by one, the attackers threw down their spears, but kept their shields high.

"Mercy, Lord Marshal." Prince Brion struggled up to his knees, hands upraised.

"Mercy?" The marshal glowered down at him. "Wherefore should I show mercy to a traitor and a would-be parricide?"

"Mercy for my men and knights!" Brion cried. "This is no work of theirs! No will of their own has driven them to fight their king, only loyalty to me!"

The marshal towered above him, immobile as a rock, for

long seconds. Then he said, "Even so. We shall show them quarter." He turned to his aide-de-camp. "Bid the knights surrender their swords; we shall hold them for ransom."

"It shall be done, my lord." The aide lifted his visor. "What of the footmen?"

"Bind them and march them back to Castle Westborn," the marshal commanded.

His footmen lowered their spears. The attackers finally set down their shields and turned their backs; the defenders drew thongs from their belts and tied wrists together. A knight with a dozen men started them back the way the marshal's army had taken, the knight visibly reluctant to miss his chance of glory in the main battle yet to come.

"Take up the march again," Earl Marshal told his aide, "and pray that we have not come too late to aid our lord the king."

The aide nodded and turned away to relay the order. As the army moved off down the road, the marshal turned back to the prince. "For your deeds, Your Highness, I should smite you down where you kneel. But you are the son of my sovereign liege, and for that I will spare your life."

"I—I thank you, my lord." But Brion could only stare up at Earl Marshal, stricken by so stinging a rebuke from so chivalrous a knight. As the marshal turned away, Brion bowed his head, for the first time doubting the rightness of his cause.

Earl Marshal spurred his horse to a canter, to overtake his own army. As he neared them, though, a soldier looked back at the sound of the earl's hooves, looked back and stared, mouth and eyes wide in shock.

The earl turned to look back even as he turned his charger, and saw a knight in blue armor riding down the trail toward the prince, who was struggling to his feet with the aid of a roadside boulder. He heard the galloping hooves and looked up just in time for the huge broadsword to strike him down again.

The marshal shouted in anger at so foul a blow against a knight unhorsed, and spurred his charger, riding to the rescue of the man he had just condemned.

Brion looked up and saw his death. He held up a hand,

crying, "Hold! Grant me this boon, since you mean to take my life—let me at least look upon the face of the man who slays me!"

The Blue Knight hesitated for a moment, then lifted his visor, revealing only darkness and emptiness within.

Brion screamed with fear, but even as the huge sword stabbed down, his cry changed to anger. He seized the steel leg of his opponent and tried to pull himself up, bellowing, "Sorcery!" Then the sword lanced into the crack between breastplate and gorget, down beneath the collarbone toward the heart. The prince's eyes rolled up as his body fell full-length into the dust of the road.

The Blue Knight turned his horse and rode away.

Seconds later the Earl Marshal pounded to a halt and swung himself down to kneel by the prince's body. He swung open the visor, but one look at the pallid face told him all. Slowly, he slipped off a gauntlet and reached down to close the prince's eyes. More slowly still, he closed the visor. He looked up as several knights reined in their horses beside him. "Take up his body and bear it in state to his father, men of mine," he told them, "for he died with honor, though he died by a foul blow."

The knights lifted their visors in respect. Then two of them reached down to help the marshal mount again, while footmen came to lash spears and a cloak into an improvised litter. They used it to take up the body of the murdered prince and hand it to the knights, who bore it gravely onward as they turned to follow the marshal to the battle.

But when they came to the plain on which the armies contended, there was no time to take the body to King Drustan, for they arrived in the midst of a melee. Queen Petronille and her army had taken their stand atop rising ground with a hillside at their backs, but their ground was not high enough, for the army of the king had surrounded them on three sides, and the fourth was too steep for horses. The queen sat her charger, armor glinting from the waist up, mail skirt hidden beneath silk, hewing about her desperately, crying, "Hold them! Strike down upon them! Hold them till their cowardly master comes to strike his own blows! Oh, where is my relief? Where is my son, my Brion, with all his knights and his men?"

At the edge of the fray Earl Marshal drew rein, holding up a gauntleted hand to halt his army.

"We have come too late," said his aide-de-camp. "Could they not have waited battle for us?"

"They have not," the marshal returned, "but we can shorten it for them. Lay the prince's body atop the hill and set knights and a dozen men to guard it! Then follow me, for we must attack the queen from the rear and shorten this battle. We may yet save some hundreds of men's lives by this!" Then he spurred his mount and charged into the melee, bellowing his war-cry. His army followed him, yelling for blood, as four knights turned away with regret to lead a dozen soldiers up the nearest slope, bearing the prince's body with them.

The soldiers, however, were not disappointed.

With the marshal striking from the rear, the battle was short indeed; even Queen Petronille saw she would have to surrender, and called for mercy. When her knights and men were disarmed and bound and she herself was hemmed about by armored men, she endured her husband's gloating as he decried her for a traitor, then jeered further at her for an unnatural mother and wife. The marshal then dismounted and approached them both, with a solemn pace and thunderous brows. Even Drustan, late arrived to the scene, realized that the news must be bad, for he broke off his sneering just as Petronille's throat was swelling with a scathing retort—but she swallowed it as she saw the Earl Marshal's face.

"What news have you for us, my lord?" the king demanded.

Ponderously, the marshal knelt and bowed his head. "The worst, Majesties."

"Call her 'Majesty' no more, for she has abdicated by this rebellion," Drustan commanded, but apprehension filled his face.

"What news could you give me that is worse than my defeat?" Petronille asked, but spoke with foreboding.

That, of course, was exactly what the marshal had intended—some slight warning, so that his sovereign and his queen might brace themselves at least a little. "It is the prince, my lord—Prince Brion."

"Tell us," Drustan commanded, his face granite.

Petronille held her breath.

Earl Marshal launched into an account of Brion's ambush and defeat, of the sparing of his life—then of the treacherous attack of the Blue Knight, and the prince's death.

"Surely it cannot be so," Drustan said, his face white.

"I shall not believe it until I see his body!" Petronille exclaimed.

"Come, then," the marshal said gravely.

Footmen helped him to mount. King and queen alike were horsed and followed. Up the hill they rode.

They found four knights and a dozen men lying unconscious. Of the prince's body, there was no sign.

"He has been stolen away!" Earl Marshal cried, then dismounted and wrenched off his helmet, bowing his head. "Strike if you will, Your Majesty, for your son's body was in my keeping!"

Then Queen Petronille began to scream.

The stick swung high. Papa lifted his own staff to block it, then swung the lower end at his opponent. The soldier dropped his own staff, and Papa's stick cracked against it a second before the soldier caught him a glancing blow on his crown with the tip.

It was only a tap, and though it hurt, it wasn't any major pain. Papa stepped back, laughing. "Well struck, Trooper Cole! I yield me!"

"Well struck yourself." The trooper lowered his staff, grinning. "Your pardon, milord, but I never expect noblemen to be as skilled with the quarterstaff as we peasants."

"I studied it quite seriously at one time." Papa remembered his army pugilstick training. "Though I own I've improved considerably since coming to this castle and always having sparring partners available. Still, I think that's enough for one morning, Cole. Shall we rest a moment and take a stoup of ale?"

"Gladly, if Your Lordship pleases." Cole grinned and followed Papa to a table at the side of the yard, where they each tapped a small mug from a huge keg. Papa sipped, reflecting that to these people, ale was only a beverage, and surely its alcohol content was low enough to qualify it as such. Soldiers frequently drank ale with their breakfasts—and lunches, and dinners. In fact, they were joining a group of other soldiers who were taking a break in their morning practice, watching their fellows who still swung and blocked in the exercise yard and discussing their merits.

"Elbert is quick, but he is still clumsy," one soldier opined.

"Aye, but improved," a sergeant pointed out. "A little more instruction, and he'll be able with a spear as well."

"Will he then be ready for the halberd?" Papa asked.

A silence fell on the group. The sergeant broke it. "Ready to *begin* the halberd, yes. Your pardon, milord, but we are still amazed that a nobleman will practice with us commoners."

That is because I was born one, Papa thought, but aloud he only said, "I may have to command you, if King Drustan brings war to this castle, Sergeant, and I believe in coming to know my troops as well as I'm able. Besides, you have knowledge that I lack."

The men shifted from foot to foot with a brief mutter, and the sergeant said, "Begging your pardon, milord, but most knights consider the quarterstaff and halberd to be below their notice."

"Until one cuts them in the midst of battle," Papa said dryly. "Still, I'm not only speaking of arms and weapons, Sergeant. For example, I suspect there is much you men saw and heard about the Bretanglian royal family that we above the salt did not."

Several of the troopers laughed, and the rest grinned. Cole nodded, and the sergeant smiled as he said, "Might be we did, milord, but I doubt you'd want to hear it."

"Try me," Papa invited, returning his grin.

"Well . . ." The sergeant glanced to both sides elaborately and leaned close to Papa, muttering behind his hand—and winning a few more laughs for his performance. "Those of us set to guard the guards who guarded King Drustan's and Queen Petronille's suite did notice that they argued whenever they were alone. Quite loudly, too."

"That doesn't surprise me," Papa told him. "You couldn't understand the words, though."

"No, we were too far away—but I think the Bretanglian guardsmen caught the odd word or two, and it made them, shall we say, nervous."

"I should think it would." Papa considered the range of topics for royal argument—adultery, control over the Merovencian provinces, adultery, which son should inherit what, adultery . . . "How long did they argue on their last night here?"

The soldiers fell silent again, finding great fascination in the patterns of their bootlaces.

"Come, come," Papa cajoled. "No one is blaming any of you—and I certainly won't say where I heard it. How long?"

"Perhaps the half of an hour," the sergeant told him. "Then, say the guards who were in the hall, the king stalked out in high dudgeon, whipping his cloak about him. But he wasn't even gone an hour!"

"Home in plenty of time to start arguing with his wife again, eh?"

"Of course." The sergeant spread his hands. "What else would they do?"

"What indeed?" Papa could have mentioned Drustan's rumored libido, and Petronille's still-vibrant beauty, but he was too busy wondering if Drustan really could have found the Inn of the Courier Snail, sneaked in to stick a knife in his son's ribs, then run back to the castle in less than an hour.

The sergeant kept his eyes carefully on his boot toes. "They say that with some couples, fighting leads to lovemaking."

"I've heard that, and seen a few," Papa agreed, "but those fights always have the quality of a game about them, keen enjoyment just in the shaping of clever phrases. Such fights are not as bitter as those between King Drustan and Queen Petronille."

"I suppose not," the sergeant agreed in chagrin.

Another soldier said, "I'd say their love has died."

"Not died, perhaps," Papa said, "but it's certainly in a coma."

*   *   *

Ordinarily, Rosamund loved rainy days. Even now, gazing through the ripply glass in the leaded panes of her window, she watched the pot-boy poling his little skiff back to shore with a string of fish dragging in the water—her supper, no doubt. The rain had caught him unawares, in spite of the lowering sky. He would probably curse it, but she blessed it. The gentle susurrus of the raindrops soothed her, and the rain's blending of the trees and bushes with the wall enclosing her country house lulled her, letting her own melancholy harmonize with the world around her . . .

. . . until the mist lifted and showed her the walls of the castle, only a hundred yards distant.

The royal castle. The castle where her nemesis, King Drustan, would live if he won the war. Rosamund imagined the king coming to call on her with news of his victory, stepping too close to her, smiling down possessively, lecherously, reaching out to touch . . .

She turned away from the window, shuddering, and prayed with all her heart for the queen to win. Without Petronille's protection, without Brion's, shorn even of the mild protection of a betrothal to the heir, she would be at the king's mercy in every way, and with no defense. She swore to herself that she would rather die. She touched the front of her bodice to caress the small hard oval of the crystal teardrop she wore between her breasts, the clear little tear in its basket of leaden strips that held the single drop of poison old Aunt Maude, her grandmother's sister, had given her the day before she left her father's palace in southern Merovence.

"God grant that you shall never need it, my dear," the old woman said, "but if it is a choice between your virtue or your life, choose virtue, for a life without it is a torment for a woman in this day and age."

Little Rosamund had shied away from the crystal drop, asking, "Is there no other way?"

"There is this." Aunt Maude turned to show her a log of wood lying on a velvet cushion.

Rosamund stared. "What good is a log? And why do you treat it with such luxury?"

"Because that is where a princess should lay her head."

Aunt Maude passed her hand over the wood, chanting a rhyme in archaic words—and the air about the log shimmered, its form seeming to melt and reorder itself, and there lay a perfect likeness of little Rosamund's own head! She cried out, hand covering her mouth, and Aunt Maude explained, "It is now no longer a stick, but a stock. Find one that is as long as you are, and it will take on the appearance of your whole body. Moreover, another spell will make it walk with your gait and talk with your voice for three days. Then the spell will wear off and let it become only a log of wood again. Come, recite the spells after me, learn them by heart, for they may someday give you time to escape. Even then, though, you may need the drop of poison, for you may be caught, and life without virtue or love is worse than no life at all."

She hadn't explained, but she hadn't needed to—Rosamund understood her full well now, had understood for several years, ever since she blossomed into womanhood and King Drustan's eye had glinted whenever he saw her. Her own future husband had been worse, for Prince Gaheris had pressed her not to wait for the wedding, whenever he could catch her alone.

"A betrothal is almost a wedding," he had protested.

"It is not," Rosamund asserted, "or you would be willing to wait for it."

Even so, she had dreaded the day it would come, for her flesh shrank whenever Gaheris touched her.

A knock at the door brought her back to the present. Her heart hammered with apprehension, but she kept her voice calm as she called out, "Who knocks?"

"Count Sonor, my princess," the rich baritone answered.

"Enter, my gaoler," Rosamund said. After all, she could scarcely deny him. She braced herself for an unpleasant interview.

"Scarcely your gaoler, my lady." Count Sonor entered. "Say rather, your host." But his smile belied his words and told her that he relished his task.

No, worse—his smile was unctuous, his eye glittered. Rosamund's heart beat more faintly at the sight, for there was a gloating air about the nobleman that made her demand, "Have you news for me, milord?"

"The best." Count Sonor's eye flashed with malice. "King Drustan has put down the rebels and will ride home in triumph tomorrow."

CHAPTER 9

Rosamund fought to keep her composure while panic screamed within her. When she could trust herself to speak, she asked, "What of the queen and the princes?"

"The king has accorded Durif Castle to Her Majesty as her royal residence," Count Sonor told her, "with a company of soldiers to protect her, four ladies to wait on her, and a dozen maids in attendance."

"Alas, my lady!" Rosamund whispered, turning away. She knew a sentence of imprisonment when she heard one. The thought of that brave, daring spirit shut up within four stone walls, never to go forth again, made her heart ache in sympathy. She had heard of Durif Castle—small, even cramped, with no courtyard and a garden only ten paces' walk in either direction. It was scarcely larger than her own moated grange— but it was all of stone, hard stone, and the only entrance was through the gatehouse.

The count went on, pretending he had not heard. "Prince John stands by his father's side in victory, even as he stood by him in battle."

John, stand courageously in battle? Fighting like a cornered rat, perhaps—but that Drustan had made him stand near, Rosamund didn't doubt; it was the only way to make sure the savage little weakling wouldn't run and hide.

"What of Brion?"

Count Sonor fought down a vindictive smile. "As Prince John stands with his father, so Prince Brion stands with his grandfathers and their grandfathers."

Rosamund spun to face him, aghast. "You do not mean he is dead!"

"He rode upon the Earl Marshal from ambush," Count

Sonor told her. "The earl left him afoot and unarmed, but alive—yet before he had ridden out of sight, a knight in blue armor came riding from hiding and slew the prince with two strokes of his sword. None knows who he was, for he rode away into the mists from which he'd come."

Rosamund didn't even know if she had turned away, for the whole world darkened, and there was a roaring in her ears. She did know that she fought to stay on her feet, reached out and caught hold of something hard, leaned against a wall. Her world had fallen apart, for her enemies lived, and the queen and prince who might have protected her were imprisoned and dead.

Dead! Brion could not be dead! That great, capable, brave loon who could scarcely talk to a woman without stammering, but who could face a dozen common soldiers with only his sword and shield, and win! She had seen him do so, could remember the scent of him, the feel of him as she unwillingly took his arm when he escorted her in his brother's absence—Brion dead! It could not be!

"Milady?" Count Sonor's voice finally penetrated the roaring, for it was diminishing, and the world seemed to be lightening again. Looking up, Rosamund saw that it was his arm she had caught in her blindness, his armored chest against which she had leaned. She stepped away quickly, though her feet were still unsteady, and saw the mockery in his eyes, the veiled satisfaction at her discomfiture.

"Is there anything you require?" the count asked.

"Wine," she said, and shivered, drawing her shawl about her shoulders. "Mulled wine, and a log as long as my hearth is wide, for I am suddenly chilled."

"Very good, my lady." The count gave her a slight bow, and she saw a reluctant respect in his eyes. He stepped out and closed the door behind him. She heard the key grate in the lock.

Not that it mattered. Not that anything mattered anymore. She turned away and rested her forehead against the cold glass of the window, closing her eyes and letting the despair take hold of her, but dizziness came with it, and she forced her eyes open in fright. Now more than ever, she must keep her wits about her!

The raindrops spattered against the leaded pane, and Rosamund could only think how much they were like the tears that sprang from her own laden pains. Overcome with grief, she admitted to herself at last how much she had depended on the great bumbling hulk that had been Brion, so graceful and confident in war, so uncertain and awkward with herself! If only he could have been a bit less of a prig, a little less sure of the rightness of his chivalry and a little more willing to step an inch beyond its boundaries, willing perhaps even to kiss the hand of his brother's betrothed! If only he had not been so arrogant and so condescending toward her! But now when it was too late, now she could admit that she had relied upon him to take her side against his brothers, to shield her from their advances, to comfort her in her loneliness, if only with his inept arguments.

But he was gone, Queen Petronille was imprisoned, and she stood alone and defenseless against the importunings of King Drustan. Worse, she would now surely be wedded to that slug John, for he was the heir—but he would never dare say nay to his father, even if it were to defend his betrothed from becoming one more of the king's conquests! She could not endure it, she would not endure it! Her fingers touched the cold lump of the poison vial at her breast, but she forced herself to strength, reminding herself that Count Sonor might lie, that Brion might still live—so she must, too. She was not quite completely without defenses yet. Like all noblewomen of her time, she had been taught the rudiments of swordplay, for when married, she would surely be called upon to defend her husband's castle at one time or another—and she had learned a few spells, though none but she and Aunt Maude knew of them.

Someone knocked at the door. "Enter," she called, not caring who it was.

Two soldiers, hardly more than boys, wrestled a huge log in through the doorway. "You called for wood, my lady?"

"Aye. Set it in the grate." Rosamund drew her shawl about her again, once more shivering.

The soldiers rolled the log onto the andirons, then bowed and left the room. She barred the door behind them, drew the curtains closed, then took off her gown so as not to dirty it, and somehow, she never knew from where she found the strength, wrestled the huge balk of timber out of the fireplace. When it lay upon the cold stone of the floor, Rosamund walked its length, waving her hands in the pattern her great-aunt had shown her so many years ago and chanting the antique words she had memorized, only half aware of their meaning.

Mist seemed to gather about the log. As though it were heated wax, its form wavered, remolded itself, bleached— and a naked duplicate of Rosamund lay on the cold flags, so lifelike that it made her gasp. She glanced at her body to make sure she still stood. Reassured, she walked back along the stock, waving a new set of patterns and chanting the second spell. Then she turned anxiously to see if she had succeeded.

The molded eyelids fluttered, opened, revealed blue orbs so much like her own—but lifeless, dull.

An eerie feeling washed over Rosamund, but she shook it off and commanded the stock, "Arise!"

The wood-woman stood, awkwardly but well enough. Rosamund dressed it in her own gown, her skin crawling at its touch. When she was done, she stepped back and commanded it, "If anyone knocks, say 'Enter!' If they speak words to you, nod your head ever so slightly! When the room darkens, take off the gown and go to bed. When the room lightens, arise and put on a different gown from that rack." She pointed to a wardrobe.

The stock began to take off the gown.

"Not yet!" Rosamund snapped, and ran to open the drapes. She turned and gasped, for in the light the stock looked even more like herself—and if it seemed dead and lifeless inside, what matter? None would care, least of all King Drustan!

Turning to the wardrobe, she took out a traveling dress, boots, and a hooded cloak, and dressed. Then she positioned the stock by the door where it would be hidden by the opening of the panel and commanded it, "When the guard lifts his helmet, strike his head!" So saying, she rapped upon the door and stepped back.

The guard came in, frowning. "My lady?"

"Do you not uncover and kneel when you speak to your princess?" Rosamund demanded coldly.

The soldier sighed at the woman's whims and knelt, taking off his iron skullcap.

The stock stepped forward and struck with its little fist—small, but still of wood. Without a sound, the soldier's eyes rolled up, and he fell.

"Guard!" Rosamund called in pretended exasperation, "show this fellow his manners!"

But no one came. Greatly daring, she peeked out, and saw the hallway empty. Elation soared; the soldier would waken and see only the stock and the door, closed now, and think himself a fool for submitting to her whims—but he would never dare tell how his prisoner had outwitted him. Most likely he would curse the stock and take up his post again, and no one would know.

Then Rosamund stepped out into the hallway, looking to left and right, and crept away, her heart hammering. What followed was a harrowing half hour as she crept from darkened doorway to dim-lit hall, thankful that it was raining and the whole castle dimmed thereby. Thrice she barely hid in time as guardsmen passed; twice she almost stumbled upon a servant carrying wine and meat to the count, or scrubbing the floor. At last, though, she dodged through the screens passage and out into the cold, sharp air of the waning day. Wet or not, it tasted of freedom.

Sure enough, the pot-boy had left his little skiff tied by the kitchens. She stepped in, loosed it from its mooring, and set the oars in their thole-pins, remembering afternoons on the river with her father. As silently and quickly as she could, she rowed across the moat, praying to St. Jude to aid her. He must have heard, for she gained the farther shore without a single cry from the grange. She set the oars back in the skiff and shoved it away into the moat; people would think it had simply pulled loose from its pier during the storm.

She could have shouted with triumph, but reminded herself that she was still far from free. Off she went into the rain, welcoming the drubbing it gave her, blessing the mud that squelched beneath her boots, off into the dimness of the weather until she came into the shelter of the deer park, tall trees gathering close to hide her. There she let herself rest for a few minutes, let the shivering of close escape take her, then remembered that she should feel victorious, for she was free, and no matter what dangers she faced, they could not be worse than King Drustan and his puling son.

Off into the wood she went, the rain only the occasional drop striking through the leaves, off to hide herself in the deepest forest she could find, and remember all her father had ever tried to teach her about hunting and fishing.

The footman poured mulled wine into the goblets, bowed to Alisande, and backed out of the room. She watched him go, frowning and toying with her standing cup. "I do not know if this Latrurian conceit pleases me entirely. A subject should be able to bow and turn about so that he can see the door through which he goes."

"It is a mark of respect, my dear," Mama reminded her.

"Respect? If King Drustan had done it to me, it would mean only that he did not trust me behind his back!"

"Wise of him," Papa said.

"Indeed." Alisande's lips thinned. "But are my subjects not to trust me? No, I think I shall return to my father's protocol. I never asked for this, after all."

"Odd that your noblemen should feel the need for more elaborate ceremony," Papa said.

"They have begun it only because Queen Petronille insisted they behave so to her—but she was reared much closer to Latruria than I. No, I think I shall insist on northern ways."

"She has played havoc even with your domestic arrangements," Mama sighed.

"What greater havoc could she play than beguiling my husband and your son away from us?" Alisande demanded, then softened. "Though I cannot fault the poor dame, when she has lost a son of her own!"

"I cannot believe she had anything to do with his murder," Mama stated.

Papa nodded. "By the guards' report, she stayed in her chamber from the finishing of our conference till the horrible news of the tragedy came, and she quarreled with King Drustan for the first hour of that time."

"Only the first?" Alisande caught the discrepancy immediately. "Did they finish their dispute so quickly?"

"I doubt that it ever ends," Papa said with irony, "but King Drustan did stalk out in wrath, to walk abroad for most of the second hour."

"Surely that would not have been time enough for him to murder his son and come back!"

"I should think not," Papa agreed, "and the guards have inquired, and assure me that he did not pass through the gatehouse or the postern in that time. Wherever he stalked, it was inside the castle."

"Prince John was in his chamber all the while," Mama sat a little straighter, her whole body expressing disapproval. "We have a witness to the fact."

Alisande glanced at her, caught the message of her body language, and did not ask for particulars. "And Prince Brion?"

"So far as I can tell," Mama answered, "he went out wenching with his brother, but was too much imbued with the ideals of chivalry to patronize a prostitute."

"But perhaps not too chivalrous to stab his brother in the back?" Alisande shook her head. "It is far too unlikely. Did no one see him at the Inn of the Courier Snail?"

"None I have talked to saw him there," Papa told her. "I can only think that he went to a different inn."

"Or came in disguise with a dirk," Mama said, troubled. "I think he loves Rosamund, but will not admit it. Still, Gaheris treated her most rudely, and Brion might think of killing Gaheris as defending Rosamund's virtue."

"He might have been right to have thought so," Alisande said grimly. "Did no one see the stabbing?"

"None," Papa said. "The assassin struck from behind, and none saw the blow itself. We only know that a Bretanglian guarded Gaheris' back as long as he could. Minutes after that soldier fell, Gaheris died."

"Brion, in a soldier's garb?" Alisande shrugged. "If they were to disguise themselves as commoners, it would have been the habit he would have preferred. Still, I cannot believe he would have fought to protect his brother one minute and stabbed him in the back the next."

"It is hard to believe," Papa said noncommittally. "Still, on the face of it, none of Gaheris' family struck the fatal blow."

"Nor did Rosamund," Mama said, "for she, too, was in her chamber all that time. None actually saw her sleeping, but none saw her come out, either."

"I think we must assume that if any of the family were involved at all, it was by hiring the assassin," Alisande said, "and Matthew's Man Who Went Out the Window is still the most likely to have been the actual killer, no matter his denial."

"What murderer would boast of his deed to the queen's husband?" Mama agreed.

"Or her Lord Wizard," Papa seconded.

There was a knock at the door. There were several knocks, then a storm.

Alisande rose and turned to face the portal, calling, "Enter!"

The door opened; the guards stepped in, and between them came a man in stout broadcloth leggins, tunic, and cloak, still coated with dust, his face lined with fatigue. "Your Majesty!" He sank to one knee and almost fell.

A guard caught him.

"Rise," Alisande commanded, and the guard helped the courier to his feet. "What news?" the queen demanded.

The man's words fairly tumbled over each other in his urgency. "The war is done, Your Majesty!"

"Done?" Alisande stared. "It has scarcely begun!"

"The king met the queen in the field, with an army six times her number," the messenger told her. "Prince Brion ambushed Earl Marshal on his way to the battlefield, but the marshal struck him down, vanquished his men, and took the prince's sword."

"He let Prince Brion live, though?" Alisande demanded.

"He did, though unhorsed—and before the marshal's men had ridden from sight, a knight in blue armor came riding out of the mists and slew the prince. Earl Marshal carried his body to the battleground, but someone stole it away during the fighting."

"Stole a dead body?" Alisande stared. "Why?"

The spy shook his head. "Your Majesty can imagine the reason far better than I."

"I can indeed." Alisande's face darkened. "We shall soon hear rumors that the prince was not slain, but lives, and gathers an army in the hinterland to free his mother and claim the throne. Queen Petronille is imprisoned, is she not?"

"She might as well be," the spy told her. "The king has sent her to Castle Durif, where she will have a score of servitors and every luxury but freedom."

"A gilded cage," Alisande said grimly. "What of the king and Prince John?"

"Prince John stands by his father's side in victory, even as he did in battle," the spy told her, "though Rumor says he fought like a cornered rat, not like a loyal knight."

"What else does Rumor say?"

The spy tossed his head in disgust. "That Prince Brion's body was stolen away by fairies, which I highly doubt . . ."

"But thus is discontent kept alive and given hope," the queen said, "and the next rebellion born. What else?"

"That the king won by sorcery," the spy said, "and will repay the sorcerers by letting them spread their heathen rites across the land."

"What need for sorcery, with six-to-one odds and the Earl Marshal by your side? Speak on!"

"There are folk who wonder why the Earl Marshal spared Prince Brion's life," the spy said darkly.

"Why, because the marshal is a chivalrous knight and a loyal servant of the king who would not slay his suzerain's son! What does Rumor hint?"

"That the marshal had a more personal reason. That is all, only a hint, but it will grow."

"Soon we shall hear that the earl was secretly in league with the prince, or left him alive because he had hired a murderer to slay him," Alisande said with scorn. "You do not believe any of this, do you?"

"Not a bit," the courier confirmed. "I know no details of the battle, but I would not believe them if I did. It will take weeks to thresh the kernels of truth from the chaff of gossip."

"Is there any rumor that you do believe?"

"One," the spy said slowly, "that Princess Rosamund is

a prisoner in a moated grange near the king's castle at Woodstock."

"Alas, the poor child!" Alisande squeezed her eyes shut. "Is there word of her betrothal to Prince John?"

"Not even rumor, Majesty—but there is gossip as to the king's intent in keeping her so near to his castle."

"Even I do not need to hear the substance of that gossip!" The queen spun away to her writing desk and took up a quill. "I shall send to demand the princess be returned to me at once, since she is no longer betrothed to any prince of Bretanglia!" She paused with quill on parchment and turned back to the messenger. "Great thanks for your news, good fellow. Take food and drink, and sleep for a few days. Then back to Bretanglia with you, for I must have more news of what transpires there!"

"As Your Majesty wishes." The man bowed his head, his delight at her praise glowing through his weariness.

He turned away, but stumbled, and Alisande told a guard, "See him to food and a bed."

The guard took the agent away, but Alisande directed the other guard, "Send word to the Chancellor of the Exchequer to lay aside ten pieces of gold for that man, and to send him a note saying it is held for him."

The guard bowed and stepped out, closing the door behind him.

Alisande scribbled a note, sanded it, and said, "That will be set into proper form in the morning, and dispatched to the king."

"Do you not risk war?" Papa asked, frowning.

"Risk?" Alisande laughed bitterly. "Drustan will declare war on us himself, as soon as he has rallied his forces and buried the dead. He has sought an excuse to capture away from us those provinces he feels should be his. It will probably do no good to demand the return of Rosamund, but it can do no harm, either. At least this spat between himself and Petronille has won us a month or two more to prepare for war."

"That will not help the princess, though," Mama pointed out.

"Yes, and if the rumor of her imprisonment is true, she will need help most sorely." Alisande scowled. "What can I do, though?"

"For one thing, we can discover whether or not that rumor is true," Mama told her, "or whether she is safely gaoled with Queen Petronille."

"I doubt that," Papa said darkly.

"I, too," Alisande agreed, "and I am troubled about these 'details' that my agent did not yet know. Mind you, he did right to bring me the great news at once—but the small news can hide great problems."

Mama glanced at Papa; he nodded. She turned back to Alisande. "If you wish, we can go among the people of Bretanglia and learn what news there is."

Alisande froze, glowering down at her desktop.

"I dislike leaving you alone," Mama said gently, "but surely the situation is now grave enough to ask Saul to come guard the castle from evil magic."

"It is grave enough that I need you here! Let the Witch Doctor go among the people!"

"He is young," Mama explained, "and less skilled at prying information from the unwary. Then, too, folk are more likely to confide in mature people."

Alisande had to admit that was true—Mama's motherly air had induced her to confide more than once.

"Then, too," Papa said, "it is perhaps more important that we do what we can to keep war from coming to Merovence, than help to win it once it does."

"Keep the war away?" Alisande looked up, frowning. "How can you do that?"

"For one thing, we can find our son and make sure he doesn't work himself into greater trouble than he can handle," Papa said with a smile. "More to the point, we may be able to find ways to distract King Drustan—say, by using magic to free Queen Petronille and spirit her away."

"He will not attack if he fears rebellion at home while he is gone," Alisande admitted. Her voice gained an edge of desperation as she asked, "But why must you both go? Surely Papa Mantrell is enough of a spy by himself!"

"He is quite capable, of course," Mama said carefully, "but you know as well as I that women know things men do not, and are reluctant to speak of them to any but other women. Matthew certainly will not be able to learn such secrets, nor will my Ramon."

"There is truth in what you say," Alisande admitted, "particularly news regarding Queen Petronille and Princess Rosamund. Yes, there is some chance you may be able to keep Merovence safe from war."

The older couple relaxed. If it was better for her country, the queen would let them go.

The queen went to the door, opened it, and told the guard, "Summon Ortho the Frank."

Mama smiled at Papa and squeezed his hand. Ortho was Matt's assistant, and a powerful wizard in his own right. If he pronounced the castle safe in their absence, they would go.

When Ortho came, he listened to Alisande gravely, then sighed. "Ah me! War again! Well, if we must face it, we must. But surely King Drustan will give us some warning—an embassy with a declaration, perhaps."

"He is chivalrous enough for that," Alisande admitted.

"Then I shall send to inform the Witch Doctor of events, and ask him to hold himself ready to come. There will be time enough to send for him once war is declared."

"But if evil magic is directed against us before that?" Alisande couldn't help glancing in the direction of the nursery.

"I can deal with it," Ortho said, with a quiet smile that bespoke a wealth of confidence, "or should I say that I believe I shall be able to cope with any magicks that are likely to be thrown against us, especially with the new spells Lord and Lady Mantrell have taught me. Surely if enemies attack, the ones that conjure defense by the name of El Cid should be particularly useful." He acknowledged his colleagues with a bow of his head.

They returned the nod, smiling. Mama said, "The *Song of the Emperor Hardishane*, which you have taught us, will doubtless prove most useful if we encounter difficulties, Master Ortho."

"Let it be done, then," Alisande sighed. "Go forth in disguise, lord and lady—go forth to protect your son and my husband and to discover the true nature of what passes in

Bretanglia." Then her face creased with anxiety. "Though Heaven knows, I shall miss you both sorely!"

Mama rose and went to her, and Ortho had the good sense to leave without asking his sovereign's permission.

Three days after Rosamund's escape, the guard threw her door open and bawled, "His Majesty the King!"

King Drustan marched in, resplendent in velvet cloak and satin doublet, crown on his head and a gleam in his eye. "My dear, good news! We have won!"

He saw Rosamund standing at the window in a cream-colored gown embroidered with pale roses—only gazing out at the moat, nothing more.

Drustan frowned at the lack of response. "Do you not rejoice with me?"

"Rejoice with you." The voice was dull; its owner raised dull eyes to his.

"Come now, is that any way to greet the conquering hero?" Drustan chided. He stepped over to her, snapping at the guard, "Close the door!" As it shut behind him, he cupped Rosamund's chin and lifted her lips to his. They were cold, unresponsive, but not repelling him, either. Somewhat surprised, he tried a deeper kiss, and again received no rebuff, but no response, either. Still, the flavor pleased him and he drank deeper.

His hands began to shake with years of desire as he caressed her more and more intimately. The taste of her was sweet, though it would have been sweeter if she had returned his ardor or, better still, tried to fight him off. Nonetheless, he was glad of her resignation, glad that he would finally make her his own, no matter who married her. With trembling fingers he stripped her gown, caressing as he went, stepped back to admire her naked body—though its contours were not quite as rich as he had hoped—then swung her up in his arms and carried her to the bed. He was amazed at her weight.

She watched him calmly, with a composure that was almost unnerving, as he undressed, and seemed to find the sight of his nudity neither repelling nor inflaming. Drustan frowned, determined to make her gasp with pleasure, and lay down beside her, saying, "You'll learn now the delights of royal lovemaking, my dear, and I'll not let it cease till I hear you moan with longing." He reached out to touch her breast as the last rays of the setting sun colored her pale flesh, pale flesh that suddenly hardened, roughened, darkened, and Drustan froze, staring at shaggy bark. He shot a glance up at Rosamund's face, but saw only a single knothole and the roughly sawn end of the log.

CHAPTER 10

Superstitious fear froze King Drustan for several moments. Then he sprang from the bed, shouting angry curses.

The guard hammered at the door, his muffled voice crying, "Majesty! Are you well?"

"Well enough!" Drustan cried, and dove for his clothes. Dressed, he turned to the door, then with a last thought turned to kick Rosamund's gown under the bed. He turned back to yank the bar off the door. The guards tumbled in, weapons at the ready. "Who dares strike at Your Majesty?"

"A witch!" King Drustan pointed a trembling finger at the log. "Or perhaps that puling Lord Wizard of Merovence!"

The guards turned to stare, then paled with fear of the supernatural, making signs to ward off evil.

"Oh, be done with your womanish fears!" King Drustan snapped in disgust, all the greater because of the reminder of his own brief terror. "Send men out to seek for the princess! Send more to discover who has kidnapped her! Find me a wizard of my own, to discover whose work this is!"

The soldiers bowed and ran from the room, all too glad to get away from the scene of witchcraft. Drustan stood his ground, glaring at the log and fuming. He didn't really believe that Matthew Mantrell had done this, but he would learn who had, and they would suffer for his embarrassment!

It was another night and another inn—but this time they were in Bretanglia, for during the day, they had crossed the Calver River, the border between Bretanglia and Merovence. Matt was constantly on edge now, and acting all the more casual because of it, very much aware of being an alien in his enemy's land. At least he was accompanied by a knight who had acquired the accent of Bretanglia's nobility, when he chose to use it, and a peasant who had been born with the burr of the village folk of the North Country.

The common room was full, peddlers and carters jostling elbows with the local farmers as serving wenches threaded through the maze of tables with handfuls of mugs and laden trays. The companions elbowed their way through to a few seats and wedged their way onto the benches.

"Good e'en to you, travelers!" A jovial carter raised his mug in welcome. "Have you come far?"

"From Bordestang, good fellow," Sir Orizhan told him.

The man sobered at hearing his accent. "A weary trip, sir."

"Weary indeed," Sir Orizhan agreed, "but liable to prove unhealthy, if we had stayed."

"So!" The carter raised his eyebrows. "The rumors are true, then?"

"Which rumors?" Sergeant Brock asked.

"That Prince Gaheris was murdered in Merovence, and King Drustan may make war upon Queen Alisande in revenge?"

"True enough," Sergeant Brock said, "though who can tell how a king thinks?"

"But there's no proof that he has call for revenge," Matt said. "The killer might not have been a man of Merovence."

The carter turned to him, frowning. "You've an odd way of speaking, friend. Where is your home?"

"I grew up far to the west," Matt said, "very far."

A peddler next to the carter leaned in and said, "We have heard it was a Merovencian sorcerer what struck the prince."

"It might have been a sorcerer," Matt agreed, "and it might have been a Merovencian—but the truth is that no one saw it happen, or who did it. They only know that a man leaped out the window right afterward, and he was both a sorcerer and a man of Bretanglia."

"Was he! We've not heard of that!" the carter said.

But the peddler frowned. "Where have you heard this, fellow?"

Matt forced himself to ignore the "fellow"; after all, he was disguised as a peasant. "From those who saw it," which was true enough.

"Did they?" Another peasant leaned in, his hood still up. "How did they know he was a sorcerer?"

"Someone saw him work magic." Matt didn't feel obliged to say whom. "As to his being a man of Bretanglia, that was his accent."

"Phaw!" the third peasant said in disgust. "Any man can fake an accent!"

Matt shrugged. "It's all just rumor, as our friend the carter said. But what news have you heard? There must be some folk come down from the north with word of the war there."

"Ah." The carter glanced to left and to right, checking who was in earshot, then leaned even farther forward and said in a conspiratorial tone, "They say that when the Earl Marshal left Prince Brion alone, on foot and unarmed, one of his troopers turned back and saw a blue knight come riding down upon the prince and slay him."

Sir Orizhan and Sergeant Brock sat stiff with shock, but Matt's mind leaped past the emotion and onto what was, to him, just as important. "Prince Brion was slain? And there was a witness to it?"

"Aye, but he says the prince claimed the right to know who slew him, and the Blue Knight raised his visor."

Matt braced himself. "What face did he see?"

"None." The carter's voice was hollow with dread. "The helmet was empty. Dark, and empty."

The other peasants muttered and crossed themselves—but the one with his hood still up howled as though he'd burned his hand and leapt up from the table, stalking away.

The other peasants stared, watching him go. Then one said, "What bit *him*?"

"Guilty conscience, maybe." Matt watched, too. "He's got awfully hairy hands, hasn't he?"

They all looked and nodded. "Most marvelously hairy," said the carter. "I know a plowman who is almost as bad."

Matt made a mental note that the bauchan was allergic to the Sign of the Cross, then realized it would probably do no good if he deliberately used it as a weapon. He sighed and braced himself for more mischief.

Apparently it was going to be delayed, though. A sudden commotion of talk swept through the room. Everyone turned to everyone else, either asking or telling.

The carter leaned over to the next table. "What has happened?"

"A minstrel!" a farmer told him. "He has just said that Princess Rosamund is gone from her moated grange!"

"A minstrel! Will he sing of it?"

"Not until he has finished—there! He has swallowed the last bite of his dinner!"

The minstrel stepped into the clear space near the hearth, lifting his lute. As he tuned it, the bauchan, on his way out the door, stopped and turned back to listen. As the strains of the lute grew louder, the people gradually fell silent, and Buckeye settled down, leaning against the wall.

Matt made another mental note—that the bauchan liked music—for it might come in handy, whether he meant to use it as a charm or not.

The minstrel began to sing.

> "Queen Petronille was a sick woman,
> And afraid that she should die,
> So she sent for a monk of Merovence
> To come to her speedi-lye.
>
> King Drustan called down his nobles all,
> By one, by two, by three,
> Then sent away for Earl Marshal
> To come to him speedily."

The minstrel slipped into a slightly higher voice for King Drustan.

> "Do you put on one friar's coat,
> And I'll put on another,
> And we shall to Queen Petronille go,
> One friar like another."

The women in the crowd exclaimed in indignation, and the men muttered in agreement—everyone seemed to think that hearing confession under false pretenses was pretty low.

"Now, God forbid, said Earl Marshal,"

the minstrel sang in a deeper voice,

"That such a thing might be.
Should I beguile madame the queen,
Then hanged I would be!"

A murmur of approval ran through the crowd. The true knight had remained true.

The bauchan looked up and turned his head, frowning at the crowd's idealism.

The minstrel slipped into Drustan's voice again.

"I'll pawn my living and my lands,
My scepter and my crown,
That whatsoever Queen Petronille says,
I shall not write it down!"

"Which conveniently explains any lack of evidence," Matt muttered to Sir Orizhan. The knight looked surprised, then nodded slowly.

The minstrel went on.

"So thus attired, they both did go
Till they came to Whitehall,
And the bells did ring, and the choristers sing,
And the torches did light them all.

'Are you of Merovence,' she said,
'As I suppose you be?
For if you are Bretangl'n friars,
Then hanged you shall be!' "

"They really like hanging people in your country?" Matt muttered to Sergeant Brock.

"Just a minstrel's nonsense," the sergeant said, but he didn't look all that sure.

> " 'We're monks of Merovence,' they said,
> 'As you suppose we be,
> And we have not been to any Mass
> Since we came over the sea.' "

Matt frowned. "Why's that important?"

"Monks say Mass every day," Sir Orizhan explained, surprised. "They had only arrived that day, and after Mass-times."

"Oh, of course," Matt said, abashed. "Silly of me."

> " 'The first vile sin that e'er I did,
> To you I shall unfold . . .' "

Indignant or not, everybody leaned forward, eager for gossip. Some sixth sense made Matt look at Buckeye just in time to see the bauchan's lips moving as he made an intricate, double-handed gesture toward his mouth, then blow a kiss toward the minstrel. Matt turned back to watch, his stomach roiling.

The minstrel sang on in happy ignorance.

> " '. . . Earl Marshal had my maidenhead
> Underneath this cloth of gold.' "

The whole room broke into a furious hubbub, everyone denouncing such a vile accusation—but doubt shadowed many faces. The minstrel himself looked shocked at his own words, but his lips kept moving, as though of their own accord.

Matt glanced at the bauchan and saw him grinning. He didn't know how this was going to rebound onto himself, but he braced for the worst.

The minstrel began to sing in the King Drustan voice:

> " 'That is a vile sin,' said the king,
> 'God may forgive it thee.'
> 'Amen, amen,' quoth Earl Marshal,
> With a heavy, heavy heart spoke he.

> 'The next vile thing that e'er I did,
> To you I shall uncover—
> I poisoned fairest Rosamund
> There in her Woodstock bower.' "

The crowd went wild, and the minstrel clapped his hand over his mouth, appalled. People were on their feet, shaking their fists at him and shouting angrily—but he was a veteran and realized that he had to get them under control somehow. He kept playing until they had quieted a little, then called out over the noise, "I only sing what I have heard, good folk! But if it offends you . . ." He stopped playing and started to swing the lute over his shoulder.

Matt had to admire the man for a graceful exit from an explosive situation. It almost worked.

"No, no! Go on!" a dozen people cried at once.

The minstrel hesitated, looking uncertain.

"A penny to sing us the rest!" one man cried, and a copper flew through the air to land near the minstrel's feet.

"A silver penny!"

"A shilling!"

Coins rained on the singer. Reassured, he took up his lute again, playing while he waited for silence.

"Nice technique," Matt said slowly. "I can see minstrels are going to be singing this version of the song all over the country, if it brings them that kind of cash."

"There are a few towns loyal to the queen," Sir Orizhan said noncommittally.

"So they won't perform there. I wonder how this song would have sounded if the minstrel could have sung it the way he intended."

Sergeant Brock stared at him. "What makes you think he does not?"

Matt jerked his head toward the bauchan. Sergeant Brock looked, saw, and went stiff.

The minstrel, not one to let a good thing go, lifted his lute again and took up the song.

> " 'That is a vile sin,' said the king,
> 'God may forgive it thee.'

'Amen, amen,' spoke Earl Marshal,
'And I wish it so may be.'

" 'The next vile thing that e'er I did,
Or for which laid my plan—
I brewed a box of poison strong,
To poison King Drustan!' "

The crowd took it in stride, exclaiming in tones of delighted horror but staying in their seats. The minstrel managed to look nonchalant, as though those were the words he
had planned to sing. When they quieted, he went on.

" 'And do you see yonder's little boy,
A-throwing of that ball?
That is Earl Marshal's son,' she said,
'And I love him the best of all!' "

The crowd erupted into exclamations of excited condem-
nation.

"That conveniently explains why Earl Marshal let Prince
Brion live," Matt said, thin-lipped. "Very neat."

"Who could have invented such calumnies?" Sir Orizhan
protested.

"The bauchan." Sergeant Brock nodded toward Buckeye.

Sir Orizhan stared at the spirit, then whipped his gaze back
to the minstrel. "You mean the creature makes the words come
out of the minstrel's mouth?"

"No, he can't do that." Matt frowned, suddenly alert. "I
thought he was just putting the thoughts into the minstrel's
head, but . . . Watch the singer's lips, closely!"

His companions stared at him as though he were mad, then
shrugged and turned to watch the minstrel again. The man sang,

" 'And do you see yonder's little boy,
A-catching of that ball?
That is King Drustan's son,' she said,
'And I love him the worst of all!' "

"By my troth, it's true!" Sir Orizhan exclaimed. "His lips
form sounds we're not hearing!"

Matt nodded. "Buckeye is blocking the words the minstrel's really saying."

"So the bauchan is making up the words we do hear?" Sergeant Brock guessed.

"Maybe." But Matt wasn't so sure. He was a good American boy who had grown up on commercials and politicians' promises, and he was very much aware how well the song fitted King Drustan's purposes. He wondered if it was really the bauchan who was making up those words, after all, though he didn't doubt it was Buckeye's mischief that opened a channel for whoever really was broadcasting them. He had a sudden vivid image of the minstrel as a radio, picking up signals from someplace farther north.

The minstrel sang on:

> " 'His head is like unto a bull,
> His nose is like a boar!'
> 'No matter for that,' King Drustan said,
> 'I'll love him the better therefore!' "

> Then the king pulled off his friar's robe,
> And appeared all in red.
> She shrieked, she cried, she rubbed her hands,
> And she said she was betrayed."

Who really was transmitting? King Drustan was suddenly no longer the obvious source—that last verse favored Prince John too much, as the legitimate heir. Somehow, though, Matt just couldn't believe such an obvious loser could have the intelligence to compose a ballad like that, let alone think of broadcasting it magically to any minstrels with nothing on their minds—or coming out of their mouths, as the case might be. Also, John was a prince, not a sorcerer.

The minstrel was still singing. Matt concentrated on his words, hoping for a clue.

> "Then the king looked over his left shoulder,
> And a grim look look-ed he,

And his said, 'Earl Marshal, but for my oath,
  Then hanged thou wouldst be!' "

He struck a final chord, and it echoed in a room suddenly silent, as everyone stared, appalled, at the thought of one of the most chivalrous knights in the land suddenly transformed into a treacherous villain.

It numbed Matt, too. Somebody was trying to destroy the credibility of one of the pillars of goodness and principle in Bretanglia. He suspected sorcery in a big way—but who was a big enough sorcerer?

The Man Who Went Out the Window.

Suddenly, he was back at the top of Matt's suspect list. Matt began to see that, no matter who lost, the sorcerer won.

Then the crowd rose in one roaring monstrous wave, rolling toward the minstrel.

The man blanched and shrank into the nearest corner.

The reaction took Matt by surprise. He sat frozen for a second, appalled at the transformation from shouting to charging.

Then the shock wore off, and he leaped out of his seat, running to put himself between the minstrel and the crowd, then spinning to face the customers, drawing his sword. A second later Sergeant Brock was at his left with his quarterstaff up to guard, and Sir Orizhan was at his right with his sword out and ready.

The sight of naked steel gave the crowd pause, even a second of silence. Matt took his opportunity. "Freedom of speech!"

A roomful of blank looks answered him—the phrase was nonsense to medieval peasants.

"Let him sing what he pleases," Matt explained, "and anyone who can argue the queen's side, go ahead and argue! The rest of you use your common sense and decide who's right!"

"We know who's wrong!" A man leaped into the front rank, a man with his hood up and a very hairy forefinger pointing past Matt at the minstrel. "Stop him! He's going out the window!"

"That doesn't make him guilty!" Matt shouted, but his voice was lost in the roar as the crowd charged. Cudgels appeared, striking at the knights' swords, then snapping back as Matt and Sir Orizhan slashed. Sergeant Brock was beating a mad tattoo on three other staves and taking a few knocks himself. Matt stepped in front of him and snapped, "Out the window!"

Sergeant Brock was too experienced a soldier to argue with an officer under battle conditions. He went. Matt cut off a couple of cudgels, then snapped at Sir Orizhan, "Out!"

"I shall not leave you— Ouch!" The knight took a blow on his left shoulder.

"That could have been your right! Get OUT!" Matt stormed, and as the knight faded behind him, he whirled his sword in a figure-eight. The commoners pulled back at his sudden ferocity, pulled back but waited—wisely, too, because Matt couldn't have kept it up for long. On the other hand, he didn't need to.

"Away, away! For I will fly to thee,
Not through the window where you've clambered hard,
But on the viewless wings of poesy,
To land beside Sir Or'zhan in the yard!"

He fell a foot and a half as the candlelight disappeared, but he was ready for it and only stumbled. He looked up, saw Sergeant Brock and Sir Orizhan staring at him, and beyond them, the minstrel. "Don't just stand there," Matt told them. "Run!"

"What from?" Sir Orizhan demanded.

"From the mob!" Matt cried, exasperated. "Who do you *think* I'm running from—Keats?"

They ran.

They had a good enough head start so that they were already lost in the shadows of the village huts before the vanguard of the crowd came charging out of the tavern, howling for blood. They ran about thirty feet, then slowed, stopped, and milled about, baffled and enraged. The wind blew Matt and his companions shreds of conversation.

"Where did they go?"

"Through the huts toward the south road, most likely!"

"Road? That was a sorcerer's spell!"

"Aye! How else could they all disappear like that?"

"What sorcerer ever had need of a road?"

"Disappear?" Sir Orizhan stared back at the mob.

"We climbed out the window!" the minstrel protested.

"They saw me disappear, and found an empty corner," Matt explained. "They jumped to conclusions—no surprise, since that's what they've been doing all evening. Let's make tracks while we can, gentlemen. It's going to be another cold night."

An hour later Matt halted and pronounced them far enough away to be able to risk camping. He and his companions set about their usual tasks without even discussing them. He was surprised and pleased to see the minstrel pitch in and help— gathering wood, clearing a fire ring and rolling stones for it, and cutting boughs for sleeping. The wood he chose was very dry, so their minimal campfire gave off very little smoke. The minstrel pulled out a small kettle and went to fill it with water from a nearby stream. By the time he came back, Sergeant Brock had rigged a greenstick pothook to hang the kettle over the fire.

"I think we could all use a warm draft." Matt took out some dried herbs and crumbled them in. His companions shied a little, so he told them, "Don't worry, it's just chamomile. Congratulations on your performance, minstrel."

"I've seldom sung with so great an effect," the singer said with a wry smile. "I hope I can remember the words."

"You made them up on the spur of the moment, then?" Sergeant Brock hunched forward, intent on the answer.

"Made them up? I didn't even sing them!" the minstrel shuddered. "The words I did sing were only the tale of the queen's regrets for her son's death and her ward's kidnapping."

"Kidnapping?" Sir Orizhan pressed close.

The minstrel looked at his face and shrugged uneasily. "How else explain her disappearance from a moated grange?"

"Escape." Sir Orizhan leaned back. "My lady is far more

resourceful than most would think, to look upon her—so pale of complexion and hair, and so quiet in her manner."

The minstrel looked keenly at him. "*Your* lady?"

"He's from southern Merovence—the princess' home district, in fact," Matt said quickly. "But about your song, minstrel—could *you* hear the words you were singing?"

"Not those I sang myself, no. I knew what words I meant, knew which sounds my mouth shaped—but I, too, heard only this treacherous slander of the queen's confessing an adultery she never committed." The minstrel shuddered again. "I cannot wonder that my listeners should be so angered!"

Sir Orizhan frowned. "Why should they suddenly attack, though? These same people had already listened to the earl being blamed for deflowering the queen, though all know King Drustan was her second husband and wedded to her before she ever met Earl Marshal. Worse, they had heard him named as Prince Brion's real father, both with nothing more than shouts of outrage. Why should they turn violent so suddenly?"

Within Matt's head, Memory recited, *Peace. The charm's wound up.* Aloud, he said, "I think it was another effect of the spell."

"Spell?" The minstrel stared, eyes almost bulging. "What foul magic was this?"

"Well," Matt said, feeling sheepish, "I'm afraid part of it came from a spirit who has picked me out as the target for his mischief."

"Spirit?" The minstrel began to inch away from him.

"A bauchan," Matt explained. "I picked him up by accident when we camped in a deserted cottage. Now he won't leave us alone."

"Aye. Such is the way of bauchans." The minstrel kept inching.

"He could have created the illusion of different words coming out of your mouth," Matt said, "but I don't think he could have made up those verses."

"Indeed!" exclaimed an indignant voice behind him. "Do you think I'm lacking in cleverness, then?"

The minstrel froze, staring, as Buckeye stepped out of the shadows to hunker down by the fire, dressed only in his own hair, which admittedly was total cover. He fixed Matt with a malevolent glare. "You should know by now there's no end to my deviousness."

"Being devious doesn't mean you can craft verses." Matt thought of Auden and wondered about that. He glanced at the minstrel. The man had stopped trying to get away and was following the conversation with fascination. Matt could almost hear him thinking, *What a great song this will make!* He tried to ignore unwanted publicity and went on. "But clever or not, be honest for once. Did you make up those words, or did you just say the first thing that came into your mind?"

Buckeye glared at him, but admitted, "The latter. I thought the verses quite inspired, myself."

"Quite," Matt said dryly. "The question is, who inspired them in you?"

"Why, myself!"

"Was it?" Matt challenged. "Or did somebody put them in your head for their own purposes?"

The bauchan reared back, affronted. "Who could invade my mind so?"

"Well, for the first part of the song," Matt said, "I thought it was some sorcerer who was working for King Drustan, since the words made Queen Petronille look so bad—but by the end, the lyrics added up to making John look like the only legitimate heir. Maybe *he* has a sorcerer who worked on you." Even as he said it, he felt a thrill of discovery—John having a pet sorcerer would explain an awful lot.

"No sorcerer or wizard could scramble my thoughts so!" the bauchan spluttered. "I am a creature of the land! Bretanglia itself protects me!"

Inspiration struck Matt again. "Unless the sorcerer was himself a creature of the land."

The bauchan glared at Matt.

"It's true, isn't it?" Matt pressed. "If the sorcerer was using magic that had grown up in Bretanglia, or if he was the descendant of generations of Bretanglian village magicians, he might be able to meddle with Bretanglian spirits, mightn't he?"

Buckeye glared at him silently, but the minstrel found his voice. "Aye. He could."

"*If* I did not craft the verses myself!" Buckeye snapped. "Credit me with *some* intelligence, wizard!"

"Wizard?" The minstrel glanced at Matt, wide-eyed, then at Sir Orizhan, who gave a one-inch nod. The minstrel's gaze snapped back to the bauchan.

"If you think you're such a great poet," Matt told him, "prove it."

"I will!" the bauchan cried, and began to recite, "Whan that Aprille, with her flowers soote—"

"Foul!" Matt cried. "How do I know you're not reciting that from memory?" In fact, he suspected the bauchan was doing just that—or Chaucer had a lot of explaining to do.

Buckeye shut up and glowered at him. "How would you have me prove my cleverness, then?"

"I'll give you a list of words," Matt suggested. "You have to make a verse that uses them."

"What words did you have in mind?" the bauchan asked warily.

"Oh . . . let's say . . ." Matt thought fast. " 'Self, pelf, send, bend, spice, sand, ice, and land.' "

"Ha! Nothing easier!" the bauchan crowed. "You've made them rhyme yourself! Let me think . . . I have it! I'll craft the stave!

> "My powers I'll bend
> To favor my self
> And fairly send
> Bone, blood, and pelf
> By spicy sand
> To icy lands!"

"There!" Buckeye slapped his knee, staring at Matt in triumph. "I can craft a verse as well as—YAWK!"

He disappeared so quickly that air whooshed in to fill the space his body had occupied. Somehow the companions were left with the fading impression of eyes wide and appalled in a rubbery face.

Sergeant Brock stared. "What happened to *him*?"

CHAPTER 11

"He made a verse," Matt said, "and it worked—worked magic, that is. It transported him somewhere very far to the north—or maybe very far south, where there's ice and snow all year 'round. Don't worry, he's built for it. All that body hair . . ." Matt wondered if bauchans were related to yetis.

The minstrel grinned. "He forgot that verses work magic, didn't he?"

"Right," Matt confirmed. "He was so intent on trying to make a good verse that he didn't pay much attention to what it meant—like a lot of poets I've read."

The minstrel gave him a sharp look. "I think it's just as well I didn't tell you my name. You were most restrained with him, wizard."

Matt shrugged. "No need to do anything more."

"You might have done something that would make him fear us enough to stay away," Sergeant Brock said. "As it is, he will only use his magic to find his way back to us. Why did you not punish him sorely?"

Matt shrugged again. "This was all I needed—to get him out of our way for the night. Besides, it was more fun to trick him into sending himself on a long trip."

"But he set that crowd against us, for surely he must have known you would leap to the minstrel's defense! Could you not have punished him enough to teach him to cease meddling?"

"No, I don't think so," Matt said slowly. "It's his nature. Anything I did would only have made him determined to have revenge." He looked to the minstrel, the authority on local folklore, for confirmation.

The minstrel nodded.

"We have trouble enough from him when he's just being

mischievous," Matt said. "Can you imagine how bad he'd be if he really wanted to get back at me?"

Sergeant Brock shuddered, and Sir Orizhan said fervently, "Your act of mercy was not only chivalrous, but wise."

"Thanks," Matt said, "but you and I both know that chivalry is wisdom, in the long run."

Sir Orizhan looked up in surprise. "I did not know you were a knight as well as a wizard."

"Oh, I've been knighted, yes." Matt decided it was best not to go into the details. "Of course, in the short run the chivalrous action often looks foolish—for example, letting an enemy live."

"It seems so, yes," Sir Orizhan agreed, "but if you can turn that enemy into a friend by your mercy, it is the wiser course of action."

The minstrel stared. "You don't mean that you can turn a bauchan into an ally!"

"I'd better," Matt said. "He won't stay gone, after all. It'll take him some time, but he'll find a way to magic himself back to us—so let's hope I can find a way for us to be useful to each other. After all, bauchans aren't *always* malicious, are they?"

"Well, they have been known to help their hosts if the people really needed it," the minstrel said, but added, "There's no way to know, of course. They are completely unpredictable."

Prince John was playing chess against himself, moving all the pawns into the center of the board one move at a time, then having the knights, bishops, rooks, and queens take turns demolishing the little men. Even with his imagination putting the faces of his brothers on the pieces, it was still boring—he'd done it too many times before.

"Your Highness."

The prince looked up, mildly interested—anything to break the boredom. "Yes, Orlin?"

His squire was pale of face—bad news. This might be more interesting yet. If nothing else, it could be an excuse to beat the chap.

"Highness," the young man said, "there is word come from Woodstock."

Prince John frowned. He didn't particularly care for Rosamund, but he did lust after her, and treasured the notion of crushing the look of disdain from her haughty features and replacing it with total, abject fear. Besides, she came with the crown—and vice versa. Betrothal would strengthen his claim, and he knew enough of court intrigue to know that, even with Gaheris and Brion dead, he would need every bit of strengthening he could gain, to make the barons accept his reign.

"Highness?" The squire's voice trembled with fear.

John smiled, liking the sound. Everyone knew his father's rages and feared his would be every bit as bad, once he had power. "Your news had better not trouble me," he warned. "Speak."

"The princess is gone, Your Highness."

"Gone?" John frowned. "What do you mean, 'gone'?"

"Disappeared, Your Highness." Squire Orlin swallowed heavily. "The news is that the king went to bring her the news of victory himself, and found a lifeless likeness in her place—a wooden statue."

John smirked, having some idea of the way in which his father had intended to bring Rosamund the news, and gloating over his discomfiture. "Where was the true princess?"

"Nowhere." Orlin was used to John's ability to ignore what he didn't wish to hear. He took a deep breath and said, "She had vanished."

"Vanished?" John frowned. "How? She had guards at her door, a wall around her grange, and a moat around the wall! How could she have vanished?"

"I have no idea, Your Highness."

John finally registered the fact that his intended—well, he had intended to have her, anyway—was gone. "Say not so, knave!" He swung backhanded at the squire. Orlin knew from long practice just how far to lean back—enough to take most of the sting out of the blow, not enough so that John would think he had missed. He fell down for good measure.

"Poltroon and liar!" John raved. "Gone, do you say? Let her jailers be jailed! Let her guards be imprisoned! How could they have failed so in their duties?" Then he froze, eyes widening. "Witchcraft, that's how! Stolen away by witchcraft—and that means Mother!"

"But—But the queen is herself imprisoned!" Orlin protested from the floor. "The queen is not a witch!"

"Not a witch? Fool, could she have cost Father so dearly in battle if she were not? No, it must be Mother's doing!" John turned away, glowering, rubbing his left hand around his right fist. "She has found a way to cheat me of my prize again, to cheat me of my rights again! But I shall have my due! I shall be revenged!"

"Upon your own mother?" Orlin gasped.

"Of course not!" John turned back to him, scowling. "What fool would risk his mother's love? No, I'll be revenged by finding the princess!"

Orlin reflected that John had lost his mother's love long ago, but was wise enough not to say so.

Mama and Papa walked the high road dressed as peasants, but Papa's staff was of rowan, and would focus his spells with the accuracy of a rifle. Mama's hazel wand was hidden in her flowing skirts. Neither expected to use them, of course—they'd found that broadcast spells worked much more effectively, though with less intensity. Still, it never hurt to be prepared, and peasants weren't allowed swords.

Papa frowned at the trees about them. "Strange to see so much ivy! I hadn't known that England grew it by the mile."

"It doesn't," Mama told him with certainty, "at least, not in any of the herbal books I've read. And so much moss!"

"I knew England was wet, but not so soggy as this," Papa agreed. "See how many of those vines are mistletoe! Almost as bad as kudzu in our universe!"

"Mistletoe?" Mama looked more closely. "Yes, it is. I didn't know you had taken up botany, husband."

"I haven't." Papa turned to her with a gleam in his eye. "But if there is one plant I will recognize, it is mistletoe."

Mama blushed and turned away, but reached out for his hand nonetheless. Lifting her gaze, she looked for a change of subject. "They are as thick as ever, Ramon."

"The ravens?" Papa looked up, frowning. "Yes, I know. I

would have expected them to cluster thickly around old towers, but there seem to be a dozen of them on every tree, too."

"And the nights are filled with the hooting of owls," Mama said. "I could swear someone doesn't want us to sleep."

"Don't swear," Papa said quickly. "You never know what it will bring, here."

"Of course," Mama said with scorn. "Oh, look! A cross-roads, and a village. It will be good not to have to eat biscuit and jerky again."

But as they came near the village green, a voice behind them called, "One side! Make way!"

They had been in medieval Europe long enough to know what that meant. They scurried to the side of the road and watched the knight come trotting past, grinning, with a dozen men-at-arms behind him. Several of them leered at Mama, but apparently decided she was too old, and turned away with scorn.

"You may relax, husband," Mama said gently. "They could see I was old enough to be their mother."

"Really?" Papa turned to her with a smile, relaxing a little. "To me, you always look to be nineteen."

Mama gave him a roguish smile, then turned serious. "Let us follow quickly, husband. There is something about that entourage that troubles me."

The knight drew up in front of the inn, crying, "A fabulous victory! A grand triumph! I stood beside Prince John as he cut down the Count Haltain! I was his shield mate as he hewed and hacked like a madman! The king is still king and has locked the queen into a castle for a prison! Bretanglia is whole again!"

"How did he spell that?" But Papa spoke absently; he was watching the parents and sons of the village crowd around the warriors with loud cries of praise while the young women turned away, not daring to run. Taken by surprise, they could do no better than turn their faces to the nearest wall.

From his mount, the knight caught sight of a form that was shapely even in the baggy peasant skirt and blouse. He pushed his horse through, grinning at the lone despairing cry, and leaned down to catch the peasant girl by the shoulder and turn her around. "Here, lass! Let's have a look at your face!"

The girl tried to twist away, but the knight caught her chin and held it fast. He wet his lips and nodded. "Not bad, not bad at all." He dropped her chin, caught her by the arm, and tossed her to one of his men. "Here, Sergeant! Bring her to my chamber! Landlord, take me to your finest room, and quickly!"

But the girl managed to twist free from the sergeant's hold and dodge behind the broad back of the innkeeper. "Father, no! Hide me!"

"Oh, she's your get, is she?" The knight grinned, reveling in the double pain he would cause. "Well, you should be honored to send her to a knight."

"Nay, sir!" the innkeeper protested, looking up at the knight. "She is still a virgin!"

"What, at her age?" the knight said in scornful disbelief. "She can have one of me or twelve of my men, innkeeper. Choose!"

"Why, you scoundrel!" Mama cried, and ran to put herself between the knight and the innkeeper. "How dare you call yourself a man of chivalry when you would debauch a virgin?"

Papa stiffened in alarm, but the innkeeper, with vast relief, turned to a boy nearby and snapped, "Friar Thomas! Run as you never have!"

The boy sped away, even as the knight turned purple and roared, "How dare you so address a belted knight, fishwife? Aside!" He swung a backhanded blow at her.

It struck hard against Papa's staff. The knight howled and cursed, then called to his men, "Strike down this impertinent cur!"

Mama whipped out her wand and chanted a quick Spanish couplet.

The men-at-arms shouted in anger and charged Papa—but he swung his staff in a circle, hand over hand like an airplane's propeller, and a series of knocks sounded as the first three men reached him. They fell back into the men behind them, who jammed back against the six still trying to get forward, and the whole dozen churned into a scrambled, shouting mass.

"Witchcraft!" the knight cried, whipping out his sword.

"Overconfidence, more likely," Papa replied. "Haven't you taught your men never to underestimate an enemy?"

The knight froze with his sword high, glowering down from his mount in suspicion. "You do not talk like a peasant."

"A man's rank should make no difference to a true knight," Papa lectured. "Chivalry extends to all regardless of rank, and a virgin peasant should be as sacred to you as any lady of the highest station."

Anger warred with wariness in the knight's face. "Who are you to school me so?"

"A schoolmaster and scholar indeed," Papa replied, and probably would have gone on at some length if a lanky man in a brown robe hadn't come running up, the top of his head shaved in a tonsure. "Here now, Sir Knight!" he scolded. "Would you break your vows of chivalry by robbing a woman of her virtue?"

The knight looked up in surprise, then darted a glare of pure venom at the innkeeper. He turned to the friar, snapping, "It is no concern of yours, shave-pate!"

"The welfare of every soul in this parish is my concern!" The friar took up a stance between Mama and the knight. They stood four deep between him and his quarry now—the friar, Papa, Mama, and the innkeeper. "You are in my parish this moment, so your soul, too, is in my care! Remember the Commandments, O Man of Might! Remember especially the Sixth Commandment!"

"She isn't married, if she's truly a virgin, as her father says," the knight grunted. "That's not adultery."

"No, but it is fornication, which is almost as bad, and the despoiling of a virgin makes it far worse! Then, too, if she is not willing, which she plainly is not, you speak of rape, which is worse than either! Our Lord Himself has commanded us to refrain from fornication—and scandal! If your actions lead a child into sin, it would be better for you to be cast into a river with a millstone tied around your neck!"

The knight swung his sword high with an oath. "Who says so?"

"Our Lord said so!" The friar stood stiff and unflinching before that blade. "What, Sir Knight! Will you imperil your immortal soul for mere amusement? Will you send yourself to an eternity of torture for a few minutes' pleasure?"

The knight sat his horse, sword poised, wavering.

Mama made a small set of gestures, and her lips moved, but her voice came from the middle of the crowd, behind the knight's back:

> "Amazing grace,
> How sweet the sound
> That saved a wretch like thee!
> You once were lost,
> But now are found,
> Were blind, but now you see!"

Everyone looked up and about, startled by the sweet sounds, eyes widening as joy burst within them—and even the knight's face was transformed. He sheathed his sword, nodding in acceptance. "Even as you have said, Father! Nay, let the lass stay whole—and I thank you for saving my soul!"

He turned to his men. "Away and go! We'll spend this night at another village's inn!"

A murmur of relief swept through the crowd as the entourage rode away—but the friar beckoned the little boy to him and said, "Take two friends and run to Renved Village by the beeline through the woods. Tell Friar Nollid there to welcome these men as they come into his parish, or there may yet be mischief this night."

The boy dashed off, feeling very important, and the friar turned to the innkeeper. "You are safe now, Goodman Dalran, Maid Darsti."

"Yes, thanks to you, friar!" The innkeeper wrung the clergyman's hand, then turned to Mama and Papa. "And to you, good friends! By what magic you held the knight at bay until the friar could arrive, I know not, but I thank you deeply!"

Darsti caught Mama's hand and covered it with kisses.

"It was our pleasure," Mama assured him. "No woman should be subject to the whims of such a bully, virgin or not!"

"No woman should be forced, most certainly," the friar said with feeling.

"You must be my guests this night!" the innkeeper said.

"It shall be my honor to serve you myself," Darsti assured them.

Mama and Papa exchanged a glance; then Papa turned to the innkeeper. "Under the circumstances, I think we will accept your kind offer, mine host—but we were glad we could help."

A few hours later they finally managed to close the door of a private room on their grateful hosts. Papa poured them each a glass of wine and said, "A most interesting afternoon, my dear."

"It was indeed," Mama agreed. "At least the brutes still respect the clergy."

" 'Still' is the word," Papa cautioned. "I have difficulty believing the knights of this land have always been such oafs."

"Not in this universe," Mama agreed. "Not if Bretanglia has been a godly kingdom for centuries, as we have been told."

"Ah, but you are speaking of the past," Papa pointed out. "King Drustan has, wittingly or not, unleashed the forces of cruelty and oppression upon his people."

"He has," Mama agreed, "but they are not very far gone in decadence yet. Friars can still defend the weak from the mighty but corrupt."

"Yes, but only because the knights and their men still have enough respect for the clergy to heed their words," Papa said. "How long can that last, my love?"

"How thickly can the ravens flock to this land?" she returned.

"Up, lazybones!" the voice shouted in Matt's dream. "Why do you lie here sleeping when you should be seeking my murderer?"

Even in his dream Matt came up fighting. "You dare to wake me up! You dare to deprive me of sleep when I've been hiking all day and seeking whatever scraps of information I can to—"

"How dare you talk so to a prince!"

"We've been through that already," Matt said through his

teeth. "Do I have to recite an exorcism verse and kick you out of my head so I can get some sleep?"

"No, no!" Gaheris' ghost said quickly. "Not that!"

"Sure, because once I kick you out, you can't get in again." It didn't take much figuring. "So far I'm leaving the mental door open because you might be able to give me information about the crime. No, I don't have anything to tell you yet—but I do have a job for you."

"A job?" the prince cried, highly insulted. "For a *prince*?"

"Any ghost would do, but you're most likely to know the party in question. Tell me, has Prince Brion showed up on the other side?"

"Brion?" Gaheris pounced on the name. "Has he been slain, then?"

"That's what I'm trying to figure out," Matt told him, "and the reports aren't exactly conclusive. It would help a lot if you could tell me you've seen his ghost roaming around looking for that tunnel of light you told me about."

"It would seek out him, not he it," Gaheris said quickly, "but he would be no quicker to go into it than I, if he'd been murdered. No, I have not seen him here . . ."

"Sure you might not have missed him in the crowd?"

"There are not so many who can or wish to resist that last journey, wizard! Besides, those of us related to one of the newly slain are drawn toward his ghost—several here have told me that! I assure you, if Brion were here, I would know it!"

"That helps." Of course, Matt suspected Brion might have been more likely to seek out that tunnel of light, and its exit to the afterworld, than Gaheris was, especially since for him it would probably be the express route to Heaven, or at least to a short stay in Purgatory. Still, Brion was worldly enough to want justice for his own murder. "Yes, that helps. Okay. Thanks. Check in now and then, and I'll let you know if I learn anything solid."

"If! You had confounded well best learn something or I'll—"

"Be kicked out of my head," Matt said, cutting him off. "Now get out of here, before I do my daily exorcises."

"But I—"

"Out!" Matt dream-shouted. "Go 'way and let me sleep!"

* * *

"Gone?" Petronille stared, her face ashen. "From a moated grange with a dozen guards and jailers? How could she be gone?"

"I know not, Majesty." Lady Ashmund spoke with tears in her eyes; she too had been fond of the princess. "I know only the news I have been given—that the king went to bring her the news of his victory himself . . ."

"And I am sure how he meant to celebrate it!" Petronille snapped.

"Perhaps, Majesty, but he found only a wooden statue. Of the real princess, there was no sign."

"No sign, is it? No sign of which he dares tell the world!" The queen turned away to the tall, multipaned windows and stared out at the courtyard, unseeing. "He has spirited her away to some secret bower where he can have her at his mercy for as long as he wishes! Oh, a pox upon this gilded prison!"

She turned to catch up a porcelain vase and hurl it into the fireplace. The crash echoed hugely in the stone-walled room, in spite of all the tapestries and thick carpets; Lady Ashmund suppressed a start of shock.

The queen strode the length of the solar and back, raving, "I have silks and satins, I have grandeur and silver and servants, but I cannot go to find the poor child who needs me! Curse the day that ever I met that snake Drustan! Curse the day that I sought a southern princess for my son! How could I ever have believed that she could alloy his spirit with some gentleness, some courtesy, some grace? All that has happened is that Gaheris taught her his roughness and hardness, and that my husband has set his lecherous course toward her! Alas, the poor lady! How shall I ever save her now?"

Lady Ashmund sought for a word of hope to give her. "Might it not be that the Lord Wizard of Merovence has rescued her by his magic?"

The queen turned to give her a stony, contemptuous glance. "You know nothing of the old, old sorcery with which this land is imbued, my lady. Even I, who have learned some magic, can only guess at the weight and mass of this cold northern runimancy! It is heavy enough to drown any magic I seek to work, I know that, and I cannot believe that the Lord

Wizard could fare better than I! Oh, a pox upon this false husband of mine! A murrain upon him, for the cruel ox he is!"

Lady Ashmund blanched at hearing the curse.

The queen raised her fists before her, calling out, "O elves and sprites of Bretanglia! O pouks and ghasts and nightwalkers all! If you hear me and can do it, strike down this false king who has foisted himself upon your land! Pouks, smite him! Ghasts, fill his sleep with nightmares! Elves, aim your bolts at his temples! One and all, hear this foreign queen he has brought to misery! Save the southern princess, save the land, and lay him low!"

The king was at dinner the next night, with Prince John at his right hand and Earl Marshal at his left. Two dukes and their duchesses sat at the head table with him, the lower table filled with lesser aristocrats. Drustan was in high good spirits in spite of the nasty surprise Rosamund had left him—he was, after all, the victor, and knew that the queen who had caused him so much frustration and pain with her deprecating remarks and encouragement of his enemies was now eating her heart out in isolation.

The Duke of Boromel, sensing His Majesty's mood and its reasons, rose and lifted his cup, crying, "A toast!"

"A toast!" the others cried, and rose, then fell silent with their cups on high.

"To our sovereign liege, who dines upon the rich fare of victory in glittering company—and to our queen, who drinks the bitter wine of defeat in solitude!"

There was a moment's shocked silence, and Earl Marshal frowned—it was a most ungallant toast. Then the king crowed with delight, surging to his feet and lifting his cup. "To the queen!"

The other aristocrats took up the cry with relief. "To the queen!" they cried, and laughed and drank.

The king set his goblet to his lips, tilted its base high—then turned rigid, eyes bulging, and let out a single hoarse cry as he fell, the goblet slipping from his fingers and dashing wine all over Prince John.

There was another moment of shocked silence. Prince John broke it with a cry of distress and dropped to his knees by his father, lifting the older man by the shoulders and feeling for his pulse.

For himself, King Drustan knew only sudden darkness that after a while lightened. He seemed to float in a void of mist, hearing voices talk around him.

"Yes, Your Highness, I am sure he will live."

"Praises be!" said John's voice, though it was shaking. "But will he be well?"

"Ah! Nicely asked," the older voice sighed. "No physician can answer that while he sleeps. We can only wait and see how he fares when he wakes."

"I am awake," King Drustan grumbled—but why were the words so slow to come, so hard to form? He forced his eyes open and saw Prince John and Dr. Ursats, staring at him. Behind them he saw the tapestries of his own bedchamber, and the curtains between them and himself were those of his own tester bed. He sat up, assuming his most arrogant posture—then realized that he hadn't, that he had scarcely stirred. Panic gripped him, and he hid it by shouting. "A pox upon you! Do you not hear me? I am awake!"

This time, though, he heard his own voice—only a gargling mixed with a sort of braying, a mouthing of vowels with scarcely a consonant. The panic surged higher, and he would have screamed, only John stepped up to him, gripping his hand. "He wakes! How are you, my father?"

"What nonsense to worry!" Drustan said, mollified. "I am perfectly well!"

But he wasn't, and he knew it. He couldn't hear the words he had spoken, heard only a sort of cawing in their place.

Now the doctor stepped up on his other side and took his hand. "I am relieved to see you conscious, my liege. Do you remember what happened?" Then, before the king could answer, "Allow me to remind you. You were about to drink a toast to the queen when you fell down, unconscious."

The king frowned, remembering.

"Suffer my impertinence, Majesty." The doctor leaned over and lifted first one eyelid, then the other, staring intently into each orb in turn. Then he straightened and said, "Squeeze my hand, Majesty."

"What idle game is this?" Drustan snapped, but heard

again only an ass' braying. Appalled, he resolved that he would never talk again. He did, however, squeeze the doctor's hand, and Ursats nodded, satisfied. He took the king's other hand from John and said, "Squeeze with this hand now, Majesty."

The king repressed the urge to make a withering comment and squeezed.

The doctor's face was completely neutral. "Have you squeezed my hand, Your Majesty?"

"What the devil sort of question . . ." Drustan heard his own cawing and clamped his jaw shut. He forced a very stiff nod.

"Yet I felt nothing," Dr. Ursats said sadly.

"What does this mean?" John cried.

"That His Majesty has been elf-shot," Ursats told him, then to Drustan, "Some malicious sprite has aimed his miniature crossbow at you, Majesty, and struck your temple with his tiny dart. Country folk find their minuscule arrowheads in the dust of a road sometimes, after a thunderstorm. This barb has lodged in your brain, though, and will be some time working its way loose."

The king stared, and tried to ignore the fear that threatened to overwhelm him.

"Until it does," Ursats went on, "your speech will be slurred, and the whole right side of your body will move only with difficulty, if at all."

The king brayed denial.

"Peace, Your Majesty." Dr. Ursats patted his hand. "Is not the life a greater thing than the body, and the body itself greater than the ability to walk without a limp?"

"No!" the king shouted, and this time they understood him.

The doctor smiled. "You see, Your Majesty? With effort, you can still make yourself understood! With practice and work, you shall one day speak again, almost as well as you did before."

"But my leg!" Drustan howled. "My arm!"

Ursats explained as though he had understood. "You shall have to work as hard as you did when first you learned swordplay, practice as diligently as when you strove to master jousting by riding at a quintain. But with constant effort, you shall gain in strength and smoothness as the arrowhead works its way free. Then, someday, you shall walk again, perhaps with only the slightest of limps!"

"Learn to walk, as though I were a toddling babe?" The king howled at the injustice of it.

John gripped his hand again. "You shall not face this daunting prospect alone, Father! I shall be here beside you every day, here to comfort and sustain you! Only tell me what you need, and I shall see it fetched!"

"Don't patronize me, boy!" King Drustan snarled.

John frowned. " 'Don't' . . . ? You said something else, then 'boy.' "

The doctor looked up with keen interest. "Can you understand him, then?"

"A little, I think. Was I right, Father?"

Drustan stared at him, gears meshing in his brain. Slowly, he nodded.

"We captured the Count of Tundin in battle," John reminded him, "but his youngest son fought in Earl Marshal's entourage. Shall we hold both father and son attainted, then?"

Drustan scowled. "Why speak of such trivia at a time like this?"

"Again, more slowly," John urged, and Drustan realized what the boy was trying to do. Slowly and with great effort he said, "Attaint the father. The son is Count."

"You say the father is attainted?"

Hope thrilled in Drustan; he nodded.

"But the son? What of the youngest son?"

Trying even harder to be clear, Drustan said, "He is now Count."

"Did you say that you declare the youngest son to be Count of Tundin?" John asked with great intensity.

One corner of Drustan's mouth lifted in a leer intended to be a smile. He nodded.

"Excellent!" John squeezed Drustan's hand with both of his own. "Thus shall you rule still, my father! I shall come to you with all the questions of state, and listen until you have made yourself clear! I shall bear all your commands to your ministers, and see that each is carried out as you would wish it! I shall come to talk to you twice a day, three times a day, as often as it takes—and at least once, at supper, only to enjoy your company!" He shivered. "For you must know, Father, how much afraid I am, without your shield to ward me! How badly I need your presence to give me the strength of will to face your ministers!"

Compassion flowed; for a few minutes Drustan's own fear submerged under concern for his son—the only son left him now! He squeezed John's hand and muttered, "Be brave, lad! I shall be here for you, ever at your call! How could I desert you, when you do my work?"

John smiled, reassured, and gave as good as he got. "Courage, my father! You have beaten many enemies, great enemies— surely now you can defeat one so tiny!"

Half an hour later John returned to his own apartments. He closed the door behind him and let out a long sigh, folding in on himself.

"Was it as difficult as all that?" asked a resonant baritone.

John snapped upright, remembering the rendezvous he had set. "It went well enough, Niobhyte. It went just as you said it would."

CHAPTER 12

John went to the side table, his steps unsteady, and poured a goblet of wine with hands that trembled from the release of tension. "The spell worked as you said it would—I understood him, but no one else could. How did you persuade the elves to shoot him?"

"There are some things sorcerers must not confide." Niobhyte didn't tell John that the stroke had been as much of a surprise to him as to everyone else. He had been quicker to take advantage of it, though. "Did I not promise you that you would rule within six months of our pact?"

"You did," John acknowledged. "I had not known it would come at the price of a war, though."

"The war would have come in any event," Niobhyte said easily. "Your parents would have made war upon Merovence if not upon one another. As it is, you can blame the elf-shot on the Lord Wizard, and claim he did it to keep Bretanglia from attacking his queen and wife."

John's eye gleamed. "Yes, I can see that would serve." He sat in a chair opposite Niobhyte's.

"I regret that your road to power came at the cost of the lives of your brothers, and your father's illness." Niobhyte's expression said that he was anything but sorry.

John waved away the half apology. "Believe me, it scarcely tears at my heart. I would have slain my brothers myself, for all Gaheris' hurts and Brion's arrogance and condescension. As to my father, he has suffered only a fraction of the hurt due him." John's hand tightened on the goblet as he remembered his mother's furious denunciations of mistress after mistress. They must have been true, for his mother had said it.

"I understand." Niobhyte nodded. "Always the youngest,

always the smallest. It is only your due if, after all, you rise to rule."

"Yessss." It was more a hiss than a word as John gazed into his cup.

"You rule already," Niobhyte reminded him, "in fact if not in word."

"Yes, I must have the shadow of my father behind me for some few weeks more," John agreed, "until all the barons have accepted my authority. Of course, I will only deliver those of my father's commands that serve my own interests, and if I issue a few orders of which Father knows nothing, who will care?"

"Quite true," Niobhyte agreed. "However, you do indeed need your father for some time yet, if your only power is as his regent."

"True, very true." John's nose wrinkled as though at a foul smell. "Curse Brion for having made his body disappear! If I could prove his death, I could be king in my own right."

"Believe me, he could not have transported his own corpse away from us," Niobhyte told him. "I would suspect the Lord Wizard of Merovence of the deed."

John darted a quick, suspicious look at him. "You blame him for all my troubles, don't you?"

"And with good reason," Niobhyte maintained. "His purpose is to keep Bretanglia too weak and too disorganized to attack Merovence. The more confusion he can create, the less the danger to his wife. No, Highness—Majesty that will be— you must wait until you have consolidated your power over the nobles and the Church before your father can pass to his reward. Whether you are crowned or not, they will rebel against you if they can. Even King Drustan has had to put down rebellions from time to time, though the people love him for making the land safe and prosperous."

"Oh, I shall make it safe and prosperous, too," John purred, gazing into the fire. "I shall make it safe and prosperous indeed—for myself."

Two nights later Matt and his companions found an inn as the sun was setting. As they were about to go in, Matt noticed something. He stopped Sir Orizhan with a hand on the shoulder.

"What troubles you?" the knight asked, then followed the direction of Matt's gaze.

"The bird." Matt pointed.

Looking, his companions saw a big black avian, like a very oversized crow, sitting on a windowsill and peering into the inn.

"It hopes to beg a crust or two, I doubt not," Sir Orizhan said.

Sergeant Brock nodded. "It was ever the way of ravens to wait for what was left."

"If you say so," Matt said, with misgivings, and started to follow them in, when the bird turned and fixed him with a bright black bead of an eye. A chill passed through Matt; he felt that he had never seen such malice in a bird's glance, such sheer gloating malevolence and eagerness to pounce.

Then the raven turned its attention back to the interior of the inn, and it was only a large black bird again. Slowly, Matt followed his companions into the inn.

They walked into a blast of noise—conversation, laughter, snatches of song, and the clattering of wooden platters. Serving wenches swiveled through the crowd, trays held high. Glasses lifted in toast.

"Quite a party," Matt observed. "What do you think they're celebrating?"

Sir Orizhan shrugged. "Life."

"Do you think we will be able to stay the night this time?" Sergeant Brock asked.

"We can only hope," Matt sighed.

"I mean no offense, Lord Wizard," Sir Orizhan said, "but this bauchan of yours is proving to be a most pernicious nuisance."

"Not so loud," Matt hissed. "He might hear, and take it as a compliment." Then, in a more normal voice, "I'm really sorry about this, guys, but he isn't my bauchan—not willingly, anyway."

"So long as he does not take us for your family, I suppose we will be well enough," Sir Orizhan said. He surveyed the room and shook his head. "We have come late—there is no table empty."

"There is one in the back corner." Sergeant Brock pointed. "There is only the one man at it."

The one man in question was hunched over, glowering at his tankard and muttering to himself.

"Not the world's most savory company," Matt said warily, "but it's the only table with any room. Brace yourselves for an unpleasant meal."

"I would say that we should go on to the next village and chance the inn there," Sir Orizhan said, "save that we have already done so, and the darkness is upon us. It may be that you should stop urging us to just one more village, Lord Wizard."

It was getting to be a running argument. "But we're going so slowly as it is," Matt protested. "We run into so many delays."

Sir Orizhan sighed. "Then we shall have to suffer the company of a drunkard."

"Pooh! We'll only listen for the space it takes him to drink three more stoups of ale," Sergeant Brock told him. "Then he'll fall asleep and we'll be rid of his talk."

"Oh, really?" Matt regarded the drunk with a jaundiced eye. "How is he going to get three more stoups?"

"Why, you will buy them for him." Sergeant Brock grinned. "Is it not a small price for peace?"

"I suppose so," Matt sighed, "and money's no problem yet. Gentlemen, be seated."

Sir Orizhan sat with him, but Sergeant Brock stared, offended. He started to speak, but caught himself.

Matt frowned up at him. "What's the matter? Sit down."

The offense turned into disbelief. "But I am not a gentleman!"

Matt felt a surge of guilt as he remembered that no one below the rank of squire counted as a gentleman in this medieval world, and gentlemen did not dine with lower classes outside of common rooms. He started to correct the error, but before he could speak, Sir Orizhan beckoned the man close. "You are my squire for the space of this venture. I raise you to it, and shall make it lasting with all due ceremony if we succeed in our venture."

Conflicting emotions warred in Brock's face for a moment—disbelief, joy, and apprehension. Matt could understand it—peasants were almost never raised to the gentry, and if they didn't succeed, this amazing prize might be snatched away from the sergeant. But he must have remembered that if they didn't succeed, they'd probably be dead, because the joy won the skirmish, and he sat down beside Sir Orizhan, bowing his head. "I thank you, Sir Knight. From the depths of my heart."

"You honor me as much as I you," Sir Orizhan said generously.

"Honor!" the drunk across the table snarled. " 'S only a 'scuse for killin'a good onezh!" He lifted his tankard, glare defying them to disagree. "Long live Prince Brion!"

The three companions exchanged glances. Then Matt said, "Long life, and we'll drink to it as soon as we get mugs."

A serving wench overheard and swirled by their table. "Would you have ale, sirs?"

"Yes, and meat and bread," Matt told her. "Dinner, in fact."

"As soon as I may," she promised, and whirled away.

"Busy place tonight," Matt commented.

" 'S'a minshtrel," the drunk informed them. "Came in f'r shupper. Landlord fed 'im while he shent boyzh out t' tell ev'yone."

"So the whole village crowded in to be ready to listen by the time the minstrel finishes." Matt nodded. "Smart businessman." Then he turned to Sir Orizhan. "Does it seem to you there are an awful lot of minstrels running around these days?"

"Far more than I am accustomed to seeing," the knight agreed. "One might almost think them to be troubadours, and us to be in the south."

A man dressed in bright clothes stood up and struck an off-key chord on his lute.

"Or perhaps not," Sir Orizhan amended.

The minstrel tuned a string, then struck the chord again. It was much better, and he nodded in satisfaction.

"Tell us the news ere you sing, minstrel!" one man called, and a chorus of voices took up the cry. "Aye, the news! First, the news!"

"Well, my songs are news enough in themselves," the minstrel said, laughing.

"If they have tunes, that is news indeed," Sir Orizhan muttered.

"Just my luck," Matt sighed, "traveling with a critic."

"Still, I'll tell you the most recent in short sentences," the minstrel went on. "Which will you have first—the bad, or the good?"

"The bad!" a dozen voices cried with relish.

"The worst of it, then, is that King Drustan has fallen ill."

A furious babble broke out as people asked each other if it could be true, and assured that it could be, wondered about the benefit-to-damage ratio of the results.

When they had quieted, and begun to realize that the damages might well outweigh the benefits, the innkeeper called out, "Then what is the good news, minstrel?"

"The good," the minstrel cried with false heartiness, "is that our loyal Prince John has assumed rule as regent! The king has spoken through his son, and appointed him to care for us all!"

The announcement was greeted with stunned silence. The minstrel tried to grin around at them all, but his smile faltered. Then the murmuring began, dark, ugly, and apprehensive.

"I've heard of it," a tinker told his neighbor, much too loudly. No doubt he'd been disgruntled at having to give up the attention of the crowd as news bearer.

"What have you heard?" a woman at another table asked.

"Why," the tinker said in a voice to fill the room, "that there is more to His Majesty's 'illness' than meets the eye."

"How do you mean?" The minstrel's tone was threatening; he didn't like having his thunder stolen, either.

The tinker's tone sank to a dramatic whisper—one that carried to most of the room. "There's some as say the queen poisoned him."

"Ridiculoush!" the drunk exploded. "Queen couldn't've! She been in prizhon!"

Matt started to edge farther away from the man. So did Sergeant Brock; they converged on Sir Orizhan, who sat across from the drunk.

"Worsht of 'em all, that Zhon!" the drunk grumbled. He

glared into his ale, but his voice grew louder and louder. "That Gaherish, he wazh a mean 'un, but wazhn't a puling little coward, at leasht! An' who wazh that blue knight that did in Prinsh Brion, eh? Just a shuit of armor with nothin' in-shide? That'sh bad magic, I tell yuh, bad! Sumthin' really bad, when only the sniveling slug of a grubby little coward'zh left t' rule ush!"

Out of the corner of his eye Matt caught movement. He turned just in time to see the raven fly away from the window-sill. Somehow, it gave him a very bad feeling. He stood up, tugging at Sir Orizhan's shoulder. "Come on. I don't think I want to stay and hear this."

"Give up housen again?" Brock protested.

Sir Orizhan started to object, too, until he saw the look on Matt's face. Then he nodded and stood up. "Yes, of course. There is bound to be another inn down the road."

"Oh, I'm not good enough fer yuh, hey?" the drunk called after them. "Jus' cauzhe ol' Dolan'zh tellin'a truth, nobody wantsh 'im aroun'."

"Might have more to do with how much ale you've drunk," Matt told him as he hurried his friends toward the door.

The innkeeper rushed to intercept them. "No, goodmen, by your leave! Stay! I'll toss out that fool Dolan! I should have done it long ago!"

But Dolan had no doubt been paying for his drinks. Still, three dinners would bring the innkeeper more than a dozen stoups of ale.

Sergeant Brock sighed. "I would dearly love to stay in an inn for the night," he said.

"All right, we'll stay." But Matt felt a twinge of sympathy. "You don't have to kick him out, mine host. Just tuck him into the inglenook, okay?"

"And keep feeding him ale," Sergeant Brock added. "My . . . employer will pay for it." He nodded at Matt.

"Well, if it's the price of a good night's sleep, okay," Matt said, and they went back to the table. The landlord preceded them and hustled Dolan off to the inglenook, protesting every inch of the way. As they sat down, Matt wondered if maybe he really would have been doing the man more of a favor to let the landlord kick him out.

He thought so even more after dinner, when the soldiers burst in.

They came following a hound that looked to be more wolf than dog, its cry more a howl than a bark. It padded straight toward the inglenook. The patrons exclaimed in horror and fright and leaped out of its way, overturning chairs and tables in their haste.

Dolan looked up and saw the hound coming. "Nooooo!" he wailed, hands up to shield him. "Save me, goodfolk!"

But the dog stopped inches from him, growling a threat. Dolan climbed up on his stool and pressed himself back into the inglenook, still wailing his denial and staring at the beast in terror.

"Down with you, then!" A soldier struck his knees with a spear shaft, and the poor man fell with a scream.

The soldier yanked him upright, and Dolan yammered, "But I've done nothing!"

"You've spoken against the prince!" The sergeant's voice rang through the great common room. "Don't try to deny it! We know!"

"Sit down, my masters," Sergeant Brock muttered, yanking at Matt's sleeve.

Matt looked down in surprise; he hadn't even realized he'd stood up. Sir Orizhan stared, too, looking down at himself.

"We can't let them haul him away just for being drunk," Matt muttered, but it was halfhearted.

"You can't throw away a kingdom for a single drunken fool!" Brock hissed. "Sit down, my masters, for if you fight the king's men-at-arms, everyone will know you for what you are!"

It was a point well taken—they couldn't compromise the whole mission, and risk the war they might prevent, to save one single man. Matt forced himself to sit, and Sir Orizhan, equally reluctantly, sat, too, and watched the soldiers drag Dolan out, wailing and weeping.

"Be calm, Sir Knights," Brock muttered. "We do not know what punishment they will give him, after all."

"True," Matt said stiffly. Since Dolan was just a drunken

loudmouth, presumably the punishment wouldn't be terribly severe.

"It is not as though he were really talking treason, after all," Sir Orizhan muttered, but he didn't look convinced.

The door closed behind them all, dog, soldiers, and victim, and the patrons turned back to talking to one another, trying to strike up conversations again—but their efforts were subdued and listless. Finally the innkeeper called, "Your songs, minstrel! Are you not one who has the gift of raising folks' spirits?"

"I shall try, mine host," the minstrel answered, and struck some chords from his lute, then began to sing "Queen Petronille's Confession."

"Amazing how that song is getting around," Matt said in an undertone.

"Yes, but it is even more amazing how carefully that minstrel sings it," Sir Orizhan answered, "as though he were afraid each and every word might bring that hound of menace back again."

It was true, and Matt saw that the minstrel, along with everyone else who had witnessed the scene, had realized its meaning—that there was to be no freedom of speech of any kind, not even the slightest hint, in Regent John's England.

Just across the border in Merovence, Mama and Papa were hearing the same song in a very similar inn that same night.

Papa frowned as he listened, and considered how to talk to Mama in public without worrying about eavesdroppers. He couldn't speak the English of his own world—being his native tongue and the first words that answered the impulse of speech, it emerged here as the language of Merovence. Then he realized that French wasn't a native language to either of them, and should emerge here as words no one else understood. *"Ma cherie, comprends-tu cette langue?"* My dear, do you understand this language?

Mama looked up in surprise, then realized what he was doing and smiled with delight. She answered in the same language, "Yes, I understand. So we can speak French here, though we cannot speak English? How clever of you to think of it!"

"Thank you, my dear. What do you think of this song we have just heard?"

"That it is slander," Mama said instantly, "and the proof of that is that it makes John out to be the legitimate heir, even if Brion had still been alive."

"I knew it was slander, but I didn't think of the purpose," Papa told her. "Do you think there can be any truth to it at all?"

"That Drustan might have disguised himself to learn Petronille's secrets, I might believe," Mama told him, "but Earl Marshal is far too chivalrous to stoop to such a deed, even if his sovereign commanded him to do so."

"He is indeed," Papa agreed, "and too chivalrous to commit adultery, even if he had been in love with Petronille—the kind of love the troubadours praised was love from afar."

"Well, sometimes not," Mama demurred, "but when it was anything else, it involved years of courtship. No, I think we can safely rule out Brion's being anyone's son but Drustan's—especially since John needs to sway the people to his side, and it would be amazingly convenient for him if Brion, the people's darling, turned out to be a bastard, dead or not."

Papa nodded. "A propaganda piece, then. And to think our politicians think they invented mudslinging!"

Mama stood up, blazing with indignation. "We must tell everyone the truth!"

"No, wait." Papa forestalled her with a hand on her arm, and jerked his head toward the rafters. Looking up, Mama saw two ravens squatting on the beams, glowering down at the people.

"Hugi and Munin?" she guessed.

"Like them, at least. They may not be spying for Odin, but I feel sure they are someone's eyes and ears. We know there is a sorcerer involved in this affair somewhere, my dear."

"Yes, we must assume the worst." Mama sat down and looked out over the room with a stern gaze. "And we dare not put those birds to sleep, or we will reveal that there are master wizards here."

"I had not thought of that, but you are certainly right," Papa said, frowning. "No, my dear, for the time being, I'm afraid we must watch and learn, and wait for the time to use our knowledge."

"And hope those ravens do not speak French," Mama replied.

The road opened out into a huddle of huts before the companions, and Brock reminded Matt, "You said we should stop at the next inn."

"Yes, but there's a good two hours of daylight left!" Matt protested.

"Who says that they will be good?" Sir Orizhan asked airily. "Besides, we might not find another village with an inn before midnight."

Well, Matt doubted that—the villages tended to be about two hours apart, even by the back roads they were traveling— but he gave in with a sigh. "Okay. If there's an inn here, we'll stay the night."

They sauntered down the single dusty street, with wary eyes watching them from every window and women's cries warbling from every door. Children heard and scurried for cover behind their mothers.

Sergeant Brock grinned. "Cautious, but not frightened. The war has spared this place."

The cottages opened out into the village green, with a two-story thatched inn at one side and the church at another. In the center of the green a man in white robes and sandals stood atop a small knoll, his head wreathed in mistletoe. He held high a staff carved into a snake as he cried, "Come at sundown, come! When your day's work is done! Come to the gods of your ancestors! Take up again the Old Worship! Come with Banalix the Druid, to honor Toutatis!"

A score of villagers surrounded the man already, and housewives were drifting closer. The men coming in from the fields looked up with interest.

"What have we here?" Sir Orizhan looked up, on his guard.

"Someone trying to bring back that Good Old-Time Religion," Matt said slowly. "Talk about a revival meeting!"

"He is a druid," Brock said with certainty.

Something in the tone of his voice made Matt turn to study

him. He was somber, but not angry or contemptuous—and Matt realized he had expected the sergeant to be so. Why? He looked at the so-called druid again, and caught the flash of something bright at his belt . . .

A gilded sickle.

Suddenly Matt remembered the sickle in Sergeant Brock's pack. If the soldier really had fought these latter-day druids, he should be angry at the mere sight of Banalix, the more so because the man was standing boldly forth in broad daylight and openly calling people to his religion in defiance of the Church.

"The Old Gods knew the ways of war!" Banalix orated. "They shall protect you from the bloodthirsty hordes of Merovence!"

Sir Orizhan stiffened. Matt took umbrage himself.

"The Old Gods shall lend skill to your hands and show you once again the use of weapons, not merely the handles of a plow! Come to the Old Gods! Grow strong again!"

"You lie, rogue!" thundered a voice from the church, and the village priest came striding forth, his face red with anger. "There is great strength in the Christian God, but His strength is tempered with mercy!"

"Strength?" Banalix turned to meet the attack with a relish that spoke of success; he had meant to provoke this cry of defense. "When did the Christ ever wield a sword?"

"He stood barehanded against blades, for He told us that any who live by the sword must die by the sword! Yet He had the courage to stand unarmed before soldiers!"

"Surrendered himself meekly, you mean!" Banalix sneered. "When did He ever fight?"

"When He threw the moneychangers out of the Temple! To cleanse the House of God! For a good and godly reason, Christ fought, as must we all!" He turned to the crowd, raising his arms. "Fight against the seduction of this man's lies! Fight in your hearts for the salvation of your souls!"

"Fight?" Banalix jibed. "What weapon did your Christ ever use? Only a whip of knotted cords!"

"That, and the force of His anger, against which no man can stand!" the priest declared. "Beware, impostor, for that anger shall be directed against you!"

"I am not an impostor!" Banalix cried, reddening. "I am a true druid!"

"There are no true druids anymore," the priest shot back. "They all died, because they had no worshipers to wait upon them and feed them!"

"As your worshipers wait upon and feed you!" Banalix returned.

"I feed my flock, not they me!"

" 'Tis true!" an old woman cried from the back of the crowd. "Friar Gode sees that none of the poor starve!"

"Say that your neighbors and the viscount feed you, for it is they who give me food to bring you." But the friar flashed the old woman a smile of gratitude. Then he turned back to Banalix. "This is the strength of the Christ—that people care for one another, help one another in their hour of need!"

"Care for one another? Aye, and slaughter one another in battles!"

The friar smiled. "I thought you said that Christians did not know how to fight!"

The so-called druid scowled. "How many of your sheep could fight off a wolf?"

"All the men practice at the archery butts every Sunday, as you know!" Friar Gode turned to the crowd again, his arms upraised. "You have heard it! He will say any lie he finds to blind you, then counter it with another lie to confuse you! This is no priest of an ancient religion, but a rogue who seeks to enslave you by using only those parts of the heathen faith that entice you!"

"So you admit the Old Gods are enticing!" Banalix snapped, eyes glittering.

"Say rather that it is you who make the Old Gods seem enticing—all your doing, for the heathen gods never existed as anything more than stories to warn children!"

The people moved back a little, muttering fearfully at such a denial.

"But your enticement lasts only until you have them enslaved!" Gode turned to the crowd. "Then he will tell you that his gods demand blood! You have all heard the news, even if it is only whispered, never said openly—how his kind kidnap virgins to slay on their bloodstained altars!"

"They are hard gods, but they bring power and prosperity!" the "druid" thundered.

"They bring death and destruction to those who worship them," Friar Gode countered, "or their false priests do!"

"Beware," Banalix cried, "for my sickle is not false, but sharp and hard!"

"Whoever heard of gold that was hard, or could hold an edge?" the friar returned. "It may be gilded, but it is not gold—false, like its owner!"

Matt glanced at Sergeant Brock. The man's face was impassive, hard as rock.

"False? You dare call me false, when you worship a man whose disciples stole his body and claimed it had come back to life?" Banalix was getting carried away now. "Disciples who made up stories about his walking on water and feeding thousands with seven loaves and two fishes? Aye, you must know falsehoods well!"

The people murmured and backed away farther, fear sharpening.

"Those were no lies, but true miracles!" Friar Gode returned. "True miracles, such as His saints work even today by His power! Now you are not only a liar, but a blasphemer as well!" He folded his hands and looked up to Heaven, silent for a moment as he calmed his soul and focused his thoughts on prayer. All the villagers were mute with apprehension, for in this universe, a friar's prayers were powerful indeed.

Brock leaned close to Matthew and muttered, "We must stop this!"

"We can't let them know who we really are!" Matt muttered back.

"O God!" Friar Gode cried. "O Great and Powerful Father of All! O Jesus, Who art both Man and God!"

Banalix began to swing his hand in a circle, muttering.

Matt stiffened, and began gathering verses to chant.

"Suffer not untruth to prosper, I pray thee!" the friar cried. "Expose all lies, strike down all enemies of Right!"

If Matt hadn't been watching closely, he wouldn't have seen Banalix's left hand open the small ceramic box at his belt, wouldn't have seen the right hand dip in, then circle twice more before he hurled a fireball at Friar Gode.

The ball struck, and flame exploded over the friar's robe. He screamed, running, batting at the flames—and, of course, making them worse.

"Behold the power of Belenos!" Banalix cried in triumph, but the crowd only pressed away from the burning friar, moaning.

"Help me!" the friar howled, running toward his parishioners. The flames roared higher, and the villagers flinched even farther away, moaning.

But Matt was running, too, shouting, "Fall down, friar!" and whipping off his cloak.

The monk didn't hear him over his own screaming, only went on running from one villager to another. Matt knocked him to the ground and dropped his cloak over the man, rolling him in it and rolling again and again until all the flames were out.

"See how Belenos triumphs over the Christ!" Banalix cried.

"With the help of a little naphtha." Matt wrinkled his nose at the smell coming from the poor burned friar.

"Do you question whose magic is more powerful?" the false druid demanded of the crowd.

His answer was a low moan.

"Come to the worship of Toutatis and Belenos!" Banalix urged. "Return to the gods who are strongest!"

Most of the people started toward him, then glanced at their neighbors and hesitated. Everyone hesitated, in fact. Then the whole crowd pulled back, shame-faced and sullen.

"How fearful you are!" the druid said scornfully. "But I warn you, Belenos' wrath is more to be feared than the disapproval of your neighbors or the scoldings of your priest!"

Even burned and in pain, Friar Gode managed to turn his moans into a cry. "Already he begins his threats!"

The villagers glanced at him, startled, then frowned at Banalix, unsure.

The false druid at least knew he'd pushed it as far as he could. "I shall go now, but Belenos shall stay with you! Toutatis shall watch you! You shall never be free of your ancestors' gods—but then, you never have been!"

One boy stepped closer to Banalix, greatly daring, no

doubt urged on by his friends—and as the false druid turned away, his hand flashed out and caught the boy by the arm. The child yelped with fear and tried to pull away, but Banalix pressed something into his palm. The boy froze, staring at the first gold coin he had ever seen—tiny, but really gold. Banalix drew him close and said something softly to him, then turned him around and sped him on his way with a pat. Then Banalix strode off toward the woodlot beyond the village, head high, moving swiftly, certainly appearing to be a druid. The villagers gave way, pulling back to leave a channel down which Banalix went, between the huts and into the woods. The people stared after him, silent a moment, then began to drift away to their huts, talking in low tones. One or two glanced guiltily at the friar but saw he was in someone's care, even if that someone was a stranger, and took the excuse to hurry away to their homes.

Sir Orizhan and Sergeant Brock, though, came closer, their faces grave. They winced at the friar's groans and wrinkled their noses at the stench of the naphtha.

"A bucket of water, please, Sergeant," Matt said, then turned back to stripping the remains of his cloak off the friar. "Lend a hand, Sir Orizhan."

The knight stepped closer, face a mask against the sight of the burns, and helped Matt strip charred scraps of the friar's own robe from his body.

"Not my loins!" the friar cried. "Sweet modesty!" But he stirred too much as he said it, and cried out with pain.

"By your leave, friar, we have to heal the burns wherever we find them," Matt told him.

Brock came up with the bucket.

"Pour it everywhere you see a burn," Matt told him, "but gently, mind you."

Brock poured, and Matt sprinkled a powdered herb on the wet flesh, muttering,

> "Chest and arms,
> Grow skin, new skin!
> Thighs and groin, heal cold!
> Back and sides and calf and shin,
> Be healed of burns and scalds!"

He kept muttering and sprinkling as the friar's groans slackened, until every burn had grown new skin and the friar sat up, looking at his arms and chest, amazed.

Sir Orizhan's lips shaped a soundless whistle, and Sergeant Brock stepped back, the whites showing all around his eyes.

The friar stared up at Matt. "What manner of man are you?"

"A healer, among other things." Matt figured the obvious couldn't hurt. "You were lucky we got to you quickly—though the burns were only superficial, or I might not have been able to mend them so fast."

"Not luck, but Providence!" The friar started to stand up, then remembered his nudity and sank back with a cry of distress.

"Yes, there's still some pain," Matt said grimly. "Sir Orizhan, could the good friar borrow your cloak for a little while? I seem to have lost mine."

"It shall be replaced!" the friar assured him.

"Call it a donation," Matt told him.

Sir Orizhan held up his cloak, and Matt helped the friar rise into its folds. He cried out as it touched his shoulders, then clamped his mouth shut.

"I know, it still hurts," Matt commiserated. "Be careful, friar—that's new skin, and it will be very sensitive for a while."

"I shall be most careful indeed! Bless you, stranger, for a good Samaritan!"

"I have a stake in your cause," Matt told him.

"My cause!" The friar buried his face in his hands, moaning. "I have failed my Lord! Both my Lord and my flock!"

"You haven't failed yet," Matt said grimly. "This was a battle, friar, not a war. No, not even a battle—just a skirmish."

Sergeant Brock looked up in surprise. Sir Orizhan looked up, too, but only smiled and nodded slightly.

The friar stared at Matt, and hope began to rise in his eyes again. Matt turned him away gently and began to walk him toward the church. "Lucky your feet weren't burned."

"This is not the end of the matter, then?" the friar asked. "Have you any real knowledge of that?"

"Sure," Matt said. "You pushed that Banalix to his limit,

friar. All he could find for an argument were clichés that were worn thin by the time the gospels were written. He had to resort to trickery to shut you up."

"Trickery?" The friar halted, staring up at him. "Not true magic?"

Sergeant Brock stared, too.

"Not a bit," Matt assured them. "I saw him pull that ball of wax out of his sleeve while he was making those sham magical passes. I saw him light it in the coal-box at his belt, too, and I know what he mixed with the wax to make it burn that way—I recognized the smell on your charred robe. Believe me, there was no way you could have won that encounter—that would have taken a real wizard."

Both his companions looked up, startled. Matt gave them a wink and a slight shake of the head.

Friar Gode turned away and started walking again, head bowed in thought. "But why wasn't prayer enough?" he asked, bewildered.

"You should know the answer to that one better than I, friar." Matt smiled. "It's because we have free will—so God and the saints leave us to fight our own battles, and won't interfere directly, though they'll give us all the help they can. The Devil doesn't feel any such scruples, though. The only thing that stops Hell's minions from coming out in the open is that if they do, the saints feel fully justified in stepping in themselves. So the Devil keeps his imps hidden, and the saints watch ready to pounce, and that leaves it up to us to fight the battle. But the Devil gives his agents all the ammunition they need—in this case, a recipe the Greeks knew but most people today have forgotten."

"Save my people from this druid!"

"I'll do what I can. Shouldn't be too hard; Hell wouldn't be helping a real druid."

Friar Gode's face lit with relief and joy. "You, too, think the man to be an impostor, then?"

"I'm sure of it. The druids were very religious people in their own way, and the Devil's trying to destroy religions, not help them."

Friar Gode froze, staring at him in shock.

Matt kept on walking, though slowly. "I'll bet Banalix

doesn't even speak Gaelic, and that sickle was only gold plate over very real steel. Besides, real druids didn't use fake fireballs."

The friar hurried to catch up with him, then looked up at the church. "We are come to the House of God. Will you take supper with me? It is all the thanks I can show."

The thought of food suddenly sounded very good. "Why, yes, thank you. Sir Orizhan, Sergeant Brock?"

The sergeant looked wary, but the knight said easily, "I shall accept your hospitality with thanks. If we are to have another night in a cold field, hot food would be a blessing."

"In a field?" The friar looked up, startled, then glanced at the inn. "Of course—you cannot be sure of your welcome at the hostel now, can you? Well, I have only the one hard bed, but if you wish to spread your blankets on my floor, I would be honored."

Inspiration struck. "Thanks very much, but, uh . . . would it be too much to ask if I could sleep in the church?"

"In the church? But the floor is stone, as is all the building!" The friar gave Matt a searching glance. "Of course, if you wish it. The House of God is open to all, at all hours."

It made a nice contrast to late-twentieth-century America. "Thanks. I think I'll sleep much better there."

"I'd liefer have a wooden floor, if you will allow it," Sir Orizhan said.

"I, too." Sergeant Brock seemed relieved.

"Then let us dine. My housekeeper should have the evening meal ready." The friar's lips quirked in a sardonic smile. "If she still cooks for me, that is."

She still did, and though the meal was Spartan, it was hot and very good—only bread, fish, and ale, with cheese and apples after. When they were done, Matt took the friar aside and said, "If you don't mind, mine host, I know a few simple spells which might be of use to you in the future."

"Spells?" The friar stared. "Are you a wizard, then?"

"Every traveler should know enough to repel bandits and guard against night-walkers," Matt told him. "Now, here's a defense against fireballs, since we've seen you may need it . . ."

Friar Gode proved to be a better student than Matt was a

teacher, and within the space of an hour could repeat the verses and gestures of four spells perfectly. He could quench fireballs, ward off malice and spite, protect himself against weapons of any kind, and, most importantly of all, cancel the effects of spells cast to harm him.

"I'll feel a little better about you living on your own now," Matt told him.

"You are not a guest, but a blessing!" the friar declared. "You must have my bed—I shall sleep on the floor!"

Matt smiled. "Well, thank you, friar—but I'd still rather sleep in the church. It's dark now, though, so it must be your bedtime. If you don't mind, I'll take a little walk before I sleep."

"Anything that pleases you!" Friar Gode turned to Sir Orizhan and Sergeant Brock. "Please, my friends, do not delay on my account! Spread out your blankets and rest!"

"I thank you." But Sir Orizhan's gaze rested on Matt. "Perhaps you should not walk alone, my l—good sir."

"Oh, I think I'll be fine. You two lie down and sleep while you can. Don't worry about me, I'll be safe as houses."

"Houses of God, at least." Sir Orizhan smiled faintly, but his eyes were still worried.

Matt went out and began his stroll, listening to the night sounds for the hoot of an owl. When he heard it, he took a packet of powder from his belt and sprinkled a sparse, almost invisible stream beside him, chanting,

> "Around this church and cottage low
> The certain knot of peace be bound,
> That rest to care and balm to woe
> And sleep in safety may be found.
>
> Let holy warders in the dark
> Protect this building consecrate
> That ministers of grace may mark
> A place where crooked paths go straight."

He walked around the church and the hut of a rectory attached to it, sifting powder and chanting rhymes. He had almost finished the circle when a voice beside him said, "That won't do much good, you know."

Inside his skin, Matt jumped a mile. Fortunately, the outside of his skin stayed right where it was and kept on chanting and moving its feet as he sprinkled powder.

"That charm, I mean," Buckeye said. "There is no spell you can lay that can keep me from you, no warding circle I cannot cross, for you have bound me to you by the naming of magic."

Matt closed the circle and wrapped up the packet of powder, tucking it back inside his pouch.

"You cannot keep me out." The bauchan sounded miffed by Matt's silence. "Not even ignoring me can fend me off, the more so as I know you hear."

Finally Matt turned to him, grinning. "Who said I was laying the warding circle against you?"

"What . . . ?" Buckeye stared, taken aback. "But—But—what else has beset you?" Then anger gathered. "Does someone else wreak mischief upon you? Nay, tell me the name of that foul sprite!"

"Not on me," Matt corrected. "I do occasionally take the side of someone else who's being bullied, you know."

"Someone else?" Buckeye stared. "When you yourself are not hurt in any way?" The concept was clearly foreign to him.

"Even when it doesn't affect me at all." Matt frowned, thinking that over. "No, that's not true—I have the naive notion that anything that affects anybody else has some effect on me, too, no matter how small."

"Outrageous!" Buckeye struggled with the concept, and lost. "What a positively outlandish notion!"

"Well, at least you realize it's positive." Matt pointed to the rectory. "There's a good man inside there, a friar, and a fake druid has just popped up to plague him. He threw a fireball at Friar Gode this afternoon, and I'd like to make sure this Banalix can't hurt him again in any way."

"Banalix!" The bauchan's face wrinkled in disgust. "A false druid indeed!"

"Oh?" Matt looked up with interest. "How do you know?"

"Och, I remember the true druids, mortal! Five hundred years ago and more, and they were the salt of the earth, the sap and the fruit and the branch of the forest, and the forest of them! They treated me with the reverence that was my due, as they treated all the spirits! But they are gone, alas, except for the few left in that isle off the western shore—gone, and only you milk-blooded folk in their place, who idolize the plow and try to deny the forest!"

"Well, farming does provide more food, and thereby keeps more of us alive." Matt spoke bravely, but he shivered inside at the thought of talking to a creature who was five hundred years old. He clung to the one fact that offered some promise. "You've heard of Banalix, then?"

"Of course! Would I let something so obscene as a false druid slip by me? He is bound for the oldest oak in the center of the woods this minute, for he has spread word through the village that all the folk who wish to bring the Old Faith to life again may meet him there!"

Matt just stared at him for a minute—two minutes, four.

Buckeye actually grew nervous. "Wizard? Have I hit upon words that can turn you to stone?"

"No, I'm attuned to a completely different kind of rock," Matt told him. "You know, I was just going out for an evening stroll before bedtime anyway. Which way did you say this old oak was?"

CHAPTER 13

Mama and Papa woke with the sun and were on the road early, but the peasants were already in the fields. The couple left the village, following the track, talking happily with one another, for it was a beautiful morning and they were both feeling at peace with nature.

Just beyond the village, though, the road crossed a small river. There was a ford, the water only two feet deep and the riverbed floored with extra stones to give a firm footing for crossing—but at the moment the women of the village had gathered there to do their laundry. There was a cheerful hub-bub of talk as they lathered the fabric with soap and scrubbed it on the rocks.

"Washing day! What a happy chance!" Mama cried.

Papa frowned. "For what?"

"For gossip! Quickly, Ramon, give me the shirt off your back!"

"Always and willingly, my love," Papa sighed. He shrugged out of the shirt, pulled his vest back on, and stepped aside into the trees. "I assume it would be just as well if I were not seen."

"You are so understanding." Mama stretched up to kiss him on the cheek. Then she turned away, singing a little song, and Papa faded back under the leaves, watching.

As she came up to the ford, silence fell, and the women looked up at her.

"Good morning," Mama told them cheerfully. "This is fortunate—I have been wondering how I should wash my husband's shirt when we are traveling every day."

"Travelers?" A young woman looked up with keen interest.

"Be still, Meg," an older woman snapped, and the girl

192

turned away, reddening. The older woman said to Mama, with a little frown, "You are of Merovence, by your speech."

"Of Merovence, yes," Mama said, kneeling down and taking off her pack. "We have lived there for three years. But we came from much farther away, to the west."

"Ibile?" Meg looked up, eyes wide with excitement.

"Theirs is my native tongue," Mama hedged.

"She has come a long way, Judy," another woman said.

"Very long." Mama wet the cloth and the soap.

"What could have brought you so far?" a fourth woman asked.

"This is not the safest of times," Judy added.

"Indeed not, with the poor queen locked up in her castle!" Mama said indignantly. "But when my husband's father was young, he was a footman at the castle of Petronille's father, the old Prince of the Pykta, and would never forgive Ramon if he did not go to deliver what help he could."

"A noble thought, Alys," Judy said.

"Aye," Alys answered, "but a foolish one, for her husband has come too late to be the queen's soldier."

"Why would he bring you with him on so perilous a journey?" a grandmother asked, frowning.

Mama gave her a dazzling smile. "You do not think I would let him go without me, do you?" She turned back to rub soap into the shirt. "Besides, our son is grown, and I waste away at home."

"You are young to have a grown son!" a fifth woman exclaimed, staring.

Mama gave her a wink. "It is more a matter of washing the skin every day, and staying out of the sunlight whenever you can."

"Only the one son?" The grandmother spoke in tones of pity.

"Only the one child," Mama sighed. "We wished for more, but God gives as He gives, and Heaven knows I am grateful that He gave me my Matthew!"

"Indeed, each child is a blessing." The older woman looked smug. "I have five."

"And your husband still lives, Jane," Alys reminded her.

"We're all blessed in that, especially with another war just rolled past us."

"I have heard it was your queen who brought that war," Mama said, frowning. "I could not believe it."

"As you should not!" Jane exclaimed indignantly. "Was it Queen Petronille who took one lover after another? Was it she who tried to deny her second son his heritage?"

"The Pykta was her birthright," Judy maintained. "By what right did the king give it to his youngest?"

"Aye," Jane agreed. "Any woman would be right in taking any measures she could, to defend her child so!"

"And punish so wayward a husband," Alys said darkly.

Meg only listened, eyes wide.

Mama could almost see her revising her ideas about marital love, and interjected quickly, "Did Petronille lend no fuel to the quarrel? I have heard she has a sharp tongue." Had heard that tongue's sharpness herself, in fact, but she didn't say so.

"A queen *should* have a sharp tongue, if her husband seeks to lord it over her!" the grandmother said stoutly.

"We are poor, defenseless creatures," Judy said, "and must try to make our way through this world in any way we can."

"I cannot agree to so sweeping a statement," Mama said. "I have heard her sons were lacking in chivalry, except for Brion."

The women exchanged glances. The grandmother said, "I have never thought it good to lavish praise on one child, and tell all the others that they should seek to be like the favored one."

"It is true," Alys said. "She did make Brion most obviously her favorite, paying little attention to Gaheris and almost none to John."

"Who can blame her for that," Judy argued, "when the eldest is so odious, and the youngest such a horrid little man?"

"Perhaps they would not have been," said the grandmother, "if she had given them more love."

"It was amazing she gave as much as she did to Brion," Judy countered, "considering that her husband was forever dragging her all about the realm, and off to the Pykta or Deintenir with no warning. It was all she could do to bring one lad with her!"

"The others were safer here at home, in Dunlimon Castle," Alys agreed.

Meg, listening wide-eyed, shivered at the thought. "To be separated from her babes for so long!"

"They had excellent nurses," Judy told her.

"Still, she might have let them take turns accompanying her," the grandmother pointed out. "She is skilled in healing, after all—surely she must have some notion of the hurts given the heart!"

"She is a wise woman, not a witch," Alys said scornfully, "a healer, not a sorceress."

"Could not a woman so skilled heal also her sons' hearts?" the grandmother countered.

"There are skills, and there are other skills," Mama said. "Skill with herbs does not mean a woman has the skill to read the hurts that do not show."

"There is some truth to that," the grandmother admitted. "Still, she is supposed to be so very adept, even in elf-lore and spirit-lore, that I should think she would be skilled in the matters of human spirits while they are still within their bodies."

"Or perhaps out of them," Judy said darkly.

The women fell quiet, and the grandmother looked up, frowning. "What rumor have you heard that we have not?"

Judy glanced about, as though to make sure no spirits were listening, then whispered, "I went to the wise woman yesterday, for her potion to ease my monthly pain—and she told me that Prince Brion was not quite dead when the marshal left him under guard on the battlefield. She said that it was Queen Petronille's men who stole him away, and that when the battle was done, she fanned the coal of his life to a flame."

"Surely you do not mean that she was so skilled a healer that she could raise the dead!" Mama exclaimed—but also in a whisper.

"She *said* the prince was not quite dead," the grandmother snapped.

"Not fully dead," Judy agreed, "nor could the queen bring

him fully to life. She sent his body secretly to the cathedral at Glastonbury, where he sleeps while he waits for a greater sorcerer to waken him."

Half an hour later Mama was walking down the road toward the next town, telling all the gossip to Papa, who seemed somewhat dazed by it. He did manage to say, though, "Thus legends begin."

"And thus they grow," Mama agreed, "as they are passed from person to person."

Papa smiled, amused. "Before long, they will have the sleeping Brion be waiting for love's first kiss to waken him."

"No doubt," Mama agreed, "at least, according to Rumor."

Matt never knew where Buckeye had hidden his peasant's clothing. He only knew that he looked up toward a nightingale's song for half a minute, and when he turned back, the bauchan was wearing his disguise. Matt blinked, but knew better than to ask. Besides, it would probably gall Buckeye no end when he didn't.

An owl hooted almost overhead, making Matt jump, but when he looked up, he couldn't see any kind of bird anywhere. He shivered and walked a little faster, a little closer to Buckeye—he wasn't the only spirit abroad in the wood that night.

Then it occurred to Matt that the deeper they went, the nearer to primeval forest they came—the forest that had been there a thousand years, oaks that had harbored mistletoe for the original druids. He shivered again and stepped up right behind the bauchan, wishing for a little light. It occurred to him that if Buckeye really had a nasty sense of humor, the bauchan could just disappear and leave him stranded in the midnight forest.

Fortunately, the bauchan seemed to be planning on a more elaborate joke than that. He led Matt silently onward until suddenly the wood opened onto a broad clearing with a ghost floating at one end, surrounded by fairy lights. Ancestral superstitious fears yammered in Matt for a second before twentieth-century skepticism came to his rescue and made him look more closely. The fairy lights were of course only fireflies, and the "ghost" was a synthodruid in a white robe made luminous by moonlight, standing atop some sort of pedestal or platform, as dark as the huge old oak behind it. Matt stared—that certainly was a grandfather of a tree, at least five feet thick, its branches covering the whole far end of the clearing.

He scanned the rest of the open space, noticing there were fireflies all through it—then saw what else was there, with a nasty shock. Faces, scores of faces. Moonlight-scatter showed him their clothing, a darker mass beneath their faces. There was at least a quarter of the village there.

"A comforting sight, is it not?" Buckeye asked, grinning.

"For whom?" Matt demanded. "Belenos?"

"Is that what they would call the human who has organized and begun this travesty of the Old Faith?"

"I don't know." Matt turned to him with a frown. "What would you call him?"

" 'Your Majesty,' perhaps?" the bauchan suggested.

Matt stared, then said, "I very much doubt it."

But it did make sense, when he thought about it. The Church always had been the biggest single obstacle between the Crown and absolute tyranny—a counterpower that served as a restraint upon the despotism of a monarch. How more easily to remove that obstacle than to replace it with a religion of your own, securely under your control?

Of course, that was assuming that after the synthodruids became established, they wouldn't try to assert their power themselves, to counteract the king's—maybe even to try to control him. On second thought, it seemed like a long shot.

The druid raised his hands and called out, "People of Belenos! For so you are; your forefathers were, and you are of them, so you must be of Belenos, too."

The people murmured to one another in surprise, then apparently decided they were indeed people of Belenos, and turned back to the druid with a bit less wariness.

"People of Belenos! It has been long since anyone from this village worshiped as you should! Therefore I shall lead you in prayers to the Old Gods, and you who do not understand the rituals may watch without the need to pray."

"Good way for him and them to pretend they belong here, when they're really just feeling it out," Matt muttered to the bauchan. There was no answer, and Matt glanced over at him, surprised to discover that Buckeye had disappeared. He couldn't suppress a shiver of apprehension, and wondered what kind of mischief the bauchan was preparing.

"Do you know this song?" the druid asked, and sang for them,

> "Summer is a-coming in,
> Loud sing, cuckoo!
> Groweth seed, and bloweth mead,
> And springs the wood anew."

The people stared, then nodded, and a few began to sing with the druid.

"I see that you know it!" Banalix cried. "Sing it with me, then!"

The people joined in for the second verse and a chorus.

"That is a song of the Old Gods!" the druid cried, and the people exclaimed to one another in wonder.

Matt wondered, too—at the man's audacity. "Lhude Sing Cucu" had been a hit song only a hundred years before, and the druids had known it about as well as they had known Gothic cathedrals.

Banalix let them talk a few minutes, then cried out, "Aye, of the Old Gods, a song for May Day, a sacred festival! But since it mentions none of the Old Gods by name, your Christian priests let you keep it! Sing it all, now!"

He led them in a rousing rendition of the song, and Matt had to admire his musical abilities, or those of whoever had arranged this particular version—it had a driving beat he would never have expected.

When they finished, the "druid" cried, "Belenos!"

The people fell silent.

"Come, come," Banalix urged, "if you do not believe in them, you are only making noise! Shout their names with me! Belenos!"

"Belenos," some of the people muttered.

"You can call more loudly than that!" Banalix urged. *"Belenos!"*

"Belenos!" the people answered.

"I cannot hear you!" Banalix cried. "Louder, now, louder! BELENOS!"

"BELENOS!" the people thundered.

"Good, good! Now see if you can call as loudly for the rest! TOUTATIS!"

"TOUTATIS!" the people cried.

Banalix pulled a flask out of his robes. "Behold the holy elixir, the mead of the gods! Drink of this brew, that it may elevate your spirits!" He tossed the wooden bottle down to the front row. A man caught it, unstoppered it, sniffed suspiciously, took a sip, then took a longer sip. His neighbor took it from his hand and drank even more.

"Another for you, and for you!" Banalix pulled bottle after bottle out of his robes, tossing them down to the people. "Pass them from hand to hand and quaff as you chant the names of the gods! LUGH!"

"LUGH!" the people shouted.

"MORRIGAN!" Banalix caroled.

"MORRIGAN!"

He led the people in roaring out the names of the gods as they drank from the bottles of holy elixir. Curious, Matt stepped in among them and noticed that Banalix kept tossing down bottle after bottle from an apparently unlimited supply—though he was taking them from a pile in the shadows now, not from his robe. Someone passed him a bottle, and Matt sniffed warily, then took a sip and let it roll across his tongue as he passed the bottle on. It was sweet, very sweet—Banalix hadn't been kidding when he called it mead. It did seem to be made of fermented honey, but the aftertaste flared along Matt's esophagus and lit a glow in his stomach. The drink may have been honey wine at some point, but it had been boiled and condensed into something much stronger, a sort of honey brandy. Matt wondered who had invented distilling here, and had a notion it hadn't been the real druids.

Banalix had worked the crowd up to a regular chant now, reciting the names of the Druid gods, not shouting, but calling only a little louder than their normal speaking voices, with a hard driving rhythm, and Matt realized what Banalix had done. The ceremony thus far had been carefully designed to make the people stop thinking as individuals and start thinking as a mob. They'd be much less likely to worry about right and wrong now.

"The gods have given you their blood!" Banalix called. "They have given it to you in the bottles you have held, and it has been sweet. See, now! I give of my blood to the gods!" He produced a twisted dagger, carved to look like a snake, and pricked his finger, then squeezed and let the blood drip down to the grass of the meadow.

A murmur of wonder ran through the crowd.

"Those of you who wish to give in return for what you have gained, do likewise!" Banalix called. "Step forward, those of you who have the courage to give of your blood to the gods, so that all may see and honor you!"

That was obviously too much. No one would go that far so soon, Matt was sure—until he remembered the liquor. Even so, he stared in disbelief as half a dozen men stepped forward right away and pricked their fingers, then let blood drip onto the grass.

"Behold the holy libation!" Banalix cried. "Who else wishes to do as they have done?"

A dozen more men stepped forward, and even three wild-eyed girls, old enough to be caught up in the communal mania, young enough not to know better. Knives pricked in the moonlight; drops of blood welled to the grass.

"Honor what they have done!" Banalix beckoned, palms upright. "Hail, O Grateful Ones! Hail, they who give for us all! Hail! Hail!"

"HAIL!" the crowd roared. "HAIL!"

Matt had always known some people would do anything for attention, and Banalix made sure they received it. A score more of people stepped forward, drawing their knives, but Banalix was moving on. "Now dance," he cried, "for dancing pleases the Old Gods! It is part of the worship they desire! Dance like this!" He held his arms curving up, snapping his fingers as he moved left foot across right, then right behind left in a chain. He stepped back and reversed the chain, then stepped forward, completing a rectangle. "It is simple, but it honors the gods!"

The ceremony, Matt realized, had been made up out of whole cloth, and the pattern-maker had designed it like a television commercial, showing all the good things about the "old religion" and none of the unpleasant ones they might find distasteful. Well, not none—there was that bloodletting, but it was minor, and no one had really seemed to mind. In fact, they had started competing for the honor and the praise of their fellows. But step by step he was leading them away from reason and independent thought, and into a group-mind, group-body state. How far would he lead them tonight? He had brought them from group chanting to individual bloodletting, but now was leading them on into group movement, the dance inducing everybody to move as one.

Banalix jumped down off his platform—only a very wide stump, Matt realized—and strode out into the midst of the crowd. "Form a circle about me! Aye, for the circle is the sign of the whole and of emptiness, of totality and annihilation, of all and of nothing!"

Murmuring in wonder and confusion, the people lined up in an oval, filling the clearing.

"Music!" Banalix cried.

A piper stepped from the crowd with a small set of bagpipes—dance pipes, not the great drones of war—and began to play.

"Fancy just happening to have a piper at hand," Matt muttered, then remembered that the bauchan had disappeared, and foreboding struck. After all, who else knew he was here, let alone where he was? Matt began to move around the clearing as silently as he could, but didn't for a minute think he was fooling Buckeye.

"Dance, then!" the druid told the people. "Dance to honor Toutatis!"

They stared, amazed at the notion of dance as worship—but this jury-rigged ceremony was so alien from anything they knew as religion that they began to move their feet as he had shown them, in time to the slow urging of the pipes.

"Move around the circle as you dance!" the druid cried, and indicated the direction of turning with a finger. "From west to east, so that you may move time back to the days when the Old Gods held sway!"

The people swayed indeed, and the whole circle began to rotate slowly, opposite to the sun's path—but Matt knew that direction as widdershins, and its associations with evil magic. The bottles passed from hand to hand, too, also widdershins, faster than the people danced. The piper began to play faster and faster, and the circle accelerated with the music. The druid danced with them, smiling and nodding. Then he gestured to the piper, and the tune ended. The circle stopped, the people murmuring, confused.

The druid held up his hands. "O People of Toutatis! Let not your cares mask the joy of life that rises within you! Sing and dance, caress and kiss! Know that life should be pleasure, and pleasure lively!"

Murmurs of incredulity ran through the people, and beneath it, concern.

"I know, I know, you are troubled by the thought that children might be born of your pleasure, and bring shame upon you!" the druid cried. "But for the Old Gods there can be no shame in a child coming into the world, for the more people there are, the more worshipers they have! Dance, drink, laugh, and love, for this pleases Toutatis, pleases Belenos, pleases all the gods of the Gaels!"

The people exclaimed in wonder, and the druid gestured to the piper, who began to play again. The people joined hands and began to dance again, faster and faster and wilder and wilder. Men gave women lascivious glances, and the women blushed and lowered their gazes, then looked up, their eyes huge. Women batted their eyelashes at men, glancing at them sidelong with inviting smiles, and the men grinned and moved closer in the dance. The circle broke up into smaller circles, with here and there a couple dancing alone. More and more couples stepped aside to dance, their movements becoming more and more erotic, while here and there a pair slipped away among the leaves.

Matt realized that this was one cult that was sure to catch on. Give people what they wanted—a sense of belonging mixed with booze and free sex, plus an excuse not to feel guilty about any of it—and they would join in droves. How the women would feel about it nine months later was another matter. Besides, Matt had a suspicion that where the letting of human blood was involved, no matter how voluntary, sooner or later human sacrifice would follow, and the victims wouldn't be all that willing.

He couldn't let things go that far. Stepping away into the bushes, he stripped off his doublet. Then he yanked down a vine from the nearest oak, hoping it wasn't poison ivy—and saw with delight that it was mistletoe! He twisted one end into a crown, set it on his head, wrapped it to frame his face, then looped the rest of the vine around his arms and torso. A good beginning, he decided, but not impressive enough. He looked about him, found a firefly, and tracked it with cupped hands until he clapped them shut around it. Then, peering through the aperture between his thumbs, he chanted,

> "Little fly of fairy light,
> Lend your glow to me this night!
> Tinge me with your photon essence!
> Make me shine with phosphoresence!"

His hands began to glow, and as he watched, the shining spread up his arms and all over his body. Somewhat shaken, he let his diminutive captive go with a muttered word of thanks, then turned to confront Banalix on his own territory.

Exactly on his own territory, as it turned out—his edging around the clearing had brought Matt up behind the grandfather oak. Using it to shield him from the dancing, chanting crowd, he sprinted first to its huge trunk, then edged around and dashed to the broad old stump that Banalix had used for a speaker's platform. Matt climbed up on it, then slowly raised his arms, chanting to himself,

> "Now by chambers of reverberation,
> Make my voice a huge sensation.
> Amplify each word and phrase
> With echoes of ten short delays!"

Then he raised his voice and cried, "Now I call HALT!"

His words reverberated through the clearing, loud as a thunderclap, and the people stopped and stared in sudden fear. Even the piper stopped his droning, and Banalix looked up and froze, wide-eyed.

"People of Morrigan and Lugh, give heed!" Matt called. "I, who love the trees and dwell in and by them, tell you to cease this blasphemy! You desecrate the spirit of the forest!"

A low moan began among the crowd. It jolted Banalix out of his stupor. His face contorted in anger. "Desecrate! It is you who desecrate our ceremony! Who are you who dares interfere!"

Matt's brain shifted into high gear, searching for a name and finding one. "I am he who stands for Oak, Ash, and Thorn! I am he who knows the heart of the woodlands! I am he who knows how the true druids worshiped—and knows what a mockery you have made of their services!"

"Liar!" Banalix screamed. He didn't use dramatic gestures this time, only pulled the naphtha ball from his sleeve, yanked the lid off the coal-box, and lit as he shouted, "No one living can remember the ceremonies of the Old Ones! Deceiver you may be, but you cannot lie your way out of *this*!"

The ball burst into flame. Banalix hurled it, and he had a good arm—but Matt was already reciting,

> "If I quench thee, thou flaming minister,
> I can again thy former light restore.
> Yet why should I your fire rekindle?
> Be dark and cold forever more!"

The fireball shrank in on itself as it cooled, then flickered and went out. No one else could see the dark little ball that bounced off Matt's chest. A murmur of awe passed through the crowd.

"Charlatan!" Banalix bellowed. "Taste true magic now!" He gestured, reciting something that sounded like Gaelic, and Matt realized, with a chill, that he was pantomiming the tying of a noose. Matt remembered that one of the druids' forms of human sacrifice had been hanging, then throwing the body into a peat bog. Quickly, he chanted,

"Naked to the hangman's knot
A neck's set for abuse.
But vertebrae should stack intact.
Be good! Rope, be no noose!"

Something seemed to brush his neck, tried to tighten, then was gone.

Banalix stared, fear shadowing his eyes.

"Cease your cowardly attacks!" Matt boomed. "They avail you naught!"

Banalix's eyes narrowed. He blustered to hide his fear. "Coward yourself, coward and trickster! By what magic you opposed my spells I know not, but taste this assault!"

His lips poured out a torrent of words as he pantomimed tossing, stiff-fingered, left hand, right hand, left hand, on and on.

Matt didn't know what he thought he was throwing, but he did think it was a good idea to turn aside anything he couldn't see.

"Deflect! Avaunt!
Come nowhere near!
My unseen shield, hold sure!
Whatever's thrown shall thus be seared
By wards both tough and dur!"

He didn't even feel the impacts. All anyone saw was a sudden burst of lights in front of Matt as unseen missiles flared against his shield and burned out.

The crowd murmured in fear and pressed away from Banalix. The false druid stood panting, staring at Matt, suddenly haggard.

Matt knew his chance when he saw it. "People of the Church! You have seen this impostor for what he is, a feeble and powerless trickster! Avoid his snares, avoid his web of deceit, for you know the source of lies and traps! Go now, go quickly, and never hearken to this man or any like him again!"

That galvanized Banalix into action as he saw all his gains slipping away from him. "Deceiver yourself!" he screamed. "You claim to be of the forest? Then let it judge you!" He chanted in the foreign language again, pointing up at the ancient oak, and a branch the size of a grown tree groaned downward to swat at Matt.

CHAPTER 14

With a horrendous cracking, the branch began to split from the trunk. It wasn't just going to swat at Matt, it was going to fall on him! Quickly, he chanted,

> "Oh, will this limb rejoice, or break?
> Decide this doubt for me!
> Close up the wound without an ache,
> And heal this fractured tree!"

The fall of the branch slowed, then stopped, one huge burl only inches from Matt's head. Then, incredibly, it started to rise again, the base cleaving to the trunk, shaking, trembling, then stilling, and the branch stretched out whole again. Matt told himself he must have been imagining the huge sigh of relief that seemed to surround him.

The crowd burst into cries of awe—and fear. Those closest to Banalix tried to crowd farther away.

The false druid pointed at a dead tree behind Matt and screamed a verse. A groan began, softer, then louder and louder, as the tree leaned to fall on Matt.

> "I leaned my back unto an aik,
> I thought it was a trustie tree,
> But first it bowed, and now it creaks,
> To crush the one who made it break!"

He hoped Cowper's ghost wasn't listening.

The trunk seemed to roll, changing the direction of its fall. Banalix stared in horror, then turned to run crosswise, out of the path of the tumbling skeletal branches—but the tree swung about, following him, tracking him, as it fell faster and faster, then slammed down on top of him. Banalix screamed in pure terror, then screamed again and again, for the tree had enough branches left so that it hadn't crushed him, only formed a prison around him. He grabbed the dry old sticks and shook them, trying to break them, but they must not have been quite as dead as they seemed, for they held him penned in.

"Go now, quickly!" Matt boomed. "Go back to your cottages, back to your beds, and never follow such a deceiver again!"

The crowd broke and ran, howling with fright. Their voices faded away, and the clearing was still, except for the sobbing coming from the hollow tree.

Matt stood still, absorbing the whole of the night, letting the adrenaline ebb. When he trusted himself to be gentle, he whispered,

> "The game is won, the quarry's fled,
> The night regains its peace.
> Let effects from my voice all be bled,
> And sound processing cease!"

"Can you hear me, Banalix?" he said softly, but the spell seemed to have worked—he could scarcely hear himself, and the druid kept whimpering with no sign of having heard him. Matt jumped down from the stump and went slowly toward the dead tree, where he knelt down and gazed in at the prisoner.

The man stared at him for a frozen moment, then recoiled, hands up to defend, crying, "Who are you?"

"A wizard," Matt told him, "one who's on the side of the Church at the moment—and who knows what you're trying to do."

The man stared, then whispered, "For the Church? You are a godly wizard, and you defeated the powers of the Old Gods so easily?"

"Sure," Matt said. "They don't really exist, you know. The only power you had was some minor spells your boss taught you—and their impact comes from the music of the old language, not the strength of the old gods."

Banalix began to tremble. "But he told me the Old Gods live!"

"He lied," Matt said simply. "He's out to gain power, and he saw that he could do it by reviving his own version of the old religion. He even put together a mixture of excuses for people to do all the things they enjoy, but that have bad effects later on—guaranteed to win him converts, and by the time they realize all their partying has brought trouble, your boss figured he'd have them so securely under his thumb that they couldn't get away if they wanted to."

He almost felt sorry for Banalix as he watched the expressions that chased each other across his face as his wonderful new world collapsed around him. Finally he groaned, "I am lost!"

"You can find a way to rebuild," Matt told him. "For openers, tell me what I want to know, and I'll release you."

"Tell you . . . ?" A crafty look came into the druid's eyes.

"Don't think you have anything to trade," Matt said quickly. "I have plenty of other ways of finding out, and I won't at all mind leaving you here to starve."

The last part was a complete lie, of course, but Banalix didn't know that. He stared at Matt in horror for a minute, then quavered, "The Chief Druid! Surely you know that!"

"Yes, I guessed that much," Matt agreed. "Tell me his name."

"I dare not! He will discover it, he will smite me down!"

"You can't really believe that." Matt's smile held a little contempt. "You know that most of the 'magic' he taught you was only trickery, don't you? And the few genuine spells are pretty feeble. I doubt very highly that he'll know if you tell me his name."

Banalix stared at him a moment, then whispered "Niobhyte" very softly.

The name meant nothing to Matt, but he couldn't let Banalix know that. "Very good. Now, tell me—what's your real name?"

The man flushed and looked away. "Jord," he said.

"Jord." It was a peasant's name. "And what did you do for a living before Niobhyte conned you away?"

"I was a serf on the estates of Lord Manerring," Jord said reluctantly.

Matt nodded. "Well, then, I would recommend you go back to your home village and stay there, at least until this is all over."

"I dare not!" Jord seized two branches and shook them, trying to break out. "Niobhyte will slay me if he learns I have failed and gone meekly home!" He shuddered. "And I will roast forever in Hell, for I have blasphemed and lured people away from God!"

Matt stared at the man a moment, then asked, "You mean you didn't believe a word of what you were telling those people?"

"I believed it," Jord told him, "but now that I have seen the power of the Old Gods so easily defeated, I can believe no longer!"

"So you fall back on the religion in which you were raised." Matt nodded. "Well, then, repent and confess your sins, and you should be safe from Niobhyte's power."

"But he is a sorcerer! A real sorcerer! Repentence will not save me!"

"It will save your soul, at least." Matt was beginning to have misgivings about having busted up Banalix's act—but could he really have let the man suck other people into the kind of tyranny he himself seemed to fear? "It might save your body, too, if you stay in the sanctuary of a church until this is all over."

Jord stared at him for a moment, then said, "Might."

"There are no guarantees in this life, I'm afraid," Matt told him, "especially when the country is in such upheaval. But I know a church that should be safer than most for the duration, and maybe when it's over, Niobhyte will have lost. If he has, he won't be in a position to hurt anybody."

Jord studied his face, realizing what he meant—what the options were for where Niobhyte would be. Finally he said, "I'll thank you, then, and hope. Take me to this church, and a priest."

"Okay, then." Matt grabbed a stout branch and stood up, heaving with all his strength. The trunk rolled, and Jord scuttled free.

He stared up at Matt, face pale in the moonlight. "You are as strong as a knight!"

"That's because I am a knight." Matt slapped him on the shoulder, turning him toward the village.

"A knight *and* a wizard? I've never heard of such a thing! Except for . . ." Jord's voice trailed off as his eyes widened and he realized to whom he was talking.

"Keep it to yourself," Matt told him severely. "We've got half a mile to cover, and I'd rather not attract any more attention than necessary."

A wind blew up out of nowhere, moaning in the treetops.

"Too late," Jord groaned. "Some spirit has heard me, or heard the name of . . . the Chief Druid. He is gathering his companions to punish me."

"You're reading an awful lot into a breeze," Matt snapped. "Come on, let's get going. Maybe we can beat the storm."

But it seemed to follow them, the wind moaning more and more loudly, though they didn't feel it at all. Tree branches began to whip about them, slapping at them from ahead in front, swinging at them from behind.

"No wind makes them move that way," Jord cried. "The spirits are coming for me!"

"Then let's give them a run for their money! Come on!"

But the moon darkened, and Matt began to feel as though someone was watching him—someone, or something. He hurried Jord along the trail, glancing up to see if he could catch a glimpse of the sky between whipping boughs. It was clear as a bell, stars bright in their scatter—but where the moon should have been was only darkness. Matt didn't know how Niobhyte had done it, but he was beginning to hope he wouldn't meet the man—if he was a man. Even more if he wasn't.

They hurried down the trail. Matt caught sight of things moving at the edges of his vision—huge dark forms, shadows within shadows, not clear enough to recognize. He thought he could make out roughly human shapes—head, arms, and legs—but wasn't sure; whenever he tried to look directly at one of them, he saw only darkness and brush. He muttered,

"From ghosties and ghoulies
And long-legged beasties
And things that go bump in the night,
Dear Lord, preserve us!"

Then the laughter began.

Low and ominous, it sounded behind them, and Jord started to run. Matt caught him, snapping, "No! Show fear and you put yourself in its power! Walk fast, but walk!"

They strode on through the darkness, setting a record for cross-country hiking, with the laughter building to the sides, then in front of them, finally echoing all about. Other voices joined in, laughing maniacally, gloatingly, insanely, giggling, gibbering, and the almost-seen shapes pressed closer, but seemed unable to touch them. Jord began to whimper, and Matt felt like joining him.

Then, suddenly, they were out of the trees with cottages before them. "Hurry!" Matt snapped, and they rushed down an alley between houses with the laughter slapping off the walls and the unfelt wind howling overhead.

"Can not the people hear?" Jord cried.

"I doubt it," Matt called back. "Besides, if you were safe inside a house and heard something like this, would *you* look out?"

"I am afraid to look out already," Jord whimpered.

Then they were out of the cottages and crossing the village green. Jord looked up, saw the church, and dug his feet in. "You're taking me to the priest I burned this afternoon!"

"He's human," Matt admitted, "but he's a priest, and he believes in forgiveness. Besides, I healed his burns. Move! Or do you want to stay here and wait for whatever's around us to close in?"

With a wail, Jord gave in and let Matt's arm pull him over the green and toward the waiting chapel. Matt still wouldn't break into a run, but he felt a presence following him, something bigger, something more powerful, something much worse than the half-seen night-walkers that shadowed them to either side. He muttered prayers under his breath, wondering if Banalix's mockery of a ceremony, and his own interruption, had wakened some form of elemental with which Niobhyte had nothing to do. They strode toward the church.

Mama and Papa came to the next town about noon—and a town it was, no mere village; they could see down the main street to shop after shop with the emblems of trade hung over their doors—a half-dried bush for the tavern, three gilded balls for the goldsmith's, a red-and-white-striped pole for the barber/surgeon, and so on. The church's steeple towered twice as high as that of any village chapel they had seen, and there were four two-storied buildings with their lower halves built of stone. As they neared the first hut a voice behind them shouted, "Make way! Make way for the Baron Fontal!"

They scurried to the side of the road just in time, for the baron and his score of men-at-arms weren't about to wait for anyone—they came galloping by, past Mama and Papa and into town.

Mama looked up indignantly as the last went by. "I know we are disguised as commoners, but the aristocracy could still have more respect for their people than that!"

"There is more to their hurry than arrogance." Papa clasped her hand, frowning. "Let us go quickly into this town, Jimena. I fear mischief."

Mama looked up at him in surprise. "I thought I was the in-tuitive in this pairing."

"You are, you are," Papa agreed, hurrying her down the road. "You have amazing intuition, my dear. I only have hunches. Come, let us hurry."

At least that explained their intuitive son. Mama sighed and did her best to match Papa's pace.

By the time they arrived at the town square, two of the men-at-arms were dragging a tradesman out of his shop while a crowd of his neighbors gathered—but at a wary dis-tance. The poor man bawled for help, and as Mama and Papa came up, another merchant told a small boy, "Fetch the priest, and quickly!"

The boy took to his heels as though his own life depended on it.

The men-at-arms slammed the tradesman up against the wall of his shop and held him pinned there while three others gathered around, looking menacing. Here and there in the crowd, a man tightened his hold on a staff or a flail, but a glance at the glowering men-at-arms still on horseback was enough to make him loosen his hold again.

"Now, Master Gilder," the baron said, "how is this? My steward tells me you refused his request for a loan of fifty pounds of gold, though it was given in my name!"

"Gold?" Papa turned to Mama with a frown. "He must be a goldsmith."

Mama nodded. "Who else would have such a sum?"

"But—But Your Lordship, I have given you such loans three times before!" the goldsmith protested.

"Nonetheless, I require it again," the baron said, his tone iron. "Do you dare tell me you fear I will not repay you?"

"I—I—" Gilder glanced at the halberd aimed at his middle and swallowed thickly. "What I fear, my lord, is the loss of my trade! I have only forty-three pounds of gold left, and if I give you that, I shall have nothing left with which to craft the ware I sell to make my living!"

"Then you shall have to do your smithing in silver," the baron grated. "I require the rest of your gold!"

"One side! One side!"

Everyone looked up, to see the village priest come panting up. He was a middle-aged man, a little portly, and his tonsure may have owed more to baldness than to a razor, but he looked to be as stalwart as any of the men-at-arms. His robe was charcoal-gray, but aside from that, he looked very much like any friar.

"How now, my lord!" he cried. "Do you seek to rob this poor man again?"

"Do not seek to catechize me, peasant!" the baron snarled. "I know far more of the world than any shave-pate."

The priest halted dead, staring, appalled by such disrespect. The crowd murmured, half in shock, half in anger. Then the priest's face darkened. "A peasant I may be, my lord, but I have learned to read and write, and know the law of God! I must insist that you leave off this theft!"

"Theft?" The baron turned his horse to the priest, a dangerous glint in his eye. "Do you call me a common thief?"

"Not common at all," the priest protested, "but still a thief, for you have had three loans from this goldsmith, and when have you ever repaid him an ounce?"

"He shall have his due in good time! I promise to repay, and therefore is it a loan, and no theft!"

"If it were not theft," the priest returned, "you would not need to do it at the point of a halberd. It is a direct breaking of the Seventh Commandment, my lord, and therefore a mortal sin! Worse, you threaten the poor man with harm to his body, and that breaks the Fifth Commandment! For the welfare of your immortal soul, I bid you leave off!"

"I am no Christian anymore, priest, and therefore do not fear your Christian Hell," the baron snarled.

The people burst into a babble of scandalized confusion. Mama and Papa stared at one another in shock, then turned back to the baron.

"No longer a Christian?" The priest seemed as shaken as any of them. "Surely you do not deny the existence of God!"

"Of the gods, say rather," the baron snapped, "for I have returned to the faith of my ancestors. My holy men now are druids, who tended the souls of this island before your kind came, and who will tend them again. And the Old Gods do not pretend that there is anything wrong with the strength of a man's arm or the edge of his sword! They bestow power and glory upon the warrior, and give him dominion over his fellows."

The priest recovered enough to glare. "Do you say that might makes right? If so, you are very wrong, and your immortal soul—"

"My immortal soul shall rule yours in the Land of the Dead!" the baron shouted. "Men of mine, I weary of this priest. Shut his mouth for me, and be sure he shall not speak again till I am done!"

Papa started forward, but Mama caught his arm and shook her head, then nodded toward the goldsmith's shop. Papa, understanding, nodded, and they faded back among the cottages, then moved behind them.

One of the men-at-arms advanced on the priest. The people, seeing his intention, closed ranks with a roar, barring the way between soldier and priest with their own staves and cudgels. The warrior hesitated, but only long enough for four of his fellows to join him. Then they plowed into the crowd, shouting battle-cries, and knocked peasants away to left and right. The priest stood his ground, glaring at them and holding up the crucifix on the end of his rosary—but a pike butt cracked his knuckles and made him drop it, and a second slammed against his skull, knocking him out.

"Now fetch out your gold!" the baron thundered at the goldsmith.

"Yes, my lord!" the man cried, almost tearfully. He glanced at his fallen priest with a piteous expression, then turned back into his shop. Two men-at-arms followed him closely.

In they came, and the goldsmith stopped short, staring. So, perforce, did the soldiers, seeing as he did the strongbox with the hasp and lock wrenched askew, turned on its side with its top thrown open, its emptiness for all to see.

Then the goldsmith ran to the chest with a piercing cry, dropping to his knees and running a hand around its inside. "It's gone! My gold is gone! While your lord howled and berated a priest, a thief came in and stole my gold!"

Mama and Papa found a woodlot a quarter of a mile past the town and hid in a thicket. They were just in time; ten minutes later the lord and his men came thundering by. When they were gone, Mama said, "We can bring the gold back when it has been dark for an hour."

"Yes, and check on the priest, too," Papa said. "I saw through the window how the soldier swung that pike. I don't think he gave the reverend a concussion, but you never can tell."

Matt and Jord were halfway across the green when the presence struck in the form of a sudden baying and tattoo of soft feet. Half a dozen huge dark forms swept past them and slowed to a halt in front of them, gray fur luminous in the starlight against the darkness of the night, teeth flashing a startling white in long muzzles.

"Wolves!" Jord raised his druid's staff, but the baying was behind them, in front of them, all around them.

"Back-to-back!" Matt snapped, drawing his sword. The wolves drew back at the sight of cold steel, giving Matt time to pivot and set his back against Jord's. At this slight sign of retreat, the wolves snarled and leaped.

Matt slashed, and dark blood spurted. Behind him, he heard Jord howling with fear, but also heard the staff knocking against skulls. He hewed and slashed and chopped. Wolves fell back, wounded, and their fellows turned on them with a massed barking snarl, but more pressed in. He slashed and hewed, but his arm began to feel heavy, tiring. He howled as teeth closed on his lower leg. He slashed, and the teeth sprang away, but more teeth soared at his face, and he barely managed to swing his sword around in time. The wolf fell back, but another sprang and bit his left arm. He screamed and lashed a kick into its stomach.

The massed snarl sounded behind him; he knew Jord had lamed one of the wolves, and the others were turning on it. It might give the false druid a moment to snatch a breath, but it was just a question of time—there were so many of the blasted animals! How could the whole forest have held so huge a pack?

Then something dark shot through the wolves, blurring with speed, and some fell. Their mates turned on them, snarling and fighting over them, but the shadow whizzed among them again, and more fell dead. The rest, finally scenting whatever it was, turned tail and ran howling with fear.

Matt let the tip of his sword fall, panting, unable to believe his luck. "They're running, Jord! We're safe!"

His answer was a raging scream. Matt spun again, sword snapping up, and saw the former druid facing him, staff swinging high to strike, his face contorted with fury, almost demonic.

Demonic! In a flash Matt understood the tactic. If Jord slew him, that ended the threat to the Chief Druid. If he slew Jord, the Devil had one more unshriven soul in Hell. Niobhyte or Satan, the goals coincided—to keep Matt and Jord away from that church. Somehow he knew it wasn't Jord himself who was in control of that body now.

He leaped back, sheathing his sword, and the staff whizzed by. Matt had to take it away, had to subdue Jord, but Jord was swinging the staff in a blurring circle now and howling.

Matt took a chance, lunging in a feint. The staff whizzed

down, and Matt darted back, not quite quickly enough—the staff cracked against his shin, the same leg that was bleeding from wolfbite. The leg gave way, and Jord screamed with triumph, swinging the staff high for a killing blow. His arms, his whole body, jerked forward—and jolted still. Behind him towered another dark form, holding the end of the staff. Not seeing it, Jord strained against it, cursing.

Matt snapped out of his daze and shouted,

> "The log was burning brightly—
> 'Twas a night that should banish all sin,
> And all evil spirits who with it
> Try to block goodness from men.
>
> "What! Would the spirit possessing
> Wrestle with power obsessing?
> Allies unseen all around us
> Shall strike with a strength to astound us!"

Suddenly the evil presence was receding; Matt could feel it speeding away. Jord's eyes rolled up; he went limp and fell, crumpled at the feet of the dark form, which instantly shot away, blurring with speed.

Matt stared after it, not understanding his sudden rescue. Apparently the dark form had nothing to do with the evil presence—of course not, if it had been trying to restrain Jord and had scattered the wolves.

But the presence was still there, distant, gathering strength again. Matt recited a quick healing verse:

> "Mad dogs and Englishmen
> Go out in the midday sun,
> But not a North American
> Whose task is still undone.
>
> Mad wolves and hydrophobes
> Go 'bout in the dark midnight,
> So also does their wizard foe,
> Healed of all their bites."

He could feel strength returning to his leg. Stooping, he managed to wrestle Jord's torso over his shoulder, then ducked his head under the man's midriff, gathered a wrist and a leg together, and heaved himself up, Jord over his shoulders in a fireman's carry. Turning, he saw a flame in the night, then realized it was on the steps of the church. He lurched toward it, carrying Jord and wondering who or what the dark blurring had been that had helped him.

As he went he heard noises gathering around him, the padding of huge feet stalking, approaching. He was about to run when barking and roaring broke out, the snapping and cracking of brush, the impact of a heavy body. He stumbled into a run, hearing huge claws tearing up the village green, coming closer and closer—but they ended in a scream of rage and the sound of blows, then the impact of something else huge.

Matt didn't stop to look, just lurched toward the church, blessing his unseen protector.

Suddenly, the feeling of the unseen presence was gone; suddenly he knew he was completely safe, and knew he had crossed the line of the warding circle he had laid himself, hours earlier. He lumbered up the steps of the church, panting and staring in amazement. "Friar Gode! How did you know we needed you?"

"There was a deal of noise following you," the friar answered. "I could not see who fought whom, but I prayed for those who love God to win."

"You may have helped more than you knew." Matt rolled Jord off his shoulders and laid him out on the stone step. "I'm about to put you to the test of your convictions, though, friar. Here's a man who needs your mercy."

Gode dropped to one knee, frowning down, then stared. "It is the false druid!"

"Yes, but he's seen the error of his ways," Matt said, "rather forcibly, too. He wants to repent—at least, he did before—" He swallowed, remembering the demonic face behind the swinging staff. "—before this happened."

The friar's face turned stern, but he said, "If he wishes to repent, he shall have his chance." He patted Jord's cheek gently. "Waken, brother! The night is long, but the day always comes! Waken, and tell me how your soul fares."

Matt looked up in surprise, and saw that the sky was indeed lightening. He wondered just how long he and Jord had been fleeing through that nighttime forest.

Eyelids fluttered; Jord peered upward, frowning against the pain in his head. Then he saw who bent over him, and stared in fear and horror.

CHAPTER 15

Jord shrank into a ball, hands up to protect his face. "Spare me! Forgo your revenge!"

"Why, so I shall," Friar Gode said. "Do you come to attack the church of God, or to pray?"

Jord peered over his hands, saw the gentle, grave expression on the friar's face, and lowered his guard. "I come to pray."

Something howled out there on the village green. Something else answered it, yammering in anger.

Jord cringed. "I come to pray! I come to repent! Save me, friar! Save me from the sharp white teeth in the night!"

Heavy panting sounded, coming closer, spreading wide on all three sides.

Jord seized the friar's robe and pulled himself up, crying, "Save me! A fury filled my soul only minutes ago, thirsting for blood, shooting agony through every part of me! My soul gibbers at the thought of being so possessed again! Save me from that horror, friar!"

"Why, so I shall." Gently, Gode pried Jord's hands loose and slipped a roll of cloth from his robe. He shook it out into a strip with a cross embroidered at each end, and placed it around his neck. Matt saw it was a stole, the badge of office that every Roman Catholic priest wears when he is administering the sacraments, the sign that he is functioning in his official capacity rather than his private one. The friar looked up at Matt. "Go farther off, goodman. I must see this man reconciled with God before he comes into the church."

Matt nodded and paced away, down the steps to just inside the invisible boundary of the warding circle. He stiffened, feeling the malignant presence return, towering over him,

221

ready to fall on him, but he stood his ground, glaring defiantly upward into the gloom. He never would have had the courage to do it in his own world, but he had plucked up the nerve to face his enemies in Merovence, and was knighted for his pains. With the knighthood had come far more bravery than he had ever known, so he could stand with narrowed eyes, trying to stare down a malignancy he could not see, even though he felt another gathering close to it on one side and a third on the other side, then another and another. But he stared unafraid, for he stood on consecrated ground bordered by his own warding circle.

He paced its arc, hearing behind him Jord's murmured confessing of his sins. Matt tried not to listen, not that he could have understood a word anyway—he was too far from them. The presences moved with him, and he realized it was himself they had come for, though if they did manage to over-whelm him, Jord and the friar would be engulfed right after him. He wished the former false druid would hurry up and finish his confession. He also began to understand why the Devil tempted people to desecrate holy places.

Then, somehow, the malignancy seemed to lighten. Matt turned to stare outward, wondering what had happened—and Buckeye stepped out of the gloom. "You could at least thank me for safe conduct."

Matt stared in amazement. "So it was you fighting off the monsters I couldn't see!"

"Yes, and you burned my hide for it," Buckeye said indignantly, and turned his back to show Matt a patch of singed fur. Matt swallowed, feeling horrible. "Sorry. I didn't know my helper was vulnerable to blessings. Look, at least I didn't say whose blessing I was calling for."

"Thanks for small favors," Buckeye sniffed.

Matt felt suddenly apprehensive—if the bauchan had been able to defy the invisible evil entities that surrounded him, it had to have stronger magic than he had thought. Matt hoped Buckeye didn't want to get back at him too badly. "Did you fight off the wolves, too?"

"Wolves!" Buckeye said with contempt. "They are nothing. Know that we creatures of the forest understand one an-other, mortal, and if I comprehend the viciousness of their packs, they in return know the danger of my magic and my whims. The night-walkers, now, they are another matter, but there is enough malice in me to let me walk among them, and enough goodness to shield me. Spirits fear one another, too, mortal man, and know one another's power."

"Standing up to them must have taken a lot of courage, then," Matt said.

Buckeye seemed to still inside, and for a moment there was nothing of the bantering or mischievous about him. "Some bravery, yes. I knew I could master any one of them, after all, but I could not be sure they would not league against me." Then the moment passed, and his grin flashed forth once more. "But they did not—they are creatures made solitary by their spite and jealousy, and will not ally with one another if they can avoid it. In this case, they were too slow to recognize necessity, as I had thought they would be."

"It was still taking quite a chance. Thank you for braving the risk. Were they sent by the Chief Druid?"

"Chief mocker, you mean, if you speak of Niobhyte," Buckeye said with contempt. "Nay. They were sent by an evil far greater than his."

"For Banalix, or me?"

"For you." The bauchan grinned. "They thought to frighten you away from the protections of—" He decided not to use whatever term he'd had in mind, and said instead, "—from your usual protections. They did not know that you had also the protections of a spirit far more earthly."

"Meaning yourself." Matt swallowed thickly. "Why did you help me?"

The bauchan shrugged. "I was bored, and it lent the night some interest. Besides, who would I have to torment if you were slain and I had not yet met your family?"

"I see," Matt said dryly. "You were defending your property."

The grin turned to a leer. "You might say that, yes."

Matt decided he'd better keep his bauchan amused. Then his heart sank as he realized he'd thought of it as "his."

"Goodman," Friar Gode called, "you may come back within."

"Coming," Matt answered, then turned back to Buckeye. "Thanks for bailing me out."

"I shall be glad to do so again." The bauchan's eye glittered wickedly. "If the whim should take me."

Matt was tempted to wish something else would take the creature, but he had the sense to throttle the thought, if not the feeling. He turned back to mount the church steps in the first rays of sunrise.

Matt found Jord inside the church, thoroughly chastened and gazing about him in disbelief.

"He is reconciled with God," the friar said by way of explanation.

Matt said to Jord, "You look as though you'd never been in a church before."

"All my life," the ex-druid returned, "until Nio—until the Chief Druid beguiled me away with tales of power and pleasure." A smile lightened his face for a moment. "They were true, too." Then he frowned again. "But he did not tell me what awaited failure." He shuddered. "I cannot say which was worse—those huge padding feet in the night, or the hoarse breathing of they who walked."

"The feeling of them inside your mind and heart," Matt told him.

"Aaiiee!" It was short, but it was a scream, and Jord buried his face in his hands. "Heaven protect me from ever suffering that again!"

Matt set a comforting hand on the man's shoulder. At least, it was meant to be comforting, but Jord gave such a start, Matt would have thought he'd been hit with a jolt of electricity. He took his hand away. "Don't worry, you're safe from them now, as long as you stay in here."

Jord calmed considerably, looking about him and drinking in the tranquility of the church. "None can come in here?"

"No spirits," Matt told him. "I made sure of that."

Friar Gode looked up at him, startled, but Matt gave him a wink.

Jord, though, had caught the qualification. "But things that are not spirits *can* enter?"

"Evil men can," Matt admitted. "There's always the chance of that. Whenever pagans come to loot, the church is one of the first places they look."

Jord shivered, but said manfully, "Even so, as you say,

there is always such danger. I must only hope that the Chief Druid and his followers dwindle and fade."

"They are the pagan threat of the moment, yes," Matt agreed. "The more we know about them, the more quickly we can rid ourselves of them. What can you tell me about this Chief Druid?"

Jord was silent and began to tremble again.

"Come on, you know he'll kill you just for losing the gamble to steal the friar's congregation," Matt said, "if he can. Help me make sure he can't."

"None knows where he came from," Jord said, his voice low, "but he speaks with the manner and accent of a lord."

That, Matt automatically discounted—such things could be learned, as any good con man would tell. "And he's a sorcerer?"

Jord shuddered. "Yes, a most powerful sorcerer! He taught us a few spells and promised us more, but we knew he would never teach us even half of what he knew."

"Us?" Matt picked up on the word. "Who?"

"The half dozen of us who sought to become druids in our own right, not acolytes only," Jord explained. "That's how we began, as a group of worshipers following Nio—his lead. He promised us power, and his glowing accounts of the power and luxury, the silken bodies in our arms and the acclaim of the crowds, swayed us all to become druids in our own right and go out to win more worshipers for the Old Gods. I have converted sixteen villages and four towns already." There was a touch of pride in his voice; then he remembered the preceding night, and hung his head. "No more."

Matt wondered how long Jord would stay repentant, how soon the memories of willing women and awe-filled men would sway him out to his own form of preaching again. He wondered, too, how long this Niobhyte would let him live. "He taught you what he claimed was the Old Religion?"

"Yes—the names of the gods; the symbols, such as the golden sickle, mistletoe, and holly; and the ceremony of worship, of drinking to free the impulses of the heart, dancing to please the gods, copulation, and bloodletting."

"Bloodletting, right. Completely voluntary, but when you have a congregation fully committed, the cuts go deeper and deeper and the blood flows more freely and less willingly, doesn't it?"

Jord nodded. "We have sacrificed eleven virgins and half a dozen young men already. Niobhyte says it pleases the gods."

"I'm sure it does, except that the only one he's really having you worship isn't a god," Matt said. "The old gods are only dreams, even in this—" He nearly said "universe," but caught himself in time. "—land. How does he say you should behave toward one another?"

"Why, that each man should strive for the highest position he can, and beat down those who seek to throw him out— strive also for wealth, and the favors of the greatest number of women."

Friar Gode's lips pressed into a thin, angry line. Matt felt the same way, but kept his voice reasonable. "How about if you want something someone else has?"

"Why, you should take it! If he is too weak to drive you away, he deserves to lose it!"

Matt nodded. "How about copulating with someone else's wife?"

"Again, if he is too weak to prevent you, it is the way of Nature, the way of the wildwood, and it is right." Jord's eyes began to glow with the power of it.

"How about if your wife wants to sleep with somebody else?" Matt asked.

"Slay her," Jord said promptly. "Him, too, if you can."

Gode cried out in protest, and Jord turned to him, instantly contrite. "Your pardon, holy man! I would not speak of such things, but this good man did ask."

"I know, and you must tell him," the friar groaned. "I, too, must know what the enemy teaches—but it is hard hearing of it."

"How do you behave toward other villages?" Matt asked.

"Why, you obey the King's Law—but if he bids you attack, you attack, whether it be another village or the land of Merovence!"

"Just happened to mention Merovence, I see."

"These are no teachings of the old gods, but of the Devil!" Friar Gode burst out.

Jord swung to him, surprised, but Matt said, "You figured that, too, huh?" Then to Jord, "The Chief Druid has told you to break every single one of the Commandments, except the one about the Sabbath."

"Oh, on Sundays we are to work while the sun shines, then drink and make merry when it sets!"

"Broke that one, too, I see," Matt said grimly, "and I don't think I have to ask what he taught you about using the name of God as a swear word. You do know who tempts you to do the opposite of what God teaches, don't you, Jord?"

Jord's eyes widened with horror. "It is as you say, it is as you say—he taught us to worship Satan! But why then did he not call the Devil by name?"

"Say it outright, and people would be warned, and stay away in fear and loathing," Matt explained. "Disguise it, and they'll listen. In the final analysis, though, you watch how they behave, and you'll know what god they really worship in their hearts." He felt rather uncomfortable saying it, thinking of people in his own world, but he knew that the vast majority of people were very easily fooled. He wondered if P. T. Barnum spoke of all the people in all the worlds.

He put the thought aside and got back to interrogation. "Since we mentioned the king, let's follow it up. What does King Drustan know about all this?"

"As little as you did before last night, I suspect," Jord answered, "though his son John is another matter."

"John?" Matt stared. "That incompetent loser? *He's* in on the druid scam?"

"I do not know what a 'scam' is, but I do know that John is a prince, and can aid the cause of the Chief Druid mightily," Jord answered.

"Especially since he's now heir apparent," Matt mused. "Maybe he's not as dumb as he looks."

"Dumb? He is not talkative, from all I hear, but he is scarcely mute," Jord protested.

"Less and less as we go along." Matt was revising his opinion of John by the second. "What does he have to do with your Chief Druid?"

Jord shrugged. "The friars and their fellow priests prevent

the tax-gatherers from gouging all they may from the peasants. They stand between the common folk, and the barons and soldiers who have won the king's war for him."

"Stand between? How?"

"Why, whenever the baron looses his soldiers to loot and rape, as is their pay for war, a dratted priest appears to command them to withhold in the name of the Lord!"

"Literally stand between." Matt felt a chill. "And John doesn't like that?"

"What prince would? How will he bring soldiers to his banner without expectation of such rewards?"

"Certainly not by the sheer generosity of his spirit, or nobility of his brow," Matt agreed. "John isn't the kind to command personal loyalty. So your Chief Druid made him an offer?"

Jord shrugged impatiently. "I know nothing of what passed between them, save that the Chief Druid disguised himself as a gardener, and thus found occasion to speak to the prince."

Matt grinned in spite of himself. "And boy, wasn't he surprised when one of his gardeners told him he could get rid of this nuisance problem of interfering clergy!"

"I expect that he was," Jord admitted. "Nonetheless, the long and the short of it is that Prince John was quite willing to give his support to the Old Religion if the druids could woo the people away from the Church. He could only pledge such in secret at first, but has promised to become more open as he gains influence, and to make the Old Religion the faith of the land if he comes to power as king."

Puzzle pieces fell together in Matt's mind. "So not only does he have a chance of actually becoming king someday— he has some help arranging it, and some definite plans!"

"With his brothers dead, it would seem so," Jord admitted.

"I know little of the druids," Friar Gode said, frowning, "but I cannot believe that any clergyman would so conspire to despoil his own flock!"

"I can't believe it, either," Matt said. "The real druids would never have approved of such behavior toward their own people. Enemies, maybe—conquered foemen are another matter—but not toward their own commoners."

"They did sacrifice people to their gods," Friar Gode reminded.

"Yes, but those were captured enemies, or volunteers from their own people, not kidnapped virgins! Besides, that ceremony I watched last night was pure hokum, with no higher object in mind than luring people to join up. I don't know much about the ancient druids' worship, but I do know it wasn't like that!"

Friar Gode nodded. "There is little that is real about these so-called druids."

"They're a synthesis of power-mongering ideas from this century, together with all the most popular human vices disguised as ceremony, mixed in with bits and pieces of Druid lore that everybody already knows about, so that the people will recognize the symbols and think the men are genuine druids," Matt said.

"Almost a mockery of them," Friar Gode said grimly.

Jord stared from one to another, more and more scandalized with every word he heard.

"Yes, a burlesque of the actual article," Matt agreed. "You might even say these synthodruids are a do-it-yourself religion. No matter what you call it, though, it's a great cover for a grassroots takeover by the forces of Evil. How can we fight them, friar?"

"By virtuous living, and thus setting a shining example before the people." Friar Gode spread his hands, at a loss. "How else, I cannot think."

"There is the possibility of telling the people what they're doing, by means of minstrels' songs," Matt said, "but I hesitate to think what might happen to those minstrels, and I'm not sure the people would believe them anyway."

"There are men and women far more holy than I," Friar Gode assured him. "Perhaps they can see how to counter this threat to the Faith better than a humble friar like myself."

"Well, holiness doesn't usually result in knowing how to fight," Matt said, "but I suppose that in the spiritual realm, a near-saint might have inspirations worth the listening. I don't know your country all that well, friar. Who do you think might be a good consultant?"

"There is the Abbess of the Convent of St. Ursula," Friar

Gode answered. "She is said to be very holy, yet a most redoubtable woman."

Well, Matt had his doubts as to how useful the abbess' holiness would be, but found her redoubts far more reassuring. "Best lead I've got, I guess, and asking her opinion can't do any harm. Thanks, friar—and thanks for the night's lodging, too."

"You are welcome." Gode managed a smile. "Not that you seem to have made much use of the latter." Then he frowned, concerned. "You have had no sleep, though. How shall you fare through the day?"

"Oh, I think I can keep going for a spell."

The doors opened, letting in a bright shaft of morning sun. "Lord Wizard?" Sir Orizhan asked. "Are you well?"

Jord's head whipped about; he stared at Matt as though he'd been betrayed.

"Of course," Matt said briskly. "Just because I'm up before sunrise doesn't mean I'm sick." Then his attention went to Sergeant Brock, beside the knight and very pale as he stared at Jord. "What's the matter, Sergeant?"

Brock gave a start, as though realizing where he was. "Is not this the druid who hurled a fireball at the friar yesterday evening?"

"I was." Jord bowed his head, ashamed.

"A druid, in a church?" Brock sounded scandalized.

"I have repented of my errors, goodman," Jord told him, "and confessed my sins."

That unnerved Brock even more than seeing Jord in the first place. He turned away, obviously agitated.

Sir Orizhan stepped close to confide, "I have seen this happen to soldiers before—discovering that their enemies are not always complete villains, and can even turn aside from their evil ways."

"It does give you a bad turn," Matt agreed, "having to revise your view of the world. I think he'll survive, though."

"I doubt it not," Sir Orizhan agreed. "Shall we break our fast, my lord?"

"I have meal and water, and can make a porridge quickly," Friar Gode offered.

Matt exchanged glances with Sir Orizhan, then turned to

the friar, nodding. "That ought to get us on the road fast enough. Thanks, friar—and maybe over a morning bowl we can talk about the route to the convent."

An hour later they started out, Matt with some misgivings. An abbess was an administrator, after all, and he was well aware that top administrators don't always rise to their positions because of virtue.

Toward noon a fourth person fell in with the three companions, slouching along beside them with his hood pulled up and his arms folded, with his hands in his sleeves. The trio stiffened, recognizing the bauchan.

Matt tried to be offhand about it, though. "Good morning, Buckeye. Thought you'd be sleeping it off."

The bauchan looked at him in puzzlement. "Sleeping what off, Lord Wizard?"

"Your night's fighting," Matt explained. "Mind you, I'm grateful, but I thought you'd need a rest."

Sir Orizhan and Sergeant Brock looked up, staring in amazement.

"He fought off some evil spirits for me last night," Matt explained, "not to mention a dozen or so wolves."

Knight and squire transferred their amazement to Buckeye.

The bauchan shrugged it off, uncomfortable with praise. "Remember that I'm a spirit more than an animal, wizard. I can manage without sleep quite well. But you have had none at all, and your mortal body must be dragging at you. What spell have you chanted to flush energy through your body?"

"I borrowed an hour of sleep from each of the next eight nights," Matt explained. "I'm probably better rested now than I'll be then."

Knight and sergeant swiveled their gazes back to him, staring harder.

"Your eyeballs are going to dry out if you don't blink now and then," Matt told them. Then, back to Buckeye, "So what brings you out to join us on the open road?"

"A beggar at the next crossroads," Buckeye told him. "I have gone ahead and seen that he will be of interest to you. Do not pass him by without a glance or a coin, wizard."

Matt gazed at him, wondering whether it was a booby trap

or a tip. "Trouble with you is, I never know when you're helping me or troubling me."

"I know." Buckeye grinned. "That's the delight of it. Take pleasure in your caution, mortal wizard." With a bound, he disappeared into the roadside brush.

"Surely we will not heed his words!" Brock protested.

"If it was good advice and we don't take it, he'll laugh his head off," Matt explained.

"The imp!" Sir Orizhan exclaimed. "He has us by the scruff, and he knows it! We dare not take his advice and dare not ignore it!"

"And he's chortling up his sleeve about it this very minute," Matt assured him. "Maybe that's why he wore clothes this time. Shall we see what's at the next crossroads, gentlemen?"

They came to the intersection. Matt stopped abruptly and cursed softly to himself.

Sir Orizhan and Sergeant Brock stared, too. The east-west road had been deliberately rerouted into an S-curve, so that it crossed the north-south road at a slant instead of a right angle.

"Prince John's taking the synthodruids a little too seriously," Matt said. "He's changed the intersection to avoid the form of a Christian cross."

"Could he really have so transformed every crossroads in the kingdom?" Sir Orizhan asked, staring.

"You can do amazing things with magic, if you have enough of it," Matt said grimly. "Come on—let's see who that beggar is, leaning against the signpost."

The beggar was a bit better outfitted than most—his clothes were dirty, but not yet reduced to rags; he hadn't been begging long. Matt stepped up, fishing in the wallet behind his belt for a silver penny. His shadow fell across the beggar, and the man looked up, holding out his bowl in listless routine. Matt froze. The eyes were dull, the face bleak, but he recognized it, and the last time he had seen the man, those eyes had been bloodshot from too much ale.

"Lord Wizard?" Sir Orizhan said behind him. "What troubles you?"

"I've seen him before," Matt told him. "So have you. We shared a table at an inn a week ago."

"It cannot be!"

But Sergeant Brock pushed past and knelt in front of the man, then rose with his face hard. "It is. When the soldiers were done with him, they cast him out to wander the roads and beg."

The dull eyes began to focus on them. The beggar frowned, trying to remember.

"Dolan!" Matt cried. "That was his name!"

The man stared up at him.

"What have they done to him?" Sir Orizhan whispered.

"Part of it is not so hard to guess." Brock gestured at a crutch lying beside the beggar. "He didn't need that when they took him away."

"They lamed him?" the knight exclaimed in horror. "For nothing but drunken mutterings?"

"Drunken mutterings against Prince John," Matt reminded him.

Brock knelt and looked into Dolan's eyes. "How did they lame you, fellow? You still have both your legs."

Dolan pointed to a large, dirty bandage on his ankle.

"His hamstring," Brock said, his face grim. "One or both?"

Dolan held up a single finger.

Sir Orizhan began to look apprehensive. "Why doesn't he speak?"

For answer, Dolan opened his mouth and made a sort of cawing. His lips writhed, trying to mold the sound into words and failing.

"He spoke against the prince, after all," Matt said quietly. "They gave him the punishment they thought fitted the crime."

"His tongue?" Sir Orizhan turned green.

Even Sergeant Brock rose and turned away. "It would have been kinder to kill him outright!"

"Yes, it would," Matt said, "but he wouldn't have been able to go hobbling through the land as a walking warning to anyone who might be thinking of criticizing Prince John." At a sudden thought, he looked up, then relaxed. "For a minute there I was afraid I might find a raven listening."

"No fear," Sir Orizhan told him. "All the carrion eaters are in royal castles now."

Matt tossed the silver penny into the begging bowl even as he said, "We can't just leave him here."

"We surely cannot take him with us!" Sir Orizhan protested. "We'd scarcely make a mile a day!"

"Oh, I think we can move a bit faster than that." Matt knelt and clasped the beggar's shoulder. "Dolan, I hereby adopt you! Sir Orizhan, Goodman Brock, you're my witnesses—from this day forth, this man is my cousin!"

"A mere beggar?" Sir Orizhan stared. "Have you taken leave of your senses, my lord?"

"Not a bit." Sergeant Brock grinned. "After all, the poor lad is in need of help, if ever a man was. Surely he is in no condition to suffer pranks."

"No, he's not," Matt agreed, and stood up to call, "Oh, Buckeye! There's somebody I'd like you to meet!"

CHAPTER 16

The bauchan came out of the trees, looking very surly indeed. "I heard, wizard! It's a foul trick to play upon me!"

"Hey, you were the one who told me to take notice of him," Matt reminded. "Buckeye, I'd like you to meet my cousin Dolan. Dolan, meet the family curse."

"This is beneath you, wizard," the bauchan complained. "He is not of your blood and bone!"

"All people are ultimately related," Matt said smugly, "and for the time being, he's a legal relation, too." He turned to his companions. "Shall we go, gentlemen?"

Sergeant Brock opened his mouth to object, then remembered that he'd been raised to the rank of squire.

"Yes, let us walk," Sir Orizhan agreed. "Did not the friar say we should turn west at this crossroads?"

"West it is." Matt followed the S-curve to the left, with the knight and squire beside him.

"Well, there's no help for it then," Buckeye grumbled. "Come, mortal, up with you!" He caught the beggar by the waist and swung him high. Dolan squalled with fright and swung his crutch up as a club—but the bauchan settled the man around his own neck and started after the companions, assuring the beggar, "Fear not, I can carry ten times your weight. You have naught to fear from me—but I'll be revenged on that wizard ten times over!"

"I'm not keeping score," Matt called back.

"*I* am," Buckeye growled, and hurried to catch up, stretching his legs—literally.

Night caught them in the midst of open fields without a village in sight. As they set about pitching camp, Sergeant Brock muttered, " 'Just one more village, Sir Knight! Surely there will be another inn only a few miles down the road, good sergeant! Just one more, lads, one more!' "

"Oh, stop grousing," Matt told him. "I thought soldiers were supposed to be used to roughing it."

"When they travel with *you*, they are."

"Hey, you've had dinner indoors three nights out of five on this trip."

"Yes, but have we been able to stay and sleep? No, for we are four when we set out with three!"

"Careful, there—Buckeye is positively gloating to hear you." Matt told himself the sergeant would feel better with a good hot meal inside him.

While it was cooking, he rummaged in his pack for a scrap of parchment and pulled a stick of charcoal from the fire. Then he sat down next to the beggar and said, "Time we did something about your communication problem. If I make a mark like this, it means I'm supposed to make a sound like this: duh. And this circle means I'm supposed to say 'oh.' Then this boot-shape tells me to say 'luh,' and this backward potbelly is either 'eh' or 'uh.' " He saw the question in Dolan's eyes and said, "How can you tell which sound? I'll explain later, when you've learned more letters. This sign is 'en.' Now, see what happens when I make all those sounds, one after another . . ."

By the time the partridges were roasted, Dolan was silently mouthing all the letters of the alphabet, eyes round in wonder.

"What silliness is this, to put so much store by chicken tracks on sheepskin?" Buckeye sniffed.

"Aye," Sir Orizhan agreed, "and to show a man how to turn squiggles into speech when he can no longer talk."

"But he knows what the words are supposed to sound like," Matt pointed out. "He can still write out the words he wants to say, if he can just learn the symbols—and if anybody ever had motivation for it, he has."

"It's a fool's task, to spend so much time learning to do so little!"

"It's not little," Matt protested, "and I'll bet he'll be able to write complete sentences in five days."

"Five for the symbols at your door," Buckeye snorted, and disappeared into the forest.

Matt had the right number but the wrong unit. Five hours later Dolan was writing complete sentences and working out a system of sign language with Sergeant Brock, too. When he had a large enough vocabulary, he told the sergeant a long pantomime, and Brock came away looking pale and shaken.

"What did he tell you?" Matt asked, concerned.

"What the soldiers did to him," Brock answered, and swallowed thickly. "It was my own fault—I asked. Let us hope I have not given the poor fellow nightmares by dredging up his memories!"

"Maybe," Matt said slowly, "but maybe not, too. Sometimes it helps to talk it through, get it out of your system. Just how bad was it?"

"As bad as anything I've ever heard," Brock told him, and looked up at Sir Orizhan. "They tied him down on the rack for a day or two, and when it had stretched his joints to constant pain, they demanded the names of those who had told him what he had blurted out. Poor lad, he'd been so drunk that he could not even remember what he'd said. They did a dozen things to cause him more pain, and by your leave I'll not repeat them—but I will say that they brought in a sorcerer to work a spell with some of his blood, which wrenched his memories from him with blinding pain. His head ached horribly for days. Then, when they had proved for themselves that he knew no other names of folk who had spoken ill of the prince, they muted him and lamed him as we see, and cast him out to live or die, they cared not which."

"A sorcerer?" Matt said sharply. "Not a druid?"

Brock gave him a long, steady look, then said, "I shall ask." He turned away to his pack.

Sir Orizhan watched him go, frowning. "How can he ask if the man was a druid, if Dolan has never seen one?"

"His armed band raided a druid sacrifice," Matt said, watching Brock. "He kept a souvenir."

Sir Orizhan's eyebrows lifted in surprise; then he turned to watch.

Brock went over to Dolan and held up his little silver sickle. The beggar frowned at it, puzzled. Brock made some gestures, and Dolan replied with an emphatic shake of his head. Brock gestured again, and Dolan shook his head again.

Then Brock made a third set of gestures, and Dolan's face went stony as he nodded.

Brock nodded, satisfied, and came back to his companions. "The man who tortured him did not wear one of these at his belt." He held up the sickle. "Moreover, he laid his spell in a chant that chopped and ground like a mill. The druids' magic tongue flows like a clear brook; I've heard it."

"So the sorcerer used a language that was full of gutturals and consonants, huh?" Matt filed the information away for future use. "What did he nod about?"

"That the sorcerer wore a dark robe with strange signs emblazoned on it. The druids wear white, as you have seen."

"So Prince John is resorting to sorcery," Sir Orizhan said grimly.

"Resorting to, yes," Matt pointed out. "He's got the synthodruids on one side and sorcerers on the other—but he isn't adept enough to do the magic himself, so he has to bring in specialists. I'll bet he doesn't even know how to use them, but has a sorcerous adviser pulling his strings."

"But you said he was in league with the Chief Druid," Brock pointed out, confused.

"I did, didn't I?" Matt said with an acid smile. "Apparently he's trying to play both ends against the middle, sorcerers on one side and synthodruids on the other. What's going to happen to him when they both demand their payoffs?"

The three were silent a moment. Then Sir Orizhan ventured, "Can he truly believe he can set them to fighting one another and himself emerge unscathed?"

"Sounds dumb enough to believe of him, yes," Matt said. "Or it could simply be that he hasn't thought that far ahead. He probably thinks that if he can just get to be king, he'll have power over everybody."

"And while he waits, the false druids and the sorcerers shall tear the land apart between them," Sir Orizhan said grimly.

Sergeant Brock's face set like stone.

Mama and Papa were hiking along the high road when Mama suddenly stopped. She laid a hand on Papa's arm and pointed at a lane that branched off, overhung by tree limbs, a virtual tunnel. "We must take that byway."

Papa looked at it. "Why, my dear? It doesn't look very promising."

"I can't say why, I only know we must," she answered.

"I will never argue with your intuition, especially in a universe ruled by magic." Papa turned off with her, and they strolled under the leafy roof. He looked up and about with a dreamy smile. "If nothing else, you have chosen a pleasant route for us."

"There is that." Mama pressed his arm close, smiling.

Then they heard the hound.

It was a strange cry, more howl than bay, and it sent chills down their spines.

"Hurry!" Papa clasped her arm more tightly and started ahead.

But Mama pulled back. "No! We must hide instead!"

Papa reined in impatience and exasperation and tried to speak reasonably—but before he could, he heard the sound of hooves approaching with the baying. "You're right—we can't outrun horses. We hide!"

Mama found a small thicket and pushed her way through the underbrush. Papa came after her, walking backward and doing what he could to erase the signs of their passage. Then he lifted his staff to guard position, with the sick feeling that comes with knowing the battle is lost before it has begun— but behind him, Mama drew her wand from beneath her robes.

The howl-baying passed the junction with the main road, though, and kept on going. The hooves thundered up, mixed with the shouting of men's voices, then faded away.

Papa let out a long shaky breath as he dropped the butt of his staff. "They're chasing someone else, poor soul!"

"No," Mama snapped, "they are chasing us—don't ask me how I know! It was only this turnoff that deceived them, but their hound will realize he has lost the scent all too soon! Quickly, husband! There is safety at the end of this road, if we can only come there soon enough!" She pushed her way out of the thicket and hurried down the lane.

Papa caught up with her. "What sort of safety?"

"I do not know, but I have never had presentiments so strong as this before! Walk as quickly as you can, and we may come safely through it!"

But twenty minutes later they heard the howling behind them again.

"Quickly, walk backward as much in our own footprints as you can!" Papa turned and retraced his steps.

"Are you mad?" But Mama caught up with him anyway. "You are going toward danger!"

"Only ten minutes or so! I have seen another hiding place! Come!"

A few minutes back on the trail, they came to a low-hanging branch. Papa made a stirrup with his hands. "Up with you!"

Mama knew better than to protest. She stepped in Papa's hands and caught the branch, then scrambled up as he lifted her foot higher. Lying full-length on the limb, she reached down for his hand. He leaped up with her help and caught the wood; she scrambled back to make room for him to lie full-length, surrounded by leaves.

They were barely in time. The howling swelled immensely, and the hound came charging by below, following their scent. It was a huge misshapen thing, with a face like a mastiff's behind the upper muzzle of a bloodhound, and legs as bandy as a bulldog's but as long as a Great Dane's. Its massive body was easily the size of a small pony, and its eyes burned with blood lust. It went past below, belling and baying and howling as though it were three beasts in one. Behind it came half a dozen soldiers, their eyes afire with the excitement of the hunt, their faces lit with gleeful anticipation. Mama looked at them and shuddered.

But the last was several lengths behind his fellows, for he was much fatter, and wheezed as he urged his horse onward. As he passed under the limb, Papa dropped to land behind him and struck with the hilt of his knife. The man slumped, eyes rolling up, and Papa shoved him aside. He fell, rolling to the side of the trail, and Papa caught the reins. The horse whinnied in fright, but Papa spoke to it in soothing tones, turned it around and brought it back, then off the side of the trail.

Ahead, the hound's belling turned into burbles of confusion. The horsemen cursed, and there was a sound of beating. The hound howled in anger, then yelped in pain, finally coming back toward them, bay-howling again.

Papa turned the horse into the brush beside the road, behind a screen of leaves, then leaped down and ran around to hold the horse's head and stroke its nose, murmuring soothing nonsense to keep it from whinnying.

The hound came charging by, following their back trail, baying as though it were new. The horsemen rode by, cursing, and Papa and Mama caught a single sentence: "Cursed magicians laid us a false trail!" Then they were gone again, not even noticing their fallen comrade under the roadside leaves, and too quickly for the horse to even think of calling to its fellows.

Papa remounted, rode out onto the trail and back to the low-hanging limb. "Quickly, Jimena! Before they realize their error!"

Mama leaped from her perch and ran to him, grasped his arm and swung up to ride in front of him. Papa turned the horse and kicked its sides gently. It sprang into motion again, galloping away down the lane.

Far behind them the belling grew fainter—for a few minutes. Then it turned into confusion again, mixed with angry shouting for several minutes, before the hound yelped as the men drove it back into the lane, and its voice began to grow louder again.

"What kind of hound is this, who can follow our scent even on horseback?" Papa asked.

"One who senses magic and those who work it," Mama told him, "and I hate to think where it came from!"

"I used magic as we were laying the false trail!" Papa exclaimed in surprise.

"So did I! Ride as quickly as we can, husband, and pray they go more slowly!"

Then suddenly the trail opened out into fields. In the distance the amber and green of crops surrounded the low beige walls of a convent or monastery, golden in the late afternoon sun.

"There is the safety I sensed!" Jimena cried. "Ride, husband, for our lives!"

But the poor horse was carrying double, and no matter how Papa urged it on, it couldn't go as fast as the steeds chasing them. Behind them the howling and hoofbeats grew louder.

"Hist!" Sir Orizhan stopped, holding up a hand, and frowned, looking back over the road they had traveled.

They were all silent, listening. Then Dolan's eyes widened, and he nodded vigorously, beginning to tremble.

"He hears it, too, whatever it is," Matt said.

"So do I." Buckeye grinned. "It is a kind of hound that sorcerers breed, half spirit and half dog."

Matt shuddered. "What's it for?"

"Tracking magicians!" Buckeye crowed.

"I think we'd better start walking faster." Matt turned eyes front and made long strides.

Sir Orizhan matched him. "We might even consider running."

"Run for a minute, walk for a minute," Matt agreed. "Can you keep up, Buckeye?"

"Keep up, forsooth!" the bauchan snorted. "I can surpass you in this as in all things! Hold tightly, Dolan!" He sprang ahead of the companions.

Matt loped after him, not hurrying.

"Dare we let him escape our sight?" Sir Orizhan asked beside him.

"We dare," Matt answered. "The question is, does Dolan? And I think the answer to that is, he'll get to safety first."

"What safety?" Sergeant Brock panted.

"The convent," Matt explained. "We're assuming it has a guest house—and if these hunters are anything like the usual run of evil spirits, they won't be able to enter consecrated ground."

"True enough," Sir Orizhan said, with some relief.

But Sergeant Brock panted, "What if . . . the hunters . . . are men?"

"Then only the hound will be stuck outside the wall," Matt said grimly, "and we may have to do a bit of fighting ourselves."

Sergeant Brock grinned and loosened his short sword in its sheath.

" 'May,' I said," Matt cautioned. "I didn't make any promises."

"You deal with . . . evil magic," Brock panted. "We shall deal . . . with evil . . . men. Sir Knight?"

"We shall indeed," Sir Orizhan said, matching Brock's grin.

They stopped to walk for a minute, then ran on toward the convent.

Suddenly, hooves pounded behind them.

"Run!" Matt shouted, and stretched his legs for all he was worth—but the horse was galloping, and caught up with them easily. Dolan waved down at them from its back, looking frightened. One hand held reins, the other held the cantle of the saddle to hold him on—and the reins of a second horse that galloped beside the first.

Matt stared. "How'd *you* get behind us?" Then he answered his own question. "No, don't answer. Silly of me. You were riding a bauchan."

"Pull back on the reins!" Sir Orizhan called. Dolan dutifully obeyed, and the horses slowed enough for Sergeant Brock to run around and catch the reins of the riderless mount while Sir Orizhan caught Dolan's. They stopped the horses and mounted, Sir Orizhan behind Dolan, Matt behind Sergeant Brock. Sir Orizhan kicked his heels into the horse's flanks, Sergeant Brock did likewise, and off they went.

"I should ask what happened to the men who were riding these horses," Matt called, "but I don't think I want to know."

Dolan shook his head emphatically.

"Ride!" Sir Orizhan commanded. "If these horses have caught us, the others cannot be far behind!"

"Yes they can," Matt called back. "These two knew where they were going. The hunters still have to follow the hound."

"It will speed soon enough," Brock called grimly.

True enough, the hound's bell-howling was growing louder and louder. Matt chanced a glance back and saw a dust cloud with several horses coming out of it, a strange, ungainly beast loping ahead of them—ungainly, but moving even more quickly than they were. He shut up and let the sergeant kick the horse up into overdrive.

"I thought troopers weren't allowed to ride," he called to Sergeant Brock ahead of him.

"We are not," Brock called back, "but not for lack of knowing. Any serf's son learns how to ride a plow horse."

They came out of the woods and into a broad plain, cut into a patchwork of fields with a variety of crops, including pastures dotted with sheep. At its center, far ahead, rose the tawny walls of the convent.

"Ride!" Matt shouted. "Safety's in sight!"

Then he saw the other horse off to their right with two riders on its back, riding hell-bent for leather—and saw the hell-bended hound behind, running at its top speed, leading half a dozen riders who shouted with glee as they chased. Looking back at his own pursuers, he heard the same sort of shouts—and noticed that the soldier in front had his hood up. He seemed much more gangly than the rest, knees up as high as the saddlebow. Matt deleted an expletive under his breath. Buckeye was leading the pursuit, howling with glee.

Matt undeleted the expletive. "Blasted monster can't decide whether he's for us or against us!"

"What monster?" Sergeant Brock looked back, then swore as only a soldier could, something involving a physiological impossibility and the questionable ancestry of the bauchan. But he recovered enough to say, "Be sure he'll not let them slay you, milord, for who then would he have to torment?"

"Don't say that word 'torment,' " Matt told him. "There's a lot they can do without killing me." He didn't add that the soldiers might treat the rest of the party to a few quick sword strokes.

Fortunately, the humans weren't the only ones the hound scared. The horses heard that howl-baying growing louder and stretched themselves even harder. Somehow they seemed to understand that the beige walls ahead meant safety, and redoubled their pace.

Atop the wall, several black-robed figures appeared. One looked up to Heaven and raised her clasped hands in prayer. The others imitated her.

Matt glanced over at the other travelers and saw that their hunters were gaining, too. Of course, it would be too much to hope for that the two packs might collide . . .

Not with a bauchan with a twisted sense of humor leading one of the groups, it wasn't. The two roads joined a hundred yards from the gate, and the other travelers galloped through the intersection just a few feet ahead of Matt's party—and as he came alongside he stared in amazement. "Mama! Papa!"

The two riders looked up, astonished, and cried with one voice, "Matthew!"

Then the two groups of hunters howled with triumph—and crashed into one another.

They bawled and cursed and bellowed, slashing at one another with short cavalry swords, while the two hounds sprang to fight with explosive barks, each trying to sink its teeth into the other first.

Buckeye broke loose from the melee and shouted, "Ride!" He even ran after to slap the rumps of all three horses before he turned back to dive into the churning mass again.

He was just in time, too. The leader of one group saw who he was fighting and shouted, "We are king's men!"

"We are reeve's men, under the prince's orders!" his opposite number answered, and they might have made peace there and then if Buckeye hadn't reached up and clobbered one of them in the kidneys. The man howled with pain and yelped, "Call off your men!"

"Lay off!" the other leader shouted, just before Buckeye stretched an arm to rabbit-punch him. "Yowoo! I thought you called for peace!"

And the two groups set upon each other again, hammer and tongs, short swords clashing on bucklers and steel caps. Buckeye danced around and through the dust cloud, timing his punches perfectly to keep them fighting one another.

The gates of the convent opened wide just in time for all three horses to gallop through, then swung shut again. A team of nuns hefted a huge bar into the brackets on the backs of the gates, and Matt turned in the saddle to throw his arms around his parents. "Thank Heaven you made it!"

"And you, my son," Mama said, returning the embrace, then holding Matt off at arm's length. "Thank Heaven indeed."

"Aye, thank Heaven," said a severe voice.

They looked up to see an older nun coming down off the

wall toward them, eyes flashing. "Who are you, who come unbidden to the Convent of St. Ursula?"

"At least we've got the right address," Matt told Sir Orizhan, then, "Matthew Mantrell, Lord Wizard of Merovence, with Lord and Lady Mantrell, my parents—" He gestured to his mother and father, then to his companions. "—and Sir Orizhan, knight of Toulenge, with his squire, Sergeant Brock of Bretanglia. This other gentleman is Dolan, an unfortunate who has suffered at the hands of Prince John's torturers."

Dolan and Brock pulled their forelocks; Sir Orizhan bowed as well as he could from the saddle.

"And whom have we the pleasure of addressing?" Matt asked.

"I am Mother Diceabo, abbess of this convent. Do you claim the right of sanctuary?"

"We do!" all six of them chorused.

Then Sergeant Brock said nervously, "By your leave, lords and ladies, may we put off the courtesies till we have done with the attackers at your gates?"

"Attackers!" Mother Diceabo exclaimed. "Have they not left off once they saw you were safe?"

In answer, five howling soldiers leaped over the wall—only eight feet high, no bar to a horseman who could stand on his saddle and vault over it. Most of the nuns screamed and ran—for quarterstaves piled in a cone by the gate. Each grasped her stick and turned to face the invaders.

But Sir Orizhan and Sergeant Brock were there before them, spurring their horses and shouting war-cries. Dolan hung on for dear life.

Sergeant Brock turned a cut from a foeman, then whirled his sword in to thrust, but the enemy blocked it with his buckler, swinging his sword up for another strike. Matt leaned around Brock and thrust at the unarmored line between breastplate and hip. He couldn't reach very far, but it was enough to make the soldier scream and clap his hand over his gut. Brock drove his hilt down, but the man was already clawing his way back over the wall.

Sir Orizhan turned his horse and swung a cut at another soldier, knocking the man's sword aside. The soldier howled and ran for the wall. Behind the knight, swords clattered against quarterstaves and the other soldiers ran bleating for the wall, dropping their blades as they ran.

Matt stared as they leaped back over—it had been too easy. He darted a glance back at his parents and saw why—Papa was gesturing and muttering while Mama sat ready to fight off any return spells. Matt wondered what the soldiers had thought they were seeing.

"Are they repulsed so easily?" Mother Diceabo declared in astonishment.

"I doubt it," Matt answered.

Sir Orizhan sprang up to the low parapet to look over and report, "They are riding to the gate . . . They are turning their horses' backs to it . . ."

"They're going to try to have the horses kick down the gate!" Matt cried. "Get 'em away from there!"

One of the nuns started chanting and gesturing as though she was swatting flies.

The horses reared with whinnies of anguish and shot away from the gates, bucking and rearing. The soldiers shouted, barely managing to stay in their saddles, and fought their horses back down, then managed to quiet them—a hundred yards from the convent.

Matt looked up in surprise. "You have some talented people among your nuns, Mother Diceabo."

"More importantly, they are pious," the abbess replied tartly. "Even I prayed for your safe arrival."

"I can't thank you enough." Matt wondered what Buckeye would say if he knew he had been part of the answer to a nun's prayer.

"They are putting their heads together in conversation," Sir Orizhan reported. "One is riding away . . . The rest are dismounting . . . They are picketing their horses . . . Most are sitting down, some lying, though one stands sentinel . . ." He looked down at Matt. "They have given up assaulting us, it seems—and I would guess the one who has ridden away has gone for aid."

"Surely they would not bring an army against a House of God!" Mother Diceabo protested.

"Maybe not an army, but probably a sorcerer," Matt said, his voice hard, "at least, as long as we're here. I'm sorry,

Mother. I hadn't meant to bring them upon you. There have been a few changes in Bretanglia lately." Matt dismounted. "Let me tell you about them."

"Lord Wizard," Sir Orizhan said, his voice tense, "I think you should—"

Matt didn't wait for the end of the sentence.

CHAPTER 17

Matt remounted and clambered up on his saddle, just in time to see that one of the soldiers had come to his feet and was strolling toward the convent—but as Matt watched, the man threw off his livery and spun about in a furry fury. With a gibbering cry, he stretched out his arms, forearms whirling in expanding circles as he rushed back at the soldiers.

They didn't wait for him to arrive—they wailed in terror and ran for their horses. They were just in time, barely managing to throw themselves into the saddles before the beasts reared, pulling up their picket-stakes, and raced away, any way as long as it took them far from the insanely howling monster who rushed at them.

"You don't have to worry about the soldiers anymore," Matt informed Mother Diceabo. "They seem to have remembered an urgent appointment somewhere else."

The abbess frowned. "What could have driven them away?"

"Something that I had better thank." Matt cupped his hands around his mouth and called, "Much appreciate, Buckeye! I couldn't have done it without you!"

"If you were truly grateful, you would invite me in," Buckeye called as he strolled back.

Somehow that rang a warning bell in Matt. "I can't," he explained. "It's not my house, and besides—"

"I know, I know—you speak words of gratitude, but do not mean them." The bauchan sauntered up to the gate—then recoiled, hopping about as though he'd burned his toes. "Avaunt! What sort of town is this in which you've taken refuge?"

"A convent," Matt called, trying to sound as apologetic as possible. "Consecrated ground. Sorry—I tried to warn you."

"Next time, I'll believe you." The bauchan kept hopping. "Oh! Ow! How long mean you to stay?"

"A night, if they'll have us," Matt told him. "Not long enough for those soldiers to bring back an army."

"You need not fear—I'm sure they'll think 'twas an evil spirit chased them, and will not be concerned about you if you're in a house of ill. Oh! Ah! Oh, I shall be revenged when you come out of that place! Owoo! Ooo!" And Buckeye went hopping off into the distance until he hit a dip and the ground seemed to swallow him up.

Matt turned back to see Mother Diceabo eyeing him narrowly—but all she said was, "I would appreciate it if all you men would enter our guest house immediately." She nodded to Mama. "I shall explain matters to you, milady, and you may discourse with them."

"Of course," Mama said, then dismounted and waved her hands at the men. "Away with you, now! Leave civilized people to talk!"

Matt led the way toward the building she indicated, growling, "So men aren't civilized?"

"Not according to women," Papa replied. "They have a point, son. Think about the lives most men would lead if they had a clear choice."

Matt thought about that as they entered the guest house.

Mother Diceabo was right behind them, already talking with Mama. They kept on talking as they sat around a plain plank table on hard wooden benches, though the abbess brought them a pitcher of mild ale and wooden mugs with her own hands.

"So the Prince Gaheris is murdered, and Prince Brion slain in battle," she said, "while the poor queen is jailed in a silken prison—and the king lies elf-shot, unable to speak to any but Prince John! Can you have any doubt who is behind it all?"

"When you put it that way, it does look pretty bad for him," Matt admitted. "Trouble is, there're a lot of other things going on in the kingdom."

"Indeed?" The abbess fixed him with a penetrating stare. "What sort of things?"

"The barons and their men have lost respect for the clergy," Mama told her. "The farther north we came, the less the friars could protect their folk from the ravages of their own lords."

"Say you so?" The abbess' stare swung to her. "Have they lost all thought of God and goodness?"

"They have," Matt told her, "because a very powerful sorcerer has cobbled together a parody of the Druid cult and is spreading it throughout the land."

The abbess' stare swiveled back to him, appalled. "How can this be?"

"Yes," Mama said, staring with Papa. "How can it?"

"Because his apprentice synthodruids are leading the people in wild, drunken parties disguised as worship services," Matt said, avoiding the abbess' eyes, "with all the, ah, vices that go with drink and wildness."

"You cannot mean—" The abbess broke off, shaking her head. "Can the land have sunk so low?"

"If it sinks any more, the sea will come rushing in between Bretanglia and Merovence," Matt said grimly.

"And Prince John is leagued with this self-styled Chief Druid," Sir Orizhan told her.

"Is he!" The abbess turned her stare on him. "Did I not say the whole coil was of his making?"

Well, she hadn't quite come right out and said it. "I think Prince John might be more of a victim," Matt demurred, "one more person lured in by the lies of the sorcerer, lies that he's scattering over the land like seeds broadcast."

"How can he do that?" the abbess demanded.

"Minstrels are abroad, singing a song that impugns the queen's reputation and claims that Brion was illegitimate," Mama said.

Matt turned to her, surprised, though he realized he shouldn't be. He'd heard the song twice himself; surely his parents had, too.

"A vile slander!" the abbess cried. "All know she has been a model of virtue since she married Drustan!"

"Since then, yes," Papa agreed, "but there seems to be some doubt about her standards before—and therefore after."

"Aye, to those of foul minds! Why, Brion is the very image

of his father, though one much purified! If any should be suspect in parentage, it should be John!"

"Shh! Not so loud!" Matt gave a quick scan of the windows and rafters.

"Aye," Papa agreed. "The sorcerer has sent ravens abroad as spies, throughout the countryside."

The abbess' eyes narrowed. "Carrion eaters were ever birds of ill omen!"

"If they hear anybody talking against John, they bear word to the soldiers somehow," Matt said, "and the soldiers come to arrest the poor talker."

Dolan shuddered, drawing the abbess' eye. "Were you one such?" she asked.

Dolan nodded.

"Poor lad!" she said. "He lamed you for it. What else?"

Dolan opened his mouth and cawed in answer.

The abbess turned away with a shiver. "There is evil in the land indeed!" She turned to Mama and Papa. "But why come you here, to the House of St. Ursula?"

"Good question," Matt agreed. "I thought you two were staying in Bordestang to defend Alisande and your grandchild."

"The war in Bretanglia made your wife see that the threat to Merovence was ended, at least for the time being," Papa said. "We offered to go north to learn more of what passed there."

Matt sighed. "So much for my plot to keep you home and safe."

Papa answered with a wolfish grin.

"Why here?" the abbess pressed.

Mama shrugged. "We have gone north by the byways, my lady abbess, to visit the small towns and villages and learn what the people say. When the hunters caught our scent, we fled, and I felt that safety lay in this direction."

"Our patron saint spoke to your soul," the abbess told her. "You must be devout, or your spirit would not have hearkened to the warning. What did you do to catch the hunters' interest?"

Mama and Papa exchanged a blank look. Then Mama told the abbess, "We saved a village lass from soldiers long enough for the friar to come and chase them away. Later, we saved a goldsmith's last ounces from a greedy baron, and healed the friar who had tried to protect him and was beaten for his pains."

"Reason enough!" the abbess said, shaken. "How is it this baron dared strike a man of the cloth?"

"He claimed he had become a follower of the druids and their old gods," Papa said, "and therefore no longer feared the Church."

"This has become far worse than I thought! How could so much evil have run through the land and I not know of it? We give hospitality to so many travelers!"

"This has happened in only a few weeks' time," Mama told her.

"Then it is well planned indeed! Perhaps it is not Prince John's work after all." She turned to Matt. "How did you attract the hunters' notice?"

"Well, I think mostly by saving a priest from a synthodruid," Matt said, "then busting up the druid's recruiting ceremony, and protecting him by magic until he could make it back to the church to confess. He's still there, in sanctuary—I hope."

The abbess stared at him for a moment. Then she said, "Yes, I think that might have attracted their attention. What sent you in my direction?"

"The friar I saved from the synthodruid. I asked him how to fight them, and he told me to ask you."

The abbess stared even wider, then turned away, shaken. "I? What could I know of battle? Prayer I know, and austerity, and the ordering of a convent—but what use is that against a lie so huge that many of the liars themselves do not know it for the falsehood it is?"

Matt bowed his head, clenching his fists, hopes dashed. Sir Orizhan stared at him in dismay.

But Mama had seen this mood before. Her gaze lingered on her son a moment; then she turned back to the abbess and said, "Have you no stories of saints who contended with the original druids?"

"We have," the abbess said slowly, "but they saw people suffering from the constant wars the druids thought pleased their gods, and showed the folk how their yearning for peace was a yearning for God. Is there such a yearning again?"

"It has begun," Mama told her, "or we would have had no one to rescue."

"Indeed." The abbess gazed at her, musing. "Have you told me all of what you heard on your way north, or was there more?"

Mama frowned, thinking. "The women are afraid for Princess Rosamund, who was imprisoned near the king's castle at Woodstock but disappeared."

"Well they might be!"

"They pity the queen, who fought a war with the king for her son Brion's right to inherit, and has been imprisoned for her pains—"

"Of this I have heard."

"—and there is a rumor abroad, that Prince Brion is not really dead, but only lying in an enchanted sleep like Arthur's, in the cathedral at Glastonbury."

"There is hope in that," the abbess said quickly, "though I would not spread the word abroad if you cannot prove it true."

"Then we must go to Glastonbury and look," Mama said decisively.

"No, not Glastonbury." Finally the abbess sat with them, hands clasped, looking off into the distance, as though she could see through the walls and all the way to the holy town herself. "That has the ring of peasants trying to keep hope alive, especially since Glastonbury is the only place of holiness great enough to withstand the onslaught of such concerted blasphemy that is also close enough for the poor folk to believe in it."

"But you don't think it's holy enough to hold out?" Matt felt hope returning, if only because the abbess was taking the rumor seriously.

"To hold out against a sorcerer and these sin-tho-druids of yours? Yes, it is that—but no holiness is great enough to withstand a troop of blaspheming knights who lust for greed and power. If they came in force to discover a sleeping prince and slay him for once and for all, no cloisterful of monks and nuns could stop them. No, if the prince's body has been borne away for protection, it would not be within Bretanglia."

"Merovence?" Matt stared in disbelief.

"No, nor in any place where knights could ride," the abbess said impatiently. "Whoever bore his body away would have taken it across the sea . . ." She turned to Matt suddenly, her gaze focusing. "The Irish Sea! They would have taken him to Erin, to the Isle of Doctors and Saints! There would be holiness enough to ward off any sorcerer, and seawater enough to delay any troop of knights, especially if they feared a wizard's power to bring a storm to overturn their ships! So even if there were truth in the rumor, neither John nor his sorcerer would concern themselves with it, for a sleeping Brion far from the shores of Bretanglia would be no threat to them—at least until they had consolidated their power."

"Yes," Matt said heavily. "First things first. Get the country securely under your thumb, *then* send an expedition to kill the rightful heir for once and for all. Sure, it makes perfect sense."

"The notion doesn't seem to delight you, son," his father said, frowning.

"It doesn't, Papa—because if there's one place where there might be a few genuine druids still holding on, it's Ireland."

"In the hills in the interior of the island?" Mama frowned, nodding. "Perhaps so. And you fear they could see this wave of synthodruids as an opportunity to revive their true religion?"

"It does sound like a great opportunity," Matt said, "and their last. Let the sorcerer take over Bretanglia, then come riding in and steal his conquest away from him—because if the people are worshiping the old gods and following the druids, of course they'll drop the synthos and turn to the *real* druids."

Sergeant Brock stared, amazed.

"The sorcerer would not give up so easily," Papa objected.

"Perhaps, but the contest would be worth the chance," the abbess admitted. "Still, that would give them all the more reason to protect Brion in enchanted sleep—so that they could present a true heir to enforce their claim."

"Brion would not let himself be used so," Sir Orizhan objected. "He might fight for the True Faith, but not for the power-lust of the old."

"With a kingdom to gain, and a true version of the old faith to drive out a cynical imitation?" Papa challenged.

"Not even then!"

"It matters not," the abbess told them. "A rumor of Brion will have as much force to raise resistance as Brion himself. Lord Wizard, you must go to Erin and seek his body. If you find there is no truth in the rumor, we must find some other way to fight these charlatans."

"And if I find out the prince really is still alive, preserved by magic?"

"Then you must wake him," the abbess said with iron resolution. She turned to Mama and Papa. "But there is some slight chance that he might be in Glastonbury. You must go there, and make sure of that rumor."

Sir Orizhan stood up, tightening his sword belt. "Then let us go quickly, before the hunters return."

"Who shall protect the convent, then?" Mama objected.

"By your leave, my lady, if we are gone, I do not think the hunters' hounds will lead them here."

"Then it isn't going to be safe for you!" Matt objected.

"Do not fear, my son." Mama smiled at him with a look that bordered on the bloodthirsty. "Now that we know the nature of our enemies, I think your father's magic and my own knack of binding enemies' spells against them will serve to send them packing."

"If you say so," Matt said with trepidation. Then he turned to the abbess. "I could at least ask my companions to stay, in case you need to fight off the hunters."

Sir Orizhan and Sergeant Brock glared at him.

"Men, and men of war, in a convent for more than one night?" the abbess protested. "Surely not!"

Matt turned to Dolan with an idea dawning. "Then let me leave you one poor beggar. I think he might be more of a help than you think."

Dolan stared up at him in bewilderment.

"A beggar will be no threat to my daughters," the abbess said slowly. "Surely we shall care for him until the land is peaceful enough for him to go his way in safety, Lord Wizard—but I cannot see what use he may be against men of war."

"Oh, he has a hidden strength," Matt assured her, "relatively speaking."

The road led away from the convent, across the plain to a forest, where the road forked. Parents and son exchanged quick embraces at the crossroads. Mama held him at arm's length, frowning. "You know I am not happy about letting you sally off without the two of us to strengthen you."

"Don't worry, Ma," Matt said, "I won't wreck the car."

She stared at him a moment, then smiled and gave him a mock slap. "Saucy boy! All right, I am silly to worry about a grown man who has survived so many battles. But see you do not let them wreck *you*!" Then she stretched up to give him another peck on the cheek, and turned her horse away.

Papa lingered to clasp him on the shoulder, looking directly into his eyes. "*Adios*—go with God, my son."

"I always try," Matt assured him. "May God be with you, too, Papa."

He set off walking beside Sir Orizhan's horse, but glanced back a few feet farther on, of course, and saw them looking, too. Both waved; then a turn of each path cut them off from sight.

Matt stopped, and Sir Orizhan reined in—they had insisted Mama and Papa take two of the horses, and that Sir Orizhan ride the third. Sergeant Brock stopped, too.

"I was wondering whether or not you were going to tell them," said Sir Orizhan.

"No need for them to know what might upset them," Matt assured him, then raised his voice. "Okay, Buckeye! You can come out now!"

The bauchan stepped forth from the roadside trees, grinning. "So, wizard! It seems you have a true family after all!"

"So I do," Matt admitted, "but you're only supposed to haunt my descendants, aren't you?"

The bauchan lost his smile in consternation. "I have never known a family where I began by haunting the son," he admitted.

"It's no time for innovation, with the country so stirred up," Matt advised, "and my adopted son is back at that convent. By the way, should I scold you or thank you?"

"Why, either one," said the bauchan, "or both, as it pleases you."

"Shouting might do me more good," Matt told him, "and I ought to scold anyone who helped those hunters stay on my trail—but I have to thank someone who scared them away for me. Why'd you do it, anyway?"

The bauchan grinned. "It was great fun."

"Wonderful," Matt muttered. "I'm fighting for my life and trying to save the kingdom, and he thinks it's fun to bush-whack me."

"Ah, but also to save you!" The bauchan held up a forefinger.

"I'm beginning to understand why your last family died of nervous prostration," Matt grumbled. "Well, I guess it's 'thank you' this time."

"This time," the bauchan agreed.

Matt thought of threatening, then thought better. Instead he frowned. "Why didn't you pull out all the stops on your magic when I sicced those bedbugs on you the first time?"

"They were mere fly-bites," the bauchan said with a depre-cating gesture, "no real threat."

Matt wondered if he were better off being a pussycat. "Well, we're off to Ireland. Guess you'll have to leave my son Dolan back there."

The bauchan's face was a study in consternation. "You're flitting?"

"I'm not a butterfly," Matt said, "but if that's what you call leaving a place, then yes, we're flitting. But we've *been* flit-ting the whole time you've known us."

"Well, aye, but not across water—and saltwater at that!"

Hope sprang in Matt's breast. "Don't be glum, chum—we've got a good fifty miles to the seashore."

"I should storm and rant and rave at you with every step!"

"Hey, that's no way to say good-bye." Matt was getting giddy with the thought of being rid of the bauchan.

Buckeye narrowed his eyes to glints. "Nay, neither a rant nor a rave—I'll find a way to plague your every step!"

But he didn't. Late that night, toward the end of his watch, Matt heard a distant sound that he first thought was thunder, then realized was the shouting of men and screaming of horses. He found that very interesting, especially since it was coming from the direction of the convent. He decided it was none of his business, waited with interest until it had died away, then woke Sergeant Brock for his watch and went to sleep. His last vagrant thought was a hope that Dolan would have sense enough to stay inside the convent's walls.

Two uneventful days later, as they were pitching camp for the night in a small clearing, screaming broke out in the woods nearby, mixed with gloating laughter.

"He's back!" Matt leaped to his feet, feeling his heart sink. "I thought we were rid of that bauchan!"

Sir Orizhan and Sergeant Brock rose, too, to face the noise—and a young girl burst from the trees, running in terror. Her gown was ripped and tattered, her face turned back toward whatever was chasing her. She turned to look forward just in time to slam into Sir Orizhan's chest. His arms closed about her automatically, and she looked up, mouth opening for a scream that never came as she stared unbelieving at his face.

"My princess!" Sir Orizhan cried.

Then the hunters broke from the brush.

Sir Orizhan stepped past the young woman, drawing his sword. Brock and Matt stepped up beside him, weapons out. The damsel shrank back behind them, eyes wide, hand to her lips.

The hunters halted in consternation. They were half a dozen soldiers with a hound, but they hadn't been expecting resistance with swords. They stared at the three companions.

"Too much risk now, boys," Matt pointed out. "Better retreat while you can."

"We are six to your one, and have horses besides," the leader snarled. "Sic him, Belle!"

The name was hugely inappropriate—the hound had to be one of the ugliest Matt had ever seen. But it sprang at his throat, snarling, and what choice did Matt have but to slash with his sword as he swung aside?

The six riders fell on knight and sergeant, who pivoted back-to-back and thrust upward at unarmored anatomy. Two soldiers screamed and fell off their horses.

The young woman darted forward, snatched a sword from one writhing soldier, and sprang back, sword raised to guard.

The hound fell, writhing and dying, even as the hunters shouted with anger and charged. But a luminous orange form rose from the dead body and threw itself at Matt again, snarling. He fell back, startled, but by force of habit the spell came to his lips even as he chopped at the spirit with his sword.

> "Get ye hence to the pit that bred ye!
> Turn upon the one who sped ye!
> Ere day doth daw,
> Ere cock doth craw,
> Ere channering worm doth chide,
> 'Gin ye must get back to your place!
> Again ye there must bide!"

The spirit howled in agony, and a jolt like an electric shock numbed Matt's whole arm, but he managed to hold onto the sword anyway.

The spirit faded, transfixed on Matt's sword, and its howling faded to silence. One of the soldiers saw, stared, and cried, "He has slain the demon-spawn!"

The other soldiers turned just in time to see the hound-body fade away, too—and Brock and Orizhan hit them from the side, swords probing under the edges of breastplates. Two soldiers howled in pain of their own, and the Princess Rosamund darted forward to stab at a third. He shouted in pain and swung at her, but she danced back out of reach of his blade, and he turned his horse to chase after his companion, who was already riding for the tall timber. The two wounded soldiers yanked on reins and sped after their mates, hands pressed to flesh, leaving a trail of drops of blood.

"We'll have to find another campsite," Matt panted. "All they'll have to do to come back will be to follow the drops."

"Sir Orizhan!" the young woman cried, and threw herself into his arms, sobbing.

"There, now, my princess, you are safe," Sir Orizhan crooned as though she were still the child she had been when he had brought her to Bretanglia. He stroked her head, murmuring soothing words.

Sergeant Brock stared as though he couldn't believe it. "But she disappeared!"

"Sure, but nobody said she died," Matt pointed out. He examined his sword, but it seemed sound enough, if you ignored the bluing over the lower half, as though it had been held for half a minute in a very hot flame.

"Surely she must have been stolen away!"

"Apparently she stole away all by herself." Matt sheathed the sword.

"How?" the sergeant bleated.

"It would seem your young mistress knows some magic," Matt told him. "How else would that particular kind of hound have picked up her trace?"

Brock stared at the princess as though he were seeing her for the first time.

She caught her breath and choked down her sobs, staring at the bright red line across Sir Orizhan's bicep. "Sir Knight, you are wounded!"

"A scratch only," Sir Orizhan protested. His mouth tightened in chagrin. "A foeman drove my own blade back against me."

The princess ripped a strip from her already ragged robe and turned to Matt. "Have you no spirits about you?"

"Far more than I like to think about," he returned, "and I think I just dispatched one—but not the kind you mean." He went to his pack and drew out a small flask. "The kind for drinking, you mean?"

"Aye! Give me!" She held out a hand.

"My lady, surely you recognize this lord," Sir Orizhan said gravely, "Matthew Mantrell, Lord Wizard of Merovence. Lord Wizard, you know the Princess Rosamund."

"Of course," Matt said, "though I hadn't quite expected to meet her here."

Rosamund stared. "The Lord Wizard? But of course! I should have known you!" She blushed, holding out the improvised bandage. "How silly of me, to seek to heal when you are by!"

"You were doing just fine," Matt assured her, and held out a roll of lint he'd taken out with the bottle. "You might like a real bandage, though. Go ahead, go ahead!"

Rosamund took the roll and the flask hesitantly, then began to clean Sir Orizhan's wound. He gazed down at her with a doting smile, the very picture of an affectionate uncle.

"I would appreciate having my guess confirmed or denied, my lady," Matt said. "Did you disappear by your own magic, then?"

"I did, my lord." She looked up at him, eyes wide in the firelight. "I knew a few spells a wise woman taught me when I was about to leave my home. I crafted a stock in my own image, used it to deceive the guards, and fled into the night. I have fled ever since, in the evening and the false dawn, ever in twilight."

"Not the safest time of day, considering the habits of the fairy folk," Matt said, frowning, "but not the most dangerous, either, especially if you have soldiers combing the realm for you. What did you do, sleep by day and keep watch by night?"

"How did you know?" Then Rosamund caught herself. "But of course—you are a wizard. Yes, I hid by day for fear of the soldiers, and by night for fear of the spirits, but when I could travel, I did, always toward the east, where the sea lay and I might somehow find a ship to bear me away from this benighted land."

"Since we're heading for the seacoast, too, we bumped into one another." Matt suspected there was more to it than that, but he wasn't privy to the plans of the patron saints of Merovence and Bretanglia. "What made you decide to escape? Hearing of Brion's death?"

"Aye, the poor dear fool." Tears gathered in Rosamund's eyes, and nearly in Sir Orizhan's, too, for he seemed to feel as she felt.

But Sergeant Brock stared, scandalized. "Fool? Prince Brion was nearly perfect in strategy and tactics!"

"But not in the things that matter most to a woman," Matt pointed out, "not that he could be, while she was betrothed to his brother."

Rosamund stared at him in amazement.

"I'm in love, too," Matt told her. "Have been for years."

"I am not in love with Brion!" Rosamund flared, then calmed instantly to musing. "But he was the only one of that family whom I could trust not to seek to use me in some way." Tears formed in her eyes again.

"And with him dead, you knew life would become unbearable?" Matt pressed.

"I knew the king's plans for me, my lord." Rosamund tossed her head. "I could not endure them. I would rather risk death at the hands of his hunters, or of bandits."

"Which you did," Matt agreed. "Risk death, I mean. Well, I'm glad they didn't find you until you found us." He rolled up his blankets. "Come on, folks. Leave the dead and take the horses. We don't want to be here when their comrades get back."

Sergeant Brock led them through the darkened woods, Sir Orizhan and Rosamund walking side by side, talking in low tones, updating each other on what had been happening. Matt, though, walked backward, sweeping away their tracks and reciting,

> "Any taint of my so-powerful art
> I here obscure, and shield from their senses
> My airy charms. Let all trace of spells I work
> Be broken, and any spoor of my strong magic
> Be buried certain fathoms in the earth."

He thought they must have gone a thousand feet when he looked up and saw, by patches of moonlight sifted through leaves, a tall and long-limbed shape a hundred feet away, backing toward him and gesturing with its loosely jointed arms.

CHAPTER 18

Matt's lips thinned; he could just imagine the kind of verse Buckeye was casting, one that would leave a taint of magic so strong that the least sensitive hound in the sorcerer's kennel would smell it a mile away. His eyes narrowed and he chanted,

> "Split a trail from this we leave,
> And since bauchans can't follow minds,
> Make him see naught but that false weave
> And track us down that alley blind."

With satisfaction, he watched as the rubber-limbed figure seemed to move along the side of the trail, then farther and farther away from it. The last Matt saw of him, he was backing away far to the left, still gesturing and presumably chanting, as Matt backed up straight, reciting his masking verse over and over again.

Rosamund insisted on helping them pitch their new camp—it seemed she had learned something about living in the field when Sir Orizhan had taken her along with the princelings on childhood expeditions. Certainly she knew how to lay and light a fire that gave off remarkably little smoke. Sergeant Brock was scandalized at the thought of a princess doing menial tasks, though, and insisted on cooking the meal, so she busied herself in cutting boughs and making pallets.

Dinner consisted of equal amounts of stew and the inside story of the civil war, at least as much of it as Rosamund had heard. By the time she was done, they were all ready to sleep, and Sir Orizhan insisted on taking first watch, sitting on a rock and beaming down at his sleeping ward. Watching his face, Matt could see he wasn't in love with the princess, but that she was obviously filling the place in his heart of the daughter he had never had. He went to sleep on that thought.

He woke up to a howling racket, but one far away. Everyone else bolted upright, too, and Sir Orizhan, on his feet, hissed, "What can that bedlam be, Lord Wizard?"

"The hunters and their hound," Matt told him, just as the howl-baying turned to a high-pitched yelping that faded into the distance, followed by the shouts and howls of thoroughly spooked human beings. Something hooted derisively as it faded after them, yowling and clamoring with the voices of a dozen beasts.

"The hound followed the most prominent trail of magic it found," Matt explained, "which led it to a very surprised bauchan who is now also very angry. Hopefully, he'll satisfy that anger by chasing them, and by the time he runs out of gas, he should be too far away to make it back to us by morning."

"What is a bauchan?" Princess Rosamund asked, and Matt lay back down while Sir Orizhan was explaining. When he was done, she said, "It seems a most helpful beast."

"Only by accident," Matt assured her, "this time, at least."

As it turned out, they were a lot closer to the coast than they'd thought. The second day saw them into a fishing village, with half the afternoon left to find a boat. The fishermen were just coming in, tying up their vessels at the long dock, and Matt went from one to another, asking for passage to Erin. Everyone he asked turned away, avoiding his eyes, shaking heads and muttering. He found out why when he approached the oldest sailor there.

"Erin?" The grizzled fellow eyed the gold coin in Matt's hand with longing. "I'd be happy enough to take you there, but the king's men came riding by yesterday and told us anyone who carried strangers across the water would die a slow and lingering death."

"Oh, did they?" Matt felt the bottom of his stomach go out. "Uh, I don't suppose there's any chance of swimming, is there?"

The old fisherman showed yellowed stubs of teeth in a

grin. "Not likely, my lad. There's a legend of a giant named Finn MacCumhail crossing once, but he waded."

"Not MacCool at all," Matt grumbled. "Anyone have a boat for sale?"

"For enough gold? Aye, if they didn't stop to think what the soldiers would do once they found out."

"That's what I was afraid of," Matt sighed. He turned away—and found an old woman in a tattered robe sitting on a piling, staring at him with wild eyes from an emaciated face framed by long, tangled hair that was blowing in the wind. Matt stopped and swallowed. "Uh—who's that old dame sitting there staring at me?"

"Who, Old Meg?" The fisherman looked up, and his face showed pity. "Oh, don't let her trouble you, lad. The sea took her betrothed fifty years ago, and she comes down to watch every evening in hopes that she'll see his boat come in, and him step off it. If she troubles you, you've but to tell her your name and home, and she'll let you pass without another word."

"Thanks for the advice." Matt went on down the dock, eyes on his own people—but as he passed Old Meg, a scrawny hand shot out and caught his arm with a grip so strong he almost cried out. Instead he said, "Uh, lady—could you go a little easier on the haberdashery?"

"Well, at least he knows a lady born when he sees one," Old Meg said, gratified. "Do you wish to cross the water, lad?"

"Cross the . . . ?" Matt stared; it wasn't what he'd been expecting. "Well . . . yes!"

"To Erin, is it?"

"It is." Conscience stirred. "But the king's men said not to take anyone."

"King's men!" Old Meg said with scorn. "What need to fear the soldiers of so weak a man? His grandfather Talorc, now—*there* was a king!"

Matt looked more closely at her, deciding she might be older than she looked. "I wouldn't want you helping us just to have your life cut short."

"There's not that much of it left, lad," she assured him. "I've a boat—not so big a one, but large enough to take you and those three friends of yours, and sound enough to take me out to catch my dinner every day. Will you sail with me or not?"

"Yes!" Matt said. "See you at first light tomorrow." He fished out the piece of gold again.

"I'll have none of your coin," Old Meg said sharply. "What I'll do, I'll do for the rightful king, not for pay—and you won't meet me any time but now." She hopped down off the piling. "If you want to sail with me, you come at once or not at all!"

Matt gulped. "A night crossing in a small boat?"

"Who was only now worrying about the soldiers?" Old Meg returned. "Will you come, or not?"

"We'll come!"

Matt followed her down the dock to his companions and made the introductions. Rosamund stared into the old woman's eyes and shivered. Old Meg only smiled at her and nodded slowly, but all she said was, "You'll do," and turned away, striding down the beach so fast Matt had to hurry to keep up with her.

Sir Orizhan matched his pace, and Matt told him, "Rare old lady, this!"

"I was thinking that, too." Sir Orizhan watched Old Meg with a brooding gaze.

She led them past the end of the village to a weathered cottage with a moldy thatch that stood at the edge of the sand. There she turned sharply and paced down the beach to a small boat with a short mast. The companions followed after, skidding and sliding in their hurry. Then Matt came close enough to see the craft, and stopped dead, staring in alarm.

The little sailboat was battered and patched, its paint chipped and peeling, its ropes frayed and worn. It scarcely looked big enough for two people, let alone five.

"It lets a little water," Old Meg told him, "and you'll have to take turns bailing, but it will take you across the water."

"If you say so." Matt gave the little boat a jaundiced eye, but he came closer anyway.

"A little help, lad." Old Meg held out her hand. Matt took it, and she climbed up the two pilings to which her boat was moored. They formed a rough staircase, and as she stepped down onto the seat by the mast, she told Rosamund, "Lady, come aboard. You men can shove off and get your leggins wet before you climb in."

Sir Orizhan handed Rosamund up—she didn't look any happier about it than Matt felt—then joined Matt and Sergeant Brock in leaning against the bow and shoving hard. Sand slipped under their feet, and Matt wondered how the old dame managed without any help—probably just climbed aboard and waited for the tide to come in.

The boat floated, and seawater drenched Matt's boots and hose. He grumbled as he hauled himself in over the gunwale and settled down on a bench, shivering and miserable already. At least he didn't have to worry about getting his feet wet in the bilge. He took up the leather bucket and started bailing.

Old Meg had managed to haul up the sail and work her way back to the aft seat by the tiller. Now the wind filled the canvas, and she turned the boat into the breeze. Matt saw, with misgiving, that the sail was even more patched than the hull. He wondered what kept the boat afloat—magic? You never could tell, with these old semi-hermit women.

The three men huddled in the bow, shivering in the night breeze with their soaking legs, their faces grim and stoic—but Rosamund sat high and dry, slippers tucked under her skirts, which were gathered around her legs, listening wide-eyed as Meg explained how to sail the boat. "If the wind shifts, lass, the boom—that's the pole that sticks out from the mast, with the bottom of the sail lashed to it—the boom will come about—that means it will swing, sometimes very quickly, and if you're not watching sharply, it could strike you a nasty blow, or even knock you overboard. Beware the change of the wind . . ."

Matt listened closely, some sixth sense telling him he was going to need the knowledge someday, but growing more and more confused by the wealth of details the woman spewed out, not with any organization, but as they occurred to her in response to her trimming of the sail and leaning on the tiller. His stomach churned with the rocking of the boat and the constant conviction that they were going to capsize, and he became more and more befuddled as he watched the village grow smaller and smaller behind Old Meg. By the time it disappeared, darkness had fallen, and Matt had become thoroughly convinced that he could never have sailed the little boat.

Then, in the darkness between sunset and moonrise, rising and falling with the roll of the sea, Old Meg dropped the sail suddenly and, as the boat coasted to a stop, turned to Matt and demanded, "Why do you wish to go to Erin?"

Matt rocked back, jolted by her tone of accusation. Caution ruled, and he said the first partial truth that came to mind. "Well, we're trying to escape a bauchan, you see, so we're flitting."

A gravelly basso from under his seat agreed, "Aye, Meg, we're flitting, you see."

Matt jumped a good six inches. It felt like a mile.

Sir Orizhan and Sergeant Brock turned and stared, astounded, and Rosamund looked alarmed, but Old Meg only narrowed her eyes and said, "A bauchan, is it? In my boat? You were not invited, creature, and you're not welcome!

> "Get you back to shore,
> And bother me no more!"

She followed the simple rhyme with a verse in a foreign language while she stirred the air with a forefinger, then jabbed it back toward the land. Something shot from under Matt's seat with a hooting and whooping and went galloping back over the water toward the village, clutching its buttocks and howling in alarm.

Matt stared after the departing bauchan in amazement. "Wow! Wish I could do that!" Then the implication of the phrase hit him, and he turned back to find Old Meg staring straight at him, her eyes narrowed and her mouth a hard line.

"You didn't tell us you were a magician," Matt said.

"Nor did you tell me you were," Meg returned, "not that I had any need to be told—and I'll warn you, wizard, not to try your magic on me, or you'll have a very unpleasant surprise."

"If you feel that way about it," Matt said, "why did you offer us a ride?"

"Out of the fear of the mischief you might breed if I left you in Bretanglia. If you'd been by yourself, be sure you'd have been dazed by a blow of magic and be lying unconscious this moment."

Matt gazed at her a minute, then turned to Sir Orizhan. "Looks like it's a good thing you guys came along."

"Not them, foolish male!" Meg snapped. "The maiden! I'd toss the three of you overboard without a thought, but I'll talk to her." She turned to Rosamund. "How say you, lass? Why do you go to Erin?"

"Why," Rosamund said, "because I seek to escape the king and Prince John, and that is where my protectors are going."

"Protectors?" Meg turned back to the men. "How do I know you mean to protect the lass, not despoil her?"

Sir Orizhan's head snapped back in outrage. "Why, because I have been her guardian these ten years, and would slay any who sought to harm her!"

Meg gazed at him a moment, then said, "A fair answer, and I feel the truth of it. But why do you travel with this wizard?"

"To learn who slew Prince Gaheris," the knight said, "for this sergeant and I had been set to protect him."

Again Meg gazed at him in silence, then glanced at Brock. The sergeant sat bolt upright, staring at her in alarm.

"There is truth again," Old Meg said, "though I sense there's some missing. Still, I'm not sure you know of it." She turned to Matt. "Now, wizard, the full truth: Why do *you* go to Erin?"

"To look for Prince Brion's body," Matt said. "There's a rumor that he isn't dead, only lying in a magical sleep. If that's so, we mean to find him and wake him if we can, then bring him back to fight the false druids who are stealing the realm from the people."

Rosamund gave a little, inarticulate cry, and Meg's sharp eyes swung to her. "You did not know of this, maiden?"

"I did not," Rosamund said. "I only sought to go as far from King Drustan and Prince John as I could, and these good men were taking me where I wished to go."

"Would you have gone if you had known they sought Prince Brion?"

"Oh, yes," Rosamund breathed. "Oh, most surely would I have gone, and with even better heart, if I had known!"

Meg studied her for a long while, then gave a nod of satisfaction. Turning, she raised the sail again. "Well enough, then, we go to Erin." She set the sail by taking a bight around a cleat with a turn of her wrist.

Matt decided to keep his mouth shut, but curiosity got the better of him. "Why are you willing to help us? This isn't your fight."

"But it is." Meg turned back to Matt, her eyes burning into his. "Know, O Wizard, that you are not alone in your enmity to the mock druids."

Matt only stared. So did Sergeant Brock.

"Learn that there were female druids, too," Old Meg told him, "and that some are still abroad in the land."

She waited while her words sank in, and to good effect— Matt had a very strange feeling, almost as though his skin were vibrating in resonance to old, arcane magic, and Sergeant Brock began to tremble.

"So," Matt said softly, "*you* are a druid—a real druid."

"I am, and can tell you the name of my teacher, and of her teacher, and her teacher's teacher, back to the days when we held the island of Mona as our right. There are true druids in Erin, too, more than in Bretanglia, though not so many as there should be," Meg told him.

Matt wondered about that "should," but only said, "Why are you helping me, then?"

"Because I hate and despise these mock druids who defame and debase our noble religion!" Meg spat. "They seek to imprison the people, not to free their hearts and minds! They seek to use the gods as tools for their own ends, not to devote themselves wholly to the deities! And in their blasphemy, they shall make the reputation of we who truly hold to the Old Gods even worse than the milksop monks and nuns have done!"

"We have a common enemy, then?"

"Aye, and a common champion, too! I have told you I seek to aid the true king, and you know my opinion of Drustan!"

"But you think his son Brion is true," Matt interpreted.

Rosamund gasped.

"True in heart, true in mind, but more importantly, true to the land and the people who dwell in it, far more true than either his father or his brothers have been! Nay, this much I can tell you—that Brion's body is indeed in Erin, and that holy men have borne it there by magic!"

"But you can't tell us whether or not he's still alive," Matt inferred.

"If he is, he looks most amazingly dead—though his body is not corrupted, unless the rumors that pass from druid to druid are false." She fixed Matt with a burning eye. "But alive or dead, he shall bring you men to help you in your quest— this I know! Go to Erin, go to the Isle of Doctors and Saints, and bring back an army of truth to help you disperse the purveyors of lies who defame my Order!"

"I'll try," Matt said slowly, never taking his eyes from her, "but it's apt to be dangerous. Maybe we should leave the princess with you—she should be safe enough."

"Oh, no!" Rosamund cried. "I must go with you to find Brion!"

"It is even as she says," Old Meg agreed. "Her destiny does not lie in a small fishing village on the shore of Bretanglia. Take her to Erin, wizard, and let her read her weird."

The room seemed gloomy, but there was no candle at his bedside, and King Drustan raised a hand to gesture as he called for light—but the hand would not rise at the command of his will, and he could hear only the harsh caw of his tongueless voice. Prince John stepped into his range of vision, and there was enough light to see him, at least. The boy bent low, his voice soothing. "The drapes are opened wide to the sunlight, Father; the room is as light as we can make it. Let the doctor examine you, and perhaps he can make the day seem brighter—though it is indeed gray and gloomy."

Drustan grumbled something affirmative and relaxed. His stomach was roiling, making him faint with nausea. It had been getting worse for days.

John stepped back, and the doctor stepped forward. He held the king's wrist for a little while, frowning in concentration, then leaned over to peer closely into his eyes. Brows bent, he straightened up and probed the king's stomach.

Drustan bellowed in agony, eyes bulging.

"It has been too long since your bowels moved," the doctor

said with false heartiness, "only that, my liege, and nothing more. Rest, drink only small beer, and wait."

But as he stepped back, Drustan's nausea spread upward to heartsickness. He gargled a curse at the man, recognizing the falseness of the tone—and his heartsickness turned to panic as an archbishop stepped up to his bedside. Drustan tried to push himself upright, mouthing denials.

"Gently, gently, Your Majesty," the archbishop soothed. "I have heard your confession every month, and given you the Eucharist every week, for six years. Surely there is no need to alter that now."

A little relieved, Drustan sank back on his bed and muttered a querulous phrase.

"It has been a month, yes, a month and more." The archbishop raised his head. "Your Highness, I beg you withdraw for some minutes. What His Majesty confesses is only for the ears of himself, myself, and God."

"But how shall you understand his words? I must explain them to you!"

"God shall understand them," the archbishop said, "and after sixty confessions, I fancy I shall recognize every word he says. Leave us, Your Highness—leave him to me and God."

John stood outside the door and fretted. When the archbishop finally came out and said, "You may go in again," John bolted through the door and smelled the aroma of the priest's scented candles. He hurried to his father's bedside and saw the gleam of anointing on his forehead. His smile had a vindictive quality as he bent over Drustan. "Gave you the Last Rites, did he? Well, that was wise of him, old man, for you're dying now, and there's no doubt of it."

Drustan's eyes widened; he gargled in anger.

"How dare I tell you that?" John grinned. "Because it's true enough, you old goat, and in less than an hour you won't be able to hurt anyone anymore! Aye, at last I'll be safe from your whims and your rages! At last I'll be able to build a life for myself! At last I'll be rid of you!"

Drustan struggled to rise, face livid, mouthing outrage.

"Behold the king!" John mocked. "Behold the mighty

Drustan, before whom all men tremble! Here, O Man of Power, hold this cup!"

He pressed a silver goblet into his father's hand, then took his own hands away. The vessel clattered to the floor.

"If you cannot grasp a cup, how shall you hold a sword? No, the days when all men feared Drustan are done, for Drustan himself is done—and no man need fear you now!"

He thrust his face close, so close the reek of his breath nearly stifled Drustan as John spat, "How can I be so sure? Why, because it's I who have done it, you poor benighted old fool! It's I who brought you your cup and bowl, I who spooned the gruel into you, I who mixed poison with wine and porridge! It is I who have poisoned you, and I wish you had not confessed or taken Extreme Unction, so that you could have gone to Judgment with your sins on your soul!"

Drustan roared with rage, anger so intense that he actually managed to start up from his bed, to lift an anvil-heavy arm and grope for John's throat. With a cry of terror, John sprang back, hands up to defend, shrinking into a corner—but the huge red swollen face before him abruptly turned white, and the king fell back, senseless, with eyes wide open.

John waited, heart hammering. He waited for what seemed an impossibly long time, then waited longer. Finally he dared creep up to the bed, dared even further to reach out and touch his father's hand, ready to leap away and flee—but the hand stayed unmoving. Daring even more greatly, John took Drustan's wrist and felt for the pulse. It was a task he had done every day for weeks, so he knew exactly where to probe—but felt nothing. At last he plucked up the courage to touch the great vein in the king's neck, felt and waited, dreading, hoping—and felt not the slightest tremor of blood moving beneath the skin. Finally, he dared to reach up and close Drustan's eyelids. Triumph began to boil up inside him; his face split in an idiotic grin; but he held it in while he fished in his purse for two pennies, then laid them on his father's eyelids. "Money for the ferryman! Copper to hold your soul away! Rest in agony, Father, as I have when I've dreaded your anger! Rest uneasily, rest angrily, rest painfully, but rest, rest, and never come back!"

There was more, all uttered in a hushed, intense tone, so

that none might hear it except the corpse. At last John ran down and stood panting as he glared at the body of the man who had humiliated him so often, and only given approval when John had learned how to fawn upon him.

Then John stepped away from the bed and threw his head back with silent laughter, forcing himself to keep his shout of victory to a whisper, fists clenched in triumph.

A tapestry stirred in the shadows. John heard the slightest rasp of wood sliding against wood and dropped his hands, squaring his shoulders, doing the best he could to look regal—but he could not quite wipe the grin from his face.

Niobhyte stepped out of the gloom into the light of the deathwatch candle. "Is it done, then?"

"It is," John told him, glee still in his voice. "He is dead, and shall trouble me no more. I thank you for the poison, Niobhyte. It did all that you said it would."

The chief synthodruid made a deprecating gesture. "It was my pleasure, as it shall always be my pleasure to serve you— if you will."

"Oh, yes," John told him. "Oh, I shall always be glad of your service, Niobhyte—and you may be sure of my patronage. I shall see your religion rise, and these stumbling-block priests torn down! The Church shall fall, the Old Gods rise again, and I shall be the first to worship them openly!"

"I shall ever be Your Majesty's faithful servant." Niobhyte knelt to kiss John's hand. "The king is dead—long live the king!"

"I thank you, my first and most loyal subject," John told him. "Now, though, you had better step back into that secret passageway, for I must bring in the doctor and the archbishop to make Drustan's passing the law of the land. Then I can begin to unmake their Church!"

"I am ever obedient to Your Majesty," Niobhyte said, and backed away with bowed head to disappear behind the tapestry again.

John listened for the sliding of wood on wood, then turned to open the door and call in both physician and prelate. The came, they stared in apprehension—then they both turned and knelt, declaring as Niobhyte had, "The king is dead— long live the king!"

* * *

"Read my weird?" Rosamund asked. "What is my weird, and how shall I read it?"

They stood on land, watching the little boat skip away over the waves, its sail filled with the morning breeze. Behind them the sun struggled to rise over Erin. Admittedly, the distance between Erin and Bretanglia wasn't great, but Matt was still surprised Meg had sailed it so fast.

"Your weird is a sort of a trap," Sergeant Brock told her.

Matt looked up in surprise.

"It is what you were born into this world to do," the sergeant went on, "the outcome of the sum and total of all the virtues and talents within you, the work in life for which you, and only you, are most singularly fitted. But you do not have to do it. You can turn away from it, if you lack the courage—or you can be too blind to see it. But if you have eyes clear enough to read it, and the courage to enter into it, your weird shall close about you, shall catch you up, and bear you onward to fulfillment in this world and joy in the next. Therefore must you read your weird."

"That has the sound of fate," Sir Orizhan said, frowning.

"Is that your southern word for it?" the sergeant asked.

"Not quite," Matt said. "Fate happens to you whether you choose it or not—and whether you like it or not."

"A weird is not always pleasant," Sergeant Brock admitted. "Your . . . the Church sings the praises of martyrs to the faith, who have endured the tortures of burning in this world in order to rise to the glory of sainthood in the next."

"True," Matt said thoughtfully, "but there are other saints like St. Francis of Assisi, who sang his way through life with joy."

"Well, he had his hard times, too," Sir Orizhan pointed out, "but what life does not? The importance of it, Your Highness, is that if you can read your weird and be brave enough to step into it, it may bear you on to joy or bear you on to grief, but it will never leave you feeling that your life was not worth having lived."

"Then I shall find it," Rosamund said with iron determination, "clasp it to my breast, let it fold about me, and go wheresoever it carries me!"

"Then let's begin by finding Brion's body." Matt turned his back on the sea and the fading dot that was Meg's boat. "She said holy men had carried him away. Let's find a bishop."

That by itself turned out not to be easy. They'd had to leave the horses in Bretanglia, of course—Meg's boat just barely managed the four of them—so they had to walk along the beach until they came to a fishing village. It took about an hour, and the old men were sitting on the dock watching the last of the fishing boats sail off for their day's work. Matt hailed them, waving, and the four gaffers looked up in surprise before their faces turned into masks.

"Hi, there!" Matt climbed up onto the dock with his companions right behind him and approached the nearest grandfather, a man who looked to be in his eighties but, given the harshness of medieval life, was probably only in his thirties. "Can you tell me how to get to the castle?" He didn't ask which one—any castle would do.

The oldster frowned, looking very suspicious, and demanded something incomprehensible—it sounded vaguely like "Bail out this Arab, go lair in her hair."

Matt didn't bother looking around for a Near Eastern woman. "Great," he sighed. "I've been living and traveling in countries that were pieces of Hardishane's empire for so long that I forgot what happened in lands that weren't connected to the continent!"

Sir Orizhan came up frowning. "What is the trouble, Lord Wizard?"

"Trouble? Oh, nothing—except that these people speak a foreign language, probably Gaelic, and I haven't the faintest idea what this old duffer's saying!"

CHAPTER 19

Sergeant Brock eyed the old man narrowly. "I suspect he speaks less and less of our language the more he distrusts us."

The gaffer may not have known the words, but he understood Brock's tone. He glared back at him and spat another unintelligible phrase.

"So is your mother," Brock said. He watched the oldster carefully, but the expression of suspicious hostility didn't change, and Brock turned to Matt with a sigh. "I fear he really doesn't understand Bretanglian, Lord Wizard. He didn't even seem to know I'd insulted his mother."

"Maybe you didn't. After all, he might have been paying you a compliment."

Sergeant Brock showed his teeth in something resembling a grin. "There is that virtue in merely turning his own words back on him."

"Okay, he's only a day's sail from Bretanglia, but how often do you think he meets people who speak our language?" Matt asked.

"Not often," Sir Orizhan admitted, "since he is only a fisherman—but there is a fair amount of trade between the lands. Surely we can find a merchant who can speak with us!"

"Good idea." Matt scanned the village. "Come to think of it, even the local priest should at least be able to speak church Latin . . . There! I suppose you could call that a steeple." He pointed to a larger-than-average one-story building with a sort of pointed bump at one end.

"A church indeed," Sir Orizhan agreed. "Do you truly speak the language of ancient Reme?"

Matt kept forgetting that it had been Remus who had won the fight for the first Latin wall in this universe, not Romulus.

"Let's say it's not too different from something I learned in school." He turned back to give the old men a cheery wave. "Thanks, guys. I think we can make it from here."

The gaffers stared, taken aback, and watched with apprehension as the companions started for the church.

The chapel was the only stone structure in town, as was so often the case, and the rectory-cottage beside it was only wattle and daub with a thatched roof. But the yard before it was neat and clean, with flowers around the border and a whitewashed fence, and the priest was sitting on a bench beside the door, reading his breviary.

Matt felt a little strange walking right up to him, so he knocked at the gate. The priest looked up with a pleasant smile that vanished when he saw strangers, and ones in foreign clothing at that.

"Good morning, Father," Matt said agreeably.

The priest frowned, cocking his head on one side, and asked a question in Gaelic.

Matt sighed and tried again. *"Ave, pater!"*

"Ah!" The priest's expression cleared. *"Ave, filius meam."*

It was a strange experience, hearing Latin with an Irish accent—but Matt had only had a year in high school and fifteen years of Mass prayers in childhood.

"Quem quaeiritus?" the priest asked. It meant, Who are you looking for?

"We wish to go to the bishop's town," Matt explained. "Can you tell us the way?"

"Do you come from Bretanglia?" the priest asked.

"We just have," Matt told him, "but our journey began in Merovence." After all, that was true for Rosamund, too—it was just that, in her case, the first leg of the trip had been done a long time before.

"What do you seek in the bishop's town?"

Matt began to feel that the priest meant to protect the bishop from these vile Bretanglians. "We seek a merchant, any merchant, who can tell us how to find a certain monastery where a—" Matt groped for a word that could describe the (hopefully) sleeping Brion. "—a certain relic lies."

"Ah! A pilgrimage!" The priest nodded, not only satisfied but delighted. He pointed along the main street of the town.

"Go three miles to the crossroads, and the signpost will point the way to Innisfree. It is the road to the right, and five miles later, the left branch of a fork."

"Thank you, Father." Matt tipped his hat and started to turn away.

But the priest held up a cautioning hand. "Be careful on the road, my son. A pouka haunts that way, and not by night alone."

"A pouka?" Matt's blood chilled, especially since the word wasn't Latin. "I thank you even more deeply, Father. May I donate to your church?"

The priest's face broke into a smile. "That would be pleasant."

But he was staring at the small gold coin in stunned disbelief as the companions walked away.

"What advice was it that made you so generous?" Sir Orizhan asked.

"He told me there's a pouka haunting the road," Matt explained.

"A pouka!" Rosamund and Sergeant Brock stopped dead, staring.

"I take it you have them in Bretanglia, too," Matt said.

"We have pooks, and the most mischievous of them is an elf by that name," Brock said.

Matt supposed the distinction between "pook" and "Puck" was pretty minor—only a matter of a vowel shift. Nonetheless, the thought made him glad he was in Ireland; he'd had experience with Puck. "Here, a pouka means a shapeshifter. It usually appears as a horse, but it can be just about anything, including a human being."

"How do we guard against it, then?" Rosamund asked.

"Well, if you see a horse by the roadside who looks as though he's just begging to be ridden—don't mount."

They had been strolling along the main street, and Matt stopped in surprise in front of a larger-than-average hut that had piles of folded nets, jars of beeswax, cylinders of cork, and coils of rope stacked outside it. A man stood in the midst of them all, pumping away at a push drill on a sort of lozenge of stone, boring a hole through its center.

"If I didn't know better," Matt said, "I'd think this was a chandler's store."

"It *is* more common to find the shop that sells supplies for boats down by the dock," Sergeant Brock said. "Nonetheless, in so small a town, this building's not so far from the sea, and more likely to stand longer by being away from the waves."

"Good point," Matt agreed, "but I'm surprised to see any kind of a shop in a town so small."

"Perhaps there is more trade here than there seems," Sir Orizhan offered.

"You mean he ships fish in to Innisfree? Not a bad idea. Wish we had time to wait and hitch a ride on the inbound wagon. But since we don't . . ." Matt stepped up to the shopkeeper and said, "Do you sell rope?"

The man looked at him as though he had come from the other side of the moon, and asked an incomprehensible question in incredulous tones.

"Let me translate," Matt sighed, and took out a silver penny. While the shopkeeper was still staring at it, Matt said to Brock, "Pick up a few coils of rope, will you? The thinnest he has . . . yes, that will do. Another coil . . . yes, that should be enough . . . a ball of twine . . . and four of those stone weights . . . yes, that's good. Now hold them up for him to see."

Sergeant Brock held up the goods. "What would you want these for, Lo—Master Matthew?"

"Just in case we find a stray horse by the road," Matt explained, and turned to the shopkeeper. "Well?"

The shopkeeper looked up and got a crafty look in his eye. He held up two fingers.

Matt sighed and took out another penny. He held it up in front of the shopkeeper's face. The man frowned slightly; the penny was copper. He shook his head.

Matt turned away, slipping the pennies back into his purse and telling Brock, "Put the stuff back where you found it."

Brock laid one coil of rope down, and the shopkeeper called something in Gaelic.

"Hold on," Matt said, and turned back. The shopkeeper had a resigned look on his face and an open hand sticking out.

"Pick it up again," Matt said, and took out the two pennies.

He insisted on carrying a coil of rope and two weights himself, so of course Sir Orizhan had to, too, though he did look disapproving.

"Are you sure you have not cheated that good man?" Rosamund demanded.

"Cheated him?" Matt turned back to see the shopkeeper caressing the pennies with a grin so wide he was fairly cackling. He looked up at the companions, shaking his head with a look that said, *They're crazy, but that's not my problem. In fact, it's my good luck.*

"No, I don't think we cheated him." Matt turned to the road again. "That's more silver than he's seen in a year or more. He thinks he made out like a bandit, and he's right, too."

"He is indeed," Brock said. "If you'd had more time to bargain, you probably could have beaten him down to six coppers—and if you could not, I surely could." He looked very unhappy at the lost chance to haggle.

Matt waited until they were half a mile outside the town, and presumably secure from prying eyes, before he called a halt, took out his knife, and began to go to work on the rope. Half an hour later he had a lariat and three bolas.

"Hold one end and whirl the other one around your head," he told his companions. "The trick is the same as in any argument—knowing when to let go." He demonstrated, and the bola wound itself around a tree trunk. Then he set them to practicing, one at a time so they could duck when the others got it wrong, while he practiced with the lariat. It had been a long time since his childhood days pretending he was a television cowboy, but the old skills came back fairly quickly, and he was surprised to see what an improvement adult coordination made. On the other hand, his motor skills had definitely been boosted by being knighted—that was the way the ceremony worked in this universe, and he'd had nothing but the best.

When he was satisfied that all three of his companions could wrap their bolas around the base of a tree twenty feet away, seven throws out of ten, he led them on down the road.

"And what shall we do if we meet this pouka of yours, Lord Wizard?" Sir Orizhan asked.

"It's not mine," Matt answered, "though we might be able to change that."

"Have you not had enough spirits haunting you for the time being?" Sergeant Brock asked.

"Yes, I have—so if you do see a stray horse, just try to make friends with it, okay?"

"Better us than you, eh?" Sir Orizhan grinned. "Nevertheless, if you say it, Lord Wizard, we will try it. My lady should not have to walk, after all."

"You are gallant, Sir Orizhan." Rosamund smiled with affection. "But where would I find a sidesaddle in this wilderness?"

"Why, I should ride behind you, and hold you on."

"If they do," Matt told Sergeant Brock, "you be ready with that bola."

"Never fear, Lord Wizard," the sergeant assured him. "But how shall we know if it is a pouka or a real horse?"

"If we can tame it, it's real," Matt told him. "If it tries to tame us, it's a pouka."

They found the signpost, followed the arrow that said "Innisfree" to the right-hand road, and found the horse about a mile farther. She looked very ordinary—medium height, tawny coat, and big brown eyes that watched them with mild curiosity as she chewed a mouthful of grass.

"Just keep walking," Matt told them.

"She might be only some farmer's mare turned out to pasture for the day," Rosamund protested. "It is the growing season, is it not?"

"Yes," Sergeant Brock told her. "The plowing's done and the reaping not yet come. There's little work for the farm horse now."

"Especially since most peasants plow with oxen," Matt said.

The horse came ambling over to see what was going on.

"Battle stations," Matt muttered.

Rosamund glanced back over her shoulder at the large brown eyes, then looked again with a tender smile. "How sweet!" She turned around and began to stroke the horse's velvety nose.

"You really should ride, my lady." Sir Orizhan went over to stroke the horse, too, along the neck and down to the shoulders, then along the back.

Matt throttled impatience and left them to it while he fingered the coil of rope behind his back. It took a while, with Sir Orizhan leaning on the horse's back, putting more and more of his weight on her, then swinging one leg up to half lie, then swinging it farther so that he sat up astride. The horse looked back at him as though to say, What are *you* doing there? But Sir Orizhan leaned down to catch Rosamund's forearm. "My lady, will you ride?"

"Willingly, Sir Knight!" Rosamund swung up before him, both legs on the horse's left—and the mare took off like a skyrocket.

"Now!" Matt shouted. He twirled the lariat, letting the noose spin wide. Sergeant Brock shouted as he loosed his bola.

The bola almost missed. It swung past the horse's rear legs completely, but one weight caught on a front leg. The other whipped about, wrapping itself three times around the horse's knees, and the mare fell, rolling onto her side with a whinny that was more like a scream. Sir Orizhan shouted in alarm, catching Rosamund to him as he shot off the horse to the left. Rosamund landed on her feet just as the lasso spun through the air and settled over the horse's head.

The mare screamed—it was far past a whinny—and reached for the rope with her teeth. Matt raced toward her hindquarters, a long arc from twenty feet away, and managed to keep the rope out of reach of the mare's head. She lurched to her feet—and promptly fell again, still tangled in the bola.

Sergeant Brock drew his long knife and paced toward her, his face grim.

"No, Sergeant!" Rosamund cried. "She is a sweet horse, and has done nothing to deserve death!"

"If she is *only* a horse," the sergeant snapped.

"If she is not, you cannot hurt a spirit!" Sir Orizhan cried as he picked himself up.

"Cold Iron can," the sergeant returned.

The horse went crazy. She screamed, she thrashed—and turned into a bear, a she-bear with Matt's lasso still around her neck, roaring as she threw herself to her hind feet and began to walk toward him, bola-bound paws rising to club him.

Matt ran to the side, straining to keep the rope taut. He didn't doubt for a second that the pouka would maul him to death if she could. He ran around a little tree to the bear's rear and pulled hard.

The bear tumbled off her feet but changed even as she fell. By the time she hit the ground she was a doe who struggled to rise but fell with her feet still tangled, then a wild ox who set her forefeet and lowered, then tossed her head, catching the rope with a horn. Matt obliged and flipped his wrist, sending a loop to wrap around the horn, then pulling hard. The ox bellowed in anger as her head tilted to the side, straight out. She tried to toss her head again, to pull the rope out of Matt's grasp, but Sergeant Brock threw himself onto the strand, too, and the ox turned into an otter who sprang through the loop of the bola. Matt shouted and pulled hard, just in time to tighten the lasso around the otter's body—and she turned into an eagle who leaped into the sky, beating her wings. But the lasso tightened even more around her body, pulling her back to earth.

"Parley!" Matt shouted. "Give us a chance, and maybe we can talk this thing out!"

The eagle glared at him—eagles have the right kind of eyes for that sort of thing. Then its form blurred—though the eyes stayed clear—growing to human size, and the whole body stretched and narrowed here, broadened there, until a young woman stood before them, gloriously naked, tossing her head to flip back the long tawny hair that might have cloaked her charms. Her face was beautiful, with a high forehead, high cheekbones, small straight nose, full ruby lips, and the huge brown eyes of the mare, though narrowed and angry now. Her only garment was the rope, settled around a slender waist above swelling hips.

Sergeant Brock stared, face lengthening as his tongue grew thick with desire. Matt knew how he felt, and fought desperately to remember Alisande in a similar state when she had just saved him from Sayeesa's clutches, proud and as full of dignity naked as she had been clothed, a sword whirling in her hand, her eyes bright with scorn. The image didn't change his responses to the pouka's nudity, but it did channel it in a more healthy direction.

Sir Orizhan, however, cried out in dismay and stepped over to the pouka, swirling his cloak around to cover her.

She batted it away with a vindictive smile, her glare still on Matt and Brock. "I thank you for your gallantry, Sir Knight," she said in a brogue so thick Matt could scarcely understand it, "but I'm not about to release these two from the torture that is the punishment they deserve for having treated me so roughly—and if they're fools enough to seek to touch me, they'll deserve what they get." Then she glowered at Brock alone and said, "Yes, you ache to reach out and touch, do you not? But you don't dare, for you know I'd likely turn into something with claws that would rip you from breastbone to groin."

Brock groaned, eyes bulging, and tried to turn away, but couldn't.

"If you hold me with a rope, I shall hold you by your own lust," the pouka declared, then turned her gaze to Matt, frowning. "You, though! I know the lust is there, but you are free of my hold! How is this?"

"I'm married," Matt explained, "and more in love with my wife than ever."

For a moment she only held his gaze, then sighed and seemed to wilt. "Would such love were known to my kind! But I've watched you mortals long enough to know how rare it is even among you. Say, then, why you have sought to capture a pouka! Not that I will admit you have, mind you."

Somehow, Matt was sure she was right—and, suddenly, he felt very much on trial, as though the pouka could slip out of his noose in an instant and turn into a tiger that could rip his vitals out before he could even move. "It was just self-defense. We're trying to go to Innisfree, and didn't want to get bewitched just for trying. Why are you keeping people from getting there?"

The woman spat a Gaelic phrase at him.

Matt sighed. "Okay, so you don't want to tell." He flipped the rope, making it loosen enough to drop over the pouka's hips and fall to the ground. "Go on, leave! But you're warned now. Even at night there's always one of us awake, and we sleep with our swords drawn. Try to attack us, and you'll get a dose of Cold Iron in your vitals. All we want is to get to Innisfree so we can ask somebody how to find the place we really need to go. We don't mean any harm to you or your land. Tell all the other spirits that, would you?"

"Nay, I shall do more than that," the pouka said, frowning. "I shall tell you that I do not seek to bar all from going inland—only those whom I fear may harm Erin, and since you are outlanders, I thought you might be such." She turned to Sir Orizhan. "By your leave, knight, I'll take that cloak now."

Sir Orizhan swirled the fabric over her shoulders, and as it settled into place, Sergeant Brock relaxed with a sigh, then a groan. The pouka eyed him with knowing amusement, chin tilted high. "I give you mercy, soldier, though I fear you would rather have your torture again."

"If you thought we *might* be a danger to the land," Matt said, "how were you planning to make sure?"

"Why, by carrying the knight and the maiden to spirits more powerful than I, who could read them and judge them. You would have followed—do not deny it."

"I don't," Matt said, "but if you knew that, you must have known we couldn't be wholly bad."

"To one another, no," the pouka said with a smile. "To Erin and its people? Ah, that might be another matter!"

"How could you be sure I am a maiden?" Rosamund asked, more curious than insulted by the invasion of her privacy.

The pouka gave her a look devoid of the slightest trace of humor or sarcasm. "I would have known, maiden. Be sure. Some things you may not hide from the spirit world—no, neither with fine fabrics and layers of clothing, nor with fair manners and layers of deception."

Matt wondered what the other unhideable things were.

"We do not seek to harm Erin," Rosamund assured the pouka, "only to find the body of a friend, to learn whether he is truly dead, or only very deeply asleep."

The pouka stiffened. "How good a friend is he?"

"Better than I knew, alas," Rosamund said, suddenly sorrowful. "When all about me sought to hurt me with their petty cruelties, he was always gentle and courteous, though so maddeningly formal that I found ways to anger him, to find the chinks in his armor."

The pouka frowned. "But if all others were cruel, how did you dare anger him?"

Rosamund smiled. "Oh, even at his most angry, he would never hurt a lady even by words."

"Any lady," the pouka demanded, "or yourself alone?"

Rosamund dropped her gaze. "I never knew." Her voice was so low that Matt could scarcely hear it.

"How long did you know him, maiden?"

"Since I was ten years old, and came to live with his parents and his brothers," Rosamund replied.

"And what will you do with him if you find him dead?"

"Bury him—or weep at his grave." Rosamund turned ashen at the thought, as though she hadn't really confronted it till then.

Before she could sink too deeply into anxiety, though, the pouka demanded, "And what will you do with him if you find him living?"

"Why, restore him to good health," Rosamund said, "and never let him out of my sight again!"

Matt turned to her in surprise, but Sir Orizhan only smiled fondly, nodding, as though finally hearing his own suspicions confirmed.

The pouka turned to Matt, one fist on a hip under the cloak while the other hand held it closed. "And what will you do with this man if you find him alive, sir?"

"Restore him to good health, as she says," Matt said, "but I'm afraid I'll have to tear him away from her and take him back to Bretanglia, so that he can cleanse that land of the corruption of the false druids who have begun to infest it."

Rosamund cried out in protest, but Sir Orizhan pointed out, "They are a corruption which, if it goes unchecked, may spill over into Erin."

"I am well aware of that," the pouka snapped. "We spirits are not completely unaware of what happens in the rest of the world." She turned to the maiden. "The man you speak of is Prince Brion, and you are the Princess Rosamund. Is this not so?"

"Y-Yes," Rosamund stammered in amazement.

"And who are you, man of knowledge who goes about in peasant's clothing?" the pouka demanded of Matt.

"Matthew Mantrell, Lord Wizard of Merovence," Matt said. He spread a hand toward his companions. "These are Sir Orizhan, protector of the princess since she left her homeland, and Sergeant Brock, who serves him as squire on this quest."

"Quest?" The pouka frowned. "Do you seek more than Prince Brion?"

"We do," Matt admitted. "We're trying to find the murderer of Prince Gaheris."

"When you do, thank him," the pouka advised, "for he has saved Bretanglia from a scourge, though not one so bad as the false druids are apt to prove."

Matt raised his eyebrows. "You don't like them either, huh?"

"I do not, and the true druids are livid with rage. They are at least as disgusted with the impostors as you are, and angry past speaking at their blackening of the names of the old gods."

"So there really are some real druids left," Matt said softly.

"Aye, and you knew that already," the pouka snapped. "Do not seek to bandy words with the spirit folk. What we do not know, we can guess, and we recognize truth or falsehood instantly when we hear it. Why do you wish to discover the murderer of a corrupt prince?"

"So we can show him to King Drustan and Queen Petronille," Matt said, "to remove their reason for declaring war on Bretanglia."

"You no longer need concern yourselves with that," the pouka advised, "for Drustan is dead, and John is king of Bretanglia."

Matt stared in shock, and the other three cried out in dismay.

"Then we had better find Prince Brion very quickly," Matt said, "and pray he is alive and can be restored, for John has the perfect combination of malice and incompetence to plunge Bretanglia into chaos. Can you lead us to him?"

"Of course," said the pouka. "What one spirit of the land knows, all know. You only had to ask."

* * *

Matt woke in the night, heart hammering, looking about him wildly. He almost thought he could still hear the voice shouting . . .

Sergeant Brock heard him rise, and turned from his sentry place at the edge of the camp, concerned. He came close, whispering so as not to disturb the others. "Are you well, Lord Wizard?"

"Guess so," Matt said. "Just a bad dream . . ."

"Ah." The soldier nodded wisely. "Surely you have had enough strains upon you to cause them—and there are unfriendly spirits about us, I doubt not."

"Yeah, I know." Matt nodded. "I expect our pouka guide is out there somewhere telling them to back off, but there's a good chance they won't listen to her."

"I cannot guard your dreams," the sergeant said. "Would that I could."

"So do I," Matt sighed. "Well, maybe I can get back to sleep. How long has it been, Sergeant?"

"Since you lay down? It may be an hour, by the position of the moon."

"Got to sleep longer, if I can," Matt muttered. "Thanks, Sergeant. Good night."

"Good night, Lord Wizard." The sergeant tugged his forelock and turned away.

Matt lay back and closed his eyes, willing himself to relax. He tried to think happy thoughts, Celtic thoughts—Osian seeking the Land of Youth—and began to grow drowsy as the wonderful old story drew him in. He drifted toward slumber . . .

"What are you doing to find my murderer, I said!" the voice ranted.

Matt managed to keep from jumping up, but every muscle went stiff.

"Aside!" Prince Gaheris' voice snarled. "He has my murderer to find first! I died before you!"

"I am your father, boy!" the first voice shouted. "I am the king! Yield precedence to me!"

"There is no precedence in the world of the dead," Gaheris said, full of venom, "and you are king no longer. If it comes to sheer force of will, I fancy my rage and bitterness are greater than yours, especially toward you, for it is you who have bred them!"

"I?" Drustan bleated. "What did I do to earn your hatred?"

"Ignored me," Gaheris snapped. "If you did notice me, it was only to berate me for my failings, or to bellow at me for not following your orders instantly. You showed your jealousy and spite in a thousand ways."

"Jealousy! What cause had I to be jealous?"

"Because I would have your crown when you were dead," Gaheris snapped, "and you begrudged it even then!"

"Uh, guys," Matt put in, "do you suppose you could go argue someplace else besides the inside of my head? I'm trying to get some sleep here."

"Aye!" Gaheris snapped. "Let him sleep, so that he can seek the man who murdered me!"

"Let him devise my revenge instead," Drustan commanded, "for I know who my murderer was!"

"Oh, really?" Matt sprang to full mental alertness, then settled his mind to listen. "Go on. This could be very interesting."

CHAPTER 20

Two minutes later he wished he hadn't said that. In fact he wished Drustan hadn't come calling at all. He was only glad that Drustan's memories hadn't included smell as he saw Prince John's gloating face from Drustan's point of view, bending over the dying king to ask, "Do you remember your philandering, Father? Of course you do, it was your pride and your boast! The number of times I had to listen to the sickening accounts of your conquests nearly made me die of nausea! But do you remember those horrible howling fights with Mother whenever she found out about your little paramours? Do you remember how she refused to live in the same castle with you? Did you even care that you drove her away and thereby robbed me of my mother, and my chance to win her love? No, of course not! All you cared about was your own pleasure, and indulging your own temper!"

A gargle of denial sounded in Matt's ears, filling his whole head, and he realized it was Drustan's response, seen and heard from the viewpoint of a dying, aphasic king.

"Do you remember how you sat back and watched when Gaheris beat me?" John snarled. "Oh, you could have told him to stop, but no—you had to yell at me to put my fists up, to block his blows, and scold me for failing! You could have protected me from Brion's contempt, from his rebukes and his lectures—but you were too busy with things of greater importance. After all, one lonely child couldn't have been all that important, could he, Father?"

Again, Drustan gargled a protest.

"Where were you?" John asked. "When I was a little boy, tormented and beaten by my brothers, where were you? Off fighting the Irish and gaining a few miserable square miles of bog, that's where! Or off wenching with one or another of your paramours! Even after you took me away from my mother, where were you? Gone on missions of state as often as not, until I was old enough to be useful as a weapon against Mother and Gaheris and Brion, by your threat to make me king!"

The king croaked something in protest; Matt, inside his memories, understood it: "But I loved you!"

"Loved me?" John's lip curled. "If you had loved me, you would have kept me with you! Oh, now and again you felt fatherly, and took me out to give me a drubbing with a stick and call it teaching me swordplay! If you loved me, you had a very odd way of showing it! But that's all right, Father—I loved you, too, and my way of showing it is to set you on the road to your reward more quickly than you would have gone otherwise."

Drustan's brows pulled down in puzzlement.

"Can't understand?" John jeered. "Where is the vaunted genius of statesmanship now? It is I who have killed you, Father—I who fed you your bowl of gruel this morning, and a dram of poison with it."

Drustan's eyes widened in horror.

"Oh yes, you understand now," John said, grinning with glee. "I've set you off on the road to Heaven, all right, but it will be a long, long road, Father, because you've committed enough sins for an army in your life, not the least of which was my upbringing! You'll burn in Purgatory for thousands of years to pay for those sins, and I will delight in imagining every wince, every torture, every scream!"

A roar rang through Matt's head, and the room seemed to tilt downward as Drustan forced himself up. John retreated in fear—but the room swung again as Drustan fell back, eyes filming over, breath rattling in his throat. The room was silent for a second; then John's face swam into view again, grinning once more. "At the end, of course, I goaded you into enough anger to make your poisoned heart burst—and to make sure you died in sin, in the sin of anger. Sleep well, Royal Father. I'll think of you every morning—think of you, and delight in your torments." He stepped up to close the king's eyes, saying softly, "Good-bye."

Darkness closed in, and Matt could feel the king's desperation and clamoring fear of the supernatural as consciousness dimmed and was gone.

In the darkness of dream and memory Matt drew a deep, shaky breath. He realized that what he had seen might have been augmented by the king's own guilty memories, but that didn't matter—it was memory, however distorted, and he didn't doubt for a second that John had really boasted of killing his father as the king was about to cross the threshold of death. He could almost sympathize with the prince, but not enough—he could have found another form of revenge, after all, such as succeeding where his father had told him he would fail.

"So I know who murdered me." Drustan's voice seemed to echo all about Matt. "I know it by his own confession—nay, his boast! Go you now and see justice done!"

"Give me justice first," Gaheris demanded, "or I'll never give you a night's peace!"

Drustan started a roar of outrage, but Matt cut him off—after all, it was his mind. "Shut up, both of you! I can't help either of you if I'm so groggy from lack of sleep that I can't think straight. Besides, why should I?"

"Because if you don't—" Gaheris began in his most threatening manner.

But Matt cut him off again. "Remember, I'm a wizard, and if I want to clear you out of my skull, believe me, I can. But it so happens that getting rid of John is now probably the only way to save Merovence from war, because if we let him have Bretanglia, sooner or later he'll attack Merovence."

"Why, that is so," Gaheris said in surprise. "The fat little toad is that envious!"

"He will lose," Drustan said with certainty.

"Sure, he'll lose, but tens of thousands of soldiers will get killed in fighting him off. No, if I can come up with a good reason for kicking him off the throne he has stolen, I will!"

"Is not the murder of his father and his king reason enough?" Drustan thundered.

Matt winced. "Hold it down, there. I can't think too well if I've got a headache, either. Besides, what proof do I have? Only your word."

"The word of a king!"

"Yeah, but anybody who hears me say it will only have the word of a wizard that he has the word of a king's ghost. Would you have believed anybody who came before you with a story like that?"

Drustan grumbled something incoherent.

Gaheris crowed with delight. "Well asked, wizard! What say you, O Mighty King? Would you have believed such a tale?"

"I have to be able to back up your charge with evidence." For a dizzy moment Matt felt like Hamlet, trying to find physical proof of what the ghost of his father had told him. Trouble was, Matt knew he couldn't afford several years of indecision. "Was there any proof that John poisoned you?"

"The doctor," Drustan said, "he who examined me as I lay dying. I saw the alarm in his eyes, then the look of soul-sickness."

"Probably from realizing he knew too much, and that John would have him killed," Matt inferred. "We'll have to find out where he is and try to keep him alive, if he still is. Where did John find the poison? He doesn't strike me as knowing enough to brew it himself."

His answer was a startled silence from both ghosts. Then Gaheris said, "He is right, Father—the little toad wouldn't know how to brew beer, let alone poison."

"It is well asked," Drustan said, musing. "I will think on it."

"That would be nice," Matt told him. "In the meantime, we do have one other way of getting John off the throne, and maybe even into prison."

"Prison is not enough!"

"Yeah, but it will keep him from doing anything worse while we dig up evidence against him."

"A good point," Gaheris said. "How will you oust him?"

"By bringing Brion back," Matt said.

Another startled silence followed, then Gaheris burst out, "That sanctimonious prig, sit on my throne? That lumbering self-righteous booby?"

"He is dead," Drustan said.

Matt was surprised to hear a genuine note of sadness in

his voice. "Maybe not, Your Majesty. Is his soul there where you are?"

A third shocked silence followed, then both voices said, "No . . . I have not seen or sensed him . . . if he is dead . . ."

"Enough!" Matt commanded. "Any chance he would have gone on to Heaven?"

"That young goat?" Gaheris scoffed. "There are several young mothers who were kitchen wenches when he met them, and have been taking his gold every month to raise his brats."

"He is a fool of chivalry who gallops off to battle at the slightest sign of a war," Drustan said heavily, "and has slain more than a few enemies on the battlefield. Besides, I have seen him go to confession often, far more often than is healthy for a virile young warrior. No, he has committed too many sins for Heaven, but not enough for Hell."

"How about Purgatory?"

"Purgatory calls to me constantly, and with voices I recognize!" Gaheris snapped. "Surely we would know if he were here!" Then, more subdued, "At least, I hope it is Purgatory . . ."

"But there's such a huge population," Matt said automatically. Most of his mind was wondering how could they be called to Purgatory if they were in his dream—but he remembered that the afterlife was more a state of existence than a place. "Isn't this a bad location for you to be looking for revenge?"

"I ask only justice," Gaheris said, his voice surly.

"I, too," Drustan grumbled, "but I am also concerned for the fate of my land. I wish to save my people from John."

"And make sure that he doesn't profit by your death, of course."

"Well, of course," Drustan said in a tone of surprise.

"Just your duty, I'm sure," Matt said sourly. "By the way, Your Majesty, if you wanted somebody to bring justice for you, why didn't you appear to the Earl Marshal or the Lord Chancellor or somebody else in your own country? Why come to me?"

"Because I knew you would listen," Drustan growled. "No one else ever would—certainly not Petronille or any of my sons."

Matt tried to suppress a stab of sympathy.

"I thought John did," Drustan's ghost said, with a sardonic echo, "but he listened only as an enemy listens—to find my weaknesses, my points of vulnerability."

"And to think he seemed such a fool!" Gaheris marveled.

"Be still, boy," his father grumbled, "and be glad you did not live long enough to learn in your own turn."

They woke with the sun, made a quick breakfast, and were just breaking camp when the pouka stepped out of the bushes in horse form. She let Rosamund ride, but none of the men. Sir Orizhan thanked her for carrying his princess, but Sergeant Brock kept his bola ready to hand.

Matt walked beside the pouka, marveling that she could have seemed so absolutely breathtaking as a woman but seemed merely pretty as a horse. Of course, a stallion might not have thought so—but it did raise an issue. "If you don't mind my asking a personal question—what's your true form?"

The tawny mare turned to him, puzzled. "What is a 'true form'?"

It was still unnerving, hearing a horse speak.

Rosamund answered from her seat on the pouka's back. "It is the form into which we are born, and from which we mortal folk can never change, except by growing."

"Ah." The horse nodded. "But if you could, you would—and therefore there is no such thing as a 'true form.' "

"Plato would disagree with you," Matt sighed, "but I don't think I'm quite up to arguing philosophy with a shapeshifter."

They wound their way through the amazingly green hills of Ireland, going steadily inland and steadily higher, steadily northwest. Finally, after three days' travel, they came to a cleft between two hills, spilling an outcrop of rocks that glowed golden in the sunset. The pouka halted, so the rest of them had to, too.

"I take it this is where we pitch camp for the night?" Matt asked.

"If you live that long," the pouka answered.

Matt was instantly wired for alarm. "If we live? What might stop us, pray tell?"

A band of stocky men in tunics, breeches, and cross-gartered sandals stepped out of the woods. They all looked tough, hardened, and resolute—just like the spears they held leveled at the companions.

"Behind us," Sergeant Brock warned, his voice tense with battle-readiness.

Matt risked a quick glance. The Irishmen seemed to have appeared out of the very roadside, and had them completely surrounded.

One man, older than the rest, with gray streaking his red beard, called a question in Gaelic.

Matt spread his hands. "How can I answer a question like that?"

"With the truth," the pouka answered. "Come down from my back, maiden."

Rosamund slid to the ground quickly.

The leader called the question once more, sounding a little angry.

The pouka changed into a woman again.

The Irishmen stared, catching their breaths. Then some of them crossed themselves and began to back away, white showing all around their eyes. The others stood transfixed.

The pouka stood poised in the glow of the setting sun for a minute, making sure of her effect on the sturdy sons of the sod, then called to Sir Orizhan, "Your cloak again, Sir Knight."

Sir Orizhan whirled his cape off his shoulders and about hers. The stupefied Irishmen blinked and shuddered, awaking from a trance of beauty. The others moaned with superstitious fear and kept backing away.

The leader called out in angry protest.

The pouka turned a level gaze upon him and answered in Gaelic, in a tone of authority.

The leader stared, then placed his hand over his heart and called back to her.

She turned to Matt. "I have told them that you are people who may be trusted, though you are foreigners. You may go with them in safety. They will not harm you so long as I am near."

"Uh—thanks," Matt said, "a lot." He looked around at his companions. "Put away the weapons, folks."

Rosamund brought her hand out from under her mantle. Matt wondered how long her dagger was. Knight and sergeant both took their hands away from the hilts of their swords.

"Okay, we're following," Matt said.

The pouka called out to the leader in Gaelic, a phrase that must have meant "lead on," for the men lifted their spear points and turned to follow the eldest through the cleft. They still formed a ring around the companions, but nobody seemed to be ready to stab anymore. In fact, each one glanced at the pouka from time to time, glances filled with both admiration and awe.

Matt followed the leader, too. After all, he didn't have any choice.

They walked a mile or so, while the sun slid below the horizon, leaving the moon to grow brighter and brighter. At last they came to a grove of huge old oak trees, heavy with mistletoe, silvered by moonlight.

Seven figures stepped forth from the trees, their white robes also glowing like silver. They stood in a V with the point toward Matt, a point that was a man with hair and beard as silver as his robes. He held up a palm, intoning a question in Gaelic.

Matt shrugged and shook his head.

"He asks who you are, and why you have come," the pouka interpreted.

"That makes sense," Matt said. "Tell him we are the Princess Rosamund and her bodyguard, seeking the body of Prince Brion of Bretanglia."

The pouka made a brief statement in Gaelic. The lead druid stared at the group in surprise, a surprise that quickly focused on Matt. He answered in a tone that sounded considerably more respectful.

"I have told him your true nature and title," the pouka informed Matt.

"Well, now I'll have to make shop talk," Matt sighed. "Ask him—"

The pouka interrupted him. "I will not. You have named the princess as leader of this quest. She must speak."

"But he is truly the leader!" Rosamund protested.

"Not here," the pouka told her. "Come forth, maiden, and speak with the druid!"

Rosamund obeyed, wide-eyed and uncertain. "What shall I ask him?"

Matt started to answer, but the pouka forestalled him. "Whatever is in your heart."

Slowly, Rosamund turned to the leader and asked, "Can you tell me where Prince Brion lies?"

The druid answered in Gaelic.

"He asks why you wish to know," the pouka interpreted.

The answer came rushing out. "Because he was the companion of my youth! Because of all the brothers, he was the only one who did not torment me or insult me! Because he protected me from them, because he is and always has been honest and fair-minded! Because he cared enough that my barbs could hurt and anger him, and oh! How I wish I had never spoken such sharp-edged words! How could I ever have done so?"

"Belike because you were in love with him, but could not admit it," the pouka told her. "After all, you were betrothed to his brother."

Rosamund turned to her, trembling. "How can this druid have said such a thing!"

"He did not," said the pouka. "I did." Then she turned to the druid and spoke a single sentence.

Gravely, the druid bowed his head and answered.

"He says that of course you have the right to know the prince's fate," the pouka translated.

"What did you tell him?" Rosamund demanded.

"That you are his rightful fiancée, since you were engaged to the future King of Bretanglia," the pouka replied.

Rosamund gasped, but had no time to deny it, because the lead druid stepped aside, bowing and gesturing her toward the grove. The other six stepped aside as well, also bowing and gesturing.

"Am I to step within?" Rosamund asked.

"You know you are," the pouka told her. "Have courage."

"We'll be right behind you," Matt assured her, and was very glad when the pouka didn't contradict him.

Rosamund led them down the aisle of druids. Matt suddenly realized the pouka wasn't with them, and glanced back to see her talking with the lead druid. Turning forward again, he saw Rosamund hesitate at the pointed archway of living oak branches that formed the entrance to the grove.

"Courage, lass," Sir Orizhan said at her shoulder. "Whatever lies within is vital if you wish to save your prince."

"He is not mine!" Rosamund said hastily.

Sir Orizhan was wise enough not to contradict her.

Trembling, she went forward into the grove, step by reluctant step, and it seemed as though they were stepping into a lightless cave.

But as they passed through the leafy archway, light seemed to glow into being all about them. Myriad fireflies sparkled throughout the grove, and moonbeams shone through gaps in the leaves overhead. It was enough light to show them that the interior of the grove was clear, a broad open expanse of clover and moss. At the far end the branches interlaced so heavily as to form a roof, through which a broad shaft of moonlight struck to form a pool of silver light.

In that pool stood a bier, four feet off the floor—a bier holding a coffin with no lid, and in that coffin lay a body, skin waxen and pale, paler than the light itself.

Rosamund gave a little cry, quickly stifled by her own hand.

"Yes, it is Brion," Sir Orizhan said gravely. "But they would not leave him here if he were fully dead, my lady. Approach, and look more closely."

Footsteps dragging, Rosamund went to the coffin, trembling as though with a fever. As they came closer, Matt saw two druids sitting by the body, watching. Silently, they rose and moved back as Rosamund came up.

She stepped to the coffin, looking down, and gasped with horror. Hesitantly, she reached out to touch the long, gaping wound that showed where a sword had sheared through the mail between helmet and breastplate, driving down.

Sir Orizhan frowned, studying, then said, very softly, "The angle is wrong—the stroke could not have pierced his heart, though it let out a great deal of blood."

With a cry of despair, Rosamund threw herself on the pale, still form. "Oh, Brion, why didn't I know you for the darling you were? How could I have been so blind as not to see the gentleness, the kindness you showed me? How could I ever have denied the trembling within me that came whenever I looked upon your handsome face, your speaking eyes? Now must I suffer for my folly, suffer the pangs of heartbreak all the rest of my life, and be lonely all my days no matter how many folk I gather about me!"

The tears flowed freely now, bathing his face as she lifted her head a little to demand, "Yet give me this at least, that I should have taken in life but must now seek of your corpse—this alone, that I may treasure in my heart of hearts and imagine as having the sensation of life!" Her hair swung forward to brush his face as she lowered her own, to press her lips against his mouth. She lingered, exploring the sensation thoroughly, for the memory of it would have to last her all the rest of her days. Gradually, her lips loosened, expanded, until they seemed to devour his . . .

The prince's whole form stiffened. Then his head moved ever so slightly, and his lips opened to envelop hers. Rosamund went rigid with surprise, but never for an instant relinquished his mouth, then relaxed again, lips working around his with fervor as she wept anew, bathing Brion's face with her tears. Slowly, stiffly, steadily, one iron-clad arm rose to encircle her shoulders, but did not rest there, only touched very lightly, as though Brion were afraid she might break.

Finally, they ran out of air, and Rosamund lifted her head, eyes wide and wild, staring down at him in amazement and wonder and, yes, in fear, too—but not of anything supernatural. "I never knew," she whispered. "I never guessed . . . it could be . . ."

"And I only dreamed." The prince's voice was rusty, grating, but soft and caressing. "I could never know—but now that I do, I can only want more." Then the arm about her shoulders grew heavier, pressing her down to him, and she went willingly, covering his mouth with hers, then nibbling his lips, then kissing him fully again.

Matt stepped up beside Sir Orizhan. "He does have to breathe now and then, you know."

The knight turned to Matt, beaming and radiant, with tears in his eyes. "There will be time enough for breathing later, Lord Matthew—time enough, now that she has wakened him. Let her give him all the reason she can, to wish to live."

"Maybe we should turn away," Matt suggested, "leave them a little privacy."

Sir Orizhan shrugged. "It is you who are the healer."

"We'd better stay," Matt said automatically.

When he decided there was a distinct danger of their lips bonding together permanently, he stepped in on the next gasping break for air and said, gently but firmly, "Enough, maiden. Your kiss may have started the flow of blood again, but it hasn't given him back any of the gallon or so he lost."

Rosamund glanced at Brion's wound, then stepped back with a cry of anguish. Looking down, Matt saw blood seeping all along the sword line.

"How can . . . I . . . lack blood . . . when she has set my heart . . . to pounding so fiercely?" Brion panted.

His body tensed, but Matt pressed him back down before he could start to rise. "Just as you've said, Your Majesty. Your heartbeat slowed and became so rare that everybody thought you were dead, and wondered why you didn't start to decay. All your body's systems slowed with it, and they'll take a while to work up to their normal rate again. Push them, and you really will die."

"Lie still!" Rosamund commanded her prince, face pale with fear. She pressed him back, palm against his breastplate.

But his mailed hand still lay on his breast where she had dropped it, and Brion covered her hand with his own, beaming up into her face. "Why, so I shall, if you wish it—but I beg that you give the touch of that hand to flesh that can feel it, not to the iron that covers it."

Rosamund stared down at him in surprise, then pulled her hand out from under his gauntlet and pressed it to his forehead. "You are so cold!"

"I shall warm amazingly at your touch," he promised her.

"Yes, and if you feed him plenty of chicken soup and small beer," Matt told her, "whenever he'll take it." He took off his pack and began to rummage in it. "Sergeant, get that armor off him—but gently!"

Sergeant Brock stepped up to obey, but Rosamund said fiercely, "Touch him not! That is my office!"

The sergeant stepped back in alarm, and she relented. "You may take the pieces from me, though, and lay them aside to clean and burnish. Here."

She began to unbuckle Brion's armor. Brock had to help her lift the breastplate, it being more awkward than heavy. Then Rosamund frowned over the next problem, and opted to have him help a bit more. "I shall lift my prince, Sergeant, and you shall slide his armor from beneath him." She slid an arm under Brion's shoulders and strained, raising his torso. Sir Orizhan stepped up to help, but Rosamund said fiercely, "No! He is mine!"

"Why, so let it be," Brion murmured, his face only inches from hers, his eyes adoring. "So let it be, for the rest of my life."

She looked down at him in surprise, then blushed and looked away. "Is the plate out, Sergeant? Yes, thank you!" She lowered Brion and unfastened the chain mail about his head and neck. He sighed happily at her touch, and she blushed again.

"My turn now." Matt elbowed her aside. Reluctantly, she gave way, but not very far.

"Water, please," Matt told the druids, and one stepped up, holding a metal bowl, watching Matt curiously and closely. Matt took one of his home-sterilized cloths, dipped it in the water, and bathed the wound, with Rosamund studying his actions as closely as the druids. Then Matt said, "Hold your breath, prince."

Rosamund bent to kiss Brion.

"Well, that's one way," Matt acknowledged. He painted the wound with his home-made antiseptic, largely alcohol, but Brion didn't even stir. "Talk about anesthetic," Matt muttered, and stoppered the bottle, then put it aside. "Okay, Highness, you can let him go."

Reluctantly, Rosamund ended the kiss. She made up for it by helping Matt apply the bandage, then wind clean cloth about it from Brion's neck to his armpit, making him sigh with happiness again.

Matt stepped back, eyeing the prince narrowly. "That's all I can do. We'll have to check that dressing periodically, but as far as I can tell, all his enemy did was pierce muscle tissue and give him one hell of a concussion."

"I shall watch him closely," Rosamund promised.

"Well, maybe not so closely as all that." Matt picked up his pack and turned toward the entranceway, then turned back with an afterthought. "Oh, and get the rest of that armor off him." Then firmly to knight and squire, "Come on, gentlemen. I'm sure the druids can help her with anything else she needs."

Reluctantly, and with many backward glances, they followed him out.

There, Matt found the high druid waiting for him. Before the man could say anything, Matt dropped his pack and demanded, "Now, why did you help the son of your enemy?"

CHAPTER 21

"Why, *because* he is our enemy." The old man smiled. "All us Irish hate Drustan, you know."

"Or at least are very angry with him, yes," Matt acknowledged. "I understand he tried to conquer you and failed."

"Failed indeed." The high druid's face tightened, and his assistants turned grim, too. "He failed, but his soldiers slew a great number of our warriors, raped many, many women, and burned nearly a hundred villages before we were able to expel them. No, we have no love for Drustan of Bretanglia."

"Then why help his son?"

"Do you think us ignorant savages?" another druid burst out.

The leader raised a hand to restrain him. "We hear the news from Bretanglia only a few days after it happens, my lord, as we hear word of events in all of Europe—aye, and the rest of the world, too. Credit our magic with some effect."

"I'm impressed," Matt told him. "Did the Mongols conquer China?"

The old man blinked in surprise, but said, "By 'China' do you mean that broad country far to the east, or the one south of it?"

"The eastern one," Matt said. "I take it the Mongols conquered India, too."

"If by that you mean the land of Hind, no, but not for lack of trying. The Mongols call the eastern land Khitai."

"Cathay, in Western pronunciation." Matt nodded; it was interesting that the major social forces seemed to hold in both his home universe and this one. "Not many who know magic would think to use it to gain more knowledge—especially knowledge of the world."

"They do not live so closely to a land that has tried to conquer them before, and will no doubt try again," the high druid said, smile strong with irony.

"So you see the need to stay informed of everything that happens in Bretanglia." Matt nodded. "That means you must have known about Petronille's rebellion against Drustan."

"We did, and rejoiced," the high druid told him. "We knew also of Brion's part in that affair."

"We know, too, of his reputation for chivalry and justice," another druid said.

"He is Erin's best hope for peace," said a third.

"We could not let him die on the battlefield if we could do anything to prevent it," the leader concluded.

"So it was you who bore him away by your magic."

The high druid smiled. "There is this weakness to the pretender's plan to subvert all of Bretanglia by converting its folk to a mockery of the druid faith—that a true druid can pass among them unseen and unknown. Yes, several of us went to Bretanglia as soon as the rebellion broke out and followed Brion closely. When he was wounded, we cast a spell upon him that froze his life as it was, then bore his sleeping body here."

"A spell that could only be broken by the kiss of a virgin," Matt deduced.

"A virgin who loved him," the high druid corrected.

"I thought it might be something like that," Matt said. "You knew Rosamund would be coming, then."

"We did what we could to help her escape, and to turn her footsteps in this direction," the druid confirmed.

"Including turning me," Matt said, chagrined. "You know, I really take it as an insult when people try to move me around like a chess piece, especially when they succeed. I take it you know King Drustan has died?"

"We do," the high druid confirmed, "but from what we know of John, he is likely to be worse than his father was."

Matt nodded. "Just as much greed, but less ability. Besides, I don't think Drustan had all that much genuine malice in him—it just never occurred to him that other people had feelings. John, though, is out for revenge—on the whole human race."

The high druid shook his head sadly. "We feared as much. Besides, was this John not Drustan's favorite?"

"He was," Matt said, "but not because he was like Drustan. He was just very good at bowing, scraping, and ingratiating."

"If you suffer him to remain king," the high druid advised, "the people of Bretanglia will remember him as the worst monarch they have ever had."

"I don't doubt it." Then, remembering the history of his own universe, Matt added, "He'll be so bad that the people of Bretanglia will swear never to have another king named John."

"He is like to win that distinction merely by supporting the . . . how did you call these false druids?"

"Synthodruids," Matt said. "The 'syntho' means their chief rolled a lot of ideas that had nothing to do with your faith into his parody of a religion."

"Aptly named," the high druid said dryly. "They do not even call the gods by their British names, but mix in the Irish and Gaulish, too."

"Thanks for the vote in favor of my label. By the way, do I dare say their chief druid's name here?"

"Do you fear to attract his attention?" A wispy smile touched the high druid's lips. "Do not hesitate. His magic is not strong enough to register each time someone somewhere mentions his name, and even if it were, our warding spells are surely more powerful than his enchantments."

He said it with such total certainty that Matt guessed they'd run a test of some sort. He felt very much reassured. "So you think John's supporting Niobhyte and his synthodruids is bound to win him the Worst King Ever award, all by itself?"

"I do not doubt it," the high druid assured him. "Our spies send reports, and our scryers peer where people cannot go. The false druids have wasted no time. They have converted all of southern Bretanglia already, that neck of land that bulges out from Merovence, and have sent their missionaries into the midlands. Behind, in the lands they hold, their false priests whip the people into frenzies that make them cheer the spectacle of human sacrifice. They stretch victims upon their altars and stab their hearts with copper knives. They preach that might makes right and that whoever can take his neighbor's goods, deserves them—so every man's hand is turned against his neighbor, and the strong slay the weak, then gather their wives and daughters in to serve their own pleasure. Before, the peasants feared the looting and raping of soldiers in wartime—now they fear the knives and scythes of their neighbors, every day. The southernmost counties churn in chaos, but the midlands, drunk on the druids' wine and lured by their orgies, are deaf to the cries of anguish blown on the wind from the south."

"That's Bretanglia's problem, though." Matt frowned. "They're your enemies. Why should you care what happens to them?"

"Why should you?" the high druid returned. "Do not tell me that you do not, for you have come here seeking to aid them!"

"Easy." Matt shrugged. "I want to make sure Bretanglia doesn't bring war to Merovence—and now that I've seen what the synthodruids are doing, I want to make sure I stop them before they try to spread their madness to my own country."

"Is that all?"

"What are you trying to make me say?" Matt demanded. "That the people themselves aren't my enemies, only their king and this Niobhyte? All right, count it said!"

"Indeed." The high druid nodded slowly. "Count it said for us, too." He shrugged. "We are usually content to let the world go to ruin in its own way—only what it deserves, for having deserted our religion—but even we must draw the line at such wholesale misery-making. We cannot allow it to persist, for it offends our gods, and our very souls."

"There comes a point when you cease to be yourself if you don't take a stand against what you perceive to be evil." Matt nodded.

"Indeed," the high druid agreed. "Then, too, there is the reputation of ourselves, and our gods, to consider—that is almost as important as the sufferings of the people. These synthodruids will make the descendants of the folk of Bretanglia think of us as monsters, for they will confuse us true druids with Niobhyte's travesties."

"Good reasons for trying to stop him," Matt said with approval. "But how are you fighting him?"

"Why, we have brought you here, have we not?" The high druid smiled.

Matt felt a surge of anger at having been manipulated, but managed to contain it. "I was already trying to bring them down for my own reasons."

"Aye, but you had little strength with which to fight them. Here we can give you Brion, who is worth whole armies, for he is the rightful king."

"Worth whole armies maybe, but he'll need even more armies to win back his throne," Matt said. "False king or not, John has the power now, and will fight to the death to keep it."

"His death in battle is not wholly distasteful," the high druid mused. "As to armies, I suspect that Brion shall gather them wherever he goes, as a lodestone gathers nails. Everyone who suffers from the greed of John's tax-gatherers, or the looting and raping of Niobhyte's worshipers, will flock to his banner."

"A good point," Matt admitted, "once he's well enough to travel."

"As to that, we have been weaving spells into his body, healing him as he slept; it needed only the kiss of his future queen to make our enchantments web their virtues together to make him whole. He will be able to ride tomorrow, and will be stronger than he ever was ere you reach the shores of Bretanglia."

"Nice work," Matt said with admiration. "I wouldn't have thought of that. But it's going to take more than armies to win against Niobhyte. From all I hear, he is one very powerful sorcerer."

"He is," the high druid said with a smile, "but so are we. You shall not sleep this night, Lord Wizard, for you shall keep vigil by learning every spell we can teach you. We shall even give you one to use if all else fails, one that shall drown all the synthodruids and their worshipers."

Matt shuddered at the magnitude of the disaster the words described. His head filled with the thunder of earthquakes, the roar of tidal waves. "Isn't that a little drastic?"

"These false druids are a disaster in themselves, and only something of their own magnitude can defeat them. Have no fear—by the time you come to them, there shall be no one left in the South Saxon Shore but themselves and their most ardent believers."

"Meaning the ones who have committed themselves so thoroughly that they won't even think of resigning." Matt nodded. "Okay. I'll use it if there's no other way."

"There will not be," the druid replied, "but you are welcome to try to reason with them. A caution, though—do not reason too long, for while you talk, they shall be preparing a doom to fall upon you."

Matt heard them as soon as he reached the archway into the grove.

"Will you not lie still!" Rosamund scolded. "Must you forever be reaching for me as though I were nothing but your own private cup?"

"No cup could hold wine as sweet as your kisses," Brion protested. "Have I become as ugly as a bear in only a few minutes?"

Matt stepped in quickly. He saw Brion struggling to rise, reaching out toward Rosamund, who was backing away. "You need rest, my lord, not excitement! Nay, forfend! No one owns me save myself!"

"I do not say that I own you," Brion protested, "only that you have kissed me, and, I thought, with some pleasure!"

Rosamund blushed. "It was a lapse of moments only. Be sure it will not happen again!"

Brion stared at her, realizing that she meant it, at least as a resolution. "Ay di mi!" He sank back into his coffin. "If it shall not, then I have no wish to live!"

"Oh, do not carry on so!" Rosamund fumed. "All the world knows you are a troubadour as well as a knight, but there is no need for you to sing your laments to me!"

Brion's face darkened and he struggled to rise again.

Matt decided it was time to interfere. He stepped up to the coffin and laid a hand on Brion's good shoulder. "Gently, gently, my lord. You won't get better if you don't try to rest."

Brion sank back with a groan. "Why should I heal if love is denied me?"

Rosamund rolled her eyes in exasperation and turned away.

"Perhaps for the good of your people," Matt said quietly. "Nobility imposes obligations, you know."

Brion lay completely still for several seconds, then looked up at Matt, and the lover had submerged completely under the leader. "You are right. How selfish it was of me to think otherwise!"

Rosamund turned back, staring, uncertain whether or not to feel hurt.

"And it was very wrong of me to pursue my brother's fiancée," Brion went on, "even though he is dead—perhaps even more because he is dead." He forced himself up on one elbow. Matt and Rosamund both sprang to hold him, but he inclined his head in something resembling a bow. "My lady, I beg your pardon. It was dishonorable of me to importune you so."

"My pardon you may freely have," she said, "though nothing else of me." Still, her face could not hide her hurt.

Brion must have seen it, too, for he sank back with a groan. "I had hoped to woo you for my own, now that I am heir apparent—but it is certainly improper to come courting so soon, and my father has doubtless disinherited me. No, I have no right to seek your hand, no matter how much I may desire it."

Rosamund's face was a study in consternation, both hurt and flattered. Finally, she resolved it by snapping, "Oh, fie upon your chivalry and your honor!"

"I was near to thinking that myself," Brion said, subdued. "Even if I were able to win your love, though, we could not become betrothed without the consent of the king." He was silent for a minute, lost in thought.

Rosamund stared at him, and one hand began to reach out toward him, then pulled back.

Privately, Matt thought that Brion had come pretty close to the hub of the problem: both of them were feeling guilty about being in love. Their hearts may have been clamoring at them, screaming, "Right!" but all the conventions of their society were howling, "Wrong!" He had to find a way to resolve that dilemma for them.

Brion turned to Matt again, still frowning. "Lord Wizard . . ." Then he hesitated, which was unusual for him.

"What's the matter?" Matt asked.

"When first you reached out to heal me, you called me 'Your Majesty,' " Brion said. "That was a mistake, was it not?"

"No mistake." Matt saw what was coming, and braced himself.

So did Brion. "A prince is addressed as 'Your Highness,' my lord."

"I know."

The foreboding shadowed Brion's face. "I cannot be 'Your Majesty' unless my father dies."

Matt gave him a long and level look, then slowly sank to one knee, even though Brion wasn't his liege lord. "The king is dead. Long live the king!"

Brion buried his face in his hands and burst into tears.

Matt stared at him in amazement.

Rosamund was at his side in an instant, trying to fit an arm around his broad shoulders, gazing down at his face in anxiety. "Weep, my lord, as becomes a noble knight! Weep, for grief must out! Weep, for surely the strong may dare to show their hearts!"

Matt resolved to quote that to her later. For the moment, he waited for the first burst to slacken, then said, "But he was your enemy, Your Majesty! He was a tyrant to his sons and the shame of his wife! You fought against him in your mother's war! How can you grieve for him?"

"Because he was my father," Brion gasped. "Because I have boyhood memories of games and riding and early lessons with wooden swords, memories of a kindly though boisterous man! Him I mourn! And most of all, I mourn because he was my father!"

Inside Matt's head, a voice said heavily, *How could I have been so blind as not to see such loyalty as this? How could I have failed to perceive his love, and John's treachery? A curse upon the pride and anger that ever lost me his affections!*

Matt resolved to be the gentlest father he could be, and to discipline with caring.

But Rosamund was cradling Brion's head to her breast now, murmuring in soothing tones. Time and again she started to kiss his forehead, then caught herself, though the longing was naked in her face.

The next day, when Matt went into the grove, he heard Rosamund crying, "Stop it at once! You cannot be healed so quickly! You shall open the wound and bleed to death!"

"You saw for yourself that it was healed so thoroughly it might have been new flesh!" Brion grunted, whirling his sword and leaping in a practice slash. The sword spun in his hands, sending flashes of sunlight caroming off the leaves, as his feet wove an intricate pattern of advance, feint, and retreat. Suddenly, though, he swung his sword high and jabbed it into the ground, leaning on it and panting, "A pox upon it! I have barely begun, but already am wearied!"

"The amazing thing is that you managed it at all," Matt said.

Both young people looked up at him, staring.

He came forward and took Brion's wrist, feeling the pulse slam through it. "Healthy enough, if you don't overdo it— which you will, if I know you." He looked up at Rosamund. "Don't worry, Your Highness—the druids told me that they wove all sorts of healing spells into him. His body has been mending while he slept—the best way to keep him from trying to get up too soon."

"Truly said." Rosamund gave Brion a dark look.

"Perhaps not fit enough to fight," Brion gasped, "but surely fit enough to travel."

Matt glanced from the new king, fairly glowing with virility, to Rosamund, who seemed to exude an equal or greater feminine glow whenever she looked at him, which might explain why her face so quickly erased the burgeoning euphoria that started every time she looked at him, hiding it under a mask of defiance and anger. Guilt, he decided, could do amazing things—but so could leaving these two alone together. Brion was certainly now strong enough for them to do more than kiss, and Rosamund too filled with desire every time she looked at him, no matter how angry it made her.

Whatever their mutual destiny might be, the rules of their society made it entirely forbidden for them—yet. "Yes," he agreed, "we'd better get on with our quest—tomorrow morning. Until then, Your Majesty, back to bed. You can get up for a ten minute walk every hour, but when we set out tomorrow, you're riding in a litter."

He braced himself against the storm of Brion's outrage and waded through the outburst with grim and unyielding determination. After all, Brion might have been the rightful king, but he was Brion's physician, as well as consort to the Queen of Merovence. When the sun rose the next morning, Brion's war-horse went in front of him, and a local horse—drafted by the druids—behind, with the king lying on a stretcher between them, grumbling every foot of the way.

Matt accepted his grumbling with good grace, but Rosamund, who rode beside him, spoke sharply to him every ten minutes or so, upbraiding him for his lack of chivalry in making those about him suffer. She must have known which buttons to push, because she always managed to make Brion subside into dark muttering for five minutes or so.

For his own part, Matt kept glancing at the Irish horse at the other end of the stretcher, wondering whether it was going to turn into a person or not. However, by the end of the day it was still a horse, and the most human thing it did was to turn greedy when he put on its feed bag.

The next day, though, even Matt couldn't deny that Brion was well enough to ride. The Irish horse was quite happy to bear Rosamund, and three other horses had showed up during the night to carry Brock, Orizhan, and Matt, who rode gingerly, each wondering what he would find himself riding the next minute.

At noon they turned off the road to rest and eat—and broke through a thicket into a lovely little grotto, decked with flowers, with a brook making a small waterfall into a crystal-clear pond where brightly colored fish darted.

Brion's gaze turned distant, and he reached out to rest one mailed hand lightly on Rosamund's. "Now could I stay in this grove all my days and let the world go hang, if you were by my side!"

Her gaze snapped up to him in surprise and, since he wasn't watching her, the naked longing filled her face and stayed there.

"Could you not, also?" Brion's voice was low, seductive, and thrilling.

Rosamund shivered and admitted, her voice very low, "Aye, my lord, and be mightily content in your presence and the beauty of this place."

Matt had to do something fast. "You can't seriously mean to stay in this grotto the rest of your lives!"

"Why should we not?" Brion reached out toward Rosamund, smile glowing, eyes devouring her. "What more would we need than each other?"

Slowly, shyly, she reached out to him, but her eyes were locked on his, and her face was beginning to glow, too.

"Well, there's the matter of midwives, for one." Matt spoke a little more loudly than he needed to, just to break the spell. "Or were you somehow going to live together all your lives without having babies?"

"Our love shall be as pure as any troubadour ever sang!" Brion declared.

Rosamund drew her hand back a little, the glow starting to fade.

"There's also the minor matter of food," Matt pointed out. "I see wild grapes growing here, but that's hardly a balanced diet, and it won't last past the first frost. I suppose Brion could hunt enough meat to keep you through the winter, if you had any way of staying warm, but that's hardly a balanced diet, either."

"Must you be so confoundedly practical!" Rosamund cried.

Matt shrugged. "Somebody has to, and neither of you seem to be in the mood—at least, not that mood. But the biggest problem is that Brion is a knight, and one of the most chivalrous in Europe. How long do you think it would be before he grew restless and began to sicken for battle again?"

"Never!" Brion declared.

But Rosamund withdrew her hand completely as the glow died. "Then I must know you better than yourself, Majesty, for I see that the Lord Wizard is right in every particular. You are a knight born and bred, and would chafe and grow ill-tempered if you could not take to the saddle and ride to defend the weak and the poor."

Brion opened his mouth to protest.

Rosamund's voice sank low. "Indeed, if you were not such a man, I would not . . . esteem you so highly."

Brion closed his mouth.

Rosamund turned away. "Let us find some other place to rest, Lord Wizard. I could not abide here now, and think of what might have been."

She rode out of the clearing, back straight as an exclamation point, and Brion followed, casting a black look at Matt as he passed. Matt let Sir Orizhan and Sergeant Brock ride by before he rode after, cursing under his breath. It wasn't always fun to know you were right.

Nonetheless, later in the afternoon Matt found himself riding beside the new and uncrowned king. Brion rode with his eyes straight ahead, not deigning to give him so much as a glance.

Matt couldn't let that last, either. "I still have to learn who murdered your brother, Your Majesty. Your mother burns to make war on Merovence as long as she believes it was our fault he died."

"And you know that if I overthrow my upstart puppy of a brother, I shall loose her from her prison?" Brion nodded. "You would rightly dread her then! Yes, she might make war upon Merovence of her own accord, and I would surely march to support her."

"But not if Gaheris were murdered by a man of Bretanglia, who was trying to shift the blame onto Merovence," Matt countered.

Finally Brion turned to frown at him. "Who had you in mind?"

"Practically everybody who was there, or anybody who knew Gaheris." Matt didn't mention that the list included Brion himself. "I was hoping you might have seen or heard something that would help me learn who the murderer was, even though I know you weren't at the inn."

"In that you are wrong," Brion said. "I knew my brother of old, and followed him to that inn disguised as a common soldier."

CHAPTER 22

Matt stared. "You followed your brother because you know him? I'm sorry, but that doesn't make sense. You're leaving something out. Why did knowing him make you want to follow him?"

"I knew he would begin a brawl of some sort," Brion answered, "and so he did. I followed both to protect him from those with whom he picked his fight, and to protect those others from him. If the whore's pimp had not stepped up to protect her, I would have done so myself."

Matt's head reeled in amazement. "A belted knight, fight to save a prostitute?"

"I am sworn to protect the weak, my lord, no matter their virtue, or lack of it," Brion said severely. Then he seemed to thaw a little and added, "Besides, I have never been certain that prostitutes were not more victims than sinners."

He spoke softly, but Rosamund heard nevertheless, and looked up at him in surprise. Then her gaze turned thoughtful.

"So you saw the fight," Matt interpreted.

"I saw it begin," Brion corrected. "Once the melee began, though, and I saw the harlot was safe, I leaped to defend my brother's back."

Matt stared. "*You* defended *Gaheris*? I thought you hated each other!"

"He was my brother," Brion said simply.

Once again Matt was amazed by the medieval concepts of honor and duty.

"I turned three blows that would have felled him," Brion reported, "and stretched their assailants cold on the floor. They were common men, only enjoying a good fight. I doubt they knew Gaheris for a prince."

"So how come you didn't see who struck the killing blow?"

"Because some foul knave came upon me from behind, and laid *me* low."

Matt looked Brion up and down in one quick glance. He was taller than Matt, which made him much taller than most men of his time, and even more broad-shouldered and muscular. It was hard to imagine anyone being able to hit hard enough to knock him out, especially through a trooper's boiled-leather helmet.

"So you don't know who knocked you out."

Brion shook his head.

"Was anyone else helping you guard Gaheris?"

Brion stared, then swung about in his saddle to transfer that stare to Sergeant Brock.

Brock stared back, then frowned slightly, puzzled.

Brion turned back. "It was your sergeant! I did not recognize him until now!"

"That figures," Matt said with chagrin. "That's why he and Sir Orizhan are with me—they both lost honor when a prince who was officially under their protection was slain."

"As though any could protect Gaheris from the consequences of his own wickedness!"

"Just a matter of time, huh? But I thought Brock was fighting in front of Gaheris."

Brion shrugged. "It was a melee, Lord Wizard, a mass of confusion. Like as not the ebb and flow of battle carried him around the prince, fighting as strongly as he could, until he was beside me. However, it was not long after that the world went dark around me."

"Well, you can't fault a man for protecting his prince from every possible direction," Matt said. "Unfortunately, he's already told me everything he remembers, and that ain't much."

Brion sighed. "My brother died in combat, Lord Wizard, albeit it was a brawl in a tavern, not a battle on the field of honor. Is that not enough for you?"

"For me, yes," Matt said. "For your mother, no."

Old Meg was waiting in the moonlight with her little boat, though how she knew to which stretch of rocky beach they were coming, Matt didn't know, especially since he had steered the party well away from their original landing place on the theory that unwelcome visitors might have been waiting for them along the road they had already traveled.

They climbed into the glorified skiff, which somehow managed to hold all of them, and Brion's war-horse, too. Since it had been just barely large enough for the four of them and the old woman on the way to Erin, Matt wasn't about to ask questions. Instead, he made sure he was the last one aboard, on the excuse of saying good-bye to the horses. "We appreciate the favor," he told them. "Back to your homes, now, whether they be in the meadows or the barns." He withdrew four silver coins from his wallet and slipped one under each saddle. "That's to thank your masters for the loan. 'Bye, now."

He turned and walked away, and was about to get into the boat when the old woman commanded, "Shove off!"

Matt stared, deciding that he ought to be angry, until he realized that she meant the term literally. "Well, that's what I get for being last."

"What, Lord Wizard?" Brion asked, frowning.

"Wet clothes," Matt sighed, and set his feet. He shoved hard, and the little craft floated free. He waded out knee-high before he clambered over the gunwale, not wanting his weight to ground it again. Then he looked back at the shore, already receding—and saw a man in peasant's clothes holding all three horses. The fourth was missing.

Matt stared.

The peasant lifted a hand in farewell.

Matt waved back, then turned around to shiver with his companions.

Sir Orizhan noticed. "What troubles you, Lord Wizard?"

"I just found out that poukas can shift their shapes to include clothing," Matt said. "Makes sense—what else would they do with all that horsehair?"

Sir Orizhan glanced back at the shore, then forced a smile, though he shivered, too, as he turned back. "They came to us with saddles and bridles, my lord. Who can say what was in the saddlebags?"

"Good point," Matt acknowledged. "Me, I didn't check."

"Nor did I," Sir Orizhan confirmed. "There were other matters more pressing."

Old Meg was a very poor host, at least for the original three companions—she spent the whole crossing in quiet but earnest conversation with Rosamund, who seemed dazed by what she learned, then with Brion, and the young man's face became more grave with every sentence. Matt felt indignation mushroom within him, but tried to stifle it—the old druid priestess had paid enough attention to him on the way to Erin, after all, most of it unwelcome.

But when the ship grounded on the Bretanglian shore and Old Meg clambered out after her passengers, Matt had an even bigger surprise in store, for the old woman knelt stiffly before Brion and cried, "Hail, rightful King of Bretanglia! Long may you live, and long may your line flourish!"

Matt stared, astounded, and Rosamund's face seemed to close into a mask, no doubt resenting Meg's presuming the princess' part in the flourishing of the royal line, but Brion seemed to grow and swell with every word, becoming something greater than human. Matt realized all over again that in this universe it was no mere fable that the king became the embodiment of his people and his land.

"You have given me honor and countenance," Brion told her, "and for that, I shall name you—"

"You shall name me nothing!" the woman said sharply, glaring up at him. "I am only Old Meg, as I have been these many years, and nothing more—nothing that any king or sheriff need know of, at least."

"Meaning that you are and always have been a druid priestess," Matt said quietly.

Old Meg turned her glare upon him. "The fisher-folk know me only as a wise woman, young man. Who are you to say otherwise?"

"A wizard," Matt answered, "and one whom you sent to Erin. But if you're a druid, why do you kneel to a king of Bretanglia, and one who, moreover, hasn't an ounce of Celtic blood in him?"

Brion stared at Matt, startled, but Old Meg said evenly, "Not all of us fled to Erin or Scotland, or even Wales. I am a druid and a Celt, aye, but I am a Celt of Bretanglia, and no matter his parentage, this young man is rightwise born king of this country. By his deeds and his actions he has shown that he cares immensely about the common people and their land, cares as much as he does for the nobility and their castles— and more than he cares for the lands in Merovence from which his mother and father sprang."

"That is so," Brion said quietly. "I fought to inherit my mother's patrimony and would have taken it gladly, but my heart was truly in Bretanglia."

"Then you are the first of your line of whom that is true," Old Meg said, "since the first of those foreign hussies wed your great-grandfather and turned the eyes of your house southward. It is for that I kneel to you, not for your father's crown or your mother's heart."

"Then, Your Majesty," Matt said, "you have as much as been crowned by a bishop, for this woman is of the clergy, too, though not Christian."

Brion turned back to Old Meg, startled, but the woman rose stiffly. Sergeant Brock sprang to her aid and she took his arm gladly, smiling up at Brion with triumph. "It is true what he says, Your Majesty. I am as much a senior druid as any woman, as my age should tell, and am very much like one of your archbishops. I will tell you further that a great number of your people still follow us druids, though many of them are also Christians. That is why there was never any great chance that these mock druids would ever gain the whole land— there are too many of us who knew them for what they are. Oh, there are far more of your people who are Christians, or were before they flocked to the false priests for the pleasures and cruelties your church would never allow—but there are enough druid folk to form an army or two, and these will rise and march behind you wherever you go."

Then Old Meg stepped aside, gesturing down the beach. "Behold your first legion!"

Looking where she pointed, Brion saw a crowd of fishermen marching toward him along the sand, hard-faced and hard-handed, each with his filleting knife and his belaying pin thrust through his belt, each with his harpoon or his sharpened gaff hook in his hand. The young king seemed to expand still more, a smile glowing on his face, and when the fishermen knelt and cried with one voice, "Hail, King of Bretanglia!" he spread his arms wide, as though he would embrace them all.

Then an older man with grizzled hair and beard stood up before him. "We are come to march against the false druids and their cattle, Your Majesty! Where would you have us go?"

"Why, inland," Brion said quietly. "Let us march!"

Then two men came from the trees that lined the shore, each leading two horses. They bowed to Sir Orizhan and Matt, handing them the reins.

Sir Orizhan turned to Rosamund. "My lady, will you ride?"

"I thank you, sir," she said. "I shall."

She mounted, but her gaze was on Brion—a troubled gaze, even hurt, for he seemed oblivious to her of a sudden, mounting his huge war-horse with the help of two of the fishermen, then turning to give them a quick, encouraging speech. They all cheered in answer, waving their weapons, but as Brion turned to lead the march, he gave Rosamund one brief, dazzling smile, and reached out to clasp her hand. Almost shyly, she gave it to him, squeezed the chain-mail palm of his gauntlet, then let it go and rode after him, seeming much reassured.

Matt mounted and fell in behind her, wondering if he would ever again be able to trust any steed. Then he noticed that the fourth horse followed Sir Orizhan on a leading rein with its saddle empty. Looking around, he saw Sergeant Brock marching beside the older fisherman, already deep in conversation. Matt smiled to himself, reflecting that the sergeant had already taken his natural position as leader, whether he realized it or not.

Into the forest they rode, with a fisherman walking before them, one who seemed to know the trails well, and Matt wondered how many midnight smuggling trains the man had led down this very path.

They were deep into the woods when howls broke out on every side, and four knights charged out of the leaves with a hundred footmen behind them, spears flashing through the leaf-filtered patches of sunlight.

Matt cursed his own stupidity even as he lugged out his sword and parried the cut from the nearest knight. He had known he was fighting a powerful sorcerer; of course the man had scryed where they would come ashore and what route they would travel!

But the fishermen were proving their worth against the spearmen, harpoons cracking against spear shafts, then stabbing home through leather armor. Other spears jabbed back at them, and here and there a fisherman screamed and fell, but more of them whirled even as they jerked out their gaff hooks and swept the next spear aside, then struck the spearmen low with an iron-tipped blow.

Matt parried and thrust, crying,

> "Spirit perverse, bind our foe!
> Now is the time for favoring Chance
> To come to the aid of all good men!
> Let accidents our blows enhance!
> Let all wrong for enemies go!"

He thought he heard someone call, "Why, here I am!" but couldn't turn to look—he was too busy ducking under a slash and catching the knight's arm, yanking hard and turning his horse. Caught off balance, the knight shouted in anger as he fell from the saddle. A fisherman accidentally-on-purpose kicked him in the helmet, hard, since he happened to be passing by, and the knight went limp. His charger stepped over his fallen body, rearing and striking out with his hooves at anyone who came near—who just happened to be another knight, riding in to cut at Matt. The hooves struck him on helmet and shoulder, and the knight fell, out cold before he hit the ground.

Brion, roaring, finished dispatching the third knight by more conventional tactics—but the fourth shouted, "Retreat!" and galloped away, his men running to catch up with him. A scream of rage floated after him, and Matt, looking up, saw Rosamund facedown over the knight's saddlebow, kicking and flailing with her fists.

"They have taken the princess!" Brion cried, agony in his voice. "After them, men of mine! They must not have her!"

"Majesty, no!" Matt caught Brion's bridle. "That's just what the enemy want you to do—go chasing off over half of Bretanglia instead of standing to battle against their army! Out there, they can lay a dozen ambushes for you, slay you before you're halfway to Gloucester!"

"What matter!" Brion cried. "What use is my life without Rosamund? Let John rule, let the mock druids run rampant for all I care! Cast away my crown and my kingdom! Nothing matters, nothing has any worth without her!" He turned to the fishermen. "Run, to rescue the princess!"

The fishermen answered with a shout of determination, and Matt realized that no king would be able to keep the loyalty of his people if he couldn't even rescue his queen—or lady-love, in this case. Matt let go of Brion's reins. "Then what are we waiting for? Let's go!"

Brion's stallion leaped ahead. Matt kicked his heels into his horse's sides and took off after the king, but Sir Orizhan was already ahead of him.

They left the fishermen to their headman and Sergeant Brock as they rode pell-mell through the forest. The knight and his surviving soldiers had left a broad trail and weren't at all hard to follow. Within ten minutes Brion came in sight of them.

The rearguard heard the drumming of hooves, looked back and shouted with dismay, leaping aside from the virtual tank that was Brion in full armor on a Clydesdale. They knew he wasn't after them. But they recovered from their terror in time to jab at Matt and Sir Orizhan, who weren't armored. It was a mistake, for both men laid about them with swords. One or two footmen bled for their temerity, but the rest were smart enough to pull back.

Brion swerved his horse in front of the knight, meeting him with a body block that shivered both their horses but held them firm. The enemy knight instantly set the tip of his sword against Rosamund's back. "Strike, and she dies!"

"Coward and caitiff, to hide behind a woman!" Brion raged.

"Oh yes, you are a man of *honor*," the other knight sneered. "How much is that—"

Then the lasso settled about his neck, Matt jerked backward, and he went sprawling over his horse's hindquarters, squalling.

Brion caught Rosamund to him, pressing her fervently against himself even as he settled her on his saddlebow. "My lady, I thought you were lost, and all the world lost with you!"

Rosamund only gave a single cry of relief and joy, pressing herself against his breastplate, then shoved herself away and leaped to the ground. "Do as you must, my lord and king!"

"As I must indeed!" Brion glared at the enemy knight.

The man was just fighting free of the loop of rope, crying, "What coward's weapon is this!"

"A coward's weapon for a coward," Matt returned, "and a treacherous attack for treachery."

"I shall sever your—" Then the knight saw Brion, sitting like a mountain above the foothills of his horse, impassive and immobile, his sword raised to guard.

"I am unarmed!" the knight protested, holding up empty hands.

"Give him his sword," Brion grated, and a fisherman sprang to scoop the blade from the ground and offer it hilt first to the enemy knight.

"I would advise you to take it, sir," Matt told the man. "You know the punishment for cowardice in a knight."

Actually, he didn't, but the enemy knight must have, for he accepted the blade and held it up to guard even as he fumbled his shield up from its hook on his saddle.

"Lay on!" Brion shouted, and struck.

Five blows later the enemy knight lay stretched on the ground.

"Shell him," Brion grunted, "then bind his wounds and chain him. He may yet prove of some worth as a hostage. Heaven knows he had little enough as a knight."

Then he sheathed his sword, turned his horse away, and dismounted heavily. Sergeant Brock sprang to take the shield from him, then the helmet, as Brion turned to fold Rosamund into his arms with a glad cry. She came willingly, and he buried his face in her hair, murmuring, "My lady, I feared you were lost to me!"

"I was not," she told him, head on his shoulder. "I knew you would prevent it."

"I would defend you against all Hell's legions," Brion declared fervently.

Matt didn't doubt it, even though Brion was bound to lose—if he hadn't had several patron saints on his side.

What else they said to one another was lost to Matt and everyone else, it was so softly spoken. Of course, it didn't help the eavesdroppers that Sir Orizhan sternly pressed them back, saying, "Give them space, if you value the freedom of your country."

The fishermen moved away with looks that ranged from impatience through sly grins to tenderness.

Later, as they rode behind Brion, with peasants acclaiming him loudly at every crossroads, Matt managed to press his horse up beside Rosamund's long enough to tell her, "When they kidnapped you, he went kind of crazy."

"Crazed?" Rosamund turned to him, suddenly intense. "In what fashion?"

"He said to cast away his crown and his kingdom, because nothing else mattered, nothing had any worth without you."

"Did he truly?" Rosamund turned back to watch Brion with a slight smile and a glint in her eye. "Perhaps there is some truth to his troubadour's extravagant phrases, after all."

Nonetheless, when they pitched camp that night, and the peasants and fishermen were passing the aleskins and getting to know one another by discussing the relative merits of pruning hooks versus gaff hooks as weapons, Brion came up to Rosamund where she sat by her campfire, his armor laid aside, his manner stiff and formal. "Highness, I must ask your pardon."

Rosamund looked up at him with a glad smile that froze as she saw the stiffness of his face. "Apologies for what, Majesty?"

Inwardly, Matt groaned.

"For presuming to show you affection," Brion said, every word creaking, "when we cannot be betrothed."

Rosamund went rigid. "My pardon is given, Majesty."

This time Matt groaned aloud. "What is it with you two? Can't you see that how you feel about each other is what really matters?"

Sudden vulnerability showed in both faces, and Brion protested, "But we cannot wed without the leave of our fathers!"

It is given, it is given! howled a voice inside Matt's head.

Matt ignored it. "Her father betrothed her to the heir to the crown of Bretanglia. Do you really think he'd take that back just because the actual person has changed?"

Brion hesitated, but Rosamund said, almost angrily, "He certainly would not!"

"But there is still my father to be considered," Brion protested.

Loyalty can go too far, exclaimed the exasperated voice inside Matt's head.

"All right, let's consider your father," Matt said. "Why does his opinion matter?"

"Why, because a prince may not wed without the permission of . . ." Brion's voice trailed off as his gaze drifted away from Matt to Rosamund.

She gazed back, speechless.

"You may not marry without the permission of your king," Matt finished for him. "But *you* are King of Bretanglia now. At least, you're the rightful king, and the man who wears the crown is a usurper, brother or not!"

"Why, that is so." Slowly, Brion knelt before Rosamund and asked, "My lady, will you marry me?"

"Oh, yes, Brion, with all my heart!" Rosamund threw her arms around his neck and kissed him, tolerating no nonsense about chaste symbols.

Matt turned away to find his pallet. After all, it had been a long day.

His last thought was wondering which spirit of perversity had come to help him when he had called for accidents during the ambush.

They marched through the countryside, and as Old Meg had predicted, peasants joined him at every crossroads. Soon there were merchants with them, then squires, then knights. No lords joined them—they had estates to consider—but several of their younger sons came in.

"Doesn't that show the lords' hearts are with you?" Matt asked.

"No, it shows only that they wish to be sure that no matter who wins, their families will still keep their estates," Brion told him. "We must watch those younger sons closely, Lord Wizard. There may be traitors among them."

Matt set his spies to watching—fishermen and peasants, and a squire or two—but they found nothing suspicious about the younger sons. In fact, they reported that the young men seemed to burn with eagerness to strike a blow against John and his reeves, for they had heard of the insults he was offering the nobility, trying already to make them bow to his tyranny.

Then at a crossroads in the wood, a dozen outlaws with bows and staves stepped out of the leaves in front of the king.

Brion leveled his lance and cried, "Declare yourselves!"

"We declare for King Brion and the welfare of the kingdom," the foremost said. He carried himself like a nobleman, but he knelt, bowing his head.

"For Brion and Bretanglia!" his followers shouted, and likewise knelt even as the same slogan rang from the trees all about them: "For Brion and Bretanglia!"

Matt's scalp prickled. He realized that there were a hundred archers all around them, probably with bows drawn. Worse, he realized what those bows could do, and doubted that anyone else there did.

The leader stood. "There is not a man of us who is not sickened by the slaughter and rapine with which this self-named 'King' John treats the common folk. There are already many among us who have fled to the greenwood because his soldiers have beaten the poor to pry from them every copper coin. There are more who have fled to us because the king's druids have tortured and slain their families or sweethearts."

"They are false druids," Matt called out quickly.

Everyone turned to stare at him, but Brion confirmed, "They are false indeed! It is the true druids who saved my life!"

"Why, that makes most excellent sense," the outlaw leader said, "for no true holy man could drench the land with blood as their chief Niobhyte has done! Down with the false druids, and up with the true king! We hail Brion as the savior of Bretanglia—if you will have us!"

"I welcome you, and am right glad of your allegiance," Brion told them. "I cannot promise a pardon to every man, for I know not what crimes each has committed, or what his circumstances were—but I can promise you justice if we win!"

That didn't seem to faze a single man; apparently they were all sure of their innocence, or at least of their justification. "We will depend upon your justice," the outlaw chief said, "for you shall triumph, and the crown of Bretanglia shall rest upon your brow!"

"That shall be as God wills," Brion told the man. "We can only strive as mightily as we can, and leave the victory to Him!"

"Ah, but a victory for Brion is a victory for God," the outlaw returned. "None could think otherwise, who knew even half of what the soldiers and the druids have done." Then he spun about and punched his forearm straight above his head, calling to his men, "For God and Brion!"

The answering shout blasted from every side: "God and Brion!"

Somehow, the word spread ahead of them. By the end of the day, every new handful of men at each crossroads greeted them with the cry, "For God, Brion, and Bretanglia!"

Still, Matt couldn't help worrying about something the bandit leader had said—that anyone who knew even half of what Niobhyte's minions had done would know them for what they were. He wondered just how bad the situation had become, but wasn't sure he wanted to find out.

He learned anyway, for the company passed by a monastery, and the monks streamed out to watch and to cheer. Matt was just hoping that John's agents wouldn't hear about their enthusiasm and burn down their abbey, when he noticed the middle-aged man and woman standing at the forefront of the crowd, waving and cheering with the rest, even though they looked somewhat haggard. Matt leaped down with a shout of delight and threw his arms around them.

"Halt!" Brion held up a hand, and the whole column slowed, then stopped.

Rosamund looked down at the older couple, who were

laughing and hugging Matt with tears in their eyes. "Lord Wizard," she asked, "do you know these people?"

"Since the day I was born, Your Highness!" Matt turned to her and gestured to the couple. "You remember my mother and father, Prof—uh, Lord and Lady Mantrell!"

Mama and Papa bowed to Rosamund.

"Your apologies," she stammered. "I did not know you. But why are you dressed in peasant garb?"

"To hear the peasants' grievances, Your Highness," Mama told her, then turned to bow again to Brion, crying, "Your Majesty!"

"I must thank you both for bringing this man into the world and for rearing him so well," Brion returned, "for without him, I suspect I would still be sleeping in Erin, and the fairest gem in the land might have been lost." He reached out and caught Rosamund's hand. "Will you join our march?"

That evening, when they pitched camp, Matt made a separate campfire for his parents and, over dinner, asked what he didn't want to know.

"It has been horrible," Mama said with a shudder. "We have fought it wherever we can, of course, but it sweeps the land like wildfire."

"The false druids are preaching what people want to hear," Papa said, "that they can do whatever they wish without worrying about the consequences."

"But there are consequences," Matt said softly. "There always are."

"Always," Mama agreed, "but by the time they begin to show, the druids are too thoroughly in power, backed by so-called acolytes who are really only bullying sadists who revel in the misery they cause in their false sacrifices to the old gods."

Matt braced himself. "How bad are they?"

"Very bad," Papa said with a shudder. "They practice all the tortures that the real druids used for sacrifice on their feast-days, such as making giant wicker-work statues with living people inside, then burning them alive."

"But they have invented other obscene rites that the true druids never imagined." Mama shuddered. "I have seen the beginnings, but have managed to turn away, then chant my spells and turn their own cruelty back upon them."

"I watched while she chanted," Papa said. "I saw, and hope I shall someday forget."

Matt felt panic rising. "You should have gone home to Merovence the minute you saw you couldn't stop them!"

"We could not," Mama said simply. "There was too much suffering we could prevent."

"How?" Matt cried. "The sorcerers must have been able to tell who was interfering with their own gruesome magic!"

"Ah." Papa almost smiled. "In that, we were fortunate—I think."

CHAPTER 23

"You're not sure?" Matt stared.

"It was, shall we say, double-edged," Mama told him. "You see, a few days after we last saw you, we camped for the night in a grove. Papa went to hunt while I gathered wood, but when we came back, we found a campfire already burning."

"I'm beginning to have a bad feeling about this," Matt said.

"So did we," Papa assured him, "but we reasoned that an enemy wouldn't have done us a favor. So we cooked our dinner, and as we began to eat, a stranger wearing a tunic and fur leggins came up and asked if he could join us."

"We invited him to dine," Mama said.

Matt groaned.

"So it was true, what he told us," Papa said softly.

"If you're talking about who I think you are," Matt said, "yes."

"He said he remembered us from our meeting with you at the monastery," Mama told him, "and said he had followed our auras until he found us."

"He knew we were of your family by that aura," Papa said. "Do you have any idea what he meant?"

"Other than an inborn ability to sense DNA," Matt said, "no. Did he tell you his name?"

"No," said Mama. "He only said, 'Call me what you will.' "

Matt groaned again. "What did you call him?"

"They called me 'Whatyouwill'!" said an indignant basso.

Matt jumped a mile without uncrossing his legs—at least, inside himself. When his insides came back down to fill his outsides again, he turned slowly to his left, toward the glowering face under the tunic hood. "Furry leggins, huh?"

"They guessed quickly enough," Buckeye told him.

"So it was well that we did not give him a nickname?" Papa asked.

"Oh, you bet," Matt said. "I did, and it turned out to act like a spell that bound him to me—until I went across saltwater to Erin."

"Aye." Buckeye grinned in the dark. "But now you are returned, and so am I."

"Now I know why Erin is the land of luck," Matt said.

Papa stared at him. "The potato famine? The British conquests?"

"I didn't say what kind of luck." Matt frowned at Buckeye. "I take it you had to save their lives in order to have somebody to torment."

"Even better." The bauchan grinned. "They led me to scenes I could confuse, places where I could cause havoc."

"No wonder the sorcerers didn't figure out who was lousing up their scripted rituals." Matt couldn't help smiling. "How about I thank you, Buckeye?"

"Do not!" the bauchan said quickly.

Matt suddenly felt much more confident. He remembered the old superstition, that if you thank a helpful elf, it will disappear and never come back. Of course, Buckeye wasn't exactly helpful, at least not always, but it was worth trying—later. For the moment, though, he somehow had a feeling the sprite might come in handy. "You didn't dare treat my mother rudely, did you?"

"He did," Mama sniffed. "I believe he regretted it."

"Your punishments always fitted the crime," Matt said to her, grinning, and said to the bauchan, "What did she do—make you ashamed of yourself?"

"Nay." Buckeye grimaced. "She made a horrible taste form in my mouth whenever I used words she misliked. Even now I dare not say them."

Matt could imagine the flavor of Mama's laundry soap. Only imagine—he'd never pushed it past her warnings. "Disagreeable, but harmless," he assured the bauchan.

"It was not enough to chase me away!" Buckeye said staunchly.

"No," said Mama, "but it did teach you a very healthy degree of respect."

Matt reflected that soap, correctly applied, could be very healthy indeed, but that a medieval spirit might not see it that way. Feeling the need of a change of subject, he turned back to Papa. "So the synthodruids never even realized who was putting out the fires on their wicker forms?"

"One did," Papa told him. "He pointed at us, screaming that we desecrated the very ground, and commanded his mob of worshipers to fall upon us."

"I had a few spells to say about that," Mama said primly.

"And I a few heads to knock." The bauchan grinned. "I had them fighting each other in minutes, and struck down those whom their companions did not."

"When all his men lay unconscious," Papa said, "the druid came up to us, shaking with rage, and told us that their ceremonies were becoming so widespread that we couldn't possibly stop them all, or even most of them. 'Perhaps not,' your mother said, 'but we can stop all those we find.' " He fairly glowed with pride in his wife.

"The next sacrifice we found, I did better," Mama said. "When Whatyouwill set the men to fighting one another, I marched up to the druid and matched him spell for spell. It did not take long; I overwhelmed him easily." She smiled with contempt. "I bound him in his own chains, and when the peasants recovered from their fighting with one another, I commanded them to lock up the druids in a hut with strong walls. They did, and Papa surrounded the makeshift jail with a magical fence that their weak magic could not breach. Then we paced out of the town and called out to thank the bauchan."

"We received no answer, though," Papa added.

"I should think not!" Buckeye snapped. "I had fled far enough not to hear, I assure you."

"Wait a minute." Matt frowned. "I thanked you for helping out once—after that fracas at the monastery, remember? And other times, too."

"Aye." Buckeye gave him a toothy grin. "But I am bound to you by a name-spell. Thank me all you wish."

Again Matt frowned, as that hope crumbled. "The druids didn't stay in jail long, did they?"

"Of course not," Papa sighed. "A week later, when we stopped at an inn for the night, the gossip at the tables was all about us. We heard a glorified account of our own victory, but it ended with the druids escaping from the jail."

Matt frowned again. "But I thought you said Papa put up a magical fence that they couldn't break through."

"*They* couldn't, no," Papa said grimly.

"I went right out and scolded the bauchan roundly," Mama said, "even though I could not see him. I knew he was lurking near in the night—but he only laughed at me!" Her face darkened even at the memory.

"I found it all a delightful joke," Buckeye retorted. "Those false druids are still looking over their shoulders wondering whether I will help them or hurt them next."

Matt knew how they felt.

But Buckeye lost his grin. "Then your mother was most ungracious."

"I wished to remind him which way to choose, if he must decide between helping us and hurting us," Mama said. "You know the verses in which Prospero threatens Caliban with pinches from unseen fingers?"

"Yeah, sure."

"Well, so does Whatyouwill—now."

The bauchan looked highly offended. "I do not come and go at your bidding, Dame Mantrell."

"Not yet," Mama agreed.

Matt felt it was time for another change of topic. "So John's rule isn't exactly a roaring success for the common people."

"Oh, for the strong ones who have so far survived the sacrifices and the looting, it is excellent," Papa said. "Of course, those are the ones who have not yet realized that there will always be someone stronger than they, and that when all the sheep are dead, the wolves will turn upon one another."

"For most of the common people, though, John's reeves are as bad as the false druids," Mama told him. "They draft young men into the armies, give their soldiers leave to loot and rape where they will, and take every bit of food the peasants can raise, leaving them only crumbs for the winter. Those who try to hide some produce away are flogged within inches of their lives."

"There isn't an ounce of gold or silver in the kingdom that John's reeves have not gathered for him," Papa said, his face somber. "Even the churches have been forced to give up most of their communion vessels."

"Bad, very bad," Matt said with a shudder. "Of course, he won't let people leave the kingdom."

"No, but he has not yet thought to bar them from traveling from one part of the land to another," Mama said. "The stream of refugees has become a flood, virtually emptying the southern part of the land already."

"You mean the part that was underwater in our universe?" Matt felt a frisson of dread.

"That, and a bit more," Mama said. "There is a Dover in this universe as well as in ours, but here it is an inland town, and the chalk still lies under the soil, not exposed to the sea spray."

"And most of that land is empty?"

"There are still some thousands of people who trust in the false druids," Papa said grimly. "They do not yet realize how close they have come to being next week's sacrifice."

They had barely started to march the next morning when a peasant pointed into the sky and shouted in alarm. Everyone looked up as the flying form circled low enough to be recognizable as a dragon.

With one massive shout of fear, the army exploded in all directions, every man running for cover—except, of course, for Brion, Rosamund, Brock, and Sir Orizhan.

Brion swung his shield up and took his lance from its socket, swinging it down to the level. "What monster has the cowardly sorcerer sent against us!"

"No monster, and not from Niobhyte." Matt reached out to ward off the lance. "Please put up your weapon, Your Majesty. That's an old friend of mine."

Vast wings boomed as Stegoman struck the earth and ran to a stop. He looked about him, calling out, "Your companions are gracious, Matthew, to withdraw and leave me so much room to land!"

"Yes, they must have known you were my friend." Matt hoped he didn't sound too sarcastic. "Good to see you, Stegoman. What have you found in the north?"

"Scrawny cattle," Stegoman said with distaste, "tough and stringy. Their deer are fat and toothsome, though."

"Just don't let them sell you any haggis." Matt asked uneasily, "But how about political developments?"

"The false druids have barely begun to make headway," the dragon answered. "They can convert only a few Scots."

"Why?" Matt asked. "Can't find the highlanders in the middle of all those mountains?"

"Nay, they have not yet come anywhere near to the mountains. But those kilted men keep asking them probing questions that they cannot answer. Therefore the only druids going into Scotland are recognized as foreigners, and the Scots are gathering to march against them."

"There is one source of power that need not cause me anxiety," Brion said with relief.

"Yes, John won't have a horde of howling kilties to throw against you," Matt said, finding the thought reassuring, too. "Your Majesty, this noble dragon is Stegoman, my friend since the first day I came to Merovence."

"And till the last." The dragon bowed his head, neck forming a graceful curve. "I am honored to meet Your Majesty."

"I never knew a dragon could speak with such courtesy!" Rosamund said, staring in wonder.

"My dear, may I present you." Brion caught her hand, then turned back to Stegoman. "Noble Stegoman, may I present my betrothed, the Princess Rosamund."

A cheer went up from the whole hidden army. Rosamund blushed, lowering her gaze, and Stegoman bowed his head to her, too. "I am fortunate indeed to meet so beauteous a lady!"

Now Matt *knew* it was courtesy—Stegoman's standard of beauty ran more to iridescent scales and lidless eyes, and what he meant by "sweet breath" was a color of flame only dragon eyes could perceive.

"Even more fortunate," Stegoman went on, "to meet not only Bretanglia's rightful king, but also its future queen!"

Rosamund gave a start, then peered more closely at the dragon. "Can you see the future, then?"

"No more than any mortal who is not a wizard," Stegoman told her, "but no less, too, and seeing the zeal of the men who follow your betrothed, and their devotion to both him and yourself, I can see the future as clearly as though I read runes."

Rosamund looked even more surprised, then turned thoughtful. "I had not thought any man but Sir Orizhan was devoted to me."

"Had you not?" Brion turned to grin at her. "I assure you, love, this army follows as much in awe of your beauty as in loyalty to their rightful king."

Rosamund turned to meet his gaze, and for a moment her own was blinding.

Matt felt a need for another of his quick changes of subject. "Can you march with us?" he asked Stegoman.

"I had liefer fly," Stegoman said, "but since that would be as good as to announce to all the world where Brion's army lies, I would prefer to scout ahead and behind and to the sides, then join you at nightfall."

"A good thought," Brion said, "though I am not foolish enough to think I can keep so many men secret. Indeed, I am certain that my brother knows to the yard where I am, and his pet sorcerer with him."

For the first time, Matt found himself wondering who was the pet and who the master.

"Return, men of mine!" Brion called. "This is no enemy, but a mighty friend."

Slowly and warily the army regrouped.

They marched through the land, southward and eastward, searching for an army to fight, for druids to match spells against, but finding them strangely elusive. They did, however, find crops standing ripe in the fields with no one to harvest them, and flocks of sheep, their wool heavy and ready for shearing, but with no shepherd to guard them. Cattle grazed among the crops with no idea that they should stay in their pastures, and ravens gobbled the grain with only scarecrows to defy them.

In fact, they marched through a lovely, green-and-amber late summer countryside, but one with scarcely a human in sight. Now and then they saw a silhouette atop a ridge and knew John's spies were tracking them, but other than that the land might have been abandoned. Now and again they passed by a farmstead or village and found it burned to the ground, though there was seldom any sign of the people who had lived there. Matt didn't doubt they had been taken to sacrifice—or had run off following some stray false druid with promises of an endless supply of food and drink for the worshipers of the old gods. The wreckage of farm and town was enough to show where those druids found their provisions.

Flocks of ravens whirled overhead, filling the air with raucous cries, then arrowing away even more directly southward.

"Follow the flock!" Brion pointed at the noisy receding mass. "They go to bear word of us to John! Where they go, he lies!"

"Oh, I don't doubt that he lies," Matt agreed. "Probably never told the truth in his life."

"Seven times, I think," Brion corrected him, "though he meant the comments for insults to Gaheris and myself, and probably did not realize their honesty."

Matt frowned up at him. "What truth could he tell you that would be an insult?"

"That I am pompous, self-righteous, and arrogant," Brion said darkly. "I searched my soul when he told that to me and found all three charges true. I strive to master them, but fear I fail."

"You are prevailing most excellently against them," Rosamund said, and slipped her hand into his.

"But that is only because I have you by me," Brion told her, his eyes glowing, "and know I can never be good enough for you."

Rosamund started to answer, then hesitated.

"Don't contradict him, Your Highness," Matt advised. "That's an excellent way for him to think—excellent for your purposes, anyway."

Rosamund smiled and tossed her head, giving Brion a saucy smile. He grinned back and pressed her hand to his lips.

The army cheered.

Brion blushed, lowering Rosamund's hand. "Can we never be alone?"

"Oh, we shall," she promised him, nudging her horse nearer his, "but you must win your kingdom first."

Matt decided that she'd probably make a pretty good queen.

Two nights later, as Matt sat at the campfire with his parents and their unwelcome guest, Buckeye suddenly snarled, "This takes too long! Why, we are scarcely a day's ride from the border! Much more, and we shall have to swear allegiance to Queen Alisande! If nothing else can make these druids stand and fight, I shall!"

He stalked away into the night, and the Mantrells exchanged stares of surprise.

"What troubles him so suddenly?" Papa asked.

"It has been building for days," Mama offered. "He has been growing more and more moody with every hour."

"I think he's been looking forward to a battle where he can really cause trouble," Matt said, "and is feeling very frustrated to find things so peaceful."

"What do you suppose he intends to do?" Mama asked.

They never found out, at least not the specifics, but the next day, as Brion rode out of a woodland and into a meadow, he saw a peasant come running across the open field with a pack of howling peasants fifty yards behind him, with three men in white leading the way, shaking gilded sickles.

Behind them came a virtual army of peasants.

Not just a virtual army—it was a real army, marching double-quick and without synchronization, but marching. Knights rode in the van, on the flanks, and at the rear, as though to cut down any stragglers, and a mock druid whose white robe was decorated with gold rode before them all.

Brion turned to Matt, astonished. "How have you brought them here?"

Matt could only spread his hands and shrug. "If I'd

known they were coming, Your Majesty, I'd have given you warning."

"Would that you had!" Brion spun to his men, shouting, "Take the high ground!" then kicked his horse to a canter and rode up the side of a nearby ridge. The knights-errant who had joined him echoed his shout, "To the high ground!" and rode after, some leading the peasant army, some following and urging them on.

At the top of the ridge, the peasant army turned, faces grim and determined. The knights rode up and down the line, transmitting Brion's orders. "Spearmen in front! Aye, that means all fishermen with harpoons, and all peasants with pruning hooks! Archers to the sides—when the king commands, turn the enemy into hedgehogs! But wait for the king's command, wait for it, wait for it! Those in back, wait, and if the man in front of you falls, *then* step over him and take his place! Don't try to elbow him aside in your eagerness—there will be slaughter enough for all. Stand, don't charge! Even if they flee, do *not* run after!"

Then the bauchan came barreling straight into the center of the army. Peasants took one look at him close up and squalled, pulling away.

"Close up!" the knights bellowed.

Buckeye kept on going, all the way to the back of the six ranks and on out, up to the hillock where Matt stood with Brion and his companions, watching the chasing mob slow as it realized what it had come against. The druids called orders, and the mob turned into the van of the army, men falling into line and waiting for the mass behind them to catch up.

"What in blazes did you do to get them to come after you?" Matt demanded.

"I tracked down their archdruid and waited for his ceremony," Buckeye said between gasps; he was still panting. "That was not so much of a wait; he holds his revels every night, and slays at least one on his stone table. I transformed myself into the form of a demon and burst in as he was about to stab his naked victim. The depraved congregation screamed in terror and would have run, but Niobhyte knew me for what I was and denounced me instantly, with a spell that dispersed my illusion and showed me as I really am."

"So you ran," Matt interpreted.

"Aye, and he roared at them to follow until they caught me, for he knew that what I had done at his own ceremony I might well do at others, many others, and bring his whole charade down in fear and trembling, showing it for the falsehood it was. A dozen times they caught me, a dozen times I disappeared, a dozen times they came shouting after, and as one mob wearied and slowed, another came charging forth from the peasant horde that followed." He grinned up at Brion. "A spirit of the land has brought them to you, O King, an army of peasants against an army of peasants. What will you do with them?"

"Let them wear themselves out in charges against me," Brion said, his voice iron, "then loose my hounds upon them!"

Wings thundered above them. Everyone looked up, startled, and the dragon's great form darkened the sun. "Beware," Stegoman called down in a voice like thunder, "for half a mile behind those peasants marches a real army of veteran soldiers, and the man at their head wears a crown!"

"John," Brion hissed. Then his face turned to misery and uncertainty. "How can I slay my own brother?"

"For the good of your people and their land!" snapped Buckeye. "Can mortal folk truly be so blind? He has slain your father and your brother, and would have slain yourself if he could have! What is the punishment for king-slaying, O Monarch?"

"Death." Brion's face was still a mask of grief. "But my own brother, the playmate of my youth!"

"If he cheated then as he cheats now, the memories should not be dear," the bauchan told him, thin-lipped. "Are you a king or not? Oh, a pox upon it! Catch him first and try him later!"

Brion's face firmed with resolution. "Aye. That I can do."

"What you will do, do quickly," Stegoman advised. Then, with an explosive clap of his wings, he was up and away again, riding the ridge's thermals to gain altitude.

The attacking army saw and slowed, moaning with fear.

"Amateurs!" Sergeant Brock sneered.

The druids shouted at the peasants, upbraiding and insulting them to move forward, but Niobhyte strode ahead, hand upraised to stop them.

Matt braced himself.

"We can have these men slay one another till only a score is left," Niobhyte called up to Brion, "but in the end it will come to a duel between the Lord Wizard and myself. Why not begin with that, and spare some lives?"

"Beware, Lord Matthew!" Brion said instantly. "This is a maneuver, nothing more. He hopes to best you, and knows if he does, my army is apt to flee!"

"What His Majesty says is true," Sir Orizhan agreed, "but more to the point, if we stand and fight, we shall likely overcome his rabble, who have nothing but greed and cruelty to push them on."

"Both true." Matt's stomach tied itself in a knot. "But what Niobhyte says is true, too. If I can beat him, his side will surrender without any bloodshed. I have to try."

"Are you so sure you can win?" Brion challenged.

"No," Matt said, "but I am sure you can hold your men in place even if I'm beaten—if you start exhorting them now." Then he stepped forward, and was into the ranks of his own men before Brion could call out a command to stop—and once he would have had to make it loud enough for the men to hear, he couldn't make it at all.

A pathway opened for Matt as men pulled back, doffing their caps in respect. He strode down from the front ranks to the level ground between the two armies to meet the leader of the false druids at last.

But as he drew closer he recognized the man. He stopped, staring in outrage. "You!"

"Of course, me," sneered the Man Who Went Out the Window, "and if you'd had an ounce of brains, you would have realized it long ago."

Matt could, at least, recognize a gambit for destroying his self-confidence. He replied in kind. "A man with any real power wouldn't have had need for such subterfuge. He would have told me his name straightaway."

Niobhyte flushed with annoyance, even though he, too, obviously recognized the gambit. "You meddling fool! If you had stayed in your own country, you would not now face your death!"

"Be careful what you say," Matt told him. "If you really slew Drustan, you should remember that his son sits atop that hill listening."

"Let him hear then!" Niobhyte shouted. "Drustan was a fool and an incompetent!"

"Meaning that he wouldn't endorse your so-called religion, and even tried to execute you for it!" Matt matched him decibel for decibel. "Who do you think you are, to sit in judgment upon your own king?"

"I am Niobhyte, heir to the last High Druid!" the sorcerer thundered in anger. "Who are you to *dispute* my judgment, lowborn oaf?"

That stung. "I am Matthew Mantrell, Lord Wizard of Merovence. So all along it *was* you who had slain Prince Gaheris!"

"It was not my plan, but it was of my arranging, though not of my hand." Niobhyte smiled, enjoying himself. "All that I myself did was to steal the prince's purse while he was distracted with his doxy, then set one of my most ardent acolytes the task of actually shoving his blade in the prince's back. But I will admit that it was masterfully thought out. It was upon hearing him say it that I first understood King John's true merit."

His voice rang off the hillside, and Brion started with surprise, his face turning tragic.

CHAPTER 24

But Matt didn't even trust Niobhyte to lie straight. "Don't tell me it was really John's scheme!"

"Oh, yes," the chief druid said. "Don't believe the show of stupidity he puts on. He learned the pretense well while he was a child—it protected him from his brothers' jealousy, and from ambitious courtiers who thought he might be a threat."

"And saw other people punished for his crimes, because no one believed he was smart enough to figure out new ways of killing a cat or making dishes fall to the stone floor," Matt said grimly.

Above on the hillside, Brion's face turned gray. He began to walk his horse downhill, and the soldiers opened up an avenue for him.

"Ah, you knew of the last?" the chief druid asked.

Matt hadn't—it had just been an example of a vicious boyhood prank. But he gave a contemptuous shrug, and Niobhyte interpreted it as assent.

"Not only duplicity—he also began to learn magic at a very early age," the chief druid told him. "He fled into the wood when some courtiers humiliated him during a hunt. There, he found the hut of an old witch-woman. He threatened to bring the hunt down upon her unless she taught him magic, and thus he began. Once he had learned all she had to teach, he found grimoires aplenty—but he slew her so there might be no one to tell what he had learned."

Matt shuddered. "Nice kid."

"A lad of great promise, I assure you," said Niobhyte, with a gleam in his eye. "I heard hints and rumors from other sorcerers, and came looking for this prince who had already devoted himself to evil in order to gain power. I tempted John with the notion of stabbing and poisoning his way to power. He seized the idea like a miser finding a gold coin in the dust—but was concerned that the Church might balk him. 'Give me protection from the law,' I told him, 'and I shall build so strong a following that no Church shall be able to stand against it.' He gave me a keen glance and said, 'I had wondered what you expected to gain by helping me,' and we have understood each other perfectly from that day."

"Able to trust one another because you were each able to predict perfectly what the other guy would do," Matt said dryly.

"Whatever would gain us more power and wealth." Niobhyte nodded.

"Perfect prediction, perfect trust."

"Even so—though I still must do as he commands." The chief druid grinned. "But not much longer. I shall soon have so tight a hold on the land that John will virtually have to do my bidding."

"Wait a minute." Matt held up a hand. "*He's* been giving orders to *you*?"

"Did you think I was the master?" Niobhyte laughed, with the ring of triumph. "Fool! No, John is quite evil enough to make Bretanglia miserable all by himself—and therefore have I been delighted to take orders from him. But it will be even more satisfying to give those orders when the king has become my puppet."

Brion reined his horse to a stop, his brow thunderous. "John shall never be your servant, for I shall be crowned instead of him, and shall see you and your evil minions stamped out root and branch!"

So much for the parley. Matt groaned. Brion may have had honor, but he also had a lousy sense of timing.

"A curse upon you both!" Niobhyte recoiled, raising his staff. "So you thought to lull my suspicions with meaningless chatter while you surrounded my army and your wizard tailored a spell to hold me, did you?"

"I have not surrounded your army!"

"No, not yet! And you shall not!" Niobhyte raised his staff over his head, rattling out a verse in a foreign language that didn't sound anything like Gaelic.

Matt started chanting, too, even faster. He couldn't know what was coming, so he had to pull up something for a general purpose and hope it would give him time to shape a counterspell to match what came.

Of course, he didn't see his parents muttering their own spells and gesturing behind him.

Matt called out,

> "Then if you plan it, he
> Changes organity
> With an urbanity
> Full of inanity
> Driving your foes to the verge of insanity!"

Niobhyte's staff snapped out, pointing at Matt, shuddering with the discharge of powerful energy—but Matt felt only a wave of weakness that passed him and left him feeling weary but still able. Brion sagged in his saddle, then forced himself upright. Behind him, commoners and knights alike cried out as the wave of fatigue hit them, then exclaimed in wonder as it passed. Matt realized his mother had diffused a spell aimed just at him, so that it widened and broadened to strike the whole army, and only weakened whom it was intended to destroy.

But Niobhyte dropped his staff, clutching at his temples with a cry of anguish, dropping to his knees. "What have you done, you oaf! You have sent my brain awhirl!"

Matt dashed forward to catch up the staff.

But Niobhyte scooped it from the ground and caught Matt by the tunic. He yanked Matt's head close, and Matt found himself staring into a maniac's eyes. "It shall gain you nothing!" Niobhyte screamed. "My power is no less! I shall call the energies from the very trees and grasses to roast your army!"

Matt tried to twist away, but Niobhyte held him with hysterical strength, lips curving wider and wider with insane glee as he raised his staff higher and higher, intoning a singsong rhyme. Matt caught the occasional name of a deity, and realized the man was reciting an ancient Phoenician spell. He shuddered within—and without, too; his skin began to crawl

with the feelings of titanic energies gathering around Niobhyte, more intense than anything he had ever felt. Nausea
seized him as he realized that his own spell, driving the chief
druid nearly insane, had vastly increased the strength of his
viciousness, even though the power of the spell might burn
out his brain.

But it also might burn up Brion and his whole army. Matt
couldn't take the chance. He recited the first spell that came
to mind, and as he recited, he realized that the fate of all the
people in the kingdom really did hinge on that one verse. It
actually was the moment of desperation that the real druids
had foretold, and he thrust his face closer to Niobhyte's, his
own expression becoming more fierce as Niobhyte's became
more manic, Gaelic syllables pouring from Matt's lips to
clash against those erupting from Niobhyte's, until Matt's
voice soared to the finish, triumphantly ahead of the false
druid's chant.

The earth shook beneath them.

Men cried out.

Niobhyte chanted more loudly, voice taking on a ring of
desperation; his spell was nowhere near done.

"Down!" Matt shouted.

But Niobhyte pushed himself up to his feet with a burst of
strength, shouting out syllables as he struck Matt's hand
away, raising his staff over his head.

The earth buckled beneath Niobhyte's feet. He fell, screaming, the spell unfinished.

"Hit the dirt!" Matt shouted. "Before the earth knocks you
down!"

His parents threw themselves to the ground. The peasants,
seeing them, likewise dove for the turf. Brion dismounted,
clinging tightly to the reins as he knelt. Whinnying in terror
but obeying its training, the war-horse knelt with him. Rosamund and the other knights followed his lead.

But Niobhyte's army wasn't about to imitate their foes.
With a cry of glee, they charged Brion's men.

The earth bucked beneath their feet, then sank a yard.

Niobhyte's men screamed as they fell, kicking and laying
about at imagined enemies, stabbing one another in their
panic—but Brion's men clung to the grass, some crying out

in terror, but a few, then more and more, calling out the words of a prayer, until most of his army was praying aloud to the God who held them all in His hand, and the earth they lay on, too.

"What have you done, you fool!" Niobhyte screamed. "What powers have you unleashed?"

"Tectonics," Matt shouted back.

A huge explosion filled the air, turning into a roaring that echoed all about them, a barrage of sound that made strong men cling to the earth, howling in terror—but that very earth heaved and sank again. Then, in the distance, beyond and above the forest, he saw a huge gray mound rise up, and knew it was the sea.

It fell, and another rose in its place. Only then did the sound of its breaking batter against Matt's ears. He realized there was now a coastline where there had never been one before.

The earth stilled.

Matt scrambled to his feet. "Back!" He waved Brion away. "Back to the high ground! This neck of land is sinking, and the sea is coming in!"

"Back, men of mine!" Brion levered himself up to cling to his saddle, then barked a command at his charger, and the horse pushed itself to its feet, dragging him upright. Matt ran to help him get a foot in a stirrup and push himself aboard. All over the field, squires ran to help their knights mount, and the whole army scrambled to its feet and turned as Brion led Matt and his companions back and away from the field of battle that they had striven so hard to find.

"Away!" Niobhyte screamed at his men. "To Merovence! We can be sure the wizard would not devastate his own country! Find the high ground to the south!"

Some of his horde turned to the south, but most howled in fright and ran to follow Brion, leaving their weapons in the grass. Niobhyte whirled, howling with anger, and threw fireballs after them. They exploded, and dozens of men screamed as they died, burned in seconds.

The rest ran all the harder north, howling in fear.

"Take them prisoner!" Matt shouted at Brion. "I think they're ready to reconvert!"

Brion barked orders at his knights, and peasants and fishermen fanned out to take the enemy into custody. The synthodruids submitted meekly to having their hands tied behind their backs, as long as they were allowed to keep walking while Brion's soldiers did the tying. Behind them Niobhyte screamed curses. His former congregation shuddered, but kept on striding north.

A cry of alarm went up from the men who were hiking south. Matt turned and looked; they were lifting and shaking their feet, exclaiming in fear. One phrase rose from the hubbub clearly, from hundreds of throats in fear and panic:

"Flood! Flood!"

"Seek the high ground!" Niobhyte shrieked. "March quickly, fools, or you'll drown!"

The men started running.

"That is well advised," Brion told his men. "March quickly, before the water claims you."

Mama and Papa caught up with Matt, panting. "Son," said Mama, "what have you done?"

"Created the English Channel," Matt told her. "A real druid in Ireland gave me the spell."

"But all the people who live in that neck of land will be drowned!"

"Everyone left alive is in one of Niobhyte's bands, or fled," Matt said. "Refugee management is already a problem, right?"

"We have seen many fleeing north, yes," Papa said.

"And everyone else has been sacrificed, or killed simply for the thrill of it by Niobhyte's thugs, since he told them it's just fine for the strong to prey upon the weak. There won't be many drowned. I'll tell Brion to send his fishermen out to pick up anybody they do find floating."

Papa looked over his shoulder. "Where do you think the synthodruids will end up?"

"Stranded on some plateau that's about to become an island." Matt looked back, too. "Judging from where I think we are and the direction they're going, I'd say they'll end up in a new Jersey." He turned back to follow Brion. "Hurry, folks. The land is breaking and crumbling, leaving sea cliffs behind, and they'll stop tidal waves, but the sea will come in—more slowly and more gently, maybe, but it's coming."

"Time and tide wait for no man," Papa agreed, and walked a little faster.

"You did not tell me you had such power as this," a shaky basso said on Matt's other side.

Matt looked up to match stares with Buckeye. "You didn't ask. Besides, I'll admit I didn't know that spell when we met."

"It is not the spell—it is the ability to gather and contain so much of the magical force!"

"Well, sure, but who's counting?" Matt didn't tell him that was due to the quality of the old Celtic poetry.

"Who is counting?" Buckeye cried. "I am counting! Counting the days left to me, and mightily relieved that you have been so merciful! Nay, I'll play no more tricks upon you, or upon anyone of your blood!" He inclined his head. "Have I your permission to leave your service?"

Matt's heart soared, but caution lingered. "I might require one last service of you."

"Done! Only call, and I shall be by your side!"

"Then you have my permission." Matt grinned, holding up a hand in farewell. "It's been a very interesting journey, Master Bauchan."

"I shall never forget you," Buckeye promised, "no matter how hard I try." Then he turned away, dodged in among the peasants, and disappeared in the crowd.

Mama sighed. "If only you could solve all your problems so easily."

"Yes." Matt turned back to follow Brion and Rosamund, his face grim. "We do have one little problem left, named John—and something tells me he'll be just as hard a nut to crack as Niobhyte was."

Matt's apprehension increased as they climbed the raw stair-steps in the land that led up to the new island of Bretanglia. He felt rather guilty at the thought that even these steps would probably be part of the ocean bed in very short order.

No one came out to harry them, no army came to confront them, though they took several days marching inland, with the sea never more than a mile behind them at nightfall, nor a few hundred yards at sunrise. There was plenty of time to arrange an ambush or even a pitched battle, but no enemy army showed itself.

"I can't understand this," Matt said. "John has the professional army, the trained and seasoned veterans! All you have are raw recruits fresh from the plow!"

"John is a coward," Brion said, as though he had to force out the insult to his brother. "He will not fight me unless he has to, no matter how strong his odds. Even then he will take refuge in a castle, and hope that I will waste my strength battering at his walls."

Matt looked back to exchange glances with his parents. They nodded. He turned back to Brion. "We can do something about stone walls. But which castle will he take?"

"The nearest," Brion said. "You may be sure he was close when we met Niobhyte—near enough to look, but far enough away not to suffer."

He was right. As they neared Hastings, they found an old Roman tower, and around it were an army's tents. The army itself stood in a long line three deep between the tower and Brion's force.

Brion drew rein. "I am loathe to kill mine own people, Lord Wizard, even if they do serve a usurper—especially since I doubt not that the commoners have been forced to it. Can you not crack him out of his shell of a tower?"

Matt was about to answer when a storm of raucous cries broke, and ravens swarmed upward from the tower. Cries behind Brion's army answered, and the sky darkened with clouds of more ravens winging in to join the flock from the tower. The cawing and croaking passed overhead, and the peasants pressed hands over their ears, eyes wide with superstitious fear.

The incoming ravens joined the central flock, then all wheeled and dove upon Brion's army.

A shout of terror went up from the ranks.

Brion fought to control his and Rosamund's horses, calling, "Wizard, can you not bring them down?"

"Me? Why should I work?" Matt answered, and recited,

"Rider on the wind, come nigh!
Stegoman, now hear my cry!
Clear away this fowl bunch!
Come and have a birdie lunch!"

The answering roar seemed to shake the sky, and Stegoman came soaring from the nearby hills. He had followed
faithfully, as he had told Matt he would. A twelve-foot tongue
of flame preceded him, and the birds were singed and roasted
before they passed down his gullet. He passed through the
flock and, licking his chops, turned to pass again.

But the ravens had had enough. Squawking in fright, they
wheeled and fled. Stegoman came roaring after in glee, each
roar a four-yard flame.

They passed out of sight over the inland hills, and Matt
turned back to the tower. "Now to some serious work."

"That is my part first," Brion said, his face hard. "I am
loathe to spend men's lives, especially good men who have
had little experience of war, but it must be done."

"It is what we have come for, my liege," called the young
Marquis of Simmery Mead. He turned and called to the peasants behind him. "How say you, men of hard hands? Do we
fight or retreat?"

"Fight!" the army yelled with one voice, and lifted their
weapons.

"So be it." Brion turned to Rosamund with a courtly bow.
"My dearest one, I have no armor to fit you. I beg the favor of
your retiring to yonder hilltop, to await the outcome of the
battle."

"I suppose I must." Teary-eyed, Rosamund pushed her
horse forward and kissed Brion lingeringly, then pulled back
and lowered his visor. He saluted, but she didn't stay to see,
only turned her horse and rode away.

Brion turned forward and couched his lance—then stared,
for a dozen knights were riding forward, and the one at their
fore held a white flag.

"Majesty, will you parley?" asked Sir Orizhan.

"I will." Brion's tone was iron, hiding relief. "Give me
white cloth."

Mama took off her kerchief—not as white as it had been at

the beginning of their journey, probably, but white enough—and tied it to the tip of Brion's lance. The king rode forth, with Matt, his companions, and half the knights of the company behind him.

The other half stayed with the army, to ride to the rescue if they had to—and every archer waited with his bow strung and an arrow nocked.

But as Brion rode up to the white flag, its bearer bowed in the saddle and cried, "Hail, Noble Sir!"

It was a nice piece of fence-sitting; the phrase applied to a prince, but could apply to a king, too. Brion raised his visor and frowned, not entirely pleased. "I greet you, Duke of Easbrenn." No one asked how he knew; Brion could see the duke's shield, and every knight had all the family coats of arms memorized. "Why have you called for parley?"

"Because, Noble Sir, we who serve King John have served under constraint—all except a few who are now under guard within their own army."

"Only a few?" Brion asked, his tone skeptical. "What constrained you, then?"

"The sorcery of the chief druid Niobhyte and his coterie," the duke replied. "We would gladly leave King John's service and declare him to be a false king, if we could be sure of amnesty and pardon."

Matt caught his breath; it took a lot of courage to defy a man's ruler, false or not. It took even more to be the ringleader.

"Niobhyte may be able to work his magic from some distance," Brion warned. "I doubt that he is drowned; rather, I think him to be alive on a new-made island."

"We trust in the power of your wizards to protect us, Noble Sir," the duke answered, and bowed to Matt. "We have heard that the Lord Wizard of Merovence travels with you."

"Indeed, and I see that you have recognized him." Brion didn't bother mentioning the rest of the Mantrell family. "Very well, my lord, you have my royal word that all within this army shall have pardon and amnesty, save those we can identify as loyal to John for their own gain."

"Then we declare him false!" The duke turned, and in a voice that carried to most of his own army, called out, "Hail Brion, True King of Merovence!"

"Hail King Brion!" the army shouted, and knelt in a vast wave rolling through the ranks.

Brion sat a bit taller and couldn't keep the smile from his face. "I declare you good and loyal men—but I shall not ask that you turn against the lord for whom you fought but now. Only stand aside, that my men and I may ride through."

"We shall, Your Majesty." The duke bowed and turned, galloping back to his army, shouting orders. A wide avenue opened between Brion and the tower.

"My lord the marquis," said Brion, "let our own men form a wall on each side, to keep that channel open—and let the rest of our army surround each half of these our new allies, in case their ardent loyalty should be threatened."

"Your Majesty, I shall." The marquis inclined his head and turned away to give the orders.

"Come, my lords," Brion said. "I would as lief have you at my back when I meet my brother, for I trust him not and never have, and if even half of that which the false chief druid told us of his learning magic is true, I have no wish to face him without the benefit of wizardry."

Matt waved good-bye to his mother and father. They nodded, understanding, and stood their ground—it was for them to guard the army in his absence.

Matt turned to follow Brion into the old Reman tower, with Sir Orizhan and Sergeant Brock following them.

They could hear him a hundred feet from the doorway, though they couldn't make out the words, only the screams of rage. When they rode through the door, they found John standing on a dais before a gilded, ornately carved chair in the tower's Great Hall. Oaken rafters made the ceiling dark, and tattered banners hung on the walls, trophies of ancient battles won. But the rest of the floor was empty, and John trembled as he met his brother's gaze, then glanced away.

"Brother," said Brion, "you have taken what was rightfully mine."

"What choice did I have?" John screamed. "You were dead so far as I knew, and so was Father!"

"The king was dead by your hand, and I by your orders," Brion said grimly, "and so was Gaheris."

"You always had everything!" John screeched. "Mama loved you! Papa taught you to fight! People fawned on you, loved your singing! The women all swooned, and the men acclaimed you a perfect knight! It was my turn, mine!"

"Not by treachery," Brion said, his voice iron again. "Take off that crown."

"I think not," said a deeper voice, and Niobhyte stepped forth from the shadows behind the great chair.

Matt stared. "How did *you* get off that island?"

"Did you think I could not burn out a log to make a boat, nor direct it by magic?" Niobhyte returned. "Indeed, my followers are even now honing their skills by practicing the magical felling of trees and crafting of ships. They will land in a week's time. Did you think this battle won?"

"Slay them for me, Niobhyte!" John commanded.

"Willingly, Majesty!" Niobhyte's staff snapped down to point at Brion as he shouted a Sumerian verse.

Matt called out an all-purpose counter:

> "Defend us from ill spells, and ground
> All energies that do abound
> With malice, hate, or evil will,
> Dis-spell aggression, and do ban
> Fire and foe asbestos you can!"

He was amazed when Niobhyte's fireball exploded against an invisible shield five feet from Brion, then ran down into the stone floor. The war-horse screamed, trying to rear, but Brion calmed it and said, with a hard smile, "Our men of magic seem to be evenly matched, brother. Shall I call up my horses and my men?"

"Those who acclaimed you shall die most wretchedly!" John howled. His eyes were manic; Matt would almost have thought Niobhyte had purged his own near-madness by transmitting it to John.

He thought he'd better try to distract the false king. "Niobhyte told us you were giving him orders. I had trouble believing it."

"Why, were you deceived by my pretended idiocy?" Instantly, John was preening. "I assure you that I am well-versed in it—I learned early that playing the fool lulled my enemies and gave me the advantage."

"It almost worked," Matt told him. "I never would have believed you were the one who engineered Gaheris' assassination if Niobhyte hadn't told me when he was sure he had me cornered."

Niobhyte looked daggers at him, but the revelation didn't seem to bother John in the slightest. He only grinned, delighted to be able to display his cleverness at last. "Even more—I spoke a few idiot's phrases, whining to Mother and complaining to Father as to who should marry Rosamund. Thus I set them to screaming at one another, igniting the quarrel that led to actual warfare."

"Then you sent Niobhyte to kill Brion," Matt prodded.

"No, that was a spell of my own." John grinned, delighted with his own cleverness. "I gave the suit of blue armor the semblance of life, then gave it the command to stab Brion when all others' backs were turned and he was defenseless." His smile curdled. "It worked well enough, but it was an idiot of a puppet who did only as it was told, *exactly* as it was told, and did not make sure that Brion was dead."

Matt shuddered at the thought of a magical robot. He hoped John wasn't writing his own grimoire. "Good thing it missed."

"It struck closely enough," John snapped. "Unfortunately, Brion has done too many good works, and said too many prayers, for evil magic to kill him—but it did take him out of my way, though not quite long enough." He glared daggers at Brion. "Curse you, for coming back before my power was secure!"

"Your power would never have been complete as long as you treated the people so cruelly," Brion snapped. "What did you do with Mother? Did you slay her, too?"

"Mother? Of course not!" John's eyes glittered with contempt. "Really, Brion, you are unbelievably stupid!"

Brion strove to master sudden fury, and Matt wondered what ace John thought he had in the hole.

"I kept Mother alive, though also soundly locked in her gilded prison," John said. "Fool that I was, I had some vague hope that, with you gone, she might lavish upon me the affections she gave to you, and which I craved. Twice foolish I was, for she was still in love with Father, no matter how she railed at him, and had no love to spare for me!"

"So when your father had served his purpose and declared you his heir," Matt said, "you poisoned him."

John frowned. "How did you guess that? No matter, for you are quite right—I commanded Niobhyte to bring me poison, and mixed it in my father's wine. Then the archbishop declared me king, and I proceeded to lord it over everybody, deriving great satisfaction from seeing the ones who had treated me with contempt now fawning over me."

"Except for Earl Marshal, and one or two others who would not fawn," Brion said, tight-lipped.

"Yes, I shall tear down the earl's castle when I am done with you." John speared his brother with a venomous glance, apparently forgetting who had the upper hand—or confident that he himself did, which gave Matt cold chills.

Of course, John gave him cold chills, period, now that he had dropped his simpleton act.

"Yes, there were those who would not grovel," John said, "or who had treated me far too badly to forgive—so I had them tortured and executed. I derived a great deal of pleasure from their screams, I assure you, except for those obdurate few who were determined to spoil my fun and refused to cry out. But I gained my greatest pleasure from the sense of power, proved by caprice—making people miserable, then occasionally freeing a felon or showing mercy for no good reason at all, then hauling him back and watching him hang."

"Murderer!" Brion cried, his face darkening.

"Listen to him!" John said, lip twisting in scorn. "It matters not to him that I tried to slay his very self, but learning that I slew a blameless commoner ignites his rage! What a fool, to care more for another's life than for his own!"

Brion's face turned thunderous. He gripped his sword, moving his horse closer.

John waited, lips parting, eyes glistening.

"Yes, almost fool enough to lose his temper with you and give you an opening for hitting him with evil magic that would explode his brain," Matt said quickly.

Brion froze, and John seemed to deflate with disappointment. He turned to glare at Matt, as though counting the tortures he would visit on him.

It was so venomous a stare that Matt shuddered. "You've dedicated yourself to evil," he whispered. "You've sold your soul to the Devil."

"What, sign a bargain with the Prince of Liars?" John sneered. "I am not such a fool! No, I have sold nothing—but I have seen that power is won not by virtue or justice, but by breaking every Commandment, especially since my enemies choose to let those absurd laws limit them!"

"As I said—you've sold your soul."

John turned pale, trembling. "I have not! I am not damned!"

Matt wondered what had gone wrong in John's childhood, but realized that he couldn't know the whole of it. Some he could guess—that the child-prince had been ugly and scrawny and acquired zero social skills, so went after negative attention, and had his Oedipal feelings inverted because his mother so plainly favored Brion and barely tolerated him. That had set John to being eaten with envy, especially when she was quite willing to send him away with his father. But he had seen courtiers bowing and scraping to the king, imitated them and ingratiated himself with Drustan, and decided to become king himself by killing his brothers, which had gained him the added satisfaction of revenge.

"You can still repent," Matt told him, "though I doubt that you will, when you take such pride in having assassinated your father and your eldest brother."

"Yes, that was my doing—the planning, though not the actual stabbing." Instantly, John was preening again, showing off his cleverness. "I would have loved to stick the knife in him myself, but I had to be far away at the time so that I could avoid suspicion."

"You knew you'd have a chance when the family went visiting Queen Alisande," Matt guessed. "When your brothers decided to go wenching—"

"Decided? It was I who put the idea into their heads!" John cried. "Or into Gaheris', at least—I knew Brion's stupid loyalty would make him follow, whether he wished such pleasures himself or not. I only regret that he went in disguise and my man could not find him in the melee."

"So the disguises weren't your idea?"

"They were indeed, but who would have guessed Brion would dress as a common soldier?"

Anyone who knew him, Matt thought, and realized that John didn't—but this wasn't the time to say it. "So you sent Niobhyte to do the actual killing."

"No, only to see that it was done," John said, grinning without the slightest hint of remorse.

"As the prince commanded, I waited until Gaheris was embroiled with his doxy, then slipped into the chamber and stole his purse," Niobhyte said. "That I did myself, but could not slay Gaheris with my own hand, for I had to brew magicks that would make everyone quick to anger."

"Why did you jump out the window, then?" Matt held up a hand, the answer dawning even as he asked the question. "No, let me guess—to draw attention away from the real murderer long enough for him to escape."

"Or to avoid suspicion," Niobhyte confirmed.

"Then who committed the actual murder?" Matt asked, more at sea than ever.

John threw back his head and laughed. "If you can guess that, Lord Wizard, I shall surrender my crown here and now!"

The offer of the reward, and of all the lives saved by avoiding John's last-ditch magical assault, kicked Matt's brain into overdrive. Suddenly, the teaming of chief synthodruid and false king made him connect a series of other facts, leading to only one possible conclusion. "I'll take you at your word. It was Sergeant Brock."

CHAPTER 25

Brion and Sir Orizhan turned to stare at the sergeant.

Brock, white-faced and trembling, slowly sank to his knees, bowing his head with a cry of anguish.

Matt risked a quick glimpse at Brock and noticed, for the first time, a tall archer in a peasant's hooded smock standing in the shadows with an arrow nocked to his bow. His face was in shadow, but his leggins were furry. Matt felt his stomach sink and hoped Buckeye liked him today.

"Sergeant, you have been a good and trustworthy companion!" Sir Orizhan exclaimed. "Why have you done this dreadful deed?"

"Because he was one of the original synthodruids," Matt said. "He didn't really know what he was getting into, only liked the sound of it. Besides, Niobhyte told him battle was good and said the strong had the right to take what they wanted—very appealing, to a soldier."

"It is true," Brock said through stiff lips. "I forswore the Christ, to my shame, and followed Niobhyte with all my heart. Even when he bade me find a moment to slay the prince and promised me chaos to hide my deed, my heart sang with joy, for none wanted to live in a Bretanglia ruled by Gaheris—your pardon, Majesty . . ."

"Given," Brion snapped. "What assurance have I that you would feel differently about me?" Then he answered himself. "Yet you do, for in that cavern in Erin, you had chance after chance to slay me if you had wished. You did not, though. Why?"

"Because you are a soldier!" Brock told him, and the gaze he lifted to Brion was filled with wonder and total loyalty. "You are a skilled commander who rarely loses, and arranges the order of battle so that as few of the common soldiers as possible will be slain!"

Brion frowned. "Can this alone be reason enough for loyalty?"

"It can," Sir Orizhan told him.

"There is more." Brock turned his gaze away. "The longer I marched behind you, Majesty, the greater my respect grew, for you are not only a good prince, but also a goodly man, loyal to your friends, courageous in the face of any danger, devoted to your fiancée."

John cried out as though his heart were being stabbed, and Niobhyte snarled, "Traitor! You shall roast in wicker for this!"

"Traitor yourself!" Brock surged back to his feet, face suddenly suffused with rage, pointing a trembling finger at the chief druid. "You lied to me, to us all, you preached a travesty of the ancient religion! I learned the truth of it, heard it from real druids in Erin, aye, from a pouka's mouth, from one of the ageless spirits of the land! There is no truth in you, betrayer of thousands, and I repent the day that ever I listened to your lies!"

Niobhyte stood unmoving, but his eyes glowed with malice, as though he were memorizing every slightest feature of Brock's face and form, to work upon him a spell that would cause him endless agony.

The sergeant didn't even notice. He turned to Brion again, dropped once more to his knees. "The longer I served you, Majesty, the more I came to know that you were as good as your brother was bad, and swore in my heart to serve you. So I still swear. My life is yours, to take or to give as you will." He wrenched off his helmet and bowed his head, his neck level and naked, waiting for Brion's sword.

"How did you know!" John hissed.

"Mostly by the silver sickle he had in his pack—he didn't rank high enough to rate gold, did he?" Matt turned back to John. "He said he took it off a dead synthodruid when they raided a sacrifice and saved a maiden, and I never thought to doubt him. But seeing Niobhyte standing beside you made me realize how tightly politics and religion have been bound together in this, and Brock was the only man who was both caught up in that binding and had the opportunity to kill Gaheris. There were a host of small details, too, the look on his face when he saw Brion for the first time, the superstitious fear that fell over him now and then, his original wariness of me—a dozen of them, plus the fact that the wound in Gaheris' back was too broad for a sword, but might have been made by a sickle piercing, then hooking to cut its way out." He didn't mention that Gaheris' ghost had talked about a stabbing pain followed by a ripping, only looked down at Brock. "Niobhyte said it had to be done with the sickle, didn't he? To make Gaheris a sacrifice to the old gods."

"He did," Brock confirmed, head still bowed, "and fool that I was, I believed him."

"So you knocked out the other man who was protecting Gaheris' back—how were you supposed to know it was Brion, dressed up as a trooper? Then you fought off a townsman or two, pulled out your sickle, and stuck it in Gaheris' back. After that, you pretended to be knocked out yourself, fell down, and were just one more unconscious victim of a brawl, along with the rest." Matt turned back to John. "That's how I guessed. I believe you said something about surrendering, Your Highness? A matter of your word of honor?"

"Honor is for fools and weaklings!" John snapped. "If I had known you had the slightest chance of guessing, I'd never have said it! Niobhyte, slay them!"

"I think not," the chief druid said, though his hands began weaving a spell. "Your army has abandoned you, and it is clear I shall not triumph by supporting you. What say you, King Brion? Would you have your kingdom so securely in the palm of your hand that none dares strike against you? Would you have every subject, from high to low, tremble in fear of your name?"

John whirled, screaming in outrage.

"No!" Brion snapped. "I will never stoop to hold power through fear, with no love! And I will never lower myself to borrowing power from a man who is such a coward that he dares not strike his own blows, but must suborn others into striking for him!"

"Then die, fool!" Niobhyte raised his hand to throw a

death-spell—but John, still screaming, yanked a sword from under his cloak and stabbed.

Niobhyte fell, howling, clutching the wound high on his breast.

"He isn't dead!" Matt shouted. "Sergeant, sap him! As long as he can still chant a spell, he's a danger to us all!"

Brock stared up, amazed at still being trusted enough for an order. Then life flooded back into his face, and he leaped at the chance to serve—leaped up and over to Niobhyte as he pulled out a small cudgel and cracked his former leader over the head. Niobhyte went limp, but Matt snapped, "Tie the man up and keep him unconscious!" He knew from personal experience that it was quite possible to work magic just by thinking, if there was enough emotion behind the thoughts, and he was sure Niobhyte had some very strong feelings at that moment.

"My lord, I shall!" Brock took up station by Niobhyte, cudgel up, alert for the slightest movement.

"It is you who have unraveled all my plans!" John shrieked at Matt. "It is you who have stolen a tenth of my land, sinking it deep in the ocean! Feel the force of my hatred, fool!" He chanted a verse in an old language as he swung the sword down, but not in a blow, only pointing it at Matt, and a lightning bolt jumped from his blade.

Matt snapped out,

> "Be it live or be it dead,
> Ground this spark to spare my head!"

Light blinded him for a moment, and he felt a tingling all over his body. Then the room was clear again, and he was gasping.

"The lightning flowed down over him and into the stone!" Orizhan cried. "Yet he still stands!"

John screamed again, still in the arcane tongue, hands rolling as though molding clay, then hurling something unseen that leaped into burning light, a fireball sizzling straight at Matt's chest.

"The fire returns unto its source!" Matt shouted. "Ball, retrace along your course!"

He held up a hand, and the ball of fire bounced off without touching his palm, arrowing back toward John.

But John was already shouting another spell, even as he held up his own left hand, darkening the fireball to a cinder. His right hand snapped down, pointing at Matt. Silver streaks flashed.

"Let fire shroud the ice of hate!" Matt called. "The strength of frost in flames abate!"

Flame blazed up about the icicles. With an explosive hiss, the ice sublimed into steam and the fire went out.

"You may be a powerful magus by the standards of your fellow aristocrats, Your Highness," Matt said, "but compared to a real wizard, you're not even a squire."

John stared, his eyes wild. "But . . . but Niobhyte feared my magic!"

"He let you think so, as long as it served his purpose," Matt said, "but you saw how quickly he turned his back on you when you outlived your usefulness. I'm afraid you weren't as much in control as you thought."

"So much for magic." Brion drew his sword and strode toward his brother. "Now we shall test your swordsmanship."

"My curse upon you all!" John screamed, and threw down his own blade. Then his nose and chin bulged outward, his whole body swelled, his purple robes turned into maroon and scaly skin, and a dragon stretched its neck ten feet above Brion to blast fire down at him.

Matt's first instinct was to call on Stegoman—but he realized that the dragon couldn't fit through the windows or the door, and by the time he'd have knocked down the wall, John the Dragon would have fried them.

Brion, undaunted, swung his sword back and waded in.

The dragon blasted flame down at him, but Brion leaped forward and stabbed at its chest. The beast slid aside like a snake and blasted again, but Brion pivoted, graceful and quick even in armor, and as he swung around, his sword slashed high at the base of the dragon's neck. It writhed aside with a shriek of anger and fear, then blasted flame at Brion. He started to dodge, but the dragon blasted again, a little ahead of the knight. Brion howled with pain but sprang through the flame to stab blindly. His sword pierced scales and struck into the dragon's shoulder.

The dragon roared in fear and anger and leaped back, one clawed forefoot coming up to press over the wound. It stared down wild-eyed at its own blood leaking out, then stared again at Brion, in shock that any mere man could actually hurt a dragon.

"I doubt that I could kill my own brother," Brion told him, "but a dragon is another matter."

The dragon body seemed to melt like hot wax, reforming until it was John again, right hand pressed to left shoulder, blood leaking through the fingers. "Curse you, Brion!" he screamed.

"I have not cursed you," Brion said grimly, "but for that, I shall chastise you most sorely." He raised his sword and strode forward.

John howled and stooped, snatching his sword from the floor.

Brion halted, mixed emotions warring in his face. "It need not come to this, little brother. Repent, and I shall spare you for a life of atonement and prayer, though you shall be imprisoned in a hermit's cell."

"You call that life?" John screeched. "Fifty years in a barred stone room, when all that stands between me and a kingdom is you?"

Then he sprang at Brion, hammering blows at him from every direction, and the perfect chivalrous knight was suddenly on the defensive, parrying madly to keep up with the storm of John's strokes. Finally the usurper slowed a little, and Brion swung a counterstroke, but John parried it easily and slashed at Brion's helmet without even riposting. Again Brion staggered back, barely managing to parry, and one blow in five struck through to his armor.

I cannot be proud of his deeds, said a deep old voice inside Matt's head, *but I may boast of how well I taught him to fight.*

"Yeah, but he's fighting with the fury of a cornered rat," Matt muttered.

Brion managed to beat John's sword aside long enough to aim a blow at his shoulder, but the sword rang off steel, and armor showed through the tear.

Armor under his robes! Gaheris sneered inside Matt's head. *Ever the coward!*

John leaped back with a shout of rage and jabbed his sword straight at Brion—but it was the rash movement big brother had been waiting for. His sword blurred, spinning in a bind, and John's sword flew across the room to crash into the wall. John shrank back, but Brion followed him closely, sword centered unwaveringly on John's eyes. Still screaming, the usurper backed away and backed some more, until he jarred against the stone wall.

"He has the blood of thousands on his hands!" Brock cried in agony. "Strike, my liege lord, strike!"

Yes, strike! Gaheris said with vicious glee inside Matt's head.

Not my son! Drustan's ghost groaned.

"I cannot," Brion said, his voice agonized. "He is my brother."

John shouted with triumph and stepped away from the wall, then struck the flat of Brion's sword blade with his fist and kicked with all his might. Brion fell like a tree, his armor clanging hideously on the stone floor.

With a howl of delight, John leaped on him and wrenched the sword from his hand. He held it like a dagger and swung it high, point straight above Brion's face.

"No!" howled Sergeant Brock, and threw himself forward, diving to shield Brion's head with his own body. The sword plunged down, stabbed through the sergeant's leather armor, and bit deep into Brock's shoulder blade. He screamed with pain, and John, howling curses, wrenched at the blade, but it was stuck fast. John set his foot on the man and wrenched again.

In the shadows, the bowman with the furry leggins drew his arrow to his ear and loosed.

The arrow stabbed through John's eye. John screamed, clawing at the shaft, then fell—and for a moment silence held the room.

Then John's screams came again, but somehow not in the chamber itself, but distant, fading, fading . . .

Downward.

Inside Matt's head Drustan groaned in grief, and Gaheris, for a wonder, had the courtesy to remain silent.

Brion wrenched himself up, managed to flip over, and shoved himself to his knees. Walking on them, he went to John's body, pressed a frantic hand over his heart. "There must be a heartbeat! There must!"

"I'm afraid not, Your Majesty." Matt stepped up beside him, face somber. "Your younger brother is dead."

Brion howled, throwing his head back, a long and grief-laden keening. Then he caught his breath and looked about him, wild-eyed. "Where is he that shot the arrow! Where is the commoner who dared to slay a prince!"

They looked about them, but the archer was gone.

"Where could he have sped?" Sir Orizhan asked, his voice muted.

"He disappeared, period, and flatly." Matt gazed down into Brion's face and spoke with the full authority of a master wizard and student of mythology. "It was no common soldier who loosed that arrow, Your Majesty, but a spirit of the land. Bretanglia itself chose to save the life of its true king, at the expense of the life of a usurper."

He sent for Rosamund, and she came quickly, kneeling before Brion, holding his hands in hers, while noblemen bore away the body of Prince John, and jailors hauled Niobhyte off to a cell, already deep in a coma induced by the sleep-spell that had held Brion in stasis, recited by Matt but provided by the true druids. Then Matt went outside to pace across the meadow that could have been a battlefield, and into the trees at its edge.

There he stopped and said aloud, "It occurs to me that you can never have too many friends, but you sure can have too many enemies."

"So it would seem." Buckeye stepped forward from the shadows. "And so John has proved."

"I thank you for stepping in at the last moment." Matt frowned at the bauchan. "I have to say I'm surprised, though. Glad, mind you, but surprised. I thought you had left me."

"Not quite yet." The bauchan shrugged. "Once I do, life will be dull, and for a very long time. It is far more interesting around you."

"But much more dangerous?"

"There is some truth in that," Buckeye admitted.

"One thing I don't understand, though," Matt said. "Don't get me wrong—I appreciate your loyalty—but I would have thought John was just the kind of man to delight you."

"He was indeed," the spirit agreed. "I understood John's pleasure in caprice perfectly."

"Then why did you help kill him?"

"Ah!" The bauchan grinned, and his teeth looked to be very sharp. "Because I, too, am a creature of caprice, Lord Wizard."

Matt shivered for the rest of the day.

Matt and his parents stayed around to see Brion's coronation—under the circumstances, they wanted to make sure he was well and thoroughly established in power. They needn't have worried, if the cheering of the London crowd was any indication.

Sir Orizhan led the way, bearing the scepter on a purple cushion. Rosamund rode next, bearing the orb. The crowd knew she was their future queen, and cheered her every bit as loudly as the tall, regal young man who rode behind her, in a purple robe trimmed with ermine—Brion, their rightful king. Behind him rode all the lords who had ridden with his army on his march from the coast. After them marched the leaders of the peasant army, all in new royal livery.

Inside the cathedral, the dukes and earls waited, even those who had been loyal to John, but who had declared for Brion as soon as they could. The younger sons took their places among the older men—dukes and earls themselves now, in place of fathers or elder brothers who had been attainted in the bloodless civil war, and who had not had a chance to declare for Brion in time. They had taken up with the syntho-druids and enforced John's edicts with relish and zest. Some of them sat in prison on this day, others had retired to monasteries, but most were simply exiled to their lands at home and barred from any further use of power.

As many of the London crowd as could, followed Brion's homespun army into the cathedral. As the archbishop set the crown on his head, they rocked the rafters with their shouts of approval.

Then, though, a hush fell over the great church, for the new king commanded, "Let the assassin be brought forward!"

Two soldiers led the way with halberds, two followed, and between them came Sergeant Brock in chains, his wounded shoulder bandaged—but also dressed in new livery of fine cloth. He knelt before Brion, bowing his head.

"Did you slay my brother Gaheris?" Brion demanded in a voice that all could hear.

"Your Majesty, I did!" Brock's voice was as loud as Brion's, but still held the anguish of a man who bitterly regretted his actions. "I was fool enough to believe the lies that Niobhyte preached, thrice more foolish to do his bidding and slay your brother with a silver sickle!"

"Have you confessed your sins?" Brion demanded.

The archbishop stepped forward. "Your Majesty, he has. No matter what you do to his body, his soul will go to God—eventually."

The whole crowd shuddered at the vision of Purgatorial tortures that "eventually" conjured up.

"I have repented, and am once again a Christian, and more devout than ever for my having strayed," Brock called out. "But no confession or repentance can change the fact of what I have done! Do with me as you will! Send me naked into the forefront of battle or smite my head off here and now! It shall be as you wish, and I'll not resist, nay, not even in the slightest!" So saying, he bowed his head again, stretching out his neck.

The crowd murmured in awe and apprehension.

"To slay the heir apparent warrants a traitor's death," Brion told him, face grim, "hanging, drawing, and quartering. But you have guarded the body of your rightful king, and saved my life at the risk of your own. What the one action has lost, the other has gained, and I have no doubt of your loyalty or good faith. Rise, good sergeant, and live!"

The crowd cheered, and Brock stood up, dazed, looking about him, seeming almost sad to be alive, so ready had he been to die.

When the clamor slackened, Brion said, "But such an action cannot go completely unpunished."

Brock braced himself.

"You shall be exiled now and again," Brion pronounced. "You have served the good Sir Orizhan as squire in battle—so may you serve him on your travels." He turned to the knight, drawing his sword. "Sir Orizhan, kneel."

Completely confused, the knight stepped forward and knelt at the king's feet.

Brion laid the flat of his blade on one shoulder, then the other. "For your service to your princess and to the crown, I create you Earl of Orkney, and mine own vassal!" He sheathed his sword. "Rise, my lord!"

Sir Orizhan stood up, dazed.

Brion turned to Sergeant Brock. "An island off the coast of Scotland should be far enough to be counted as exile."

Brock finally understood. A grin a yard wide broke out on his face; he fairly glowed.

"But before Lord Orizhan goes to take up the rule of his new domain, I shall require one further service of him." Brion turned back to the new earl. "I bid you go, my lord, to Toulenge, to your homeland, and tell the princess-mother, the regent of Princess Rosamund, and all her people, that by the time you arrive there the princess shall be Queen of Bretanglia, and that if any wrong them, they shall have redress not only from the Queen of Merovence, but also from the King of Bretanglia."

The crowd cheered, and Rosamund lowered her eyes, blushing modestly.

Then Brion turned and bowed to his fiancée. "Highness, have I your leave to send your liegeman to bear word to your home?"

"Majesty," she said, "you have."

Brion turned back to Lord Orizhan. "Take your squire now, and tarry with us two more days, then be off to Merovence and the south!"

Lord Orizhan bowed and stepped back as the crowd cheered.

"It would seem they approve of the king's justice," Papa said.

They stood in the sanctuary with the highest lords, but far enough away from Brion to get away with muttering.

"He decided well," Matt said, "but he was still eating his heart out about it last night when I left him. It sort of condones the killing of the heir apparent, you see, providing you're the agent of the new king, and that bodes ill for Brion's children, if he has any."

"How did he decide?"

Matt shrugged. "I left him to talk it out with Rosamund."

"Of course." Mama smiled. "I have a feeling our princess of Merovence will have a great deal to do with the governing of this land, though I doubt she'll want it known."

"Yes—everybody and his brother would be pestering her for favors," Matt said. "Better to let Brion be the heat shield. That's what a king is for, isn't it?"

"One of the things," Papa agreed.

"What has he decided to do with Niobhyte?" Mama asked.

"He can't quite see his way clear to killing him in his sleep," Matt said, "especially since he feels any man should have one last chance at repentance and confession—but I pointed out that if he wakes Niobhyte at all, there might be hell to pay."

"Literally," Papa said darkly. "So?"

"There's a promising young wizard in the Abbey of Glastonbury," Matt said.

Mama turned to him, staring. "A monk who is a wizard?"

Matt shrugged. "We don't choose our talents, Mama, or our vocations, as you kept pointing out to me during my teen years."

"Well, that is true," Mama said, frowning.

"When the young monk is a mature monk," Matt said, "and I'm convinced he's powerful enough to handle a wide-awake Niobhyte, I'll come back and stand guard while the kid offers him one last chance at redemption. Then Brion will hold a very quick trial and an execution."

"Whether Niobhyte repents or not?"

"Right." Matt shuddered. "It doesn't feel right, but Brion is convinced it's the only way to go. Me, I just hope Niobhyte doesn't find some way to wake up before then."

"If his synthodruids are imprisoned or converted, he shouldn't," Papa said. "What will you do with them?"

"Brion is sending out all the young knights who are eager for reputation to scour the kingdom looking for false druids, and is sending the word to all his reeves and magistrates, too. If they find any, they'll arrest them fast."

"But most of them fled south," Mama pointed out.

Matt nodded. "I had Stegoman do a reconnaissance, and most of them are indeed on the new Isle of Jersey. They're going crazy without congregations to boss, trying to pull rank on each other."

"And what do you mean to do about them?"

"I've already done it." Matt grinned. "I put Buckeye into a magical sleep and hired a fisherman to row him to Jersey. He woke up as soon as the boat landed and went ashore." He shrugged. "From there on he's just following his natural inclinations. By this time next month any druids who haven't sacrificed one another should be more than ready to surrender and repent."

Papa grinned. "Then you have managed to pass the bauchan!"

"That is the one last service you asked of him, then?" Mama asked, smiling.

"Yes, and I certainly do hope it *will* be the last . . . Whup! Next part of the ceremony, folks!"

Hidden musicians pealed forth a solemn but joyous tune, and the crowd parted to form an aisle. Down it came Rosamund, dressed and veiled in white lace, a bouquet in her hands. Lord Orizhan had ducked around to take his place beside her.

As she came up to the altar, Lord Orizhan gave her to Brion, who clasped her hands, eyes wide and incredulous as he stared through the gossamer at her shining, but demure, face.

"This is how it should end," Mama said with a sigh. "This is how it should always end."

"Yes, but also how it should begin," Papa said, with a meaningful glance at his son, "for this is only a wedding. Now begins their greatest work—building a marriage."

"You don't have to tell *me*." Matt gazed at the couple kneeling before the archbishop, but he was really seeing Alisande.

DEL REY® ONLINE!

The Del Rey Internet Newsletter...

A monthly electronic publication e-mailed to subscribers and posted on the rec.arts.sf.written Usenet newsgroup and on our Del Rey Books Web site (www.randomhouse.com/delrey/). It features hype-free descriptions of books that are new in the stores, a list of our upcoming books, special promotional programs and offers, announcements and news, a signing/reading/convention-attendance calendar for Del Rey authors and editors, "In Depth" essays in which professionals in the field (authors, artists, cover designers, salespeople, etc.) talk about their jobs in science fiction, a question-and-answer section, and more!

Subscribe to the DRIN: send a blank message to
join-drin-dist@list.randomhouse.com

The Del Rey Books Web Site!

We make a lot of information available on our Web site at
www.randomhouse.com/delrey/

- all back issues and the current issue of the Del Rey Internet Newsletter
- sample chapters of almost every new book
- detailed interactive features for some of our books
- special features on various authors and SF/F worlds
- reader reviews of some upcoming books
- news and announcements
- our Works in Progress report, detailing the doings of our most popular authors
- and more!

If You're Not on the Web...

You can subscribe to the DRIN via e-mail (send a blank message to join-drin-dist@list.randomhouse.com) or read it on the rec.arts.sf.written Usenet newsgroup the first few days of every month. We also have editors and other representatives who participate in America Online and CompuServe SF/F forums and rec.arts.sf.written, making contact and sharing information with SF/F readers.

Questions? E-mail us...

at delrey@randomhouse.com (though it sometimes takes us a little while to answer).

✎ FREE DRINKS ✎

Take the Del Rey® survey and get a free newsletter! Answer the questions below and we will send you complimentary copies of the DRINK (Del Rey® Ink) newsletter free for one year. Here's where you will find out all about upcoming books, read articles by top authors, artists, and editors, and get the inside scoop on your favorite books.

Age _____   Sex ❑ M ❑ F

Highest education level: ❑ high school ❑ college ❑ graduate degree

Annual income: ❑ $0-30,000 ❑ $30,001-60,000 ❑ over $60,000

Number of books you read per month: ❑ 0-2 ❑ 3-5 ❑ 6 or more

Preference: ❑ fantasy ❑ science fiction ❑ horror ❑ other fiction ❑ nonfiction

I buy books in hardcover: ❑ frequently ❑ sometimes ❑ rarely

I buy books at: ❑ superstores ❑ mall bookstores ❑ independent bookstores
❑ mail order

I read books by new authors: ❑ frequently ❑ sometimes ❑ rarely

I read comic books: ❑ frequently ❑ sometimes ❑ rarely

I watch the Sci-Fi cable TV channel: ❑ frequently ❑ sometimes ❑ rarely

I am interested in collector editions (signed by the author or illustrated):
❑ yes ❑ no ❑ maybe

I read Star Wars novels: ❑ frequently ❑ sometimes ❑ rarely

I read Star Trek novels: ❑ frequently ❑ sometimes ❑ rarely

I read the following newspapers and magazines:
❑ *Analog*	❑ *Locus*	❑ *Popular Science*
❑ *Asimov*	❑ *Wired*	❑ *USA Today*
❑ *SF Universe*	❑ *Realms of Fantasy*	❑ *The New York Times*

Check the box if you do not want your name and address shared with qualified vendors ❑

Name _____
Address _____
City/State/Zip _____
E-mail _____

stasheff

PLEASE SEND TO: DEL REY®/The DRINK
201 EAST 50TH STREET   NEW YORK NY 10022
OR FAX TO THE ATTENTION OF DEL REY PUBLICITY 212/572-2676

HER MAJESTY'S WIZARD

Book One of
A Wizard in Rhyme

by Christopher Stasheff

Matt's graduate research turned up a strange scrap of parchment; but when he tried to read the runes, they carried him away—straight into a sorcerer's dungeon. Teaming up with the dragon he met there, and with a lust witch and a priest who became a werewolf on occasion, Matt Mantrell set out to rescue the beautiful Princess Alisande and defeat the sorcerer and his dark magics.

Published by Del Rey Books.
Available at bookstores everywhere.

THE OATHBOUND WIZARD

Book Two of
A Wizard in Rhyme

by Christopher Stasheff

Matt vows to conquer a kingdom, if that's what it takes to win Queen Alisande's hand. But in this world of magic, his oath is literally binding: now he has to win a crown, or die in the attempt! Picking out a likely tyranny is easy, but even with a well-spoken cyclops, a surly dracogriff, and a chased damsel in his corner, overthrowing an evil genius was going to be tricky...

Published by Del Rey Books.
Available at bookstores everywhere.

THE WITCH DOCTOR

Book Three of
A Wizard in Rhyme

by Christopher Stasheff

First, Saul's best friend—Matt Mantrell, hero of *Her Majesty's Wizard*—mysteriously disappears, then a spider bite sends him to an alternate universe where poetry works magic. How Saul defeats an evil queen and finds Matt—with the help of the lovely ghost Angelique, a troll named Gruesome, the Spider King, and a host of other characters—makes for a story strong enough to trap a tyrant.

Published by Del Rey Books.
Available in bookstores everywhere.